Water Weaver (Wraidd Elfennol #1)

Morgan Sheppard

Copyright © 2012 Morgan Sheppard

All rights reserved.

ISBN 10: 1518774318
ISBN-13: 978-1518774317

~ DEDICATION ~

To my husband, son and daughters – not only for their love and support; but also for providing me with the real-life inspiration for Marella and Lani.

To my family, whether through blood or bond - I love you.

To my Lady of the Moon and Tides – thank you.

"Dream your dream; and work hard to make it happen."

~ CONTENTS ~

~ ACKNOWLEDGMENTS ~

Thank you to Julie for encouraging me to start on this venture.
https://www.facebook.com/julieanafarrell

Thanks to Cathy from Ty Siriol Ceramics and Crafts for her knowledge on clay which she so willingly shared with me.
https://www.facebook.com/TySiriolCeramicsandCrafts

Thank you to Di of Adien Crafts for making the stunning necklace that I knew immediately needed to be Marella's.
https://www.facebook.com/adiencrafts

Thank you to Claire for helping me out with the Welsh translations.
https://www.facebook.com/DraigArianCards

Thank you Mae of Ye Olde Inke & Quill Editing Services for her professional advice and assistance in polishing this manuscript.
https://www.facebook.com/yeoldeinkandquill/

Thanks also to Michelle Douglass for her stunning book cover.
http://www.mdbookcovers.com/

Please note that this book is written using English/Welsh spellings and style – ie Artefacts, not artifacts and colour, not color.

~ 1 ~

Perspiration slowly made its way down the middle of Marella's back as she sat at the water's edge with trees at her sides and back, their shade providing some comfort to Mehefin's heat and the glare of the water. Strands of her honey-brown hair escaped from her braid and the blue-green net inside which it had been tucked, and played around her face in the cooling breeze from the water. Around her neck, hanging by a leather thong, was a white moonstone, etched with a spiral, which dangled as she bent forwards, busy scribbling away on a sheet of parchment with ink that shimmered in the light. On the ground was a plain silver chalice with water inside it that Marella would look at for a time, before transcribing the vision she had seen onto her parchment.

Leaning back, she stretched the kinks out of her spine and felt a tremor of pride go through her as she looked at the chalice that was down by her side. That chalice was hers; she had earned it. The trials had been passed so that she could receive it. The trials were individual to everyone, but the one thing that was constant was the secrecy and silence surrounding them. No one was allowed to talk about what had happened to them. That small, plain silver chalice was her reward to prove that she could receive the images woven by the Lady of Waters. It was a vessel of transformation, where water became vision. Silver was linked with the ultimate Feminine, with clarity, vision, and even persistence. She had proved these qualities were part of her; she'd had to, to earn it.

She looked back at what she had written and wrinkled her nose. In her rush, she had made a splodge of ink on the right hand side. *That was no good; all parchments must be presented clean and legible*, she thought to herself. She sighed as she looked at her limited stock of the ink. Someday soon she hoped, she would be shown by the Elders how to make this gorgeous, rainbow coloured ink - which herbs, berries and flowers to use and in what way.

She looked over to the water wistfully, knowing Nixie would be there and would want to play. Marella admitted to being biased, but thought he had grown into a very handsome, if cheeky, otter. His coat was a deep brown, the colour that soil sometimes was when it had been tilled. His tail was a very dark brown, with black streaks in it. Nixie's eyes were a deep black that still managed to shine with an inner light. Marella had often told him the light was the spark of mischief in his nature, to which Nixie just responded with a splash of water in Marella's direction.

Marella really wanted to enter the water, it was so very tempting, but she really needed to finish her parchment first. She heard her mother's words in her head, *"There is a time for work and a time for play, Marella. Now is not the time for play.*" She heaved another sigh, looked again over at the water, and saw Nixie flying through the water.

"*Why won't you join me?*" he asked. "*The water is warm today, just as you like it. Sitting there won't help to correct those mistakes. You need to refresh yourself and then start again.*" Marella listened to him plead with her and was still undecided. "*Come on,*" he wheedled. "*You'll feel better if you do.*"

Finally Marella stood up and dusted herself off. "You're supposed to encourage me to work," she said to Nixie. "Not to plead with me to leave it alone."

As she spoke to him, she shed her blue-green outer dress to the matching swimming outfit she wore underneath. The dress had a fitted bodice decorated with a swirling design in silver, with short, cap sleeves and, although it was long, it flared out softly and had two splits in the fabric up both sides to allow her to move freely, also with the silver design. Moving with unconscious grace, she folded her dress neatly and placed it on a nearby rock. She weighed it down with another rock to stop it from being blown away in the breeze, before she moved towards the lakeside.

"*But I am helping,*" he said in such an innocent voice she was instantly suspicious.

Marella entered the water and shivered; it was as cold as she remembered. "I thought you said it was warm?" she asked him, as her teeth chattered together.

"*It is… for me,*" replied Nixie, with mischief in his mental tone.

Marella dove underwater; having learnt from experience that it was better to do it as quickly as possible. The water rapidly warmed as she adjusted to it. Nixie came over to where she was. He was so happy to have her back in the water with him. He understood her work was important and often helped with her visions - he could still see clearer than Marella in the water, even if it was in a chalice. However, he also knew when playtime was needed. Marella could be such a serious little thing, which fooled a lot of people. Her sense of humour, when she let it go, was as wicked as he could hope for, with a tongue that could be rapier sharp.

Marella couldn't be under for as long as Nixie but they spent time chasing the air bubbles that rose and mixed in the water. They delighted in spending time together.

Nixie dove down, deeper than Marella could go, and found a beautiful queen conch shell to give to her. It was unusual to find such a cache here; it was too cold for the sea snail that lived in it. The previous owner was long gone so Nixie could only presume it had been brought from one of the warmer waters along the currents. He thought the colouring was simply gorgeous, ranging from a dark, warm orange on the spikes, to a lighter shade as it moved towards the flared lip, with the inside being a beautiful, pearlescent pink. To find one with such different and bold colours made this a rare treasure indeed.

"*Marella,*" he thought to her, "*I've found something for your collection.*" Nudging it through the water with his nose, he was able to bring it to the surface so she could see it.

"Nixie, it's gorgeous!" she exclaimed. "I wonder how it got here?" As she looked at the shell, she trod water to keep herself afloat. "No matter, I know just where I can put it," she said to Nixie. Marella swam with lazy strokes towards the shore where she placed her treasure with her clothing. She returned to Nixie, enjoying her time in the clear waters of the lake.

After a while, Nixie felt Marella had relaxed enough. Now he knew she would be able to concentrate on her work more clearly. The sun was high and there were only a few wispy, white clouds in the sky. The gentle breeze just took the edge off the heat, so he knew she would be dry and comfortable in no time. There was, however, one thing she should do before going back to the shore. "*Marella, it is time,*" he said.

Marella had been afloat, lazy with the sunshine on her skin when she heard Nixie's words. Her stomach tightened as nerves took hold once more. "*Don't worry, I'll be with you all the way,*" said Nixie, as her waves of doubt battered against his mind.

"I know you will," she replied, slightly frustrated with herself.

Marella was nervous as this was not an easy journey to make, but it had to be done; as thanks for her life, for Nixie, and for the powers she practiced every day. This was her homage to the Lady of the Waters, Lady Erwyna. It was easier to see in the bright sunshine, although she had made this journey in both day and night, and knew the stones glowed in the moonlight. As she took a deep breath, Nixie reassured her through their link, he could see mentally and emotionally that she was ready, and so they dove down towards the bottom of the lake.

Nixie led Marella to the spiral beneath the water. The stones were smooth beneath her hands; as they had been for years. Marella didn't know what they were made of, but she felt a frisson of reassurance every time she touched them.

Marella started at the outer stone and kept her left hand in touch with the stones. She started to swim around the spiral towards the centre. She always worried her breath would run out before she reached the middle, but knew from experience there would be enough.

Nixie swam alongside her, keeping pace, and watched Marella carefully. When she had first attempted the dive, she hadn't been able to make it to the centre, before she ran out of breath, and he had had to help her get to the surface. He knew her lungs had strengthened from all the swimming they did and now she was more than capable of swimming the spiral.

Marella swam slowly and respectfully, ensuring her hand remained in constant contact with the stones. As she neared the centre of the spiral, she felt the current suddenly change direction. It started to swirl around her and made it difficult for her to continue. The hair that had come free of the braid was swept in front of her eyes. With her right hand, she tried to pull it away so that she could see again, whilst still making sure her left hand touched the stones. Just as she was able to pull it away, her hand touched the centre stone.

There was an explosion of air and light within the water and Marella's body was dragged down. "*NIXIE!*" she screamed before everything turned black and her senses dulled.

* * *

When Marella regained her senses, she was lying down on a soft floor cushion. The fabric contained every shade from blue to silver. Nixie nudged her cheek with his nose. He was worried about her, but didn't seem perturbed with the situation they were in.

Marella opened her eyes and looked around. She was in a beautiful room with a tall, arching ceiling covered in murals. She turned her head and looked into Nixie's eyes. "I'm okay," she reassured him. She sat up and looked around. The room was more of a hall and its graceful arches and columns adorned the spacious interior. It was beautifully decorated and furnished, with sconces casting a warm glow upon the cold stone. Close by was a table that had some sort of food and drink on it, but Marella wouldn't be eating anything until she had figured out where she was.

As Marella gazed around the room, a lady entered through a door that Marella hadn't noticed. She was a tall, willowy woman with long black hair and the most intense blue eyes Marella had ever seen. She wore a long skirt of white, which shimmered as she walked, with blue jewels around the waist. Her top came to just below her breasts and her midriff was bare. It fastened over one shoulder and was decorated with the same blue jewels. The only jewellery that decorated the woman's body was a silver torque around the top of her arm which drew Marella's eyes to it. It seemed to be two strands of beaten silver joined together and each end was curled into a spiral, just like the stones Marella had been swimming near. One set of curls faced upwards and curled to the left, the other faced down and curled to the right. The overall sense Marella got when looking at it, was one of balance.

"Marella, I've waited a long time for you," the woman said. Her voice was full of warmth and sounded husky. She held her hands out in front of her and came over to where Marella was sat on the cushion. She took the younger girl's hands into hers and pulled her up. The woman squeezed her hands, before letting go.

Marella looked at Nixie. Who was this lady and why had she been waiting for her? Nixie seemed quite unconcerned so Marella's fears were eased on a subconscious level, but she still had questions about what had happened. How did she get here and what was happening now?

"Please, sit down, little one," the lady said and gestured towards a couple of chairs Marella was sure hadn't been there before. "I know you are curious and I have things to explain, but we don't have much time, I'm afraid."

Marella walked over to the chair and sat. Nixie strolled over and rested against her legs, leaning on them gently. She reached down and placed her hand on the scruff of his neck, as she sought the reassurance his contact brought.

"There is no easy way to do this so I will just say it. My name is Erwyna, and I am the Lady of the Waters," she introduced herself. "This lake is a favourite of mine." Stunned at the announcement, Marella remained motionless with her mouth agape. She looked at the lady and wondered just what was happening. She had heard of the name Erwyna, but had never imagined ever meeting her.

Erwyna gave a gentle smile, apparently understanding that things were going to be quite difficult for Marella to understand.

"My love, you have done so well these past few years. You coped well with the news of only one Element and showed a maturity well beyond your then thirteen years. You went through your training with enthusiasm and integrity in everything you did. You followed the training of the Water Weaver and have become a talented Weaver in a short space of time, and of course, you have your Nixie. Your accomplishments are many even though your age is yet young."

Marella blushed at hearing her life listed in such a manner and still she wondered where this was going.

"You must go now," said Erwyna. "I'm afraid our time has run out. Watch your visions well, little one. Change is happening and not all of it good. It is time for the Elements to work together."

As Marella sat there, all of the furnishings in the room and even Lady Erwyna herself seemed to wobble, just like when she looked towards the bottom of the lake. There was a strong gust of air that blew Marella backwards. The next thing she knew, her hand rested on Nixie's scruff as he pulled her towards the surface of the lake.

* * *

They broke through the surface like an arrow and Marella drew in a deep breath. She swam slowly to the side of the lake and dragged herself to the bank. She sat down and rested her arms over her knees, as she caught her breath. Nixie got out and came to sit in front of her.

"Did you know?" she asked him. "All this time, did you know?"

If it was possible for an otter to look shamefaced, then Nixie did so. *"Yes, I did,"* he admitted. *"It was one of the reasons I was chosen for you."*

"You never said a word," said Marella. She felt incredibly betrayed, but didn't fully understand why. After all, Nixie hadn't done anything wrong; he just hadn't told her he knew Lady Erwyna.

"Marella, I know you are hurt by my silence, but please understand, this was done for your best interests. If you knew that Erwyna had Chosen you as her Initiate, how would you have reacted? This was done to ensure you had a normal childhood; so you wouldn't feel any pressure. Come on, Marella, you know that I wouldn't keep secrets unless they were important."

Nixie thought all of this to her whilst staring into her eyes, his paw on her knee. He knew Marella was bewildered by what had happened, and he was sorry for his part in it. He knew once she had time to think it through; her innate sense of right and wrong would know that he hadn't really had a choice. He just wanted her to know that now, instead of taking time. He couldn't bear the thought of her hurting.

"Her Initiate?" laughed Marella. "Nixie, now I know I've lost it. I must be dreaming all of this. Initiate, ha."

"Her Initiate," he confirmed, reaching out through their bond so Marella could feel the truth in his words and understand just how important this was.

Marella stopped laughing and looked at him. "You're serious, aren't you?"

Nixie looked at her and waited.

"Nixie, there haven't been Initiates for hundreds of years. Why would I be one now? I just don't understand. I need to talk to Mama."

Marella pushed herself up and strode over to where her clothes were piled. She dressed hastily and picked up the conch shell. She set off towards home, almost skipping, as she tried to get there as fast as she could, Nixie running alongside her.

She ran up the steps towards home and pushed open the front door. "Mama, are you here?" she shouted as soon as she was indoors.

"Marella, what's the matter? What's with all the shouting?" Her father was in the kitchen preparing lunch.

"Papa, is Mama home? I really need to talk to her, it's important," she told him. It felt like all of her energy drained out of her and she dropped down into the couch. "I think I'm going crazy," she whispered, putting her head in her hands.

"She's popped round to see Murtagh; she won't be long." Edlin sat next to her on the couch and took one of her hands in his. "Marella, what's going on? Talk to me."

Marella just sat there and didn't say anything. She just didn't know where to start. What could she say that would make this any less unbelievable?

Edlin looked at Nixie questioningly. "Is this something to do with you?" he asked.

Nixie looked at Marella and knew she was in shock from what she had seen and been told. So he slowly nodded and told Edlin what had happened.

The colour drained from Edlin's face as Nixie recounted what had occurred on their morning swim and about Marella being Lady Erwyna's Initiate.

"I think I need to put the kettle on," he said, moving back towards the kitchen. He got the water on the stove to start heating up whilst he prepared a lavender tea for them both. "I think I'd better keep this out, we're going to need it," he mumbled to himself. Once the drink was made, he returned to Marella and placed a large mug into her hands. "Drink this, Marella, it will help."

Marella sat forward and held both hands around her mug as though her hands were cold. She blew gently over the top to cool the liquid before taking a small sip. They sat there in silence, while Nixie patiently watched them. This was a big thing and it would affect everyone. The least he could do was give them this time.

However, he also knew this time wouldn't last long and they really needed Riva there, so he sent his thoughts to Genna, Riva's marsh wren Partner, explaining that Riva was needed at home. Genna agreed to pass the message on and came back to Nixie almost immediately saying Riva was on her way.

"Edlin, Riva is on her way," he thought to him. Edlin stood up and went to make Riva a lavender tea so it would be ready for when she walked through the door. Just as he was turned around with a mug in his hand for her, she rushed through the door.

"What's the matter? Genna said I was needed here urgently." Riva sounded out of breath as though she had ran home.

"Genna," thought Nixie reproachfully, *"You didn't need to scare Riva. We need her input, not her fear."*

"I'm sorry Nixie," thought Genna. *"It sounded urgent so I may have passed that along as well."*

"Calm down, Riva. Marella is fine – a bit shook up, but fine." Edlin tried to soothe his wife. "Here, I've made you a cup of tea. Let's just sit down and we can explain."

Riva sat down in a chair opposite Marella and took the cup from Edlin. "So what's happened then?" she asked, looking from one to the other.

Edlin repeated what Nixie had told him whilst Marella still sat there, drinking her tea but not contributing much in the way of the conversation.

"Lady Erwyna?" gasped Riva. "But no one has heard from her in an age." She looked at Nixie, Edlin, and Marella.

"Mama, it's all true," said Marella. "Lady Erwyna didn't tell me I was her Initiate though. She said she was pleased with how I'd handled my one element and the training. It was Nixie who told me."

Riva sat back in her chair and processed what she had been told. It was connected with the conversation she had been having with Murtagh, but of course, her family didn't know that. Some of the older Water Weavers had already come to the Council of Elders with news of visions they found disturbing. In these visions, mountains overflowed with red liquid that destroyed all in its path, the seas boiled, the earth cracked and the wind tore homes apart. They didn't know what their visions were warning of, but they knew they were being given a counsel. They just didn't know by whom.

Riva shared this information with her husband and daughter, seeing the looks of comprehension on their faces as she finished explaining. "I've been talking with Murtagh and I've asked him to watch out for anything unusual. The Elders are talking to the Trainers and other members of the community to see if anything is of note. I would say this is definitely notable and needs to be brought to the Council's attention."

Whilst Marella was trying to understand the words her mother had spoken, Edlin asked Riva, "Do you think they're all involved?"

Marella looked at her father. Who did he mean? The Council?

Riva nodded at Edlin. "Yes, I do. If Lady Erwyna has made an appearance here in Ilyn, then I imagine that the others will also show. They have always acted together."

Marella realised then her parents were talking about the Lords and Ladies of the Elements - Erwyna was the Lady of Waters, whilst Daire was the Lady of the Land. Adaryn was the Lord of the Skies and Ethon was Lord of Flames. She couldn't imagine a world with them in it, "Do you really think so?" she asked her mother. "I mean, it's been so long. I know we offer our thanks to them during the festivals, but I honestly thought that was just something we did."

Riva listened with great sadness to Marella's words. "Yes, I'm afraid too many of us think that way, Marella. They are real, as you now know. They used to be amongst us more, but they decided to retreat as we became more self-sufficient. It appears they may have retreated too far. However, the visions that have occurred show a time of great upheaval and disaster. Obviously they think they need to help us once more."

Nixie came forward then and spoke to all of them. "*They are real and they appreciate your thanks at the Festivals. This is a time when you will need their help and they will need yours. Lady Erwyna Chose me to be Marella's companion because Marella is going to be Her representative in the coming months. One will be Chosen from each Element and they will need to work together if we are to survive. Make no mistake, this is not going to be easy. Our world is at stake."*

There was silence after Nixie's announcement. What could they say following that? After a moment, Riva sat up straight. "Well, if this is going to happen, then we may as well face it head on. Nothing will be gained by burying our heads in the sand. I'm going to call a Council Meeting so I can tell the others what has come to pass and to see if anything has happened with them. I feel time is of the essence."

Riva called Genna to her, and asked her to speak with the other Partners. She wanted them to meet up as soon as possible. It was very quickly arranged that the Elders would meet that night. Within a short amount of time, Riva had packed a few items and set out to Charon. She informed Edlin and Marella she probably wouldn't be back until the morning, maybe later, but would keep them up-to-date as best she could.

Marella and Edlin tried to keep busy, but there was only so much they could do. Marella kept repeating in her mind what had happened to the point where Nixie spoke. *"Marella, stop it!"* he said exasperatedly. *"It won't help to keep going over it. You know what happened, you know what Lady Erwyna said and you know what your mother said. Stop fretting and get some rest. You will know soon enough."*

"Do you know what's coming?" Marella asked Nixie. "You seem to know everything else."

Nixie looked away from Marella, hurt at her words. *"No, I don't know what's coming,"* he said stiffly, *"but I do know worrying without reason won't help. You may not like what has happened, Marella, but are you so ready to discount these past years with me? I have only ever done what I thought was right by you. I'll leave you now; I'm going to the Lake. I think you need some time by yourself."* And with those words, Nixie ran outside and headed off.

Marella sat on the top step of the porch looking in the direction Nixie had gone. She felt sorry for what she had said, but she was hurt he had kept this to himself all this time. *"What a mess,"* she thought to herself.

Edlin stepped outside and nudged Marella to one side so that he could sit down next to her. "Has Nixie gone to the Lake?" he asked Marella.

"Yes, we've had words and he said I needed some time by myself," Marella explained.

"I'll ask Torlan to keep an eye on him, he'll be okay," reassured Edlin.

"I know," Marella sighed. "I'm sorry I hurt him, but I'm having trouble getting my head around this. He knew, for all these years, he knew and he never said anything. He is my Partner. I never thought he would do something like this, Papa."

"Marella, I know this has been a shock for you, it has for me too. Can you remember back when you took your Test and you were introduced to Nixie for the first time? You were told that Nixie isn't a pet or a subordinate to you. He is his own authority and he has acted in this instance by his own authority. He hasn't done anything to put you at risk and from what you've said, he made sure he was with you during your first meeting with Lady Erwyna. Nixie hasn't done anything to earn your wrath. This is something *you* need to work past, not Nixie."

With those words, Edlin stood up and returned to the house. Marella sat in silence, mulling over all that had happened and been said. She knew she had some apologies to make, and she would, but she also needed some time by herself. Nixie was indeed right and knew her better than she knew herself at times. Marella's heart ached when she thought of the hurt in Nixie's voice when she had spoken to him.

"Nixie, I'm so sorry," she thought to him along their private path. *"I shouldn't have lashed out at you. I do know you've never done anything to hurt me and I do trust you. I'm not making excuses for my behaviour, but it's just been such a shock. I thought I had a grip on only one element but now it seems like there's more to it than I ever thought. I really am sorry. I love you. Please forgive me."*

After only a moment, she felt love flowing from Nixie and a gentle, non-verbal reassurance that he was indeed with her through everything. Marella could feel some of the tension in her shoulders easing. She really wanted to speak to Daren about what had happened. After all these years, he was still her best friend. They were still so close even though their paths had taken them in different directions. Marella decided she would ask Nixie to speak to Ula, Daren's wolf Life Partner, later on to find out when Daren would be free. She would take a trip to Bridd. She needed Daren's wisdom and strength.

The day passed slowly as Edlin and Marella tried to act as normal. Edlin was kept informed by Torlan. Through Genna, Riva's Partner, he learnt there was more to this than Marella's meeting with Lady Erwyna. Riva couldn't go into detail yet, but promised she would explain all upon her return.

* * *

The next day dawned bright and clear. Nixie had spoken to Ula the previous evening, but Daren was unable to meet with Marella for reasons that Ula didn't really go into. Marella was concerned about what could be happening with Daren. With the recent events, she may have been overreacting, but she just couldn't shake the unsettling feeling that events had been set in motion and were moving at a fast pace.

Marella and Edlin spent the next morning as they usually did, not knowing when Riva would return. Nixie spent some more time with Torlan on the Lake. Marella occupied herself with her chores and working on her small patch of garden. Edlin and Riva had given her her own piece of land in the hope she would stop killing all the house plants that Jorja gave her. It helped to soothe her mind when she was fingers deep in soil, not as much as when she was at the Lake, but Nixie was there. Things still weren't completely right between them, but they would get there.

By the afternoon, the air was hot and heavy. Marella looked up to the sky, but it was still clear and blue. *"It feels like there will be a storm soon,"* she thought to Nixie. *"Is everything safe at the Lake?"*

"Yes, we can feel it too," was his reply. *"There's something in the air."*

Marella picked up one of her towels, made her way down to the lake and checked over it. Everyone who made the lake their home was busy making sure the area was safe. She watched as Torlan helped some marsh wrens move their nest. It should have looked funny, seeing a beaver moving with bird's nest on his tail, but to Marella it was proof that their Partners were so much more than just 'mere animals'.

She decided now would be a good time to go for a quick swim to cool herself down. She stripped down to her swimming costume and immersed herself in the cool, calming waters of the lake. As she stretched her muscles and pushed against the water, she felt like things weren't as bad as she had previously thought. She heard some splashing and could see that some of the Partners were also taking a swim. A look of pleasure crossed her face. She stopped swimming and started to lazily float on her back. She closed her eyes and let herself drift away. *"Peace, little one, I am with you. Do not fret, all will be explained."* Although the words in her mind startled her at first, she soon felt an immense sensation of calm soothe her body. Marella knew that Lady Erwyna was still with her. With a renewed sense of purpose, she swam to the shore and dried herself off.

Nixie ran over to her side. *"I see you're feeling a bit better,"* he thought to her.

"Yes I am" she thought back. *"I'm sorry that I've been such a pain."*

Nixie chuffed at her while his laugh echoed through her head. *"Little one, you may be a pain but you are MY pain. I do understand your doubts and fears, I have my own. But I know in my heart, so long as we are working together, we will be okay."*

Halfway home, Genna spotted Marella and Nixie, as she flew through the trees. She chirped at them, and flew back towards the house.

"I presume Mama is back then," said Marella wryly. Genna was such a bird sometimes. She forgot that Marella could hear her even though she had been told by both Nixie and Marella lots of times.

They hurried the rest of the way home and sure enough, they found Riva had returned. When Marella walked through the front door, Riva was sat at the kitchen table, sipping a cup of lemongrass tea. Edlin raised his eyebrow in Marella's direction. "Yes please, Papa" she said.

They joined Riva at the table with their drinks and waited for her to start. Riva looked first at her husband, her rock, her strength – she needed him now more than ever because Riva was afraid. There was a storm brewing. The Weavers and Council had some information but not enough to have a clear view of what was to come. One thing, however, was clear – her youngest daughter was smack in the middle of whatever was going to happen. She took a deep breath and started with her explanation.

"The Lords and Ladies have indeed been busy. We've had word from all the main villages that one of their inhabitants has been contacted. With you, Marella, that makes one representative from each Element. It appears that those chosen are the strongest in that Element, although you are the only one with only one Element. You've all been told to wait and changes are occurring. We don't know how long it will be, but I can't see it being long."

Marella breathed a sigh as she heard her mother's words. *"One from each main village,"* she thought to Nixie. *"At least we won't be alone."* A thought occurred to her, "Mama, are you allowed to tell us who has been Chosen from each village?"

Riva smiled at Marella. "Yes, Marella, you may or may not be pleased to know that Daren has been Chosen to represent Earth; a boy called Kai, who is three years older than you, has been Chosen for Fire, and a girl who is younger than you by two years is to represent Air. Her name is Lani."

Marella mulled the names over in her mind. Apart from Daren, she didn't think she knew the others; their names weren't familiar to her. *"Nixie, do you know them?"*

"I don't know them personally, although I have heard their names. Kenna, the fox, is Partner to Kai and a hawk called Shaw is Partnered with Lani."

Riva cleared her throat to draw Marella's attention back to her. "It is the Summer Solstice in two days. Instead of us celebrating here, we Elders decided that we need to attend the one in Charon. Every village is invited and everyone who can make it is going. Others are already on their way. The eight Chosen will definitely need to be there."

Edlin looked startled at this news. He couldn't remember the last time there was only one celebration held. He quite liked the simplicity and familiarity of Ilyn's smaller celebration. Riva gave him a small smile of conciliation and held his hand on the table top. "I'm sorry, my love, but we really need to do this."

Edlin took a moment for himself. He looked at his wife and daughter who both sat still, watching him. He thought about what Riva had just told them and how this might affect Marella. He felt like a tree waving in the storm. It hadn't even started yet and he felt rocked to his foundations. Would this storm, when it reached its peak, bend him or break him?

With these thoughts he heard an old man's laugh in his head, as his beaver Life Partner spoke through their bond. *"So much drama, Edlin. Come now, you're no youngling anymore, to be scared of shadows. We will face whatever danger there may be together."* With Torlan's words in his mind, he grasped the strength and reassurance that Torlan was sending him, and combined it with his own, his momentary weakness faded.

He pushed his chair away from the table and stood up. A look of determination passed over his features as he spoke to Riva and Marella. "Come on then, slowpokes; if we're expected at Charon, we've got to get our things prepared."

He waited for Riva and Marella to stand and then gathered them both into his arms. He hugged them and felt their arms wrap around his body and hug him back.

"That's better, my lad." A smile spread across Edlin's face when he heard his Partner. *"I'll meet you there, I'll use the waterways. I'm coming to this one."*

Edlin bent his head and kissed both Riva and Marella on the top of their heads. "Torlan is going to meet us there," he told them. "We need to sort ourselves out."

With these words, he led the way up the stairs to the room he shared with Riva to start packing enough clothes and provisions for a short stay at Charon.

They arrived in Charon shortly before nightfall. They made their way to the Water Lodge to get settled in, with the help of Bradan and Orabel, his blue-winged teal duck Life Partner. Riva and Edlin were in the room next to Marella, which was very similar to hers, except it was slightly larger and had a bigger bed.

They had spoken on their way to Charon about what Riva expected to happen. The celebration was to take precedence, because no one knew for sure if anything would happen. So they were going to concentrate of the preparations and take the future as it came. For the next couple of days, Marella spent her time helping prepare Charon for the coming Summer Solstice.

This celebration was for the mid-point of Haf, when the hours of daylight were the longest. The Sun was at the highest point before beginning its slide into darkness. It was a time to celebrate both work and leisure; for children and childlike play. It was now that they would celebrate the ending of the waxing year and the beginning of the waning year, in preparation for the harvest to come. Midsummer was a time to absorb the Sun's warming rays and it was another fertility celebration, not only for humans, but also for crops and animals.

Decorations around Charon included Summertime flowers - especially sunflowers - seashells, aromatic potpourri and Summer fruits. Most people decorated their front doors with a wreath made of yellow feathers for prosperity and red feathers for sexuality, intertwined and tied together with ivy. Other decorations were abundant around the village in the colours of white, red, maize yellow or golden yellow, green, blue and tan. Sun wheels which had been made at Imbolc were now displayed prominently from ceilings and on trees, with shades of yellow and gold ribbons and Summer herbs.

During the day, the majority of the Healers would be collecting herbs and flowers as it was said they were more powerful if picked on the day of the Summer Solstice itself. There would be a bonfire in the main square, where some of the more adventurous boys and girls were going to jump over in the evening.

Marella didn't have time to find Daren as she was so busy with the preparations. She did manage to speak with Ula, just to let her know she and Nixie had arrived in Charon and would speak to him after the Solstice if they didn't have a chance before. Ula replied they would speak very soon, so Marella left it at that, knowing Daren would now know they were okay.

* * *

The day of the Solstice dawned with a clear sky. Everyone from the village had risen early to greet the sun as it made its appearance above the horizon. This was a time for quiet reflection; there was none of the music and loud celebration that would happen later. Most people meditated to reflect on the turning of the wheel and the darkness and light that was both in their lives and the world around them.

Afterwards, people mingled, catching up with friends they hadn't seen for a while. Children played and visited one of the smaller lakes for a swim. Someone had tied a rope to the trunk of a tree so the children were swinging out over the water before letting go. The atmosphere was relaxed and joyful.

Food was laid out so everyone could eat whenever they wanted. There were no strict mealtimes on this day. Foods included grilled vegetables, fresh fruit salads, fiery grilled salmon and candied ginger which the children especially seemed to enjoy. The drinks were a variety of fresh fruit juices but as the day progressed someone brought out jugs of mead and ale too. It was mid-afternoon before Marella caught sight of Ula. She had grown into a sleek, well-muscled she-wolf and her fur was still that gorgeous shade of white, although Marella could see a bit of the tan colouring that was usually hidden underneath the outer coat.

"*Hello Ula,*" she thought to her. "*Are you well?*"

"*Hello Marella, yes thank you. Are you?*"

As they got closer to each other, Marella burst out laughing and Ula jumped up and put her paws on Marella's shoulders, her tongue lolling out the side of her mouth in a wolfish smile. "*So very polite, little one, I wondered if it was indeed you,*" Ula thought as she gave her a wet lick from her chin upwards.

"*Urgh Ula! Did you have to do that?*" Marella wiped her face, although she was laughing as she did so. "*So where's Daren, I haven't seen him yet?*"

"*He's over there somewhere; he was loitering near the paprika grilled salmon when I left.*"

Marella burst out laughing because Daren's fondness for the fiery dish was well known. As her laughter peeled out, several heads turned towards her. Her laugh was beautiful and seemed to have the quality that made everyone want to smile or laugh with her.

Ula dropped down to her paws, close to Marella. "*Seriously for a moment though; are you okay, Marella? There are strange happenings going on and Nixie said you were right in the middle of it. He told me that you have met with Lady Erwyna.*"

"*Yes I did. Poor Nixie, I gave him a hard time. I was struggling to understand and took it out on him.*" Marella paused as Ula looked at her reproachfully. "*I apologised! It's doesn't make it right, but I did apologise. She didn't really tell me that much. She just said that I had done well over the years, things were changing and the*

Elements needed to work together. It was Nixie, afterwards, who told me that I was Her Chosen Initiate. I need to take note of my Visions but I've not had chance to Weave since it happened."

Ula felt the emotion behind Marella's words. The poor girl was storm tossed and had no idea which way was up or down. Ula gave an internal sigh, in this respect the Partners were so much better off. They had a general idea of what must be done, but needed to wait for further instructions. Their human Partners had no idea and were generally impatient at waiting.

"Daren will tell you more about his meeting with the Lady Daire, but trust me when I say he was as shocked as you. Little one, you are not, and will not be, on your own in this. You will have three others like you and there will be four Partners, all keeping the balance. Don't let fear bind you. Trust your heart and your intuition. After all, it's what you've done all your life."

As Ula finished speaking, she gave a gentle nudge to Marella's legs. Marella crouched down and put her arms around Ula's neck and gave her a tight squeeze. As she stood, she saw Daren headed towards them, juggling what looked like a piece of salmon in his hands.

When he saw Marella, his eyes lit up and a broad grin appeared. He rushed over towards them, but was jostled against someone's shoulder. As he did so, he dropped his piece of fish. He apologised and looked towards the ground in dismay, only to find Nixie stood next to him with the piece of salmon in his mouth. With a quick snap of his jaws, the morsel was gone, but the glint of mischievousness shone bright in Nixie's eyes.

With a sound that was halfway between a laugh and a groan, Daren finally made it to Marella and wrapped her up in his arms. "You need to control that Partner of yours," he said. "He's just stolen my salmon!"

Marella shared a look with Ula and laughed. "Nixie didn't steal it, you dropped it," she defended her Partner as she returned Daren's embrace.

Daren just grunted at her and held on tightly. He had missed Marella so much and felt awful for not being able to see her when she needed him. Ula had told him how upset Marella had been, but he just hadn't been able to go to her at that point. Marella held him just as tight, the two of them an oasis of calm amidst the crowd.

After a moment Daren drew back, but kept hold of Marella's hands. He raised them and said "Now, let me look at you. It's been so long."

Marella laughed at him and said "I'm still the same, but I think you've grown another inch or so."

Daren did indeed seem taller and his shoulders were wider. Marella whistled as she looked him up and down. "So who's the lucky lady?" she asked him teasingly.

"Pardon me? What are you talking about?" Daren asked her.

"I mean, looking like you do now, you must have someone. Or do I need to beat them all off with a big stick?" Marella laughed at the look that crossed Daren's face as he understood what she was saying.

"Shut it, you," he said and gave her a small push. "No, there's no one for me, not yet," he laughed. He sobered up and gave Marella a serious look. "Plus the fact, I don't think that this is the right time, do you?"

That stopped Marella's laughing. "No," she said, the smile disappearing from her face, "No, I guess it isn't."

They made their way over to the shade of an apple tree and sat down beneath it.

"So Ula tells me you were chosen by Lady Daire, what happened?" Marella queried.

Daren shifted to get comfortable and drank from his cup before starting. "I was practicing my Chlorokinesis, some of the plants weren't growing as well as they should, so I thought I'd give them a helping hand…" Daren said.

"Hold on, you were practicing what?" asked Marella, before grimacing as she realised she had interrupted him.

"Chlorokinesis – it's the ability to control plants, trees and stuff. I can help them to grow or to strengthen them. It's one of my Earth talents," Daren explained. "Anyway, before I was so rudely interrupted," he continued with a grin on his face, "I was practicing, but it's not something you can do on the move, or at least not that I know of. I have to sit still and meditate to find my centre before I can control it. So I was starting to relax, and about to start on the crops in front of me, when I felt a strange sensation. I tried to stand up, but couldn't move and I was sinking. It wasn't just a feeling, it was really happening. I panicked a bit because I couldn't move, was dropping through the earth, and I was worried about being able to breathe!"

As Daren spoke, Marella could see his shoulders tense up. He was trying to keep it light now, but she could see that he had been scared.

"It was Ula who reassured me. She'd been sat near me when I'd started to zone. When it started, she came up to me and touched her nose to mine. She told me to take a deep breath and then I'd be through. I had no idea what she was talking about but I've trusted her for too long to start doubting now so I did as she bid. I can't describe the feeling; it was like nothing I've ever dreamt of. I had to shut my eyes, it was just too much." Daren gave a slight shudder before continuing.

"When I opened my eyes, I was in a big room, sat on a chair. There was food and drink and everything was warm and cosy. Not what I imagined I would see as I went down, that's for sure. Then this Lady was there. I swear, I never saw her when I first looked around the room and I didn't hear her enter through a door – she was just there. I stood up and then felt Ula put her head under my hand. Honestly, I thought I was going crazy. I hadn't seen or felt Ula either since going underground, but there she was.

Anyway, this Lady was gorgeous. I'm probably not supposed to say that but she was. She was a bit smaller than me and curves in all the right places. She had long chocolate brown hair and gorgeous caramel eyes."

Marella looked at Daren in amazement. She'd never heard him talk about anyone like this before. She couldn't help teasing him, just a little bit. "Wow, Daren, you're making me hungry with this description," she said to him as she chewed on the inside of her cheek to stop herself smiling.

Daren looked up, having been lost in his remembering. He saw the look on Marella's face and burst out laughing. "Yes, I guess it would make you hungry," he said. "Chocolate and caramel – but I swear that's what she looked like. Anyway, to carry on, she told me who she was and that four were being chosen to represent the Elements. She said the world is out of balance for some reason and they don't know why. We need to put it right, but that was all I was told. The next thing I know, I'm topside again, sat in the same place and same position as before, but the crops are now fully grown and healthy. I hadn't done it. Lady Daire had."

Marella leaned back against the trunk of the tree and thought about what he'd said. "Well you got more information than I did," she said. "Lady Erwyna just told me that I had done well and she was proud of me. Then she said our time had run out, but we would meet again. It was Nixie who told me that I was her Initiate. I went home and told Mama and Papa straight away."

"I didn't get a chance to tell my folks first" said Daren wryly. "Ail was walking the fields to see how the crops were growing. He saw me disappear and then reappear. He said it was only for about thirty breaths I was gone before I came back. But I'd been down there longer than that. He gave me some bread and water and took me home. He sat down with my parents and explained parts of it first and then I filled in the missing pieces." He looked at Marella and said "Come on then, spill. What happened to you?"

Marella explained everything to him, starting with the swim and finishing with what had been said afterwards with her parents and Nixie. "I still feel horrible for the things I said to him," she finished, "but he has been wonderful in accepting my apology and helping me come to terms with all of this. I still have no idea what's going on!"

"I may be able to help," a quiet voice said, not far from them. Daren and Marella both looked around to see who had spoken and saw a beautiful, young woman watching them. She had long, golden blonde hair and big light blue, almost grey, eyes. She was wearing a white dress with light blue and yellow swirls on it that complemented her curvaceous figure, with a girdle of silver.

Daren jumped to his feet and extended a hand out towards her.

"Hello, I'm Daren," he said, "and you are…?"

"My name is Lani and I'm to represent Air," she told them.

"Hi Lani, I'm Marella. You'd better come and join us."

Lani made her way to them, Daren and Marella shifting their positions to make room for her. As they did, they heard a plaintive, rising whistle that sounded a bit like *kee-ahh*. Marella and Daren turned their heads in all directions, trying to see who or what had made that sound. "You're looking in the wrong place," said Lani. "Look up."

They looked towards the skies and saw a beautiful red-shouldered hawk circling above them. As Lani raised her arm in the air, he slowly descended until he was able to land on her bare wrist. She immediately brought him closer to her body so that she would be more able to bear his weight.

He was a colourful hawk with dark-and-white chequered wings, warm reddish barring on the breast and barred reddish-peachy under parts. His tail was black with narrow white bands. As he had flown down to Lani, Marella had seen narrow, pale crescents near his wingtips.

As Lani gently stroked his breast with her fingers, she introduced them. "This is my Partner, Shaw."

Both Marella and Daren murmured their greetings to Shaw. He watched them for a moment before pecking at Lani's fingers, and pushed himself off to fly up into the tree branches.

"So," said Daren, drawing out the word so it was almost a sigh, "you may be able to help?"

"You are to represent Air?" queried Marella.

"Yes and yes," said Lani in her melodious voice. "My meeting was with Adaryn, Lord of the Skies, and although it was only short, he still managed to give me some information."

She took a deep breath and seemed to steady herself. She opened those big blue-grey eyes and looked at Marella as she spoke. "Four artefacts have been stolen, one which represents each Element. They were under the guardianship of our Lords and Ladies, but someone was able to find them and take them. We need to find those artefacts and bring them to Charon. Otherwise the Elements will be out of balance and our world will suffer."

"Suffer how?" asked Marella.

"Wind storms, fire balls, earthquakes, tidal waves" Lani explained. "We all know the Elements; imagine them at their most destructive and that is what we're facing."

Silence followed her pronouncement.

"Wow, you really know how to get the party started," said a voice mockingly from nearby.

As Marella looked around she saw a man leaning on the tree next to them. They had been so engrossed with what Lani was saying; none of them had noticed him standing there. He was quite tall and well-built but lean, with dark brown hair that was short and spiky and deep brown eyes. He was leaning back with one knee bent up, his foot resting against the trunk, and his arms were folded across his chest.

He cocked an eyebrow sardonically at Marella as she looked at him. "Have you seen enough now?" he asked.

Marella felt a slight glow on her cheeks as she looked away.

He pushed himself away from the tree and sauntered over to them. He sat down with his legs folded and gave them all a sarcastic smile.

"Who are you?" asked Daren calmly. He didn't like how this stranger had interrupted them, but he thought he might have some idea as to who he might be.

"I'm Kai and I complete this little… circle," he said, moving his finger around. "I'm Fire."

"You mean you represent Fire," said Marella, lifting her face slightly into the air.

"No, little girl, I mean I am Fire so you'd better make sure you don't get burnt," Kai answered her.

To his surprise, Marella burst out laughing. "Oh please, do you practice saying that to get the ultimate effect?" she chuckled.

Daren gave a small smile at her words but kept his focus on Kai. Lani gave a chuckle, but quieted down when Kai looked in her direction.

Kai was angered by Marella's words. He was about to give her a sharp retort when Daren spoke.

"So you're the last one. We're all here now," he said, pushing his hair out of his face. "Did Lord Ethon give you anything that might help us all?"

"No," said Kai, abruptly.

"No?" questioned Marella. "That's it, just 'no'? Have you even *had* a meeting with Lord Ethon yet?" She turned away in disgust at Kai's attitude. She really hoped that he was wrong and he wasn't the last member.

"Oh, I've had a meeting with him alright. Pretty much the same as wind girl's over there. Item stolen, world destructing, yada yada yada. Doesn't mean I have to tell everything to *you* though. Some things are private." Kai's face was set in an angry look and his tone was clipped and sharp.

Daren tried to ease the tension that was rampant among their small group. "Come on; let's just calm those tempers down, shall we? We are all going to have to work together to succeed, and that's not going to happen if we are going for each other's throats all the time."

"And who made you the leader of this little band?" asked Kai, still as angry. "I'm the eldest so I should be."

"Oh don't be ridiculous," said Marella sharply. "It doesn't have to work that way."

"Well of course you're going to stick up for your little lover boy. How could I ever imagine anything else?" Kai retorted.

"What?" gasped Marella. "Daren and I aren't... we're not... I mean... that's none of your business!" she finally managed to sputter out.

"Whatever," laughed Kai, "I don't really care anyhow. Just keep out of my way and we'll get this finished as soon as possible and we can all go our separate ways. The quicker I can get rid of you lot the better."

"That's really pathetic," cried Marella, loudly. "This is bigger than just you, you know. We're all involved in this. How *dare* you speak to us this way? Just who do you think you are?"

By now, they had attracted quite a crowd. People stood there watching them argue and fight amongst themselves. Some shook their heads in dismay. Were these really the four human Chosen? Those meant to be the ones to help bring back the balance?

Their Partners were together by the side of the tree, watching their humans in part amusement, part disgust.

~ 3 ~

Kenna, the fox, looked at the others and said *"You know, he's not normally like this. The meeting with Ethon shook him up and then brought his foundations crashing down about his ears. I don't understand why he's being so aggressive. We've talked about this and he knows what he must do. He also knows that he must be part of the Four to succeed."* She shook her head, looking at Kai.

Nixie gave a laugh and said *"You should have seen how Marella reacted. Don't worry Kenna, they'll figure out their place and balance together. It was bound to be explosive. We need balance, but the opposites will clash before they settle."*

"Speak for yourself," said Shaw, with a chuckle. *"You'll be lucky to get Lani worked up. She's so shy and tends to go along with what everyone wants."*

Ula looked at Shaw and bared her teeth in what the humans may have found threatening but the animals knew was her biggest smile. *"You just wait until Daren sets his sights on her. I can guarantee that he'll rile her up."*

Shaw started laughing in his mind and before too long; the others were all joining in. They knew what was important and knew they had to work together. Their humans would catch up soon enough. They were in for an interesting journey and they were all looking forward to it.

~ 4 ~

During this time, the argument between Marella and Kai had continued, with Lani watching from the sidelines as Daren tried to keep the peace.

As it was building up to a crescendo, the four humans were each wrapped inside a wall of their major Element. Daren was surrounded by a wall of earth slowly moving around him. Lani had the air swooshing around her, going so fast as to resemble a tornado, with Lani as the eye. Kai was surrounded by a wall of flames that, although burned hot, didn't affect him. Marella was also enclosed in a wall of water; whereas Lani's was a tornado, Marella's was a whirlpool.

The sound of these Elements drowned out any complaints or arguments that were occurring as their other senses were overwhelmed by the walls surrounding them.

The argument between the four of them ceased once they could no longer see or hear each other. They all stood still, trapped within a circular, moving prison of Elemental magic. The gathered crowd watched in amazement as the Elements appeared.

Everyone who was within earshot heard a voice come out of nowhere. The voice was strong and loud but with a distinct echo. "What nonsense is this?" it said. "You are our Chosen Four and yet you bicker like younglings. Have we Chosen in error?"

Kai's voice rose above the noise of the flames. "No my lord, you have not. I apologise for my behaviour. I didn't mean to offend you."

"It is not us that are offended," the voice replied to him. "You have entered the circle of the Four and let loose with mockery and disdain. You have been answered in kind. Is this how you wish the quest to start? With derision? Or do you wish to work together in aid of your home? To help each other? To lighten up a dark situation or mood?

Think carefully now, all four of you. It is not too late; if you no longer wish to be our Chosen ones then you have until the phoenix rises to let us know. Once the phoenix has arisen, your position is set. Go now; separate from each other, but stay close to your Partners. Do not let this happen again."

With those final words, which had gained in volume until they boomed out, there was a loud thunderclap and the Elements dropped from around the four humans. They all stood there silently, looking at each other.

Ula approached Daren and put her head under his hand. She turned him around and bumped his leg with her body to prompt him to move. Daren walked away, turning his head back around to look at Marella, before he raised his hand slightly in farewell.

Shaw flew down and Lani raised her arm for him to land on. She looked into his eyes for a moment before quietly saying her goodbyes and walking back in the direction of the main square.

Marella and Kai were left behind, looking at each other once Daren and Lani had gone. They made not a sound, not a movement, but gazed at each other. Nixie and Kenna made their way to them and stayed at their sides.

After a moment a look of regret passed over Kai's face. "I'm sorry," he said. "It won't happen again."

"I'm sorry too," said Marella. "I don't really know how it got out of hand so fast."

"We're opposites," said Kai. "I guess we're going to clash."

"I hope that Daren and Lani don't have the same issue or this is going to be a long journey," replied Marella.

Kai lifted his hand in a gesture of farewell before turning around and walking away with Kenna by his side.

Marella stayed where she was and dropped to the ground. She drew her knees up to her chest and wrapped her arms around them as she sat in the shade of the tree. She put her head on her arms and didn't say anything further. Nixie curled up on the ground next to her.

The crowd dispersed as they continued with their own business, unsure of what they had actually seen or heard. Some swore the voice they heard was feminine, whilst others said it was male. It would take a while before they realised that the voice they had heard was the voice of the Lord or Lady of their strongest Element.

* * *

Marella spent a long time in the shade of that tree. She sat there and considered what had happened and the words she had heard. The voice she heard had been Lady Erwyna's but after hearing Kai's apology, she knew he had heard somebody else. She presumed it was Lord Ethon, but until she spoke to him, she wouldn't know for sure.

She wasn't sure why the sparks had flown between Kai and herself. From the moment he'd opened his mouth, he just seemed to annoy her. It was as if he knew the specific tone to use, the exact turn of phrase, or the precise look, to push her buttons and make her want to throw things at him. She'd never had this reaction to anyone before. Marella knew herself to be fairly easygoing, and made an effort to have a pleasant word with everyone. But somehow Kai managed to short-circuit all of her better impulses and brought her down to swapping insults and being sarcastic.

She was ashamed she had reacted that way, and to think that they'd had to be separated too. She buried her head further into her arms as she thought back over the events.

Nixie decided now was the time to speak up. He had been lying next to Marella, listening in on her ruminations and feeling the depth of her shame and regret. If he didn't put a stop to it now, she would carry this with her for a long time to come and Nixie knew things were about to become eventful, Marella didn't need this on top of everything else.

"Marella, my love, enough now," he thought to her. *"You're beating yourself up over this and it needs to stop. It has happened, it will probably happen again, but your focus needs to be on the future, not of the past. Lady Erwyna has chosen you; you will know soon enough what is expected. Learn from what happened between Kai and yourself, but don't linger on it. Learn and move on. The river does not flow in one spot constantly."*

"I know you are right, Nixie, but I can't help thinking about it. I don't understand why I behaved in that manner. I'm not a youngling!" said Marella.

"No, you are not," Nixie agreed. *"However, you've also had limited dealings with those who dwell in Hufel. Fire is Water's natural opposite, you surely didn't imagine that you were going to be best friends straight away? You have all been Chosen to go on a quest together. You need to learn to work together. No one ever said that you had to like each other."*

At his words, Marella gave a small chuckle. *"Well it's certainly going to be an interesting journey then,"* she thought back to him, with a smile in her mental voice.

"That it will be, one way or another," said Nixie. *"Come on, let's move on. Let's find your family and celebrate. It will be dusk soon enough and then they'll light the bonfire."*

Marella stood up and dusted off her backside. She straightened up her clothing, and with Nixie by her side, went off in search of her family. As she walked back to the main square, she saw Lani off to one side. Lani was sitting pretty much the same as Marella had been, but she had Shaw perched on her bended knees. Marella wanted to go over to her, but remembered the words from her Lady about keeping separate for the time being.

Looking around, she saw Daren and Kai in the distance, opposite but equidistant from each other. Marella felt a tightness she hadn't even been aware of before that moment, ease within her chest. She realised each of them had sat the same amount of distance from each other and in the direction of their Element. She was sure this wasn't something that had been planned, but it gave her hope that they would be able to work together on the quest. They were all unconsciously acting as their Element already, so Marella hoped it boded well for the future.

Marella spent the rest of the morning with her family, enjoying the festivities. There were so many stalls around, fragrant with the food they had to offer. Her mouth watered every time she walked past one, so she ate far more than she would normally. The extra sustenance in her stomach helped her to feel more grounded, which in turn, helped to ease the churning emotions within.

Jorja had also arrived in Charon for the celebration, so they had a heartfelt reunion. Although no one was really that far from anywhere else, their individual duties gave them little time for get-togethers. That was one of the reasons why so many families celebrated the festivals as the wheel turned. Their family would come from the four directions and they would pay their respects together. It was a time for love and closeness.

As the time turned towards the mid-day ritual, things quietened down. The music became softer and more soothing. This was just a lull until darkness fell and then the celebrations would become louder again. It was at this time that Jorja left the family's table. "I'll be back in a moment," she said to her mother and father.

Marella looked up at her sister as she left and caught the wink that Jorja sent in her direction. Although she didn't think anything was wrong with Jorja, she could feel curiosity bubbling inside. She thought to Salali. *"Salali, my friend, please forgive the intrusion, but I am after your thoughts. Is Jorja okay? It is unlike her to leave the celebration."*

Salali chittered from a nearby tree branch, where he was sat contentedly munching nuts and seeds. *"No forgiveness necessary. I have already told you that you are welcome to speak with me anytime. Jorja is well but has to do something. Fear not, Marella, this is a good thing."* With those words, he carried on eating.

Marella sat back and waited. Whatever it was that Jorja was doing, she was doing it with Salali's knowledge and blessing. If he was at all concerned about it, he wouldn't be sat there eating.

Within moments, Marella could see Jorja returning to their table. She turned her head and saw the excitement on her parents' faces they were trying hard to contain. She looked back towards her sister and saw she was actually leading someone with her. She stopped by the table and drew him next to her. It was a man a little bit taller than Jorja, with sandy brown hair. His hazel eyes seemed full of laughter and, as he looked at Jorja, Marella could see love in them too.

"Edlin, Riva, Marella." He greeted them with a nod of his head to show respect.

"Hello Derwen," smiled Edlin.

"Nice to see you again," said Riva, also smiling at both Jorja and Derwen.

"This is Derwen?" Marella asked unnecessarily. The question turned the smiles into laughter as they all realised Marella hadn't actually met Derwen yet.

"Yes, Marella, this is Derwen," introduced Jorja. "My apologies, sister-mine, I forgot you were training at the times I had brought Derwen home with me."

"I knew he had come down with you," said Marella. "I'm sorry, Derwen," she said to him. "I'm not normally this air-headed."

"Please, sit and join us," said Edlin, rising and clapping Derwen on his back. Marella shifted along so that Jorja could sit back next to her, with Derwen by her other side.

"Thank you," said Derwen.

"How are you?" asked Riva, "and how is Blasa? Is he here tonight?"

"I'm very well, thanks Riva. Blasa is here somewhere, getting his head into business that doesn't concern him, no doubt."

Marella was perplexed with his answer, although the others laughed in response. Seeing the confusion upon Marella's face, Derwen explained that Blasa was his Partner and was a ram. Marella was intrigued as she hadn't met a ram Partner before. "I will introduce you later," said Derwen, knowing from Jorja that her sister had a fascination for all the different Partners, and the reason behind it.

They all sat there, enjoying small talk and each others' company. From the corner of her eye, Marella saw a ram approach the table. He was a handsome fellow with a light brown coat, sturdy in the leg, and with eyes an unusual shade of orange. His horns curled up around the top of his ears, which were a darker shade of brown, before coming back round underneath, so that the tips of the horn pointed upwards. He had a mottled white and brown muzzle and a white patch on his back, just above his tail.

Derwen gestured to the ram, who came and stood next to him. Derwen looked at Marella and gave the introduction. "Marella, this is Blasa."

"Blasa, this is Jorja's sister, Marella. She can hear and speak to you, so if you wish to speak to her, please feel free to do so. It won't upset me." With those words, Derwen gave Marella a big smile. A rush of warmth ran through her as she understood he was trying to put her at ease. She had never felt comfortable talking to other Partners, even though she knew she was able to do so. The fact he had just said all that out loud to Blasa, who knew Derwen's thoughts before he had even formulated them into words, told Marella that it was for her sake that he had spoken them.

Marella bowed her head towards Blasa and said out loud, "Merry Meet Blasa, I hope you are well."

Blasa looked at Marella with those deep orange eyes. *"Hello Marella, it is nice to meet you. And yes, I am well, thank you."* Blasa's 'voice' was deep and rumbling - it made Marella think of the earth itself.

With Blasa there, Salali jumped down from the branch where he had been sat and ran towards him. With a leap and a bound, he jumped onto Blasa's back whereby Blasa turned his head to acknowledge him before looking back towards Derwen and Jorja.

"So I'm thinking, from what I'm seeing from your Partners, that you have something to say?" Edlin spoke the words to them with a twinkle in his eye. He guessed what was coming and was overjoyed for his daughter, but he wanted confirmation before he said anything. It would be embarrassing for everyone if he was wrong!

Derwen blushed before giving a small cough and straightening his shoulders. Jorja just twitched but kept silent. Marella could see from where she sat that Jorja was holding Derwen's hand beneath the table.

"Come on, lad," said Edlin kindly, "we've known each other for a fair few years now. You know you can speak with us."

Derwen nodded and looked at Jorja. What he saw in her eyes gave him strength, because he took a deep breath and said "Sir, it is with pleasure that I ask for the blessing from you both so that Jorja and I may be joined in marriage."

"Hmmm," said Edlin, rubbing his hand over his mouth. "Well, this is a serious step to take. Are you sure that you're both ready?"

"Yes Papa, we are. We've thought this through, and we have been together for years already," said Jorja eagerly.

"Edlin, you are awful," said Riva, giving him a poke in the ribs. She stood up and walked around the table. She pulled Jorja and Derwen so that they were standing and gave them both the customary double kiss on their cheeks. She then held one of their hands in hers as she completed the traditional words and actions. "I give you my blessings as the mother of Jorja, and also as the Elder of Water. It is with honour you have asked and it is with honour that you receive. May you each and together be blessed with health, happiness, harmony, and love."

She finished speaking and gave them both a hug before retaking her seat, as Edlin moved around the table to give his blessing too. He repeated the words and actions of Riva before pulling them both into a bear hug.

The tables that surrounded them gave a spontaneous round of clapping. Marriages, and the blessings that came with them, were always joyous events and everyone could see Derwen and Jorja were indeed happy together.

Jorja blushed slightly as she looked around and thanked everyone. Edlin returned to his seat and hugged Riva. He was so happy for Jorja, but hadn't realised he would feel the urge to cry at the thought of his eldest daughter taking a husband, even if he had known this day was coming for years, and thoroughly approved of Derwen.

Derwen and Jorja moved to stand in front of Marella who was smiling broadly from ear to ear, her eyes shining with unshed tears. Derwen and Jorja pulled Marella to her feet so they stood in the circle that mimicked Riva and Edlin's. Although still smiling, Marella was also puzzled as this wasn't part of the traditional blessing that she knew of.

"Little one, please would you do us the highest honour of giving us your blessing too?" asked Jorja.

"We have both agreed that although this is unusual, it wouldn't seem right to us to start our lives together without having your blessing as well," said Derwen.

Marella was amazed, siblings never got asked for their blessings. With a lump in her throat, she nodded her head. As she was about to open her mouth to say the words of the blessing, Nixie spoke into her mind.

"Don't forget Marella, you are now the Chosen of Erwyna. You need to include that in your blessing."

"Are you sure, Nixie?" Marella thought back. *"That seems a bit... presumptuous to me."*

"I am positive," replied Nixie. *"Trust me."*

Marella did trust him, and right now she was feeling a strong sense of satisfaction in him, along with the small part of mischievousness that was part and parcel of who Nixie was.

Marella gave both Jorja and Derwen the double kiss before taking their hands back in hers. "I give you my blessings as the sister of Jorja, and also as the Chosen of Lady Erwyna. It is with honour you have asked and it is with honour that you receive. May you each and together be blessed with health, happiness, harmony, and love."

There was a gasp from the tables, and Marella's parents, as she gave her blessing which changed into whispers of wonder, as from Marella's hands appeared light blue swirls. They rose from her hands and slowly surrounded the three until they were encased within a mass of sparks.

The lights moved faster and changed colour as they did so, deepening to a glorious shade of dark blue. Two swirls came out of the mass, slowed down and hovered at eye height with Jorja and Derwen. They both stood there, still holding hands with Marella, hardly daring to breathe.

Marella, moving with a surety beyond her knowledge, lifted their hands up as the two swirls slowly changed to glowing silver. Slowly, almost carefully, they landed on their joined hands, one on the back of Jorja's left hand, one on the back of Derwen's right. Their hands tingled where the symbols were sat. With a flash of blue and silver, the illumination surrounding their bodies disappeared, but on the hands of Jorja and Derwen, were the silver swirls now permanently on them.

Jorja gasped and raised her eyes from her hand to Marella. Derwen was examining his hand, rubbing his fingers over the top of the mark. A wave of tiredness swept through Marella but Nixie was quickly there to give her support. As she faced Jorja and Derwen, swaying slightly on her feet, Marella said "You have been doubly blessed this day. You have received not only the blessings of the family, but also of Lady Erwyna herself. Blessed be."

Derwen and Jorja pulled Marella into a hug as they tried to show their appreciation to her. Marella returned the hug as best she could, but was feeling weaker than she wanted to admit.

Riva and Edlin stood up, came round the table, and they too joined in with the hug as they tried to process what they had seen. By sheer willpower, Marella remained on her feet, taking in strength from her family. Slowly, she started to feel better.

The group hug separated and Marella was once more visible to the rest of the tables. Blasa and Salali moved over towards her. Blasa stood by her right hand side as Nixie stood on her left. Salali scampered up until he was sat on her right shoulder. Blasa butted Marella's hand until she placed her hand upon his head. Nixie stood on his back legs and raised himself until his head was also under her hand. Salali wrapped his tail around Marella's neck.

"Take some of our strength too," said Blasa.

"It will get easier," said Nixie.

"Thank you," whispered Salali.

"A toast," was heard through the crowd. "A toast to Jorja and Derwen to congratulate them on their upcoming marriage."

Wooden cups were filled with apple juice, the traditional drink of both Sabbats and blessings. As everyone around them drank to the health and happiness of Jorja and Derwen, Marella gratefully drank with them. Although she was indeed toasting Jorja and her beloved, she could also feel the apple juice seemingly running through her veins, filling her with strength and vitality.

Everyone sat down, those that had moved to get closer returning to their tables. Marella sank thankfully back into her seat, not quite believing what she had done or seen.

There was silence at their table as they all tried to hide their surprise at what had just happened. Marella looked around at them sat there and a feeling of warmth suffused her body. She looked at them, and the love she felt for each and every one of them showed clearly in her face. One by one, they all looked up at Marella as they felt the weight of her gaze upon them.

"I can't explain, I didn't know it would happen and, if I'm honest, I'm not totally sure what *did* happen. All I do know is that no matter what comes at me throughout the rest of my life, I will always remember this moment, and the love that I bear you all," said Marella.

Jorja reached over to Marella and grasped her hand. "Marella, I have no words to express how much your blessing meant to both Derwen and I. We had agreed that we were going to ask you, but that was before we even knew you were the Chosen of Lady Erwyna. To get the blessing of you would have been enough, it would have been perfect. To get this…" she said, looking down at the swirl upon her hand, "it's just so much more than I ever expected."

Derwen nodded his head, agreeing with his wife-to-be. "I know things are going to change for you, Marella, and I know we won't be able to go with you, but if there is *anything* that Jorja and I can do to help you, even if it is just supplies or a place to sleep, then please let us know. I will never be able to repay you for the honour that you have given us."

Marella smiled as she looked at Derwen. "You don't have to do any of that" she said. "I'm glad I was able to, even if it did turn out unexpectedly."

"Don't turn it down just yet," said Derwen. "Wait until the Lords and Ladies gather the eight of you together and let you know what is happening. You might just need what we have to offer then," he finished with a wink and a wry grin.

Edlin and Riva had sat watching their daughters talk with Derwen. They both felt very happy at what had just happened, although Riva had been pleasantly surprised when they had asked for Marella's blessing. She knew how close they had been as younglings, and it was perfect that her blessing had been sought after. To receive the blessing of Lady Erwyna on top of that made this occasion unforgettable. Riva did, however, feel a twinge of jealousy within her which she knew was uncalled for. Marella hadn't asked for this and Lady Erwyna would give Her blessing where She chose, not where Riva commanded.

"Come on now," said Edlin to his family. "We need to finish up here and make our way to the main square. It won't be long before the bonfire is lit."

Everyone nodded in agreement and set to finishing their drinks and meal before moving off.

~ 6 ~

The bonfire was set in the middle of the main square. It was here that the ritual for the Summer Solstice would be held and led by the four Elders. Marella and her family arrived in plenty of time and Riva went off to join the other Elders. The time was fast approaching for the ritual, and the square was filling up with people.

Marella stood looking at the bonfire but not really seeing it. She thought about how her life had been so far and what it would bring in the future. The Summer Solstice was about releasing negativity, amongst other things, and she was determined to put any negative feelings aside so that she could do the best she could for Lady Erwyna.

"That is all I will ever ask of you." She heard Erwyna's voice whisper in the winds.

Marella bowed her head at the words and put her hand over her heart. *"My best is what you shall have, from this day onwards,"* she thought. The slight breeze swirled around her ankles, travelling up the length of her body in a gentle caress before moving on, and Marella knew that Erwyna had heard and acknowledged her pledge.

Marella looked up and looked around at the people gathered around her. Everyone had found a place around the bonfire in the direction of where their strength lay. Jorja stood with Derwen at the north side of the bonfire, Marella could see Daren and his family next to them. Looking to the east, Lani was stood near to the front with, who Marella presumed was, her friends and family around her.

Marella forced her head to continue looking around and turned to the south where she saw Kai and the rest of the Fire village. When Kai saw her looking, he surprised her by dropping his head into a slight bow to her. There was none of the mockery she had already started to associate with Kai in that gesture and that shook her more than she wanted to acknowledge.

"I really can't figure him out," she thought to Nixie, irritably. *"He mocks us all this afternoon and now shows me a sign of respect. What is it with him?"*

Nixie let out a chuff of laughter in her mind. *"Marella, you are seeing things that the others won't. One of the reasons is because he is your Elemental opposite. Daren and Lani will have the same issues, although how they resolve it has yet to be seen, the same with you and Kai. It will take time, little one."*

The murmuring that accompanied any gathering slowly dropped to silence as the Elders all stepped into the circle. Demi, as the eldest, slowly raised her arms and held a flaming torch in the air to get everyone's attention. Only then did she start the ritual.

"We celebrate the noon of Haf with this rite held in honour of the

Blazing God of the Sun. All of nature vibrates with the fertile energies of the Goddess and the God. The Earth is bathed with the warmth, light and life of the Sun. The Wheel of the Year turns again," she said.

"Since Yule, the light has been growing ever stronger. At Ostara, the light became greater than the dark, and the light has kept growing until today, the middle of the time of light, Litha; Midsummer. From here, the light begins to fade again, until once more, the Wheel will turn to darkness and Yule will return. Today the Sun is high, the Light is bright, and the Earth is warm. As the Lord of the Sun blazes above, the Fires of our celebration shall flame below," she finished.

Demi stepped forward and laid a burning torch into the middle of the bonfire. As the flames licked and it started to burn, she said "By the powers of the Great Goddess and the Great God, by the powers of the Great Spirit of All-That-Is, by the powers of Earth, Air, Fire and Water, and by the powers of the Sun, Moon and Stars, bless us now as the rays of the Midsummer Sun nourish and bless all life."

Raising both hands into the air she said, "Let my hands be gifted to work in the Elemental ways."

Erion, Elder of Air, stepped forward and took his place near to the bonfire with his arms raised towards the skies. "Let my mind be open to the truth."

Kegan was next as Elder of Fire, and raised his arms as he said, "Let my feet ever walk along the sacred paths."

Finally it was Riva's turn. She stepped forwards and raised her arms whilst saying, "Let my heart seek the ways of the Goddess always."

With the completion of these words, they all dropped their hands at the same time. There was a moment of silence before low-level voices started up as everyone gave their thanks and blessings for what they had received and whilst some, especially those who lived and worked in the north, asked for a fruitful harvest.

It was during this silence that the bonfire started to burn more brightly than it had been doing. The four Elders all took a step back as the heat also became more intense. The voices that had been talking slowly stopped and silence yet again descended as everyone watched the bonfire. Demi, Erion, Kegan, and Riva all stepped further away from the bonfire until they were stood with the rest of their villages, watching.

As Marella watched the bonfire, she could feel a sense of anticipation. She could feel *something.* but just didn't know what. She must have made some noise, some movement, because Edlin looked down at her. "Marella?" he questioned.

She laid her hand upon his arm and then, in a sudden movement, threw her arms around his waist. "It is time," she said simply, before turning to Riva and holding her too.

Edlin and Riva watched Marella as she turned back towards the bonfire. They saw her head move so that she could see towards the north. There stood Daren with Ula by his side. Together they stepped forward until they stood in the place that Demi had just vacated.

"We are the Chosen of Lady Daire – called to represent Earth, the senses, and our ability to manifest our desires."

Daren's voice boomed out so that he could be clearly heard by everyone in the main square and sounded as deep as the earth itself. Ula let out a spine-tingling howl as she lent her voice to the occasion.

Lani moved forward, showing no sign of the shyness that had been with her earlier. "We are the Chosen of Lord Adaryn – called to represent Air, our thoughts, and our ability to have a sense of self." Lani's voice was filled with the power of the winds. With a screech, Shaw circled above her head before landing on the ground next to her.

Then it was Kai's turn and he stepped up to the bonfire with Kenna at his side. "We are the Chosen of Lord Ethon – called to represent Fire, our passion and ideas, giving us the ability to make decisions." Kenna gave a bark followed by the fox's call often mistaken for a woman in distress, known as the Vixen's Scream.

It was time for Marella to complete their circle. She looked at her parents before looking down to see Nixie by her side. "*Ready?*" she thought to him.

"*Always,*" he replied.

Together they walked into the light and felt the heat of the bonfire upon their faces. She raised her voice to the sky and said, "We are the Chosen of the Lady Erwyna – called to represent Water and our emotions, giving us the ability to be moved by feelings." Nixie gave the loud scream that was usually only used by otters when they were threatened. Marella had never heard him make this noise before and she felt it down into her very marrow.

The four humans, acting again as one, all raised their arms in the same manner as the Elders had not so long ago. They stood facing the bonfire and the crowd was silent behind them.

The bonfire continued to blaze and as they watched, the centre grew brighter and brighter, until no one could look at it directly any more. Out of the centre of the heat and light, came a flaming bird. At first the shape was indistinct but gradually the figure became clear. The bird was slightly larger than Shaw but had long, flowing, graceful wings that appeared to be made of flames. There was a crest of feathers upon her head under which her eyes shone like sapphires as she looked around at the people gathered there. Her flaming feathers ranged in colour from yellow gold, to rose, to red, and deep gold.

She stayed above the bonfire with her wings spread wide, seemingly not needing them to stay aloft. The air whipped and crackled around her but Marella and the others stayed where they were.

"I am Ena, and I have been sent here with a message for you all. There is a thief amongst you," she said to the people. Her voice was filled with the hissing of fire and yet was deep enough that everyone could feel her words within their breastbones.

"Four symbols of our Lords and Ladies have been stolen, and the very Elements themselves are in a fury. Only upon the return of these symbols will peace be amongst the Elements once more. The fate of all of you rest upon these eight. Make sure you do all you can to help them as you would help yourself. You have but a year and a day."

With these final words, she raised her wings above her head, her feathers still flashing and sparking with colour and light before she vanished with a clap of thunder and a sweet, haunting melody that faded away.

Silence reigned. No one moved, coughed, or even seemed to breathe. What had they just witnessed?

The four human Chosen, still acting as one, lowered their arms down to their sides. They all took a deep breath in and seemed to realise where they were and what they were doing. They all looked around the bonfire at each other, which was now crackling nicely just like any normal bonfire. The four animal Partners all shook down their fur and ruffled their feathers before preening them back into place.

Riva stepped forward and bowed her head to the four. "As Elder of Water, I give you my blessing on your quest and should you need anything, now or on your quest, please let me know and I will do the best I can to assist you." One by one, the other Elders came forward and echoed her words.

Marella suddenly felt exhausted. Her weariness must have shown in her face as Edlin stepped forward and put his arms around her and led her back towards the crowd. As she neared them though, they all stepped back to allow her clear passage through.

Marella looked around as she walked and saw that Daren, Lani and Kai were all being led away too.

"*Don't fret, little one, we'll all be together soon. Take the rest of this day to rest. We'll meet in the morning.*" Marella heard Ula in her mind and knew Daren had overheard.

* * *

Edlin led Marella back to the Water Lodge and it wasn't long before Riva, Jorja, and Derwen joined them. Bradan was already there, brewing some water to prepare hot drinks for them all.

Marella curled up in a chair and sipped the hot tea he had given her.

35

She was so tired, but knew she couldn't go to bed yet. As she blew across the top of her cup, she looked through the steam at her family surrounding her. They all sat in silence for a while, sipping their drinks.

One by one their Partners came and joined them. Nixie came and rested his head on the chair near Marella's legs. Genna flew in and landed on Riva's shoulder, Orabel flying in behind her before landing on a cupboard. Salali also went onto Jorja's shoulder. Blasa walked around until they could stand near to their humans before making themselves comfortable.

"So," huffed Marella "it appears this is it. I am the Chosen of Erwyna, and I'm leaving." With those words, her eyes filled with tears.

Jorja came forward and hugged her sister. "Oh Marella, I'm going to miss you so much," she said with a lump in her throat and tears in her eyes.

"We are so proud of you and we're going to miss you," said Riva, trying to hide her emotions.

Edlin, Bradan, and Derwen were all showing signs of emotion too. They had shining eyes full of tears yet to be shed and they appeared to have developed a cough which involved a lot of clearing of their throats.

After a couple of minutes, the emotional level calmed down slightly as the first of the storms passed.

"I'm afraid," said Marella, looking at them. "I don't know what I'm supposed to do. What if I'm not strong enough, what if I fail, what if…?"

At her words, Nixie sat up straight and looked at her. *Marella, if you weren't strong enough you wouldn't have been Chosen. It's not just you by yourself, remember that! There are eight of us all together. We balance each other out.*

Edlin gave a chuckle and said, "By the look on your face, Marella, I think Nixie has just answered you better than I could."

Marella gave a slight laugh. "Yes, I was just spoken to," she said, smiling at her beloved Partner.

"Marella, everyone likes to think their children are special. Jorja has proven herself in the realms of Earth to have outstanding talent in her sphere. But you, you only had Water which is so very rare; not unheard of but rare. I think we all suspected something would happen," Edlin spoke to her, using his hands to gesture around at the others as he did so.

Jorja was still sat close enough to Marella to lean over and squeeze her hands. "You always were the adventurous one," she said. "You and Daren would dare each other to do all sorts of things. I was usually there just to keep an eye on you and stop you going too far, not to join in."

"I, for one, am happy that Daren is a Chosen too and will be going with you," Riva added.

"We have gathered some items for you to take with you," said Bradan as he collected cups from everyone. He held the cups into the air. "Top up?" he questioned. At the round of affirmative responses, he disappeared in the direction of the kitchen.

"Yes," said Riva. "We have arranged a travel pack for you, items like a travel blanket, dried meat, water bottles, that sort of thing."

"A travel blanket?" asked Marella.

"It's a blanket that has wool on one side but is backed by leather on the other side," explained Derwen. "It will help to keep you warm and dry whether you lie on it or wrap it around your shoulders."

Bradan returned to the room carrying a tray with refills of the tea for everyone. "If you think of anything specific you will need, just let me know," he said to Marella.

"I don't really know what I'll need yet," said Marella. "I need to speak with the others and we need to make plans. Until then, it's all really in the air, but we don't have long. We need to find these artefacts and bring them here before a year and a day has passed."

"Then you'll need to be leaving soon," said Edlin. "At least it's the Summer Solstice, you'll have some time before the weather changes."

"But where to start?" asked Marella, feeling overwhelmed again.

"There's no point fretting about it now," said Riva, being as practical as ever. "You have agreed to do this and I can't think of anyone better suited. You need to get a good night's sleep and then you can meet with the others in the morning with a clear head. Relax and enjoy the rest of today, tomorrow will be here soon enough."

With the words from her mother, Marella stood up and drained her drink. She went to Edlin and gave him a hug. She moved onto Riva, then Jorja, followed by Derwen, and Bradan.

"Thank you for being there for me," she said to them, before they left to rejoin everyone for the rest of the Summer Solstice festivities.

Later that night, Marella made her way up the stairs to her room with Nixie at her heels. She got ready for bed and lay down, pulling the sheets up to her chin even though it was a warm night. Nixie jumped onto the bottom of the bed before curling up.

"*Goodnight Nixie*," thought Marella.

"*Goodnight Marella*," returned Nixie. "*Don't worry, I'm with you.*"

Before she really had a chance to worry she wouldn't be able to sleep, Marella slipped away on the tides of the night.

~ 7 ~

By the time dawn had broken, Marella was up, washed and dressed. She had put on a pair of blue trousers and a white lace up shirt, with her favourite black boots. She was in the main area of the Water Lodge, drinking a cup of tea to refresh herself before leaving to go and find the others. Nixie was with her, but was feeling sleepy, so was curled up on the floor near to where Marella sat.

"Marella? Are you awake?" she heard in her head, but she didn't recognise the voice.

"I'm awake," she replied. *"Who is this?"*

"My apologies, I am Shaw, Lani's Partner," he said.

"Good morning Shaw. There's no need to apologise, I'm just not used to your voice yet," Marella told him.

"Lani is awake and wondered what you intended to do this morning?" Shaw thought to her.

"I'm finishing my drink and then I was going to find all of you," Marella thought. *"We have much to arrange and not much time to do it in, if Ena was correct."*

"I'll let Lani know. Meet us by the apple tree where we all were before. See you shortly," thought Shaw before she felt his presence depart from her mind.

Marella sipped her drink. She realised how this talent of hers may actually be of more use than she had previously thought. It appeared to work both ways, if Shaw could contact her first. The thought put a smile on her face. Nixie stirred slightly as if he knew that Marella's thoughts were busy.

She relaxed back into her seat, dropped her head backwards so that it rested on the chair, and sent her thoughts towards Ula.

"Ula, my lovely," she called softly before waiting.

"Good morning, Marella," came the reply before too long. *"We were just talking about you."*

"That's never a good thing," laughed Marella.

"You know that's not true," she heard back. *"You know of our love for you so stop searching for compliments."*

Ula's candour made Marella snort into her drink. *"Shaw has just contacted me to see if we can meet this morning by the apple tree. As soon as I've finished my drink I'm going to head over there. Lani won't be long. Will you be able to join us?"* asked Marella.

There was a moment's silence whilst Ula passed on the message to Daren and then Marella felt her answer. *"Yes, we'll be there soon. I just need to get this oaf dressed and we'll be there. See you soon, little one."*

Shaw had put a smile on her face but Ula made her laugh out loud. The morning was starting off well thought Marella. Nixie chuffed as he sat washing himself in the morning sunlight. Marella then thought of the last person and Partner of the group and her smile faded slightly. She hadn't contacted Kenna before and was reluctant to do so now but knew that she had to.

She relaxed again and cleared her mind. She wasn't too sure how to do this as everyone she had contacted before she had known, either the Partner or the person.

She thought of Kai and Kenna as a pair. She thought of Kai himself and the feelings he gave her. She thought of Kenna and how she looked, the sound she had given the previous night as she accepted the challenge. In her mind, she could see and feel them clearly so she mentally moved towards Kenna until she was in front of her.

"Kenna, it's Marella. Will you speak with me?" Marella sent her thoughts towards the Kenna in her mind and hoped this was the right way to do it. She waited for a response, feeling slightly restless.

After a moment, Marella felt an unfamiliar presence in her mind, quite different from Shaw's approach, and instinctively increased her mental shield. When nothing happened, Marella relaxed but could still feel the presence there.

"That is some defence you have there, Marella," came the thought from Kenna.

"My apologies, Kenna," thought Marella. *"I reached out to you and then shut you out."*

Marella felt Kenna's chuckle in her mind. *"There is no need to apologise,"* said Kenna. *"Are we meeting up?"*

"Yes, by the apple tree where we all were before," thought Marella.

"OK, give us a moment and we'll be there," replied Kenna.

"There's no rush," said Marella, *"I'm finishing a drink, Daren's getting dressed and Lani is getting ready."*

"We'll be there soon, 'Bye." With those words, Kenna was gone from Marella's mind.

Nixie had finished his morning wash by this time and looked at her. *"Are we all set then?"* he questioned.

"Yes, we're all meeting by the apple tree soon. Come on, let's go."

Marella finished her drink and went through to the kitchen area where she rinsed out her cup and left it to drain.

As she walked back through to the main area, she saw Genna perched on top of one of the chairs.

"Genna, when Mama awakes, please tell her that I have met with the others and will return later," Marella thought to her.

Genna chirped in agreement before flying in the direction of the stairs.

Marella and Nixie left the Water Lodge and she took a deep breath of the fresh morning air before they both set off towards the apple tree.

* * *

When they arrived, Kai and Kenna were already there. Nixie ran over towards Kenna and rubbed noses with her. Kenna returned his greeting by giving him a lick over his nose which made him sneeze.

Marella laughed at their antics before turning towards Kai. "Good morning," she said to him hesitantly.

"Good morning Marella," said Kai. A smile crossed his face as he looked towards her. "I know I was an ass and we got off on the wrong foot," he continued "but we've accepted this… this… whatever this is so we need to get along. Friends?" He stuck his hand out towards her.

Marella looked at his hand before looking up at his face. All the mockery that she had seen before had gone and there was just friendliness now.

With a smile, she knocked his hand away and gave him a hug instead. "Friends," she said.

Kai stood stiffly within her arms for a moment before relaxing and hesitantly putting his arms around her too.

"This looks cosy," came a voice from behind Marella, "Can we join in?"

At hearing the familiar voice, Marella laughed and released her hold on Kai. "You get enough," she said to Daren, "but Lani can have one."

With that, she left Kai and went towards Lani before giving her a hug. Lani put her arms around Marella and gave her a quick hug before letting go.

Daren stood there with his arms open, so Marella stepped into them. Daren squeezed her tightly before letting go.

"Good morning, Kai," he said, smiling.

"Is this how we're going to start every morning?" laughed Kai.

"Usually," replied Daren. "Hugs are the common currency from Marella. It's a Water thing."

He laughed and jumped to one side, trying to dodge, as Marella punched him on the arm.

"Stop it," she told him. "Come on, let's sit down. We have things to discuss."

With those words, the laughter amongst the four of them stopped. They looked at one another before sitting down on the grass. Marella once again used the tree as a back rest.

"I brought these as I didn't know if we'd all had time to eat yet," said Lani in her soft voice. She held up a bag of apples.

"Thank you, Lani," said Daren as he helped himself to a big, green apple before taking a big bite with a loud crunch.

Lani held the bag out towards Kai who chose a red apple, and then to Marella, who took one too.

"So," said Kai, after he swallowed a piece of apple. "Ena has given us a message with not too many details."

"We have one detail though," said Lani, "We only have a year and a day to complete this 'whatever' before the time runs out."

Daren chuckled slightly at Lani's words. She turned and looked at him and Daren quickly raised his hands in the air in a placating manner. "I mean no offense," he said to her. "It's just that we've all been Chosen and accepted to do this, but none of us know what to call it."

Kai laughed too as he heard Daren's words. "I had the same problem this morning with Marella," he said to Lani. "I was talking about this and got stuck too."

Marella shook her head at them all. "I give up," she said with a giggle. "Of all the things we need to sort out, you're all worried about what this is called."

Everyone laughed together as they realised it really was the least of their problems.

"Let's call it the challenge," suggested Kai.

"Or the quest," said Daren.

Marella looked at Lani. "Which do you prefer?" she asked, "or do you have a suggestion as well?"

"I like challenge," answered Lani, "for no other reason than I don't like quest."

"The challenge it is then," nodded Marella. "I don't like quest either. That's something I read about, not participate in."

Daren groaned and clutched at his chest jokingly, falling back on the ground. "Already," he said. "We've been together for five minutes and I've already been shot down in flames. Oh the shame!" he lamented, whilst the others laughed at his antics.

"You weren't shot down in flames," said Kai. "I had nothing to do with it."

Daren laughed at Kai before sitting upright. "OK, so it's the challenge," he said. "I guess we should make some plans."

"We know we have to find four things," said Lani, "but we have no idea what they are. We can't just go anywhere, anyhow. We'll be searching for years with no ideas."

"Do we have anything else to go on?" questioned Daren. "When we were all Chosen, was anything mentioned then? There must be something."

"Nothing from me," said Marella. "I hardly had to time to find out who I was with, let alone anything else."

"I've told you what I already know," said Lani, "I just received the destruction news." She shot Kai a quick look that reminded him of how he had spoken when she had shared her news the last time.

Kai rubbed his hand over his face remorsefully. "I'm sorry, Lani, I really am."

Lani smiled at him and patted his arm. "It's okay, just don't do it again."

Kai returned her smile with one of his own before looking back at the others. "Lord Ethon didn't tell me anything either. Just that I'd been Chosen and there would be four humans and our Partners."

They sat in silence for a moment before Marella looked up, her eyes gleaming. The others looked at her and wondered about her excitement.

"Kai, repeat what you just said please," she asked him.

"Huh? Why?" he asked.

"Just do it," she said, before adding "please" in a softer voice.

"Okay," he said, looking at her strangely, "I said that Lord Ethon told me that I'd been Chosen and there would be us and our Partners."

"Exactly!" Marella snapped out the word in her excitement whilst slapping her hands on her thighs. The others just looked at her in bemusement.

"Don't you see?" she asked, "Us four and our Partners!" She looked around at them but could see the blank looks on their faces. She rubbed her hands over her face as she tried to put her thoughts in order to make them understand.

"Look, when I was Chosen by Erwyna, Nixie already knew about it. He already knew who She was. Don't you see – this isn't just us. We're all here together, some things we'll know and some things…"

"They'll know," finished Daren for her. He sat up straight as Marella's excitement started to infect him.

Lani's eyes twinkled as she looked at their Partners. "Look at them," she said. "They are all sat there so innocently." She smiled at them before looking back towards Daren, Kai and Marella. "I don't trust them!"

Kai laughed and shook his head. "Kenna," he called, "please would you come here?"

Kenna stood up and shook herself down before walking daintily over to where Kai sat.

"Do you know anything else about what we need to find or where we need to look?" he asked her.

Kenna sat back on her haunches, lifted her front left paw and licked it slowly before looking at Kai. *"Well of course I do,"* she replied. *"It's about time you asked."*

Kai snorted at her words whilst Marella burst out laughing. Daren and Lani looked at them both before looking at each other. "I'm guessing that's a yes then," said Daren wryly to Lani.

"She said of course she knows, and it's about time Kai asked her," said

Marella, still chuckling both at Kenna's words and the way she had said them.

Still laughing slightly, Kai said, "Kenna my dear, please would you mind sharing with me what you know?"

"*Fire is third, as you know. What we need to find is the Flame,*" she said.

"The Flame? What flame? And Third?" asked Kai.

Lani looked over to Shaw. "Shaw? Will you share?" she asked.

Shaw stayed where he was in a low branch on the apple tree. He gave a screech, but then responded to Lani. "*Second is Air, and it is the Feather we seek.*"

"Okay," said Lani, "so Fire is third and it's a Flame. Air is second and it's a Feather."

"Daren, you will be first" said Marella. "Ask Ula."

"First?" questioned Daren. "What makes you so sure?"

"Just ask her," said Marella impatiently.

"Ula?" Daren didn't need to say anything else.

Ula turned her head towards Daren and said, "*Marella is correct, we are first, and for us, it's the Shield, the Tarian y Ddaear.*"

"I hate it when you're right," Daren huffed to Marella. "Ula says we are first, and for us, it's a Shield."

"Which means water is last and we need to find…" her voice trailed off as she looked towards Nixie.

"*The Cauldron,*" said Nixie without any preamble.

"The Cauldron," she repeated out loud for the benefit of the others.

"A Feather, a Flame, a Shield and a Cauldron," said Daren softly.

"In the direction that the Wheel turns," said Lani.

"Exactly," said Marella, smiling at Lani. "So we have something to start with."

"It took you long enough to figure it out." They heard the words before they realised it wasn't them that had spoken. They looked around them, but Lani was the first to look up. There on the branch next to Shaw, was Ena the firebird.

"Look up," she breathed to the others.

They looked up and saw Ena. Once she saw that she had their attention she opened her wings and flew down to the ground. Marella could still see the flames that were her body, but they weren't crackling and snapping now like they had the previous night, instead being warming and gentle.

Ena stood before them, strong and proud. She preened at her feathers before speaking to them. "The four items that were stolen have probably gone beyond our borders. We may never get them back."

Lani bit her lip and looked at the ground whilst Kai shook his head. "If that's the case, then what are we doing?" he asked Ena.

43

"You need to speak to the Guardians of the Elements and ask for a token from them. Your Partners have told you the shape each item must take. It is the essence of each that will help to restore the balance but you must tread lightly. The Guardians of the Elements are an unpredictable bunch and likely to take offense where none is meant. You will have to work together and be prepared for anything."

"We now know we must go in the direction of the Wheel," said Marella. "Where do we find the Guardians?"

"Firstly, you need to go to the area of the Element. There you will find a portal that will take you to the inner realm. Beware though, as time runs differently to here. Find the King or Queen and tell them of your challenge. The rest is down to you and them; I cannot say what will happen next."

"Okay, so area, portal, king or queen, on our own," said Daren.

"Yes, Daren, you have it right. Do not forget that it will take all eight of you to succeed. I wish you all the best and send my blessings along with those of the Lords and Ladies. Go back to your Lodges and say your farewells. Time is short, my young ones. Take care and fare thee well."

With those words, Ena flew up into the air, circled around them once before flying into the sun so that they couldn't follow her movements any longer.

They all looked at each other before standing and brushing themselves down. Their Partners stood and shook themselves before moving towards their human.

"Time to move then," said Kai.

"Shall we meet back here?" asked Lani.

"Yes, it seems right," said Marella.

"Lunchtime then," said Daren. "That should give us enough time to gather what we need, and to say our goodbyes."

With that sobering thought, they each left in the direction of their Lodges.

From on high, effortlessly hovering, Ena watched them go. "Good luck," she whispered to them. "I will help where I can. Do not fail us."

~ 8 ~

When Marella returned to the Lodge, she could see and hear the hustle and bustle that happened when a lot of people were up and moving.

"Good morning, Marella," she heard. She looked around and saw Bradan walking towards her.

"Good morning, Bradan. How are you?" she answered.

"I'm fine, thank you. Just getting a few bits sorted out for you. Your mother and father are in the dining area still, if you want to catch them."

She gave him a quick thank you before heading in the direction of her parents.

Riva and Edlin were having a final drink before leaving the dining room when Marella walked in. She walked over to them and gave them a hug to greet them.

"Good morning Mama, Papa," she said.

"Good morning, Marella," they replied.

Marella walked over to one of the side tables and helped herself to a refreshing cup of tea. When she returned to the table, her parents were watching her expectantly. She sat down with them and put the cup on the table.

"We are going to leave today," she told them abruptly. She had no idea how to say it any other way, besides, they knew what was happening.

Edlin grimaced slightly at Marella's words. "I thought you'd be leaving soon," he said. "We all heard Ena mention about the time limit. What can I do to help?"

Marella looked at her father. She knew this wasn't easy for him; for any of them. "I don't know," she replied. "We're all packing and meeting at lunchtime. We now know what we're looking for and in what order, but that's about it."

Riva joined in the conversation by saying "We've arranged for a trundle truck to be filled with food; some fresh and some that will keep for the journey. It will also hold supplies like canvas for sleeping under, pots, pans, that sort of thing. It will save you carrying everything and you can get rid of it when necessary."

"Thanks Mama," murmured Marella as she drank her tea. "This doesn't seem quite real."

"It will do, soon enough," said Riva, as she made her way over to the side table to pour herself another cup of tea. She straightened before swinging round to face Marella. "I don't want you to go. I've thought about nothing else since last night. I've tried to pretend I'm okay with you going by organising things for you to take, but it doesn't change how I feel. I really don't want you to go."

"I must go," said Marella, raising her voice slightly. "I was Chosen."

"That doesn't mean you had to accept the choice!" said Riva unexpectedly. "You don't agree with everything I choose for you, and the things I choose aren't dangerous." Riva seemed to droop as she made her way back towards the table. "I'm worried Marella – about you, about the others, about what this quest will do to you and where it will take you."

"Riva," soothed Edlin, "you know Marella must do this. She was Chosen by Erwyna, not by us. You would think less of her if she didn't go."

"At least she would be here and safe," Riva snapped at him.

"Mama, listen to me," said Marella strongly, "I am going with the others and we are going to do what we can to restore the artefacts and the balance. We need to know that we are supported back home to do this. Once we are gone, we won't know how you are affected by the changes. I may be safer than you and that is something I will have to live with until this is over."

Riva stood up and put her hands flat on the table. "I'm sure you will find it easy to go, Marella, your chance to get away. Well don't expect me to wave you off on this folly's mission. I won't do it."

With those words Riva left the dining room, her back stiff. Marella sat there in shock. She never thought her mother would react in such a way.

"She will calm down," Edlin told her. "She is worried about you; we both are."

"You're not the one walking out on me though, and saying that you won't see me go," said Marella sadly.

"She doesn't mean it, Marella, you know that. You are her baby and now you're going off to the Goddess knows where. We won't see you, and you are almost certainly walking into danger. Don't you see how she wants to protect you from this? This needs to be done. As Elder of Water she understands that. As your mother, she is having a hard time accepting it."

Marella sat there as her father's words sunk in. She had never been that close to Riva so hadn't been expecting her reaction.

"She will come around and she will miss you," said Edlin, covering Marella's hand with his own. "We're both going to miss you. Promise me that you will take care and look after each other."

"I promise," said Marella, feeling her throat tighten.

Edlin cleared his throat gruffly. "Now then, how about I go and check what they're putting in your trundle truck. As I understand it, you're all getting one, so you should have plenty of supplies to start with."

He stood up and pushed his chair back under the table. Marella stood, too, and gave him a long embrace before moving away.

"I'm going to go and pack my travel bag," she said to him. "I'll be in my room for a while should anyone want me."

* * *

Marella closed the door to her room behind her and leaned against it before sliding slowly towards the floor. She could feel the warm track of tears upon her cheeks. Nixie was already in the room and came over to where she sat. He rubbed against her arm until she lifted it up and he crawled underneath and onto her lap. He put his paws upon her shoulders and came close to her face so that he could look her in the eyes.

"*This is hard on everyone,*" he thought to Marella, sending waves of love and reassurance through their bond.

"*I know,*" replied Marella. "*I just wasn't expecting that reaction from her. As Elder she knows how important this is. How can she say that I should have refused?*"

"*As Elder, she does indeed know,*" said Nixie, "*but she's not just the Elder. She is your mother as well, and she loves you deeply, even if she doesn't show it.*"

Nixie pressed his paws a little harder into Marella's shoulders, emphasising his point. "*She knows and she understands, but that doesn't mean she has to like it. Her fear for you is showing as anger. You should understand that, you do it too.*"

Marella thought back to the moment not so long ago, when she had found out Nixie had known about her being Erwyna's Chosen and her reaction to it. Yes, she could empathise with her mother's reaction, it just stung some.

Nixie watched Marella as the thoughts flashed over her face. She was as easy to read as his own reflection. He saw the moment when she allowed the feelings her mother held to have weight upon her emotions. The tears continued to flow down her cheeks as Nixie spoke softly in her mind.

"*This isn't going to be easy,*" thought Nixie to Marella. "*We are going to go places no one has been before. We've got to find or make the essence of each Element, and we have a time limit in which to do it. Your mother understands this. She trusts and loves you, but sees clearer than you just what we are up against. Give her time, she will come around. And she will be waiting for you upon your return.*"

"*She won't see me go though, will she?*" questioned Marella, already knowing the answer.

"*No, Genna doesn't think so. She is busy organising at the moment, hiding her fear behind bustle.*"

"*Okay,*" sighed Marella. "*I have things to do and I can't get through to Mama right now.*"

She sat for a moment, grabbing hold of a small sense of peace and holding it tightly. She shrugged her shoulders and sat up straight, dislodging Nixie as he jumped to the floor. She curled her legs underneath and stood up, looking around the room.

"Where to start?" she wondered to herself and then gave a short laugh as she saw Nixie's backside wriggling underneath the bed as he tried to drag out her travel bag with his teeth.

"That's a good place." She laughed as she started to gather her things to pack away.

As Marella folded clothes to put some in her bag and some to go back home, her mind wandered. She wondered what the others were doing and if any of them had had an unexpected reaction like she had. She reached out with her mind towards the other Partners.

"*Ula, is everything ok with you?*" she thought.

"*Everything is fine. Naida and Siorus are helping Daren sort through. He would take everything, if it were left to him.*" Marella could feel the love and amusement in Ula's voice.

"*Shaw? How's it going?*" she thought to Lani's Partner.

"*We're going okay,*" came the reply. "*There have been some tears but Lani is coping well. We'll be there on time.*"

Kenna was the last one. "*Kenna,*" called Marella. "*Any problems?*"

"*None at all,*" replied Kenna. "*We've nearly got everything and Kai is having a drink before starting on his travel pack. He's starting to get excited.*"

Marella gave a chuckle to herself at Kenna's words. Kai may be the oldest, but he still seemed to have the ability to get excited over things others wouldn't. She was sure that this was going to be a very interesting journey.

Before long, Marella had packed her travel pack with enough clothing to last for a while. She had one set for the changing seasons, together with her formal dress. She was sure that they would be able to find or make other clothing as necessary. She had also snuck in her favourite book to take with her. It was an old book with tales of the Lords and Ladies and the adventures they had partaken in. Somehow it seemed appropriate to take it with her.

She stood back from the bed with her hands upon her hips. "*Well, Nixie?*" she questioned. "*Have I forgotten anything?*"

Nixie looked up from where he had been lying out of the way and said, "*I don't think so. It is best to travel light. We have a long way to go.*"

Marella picked up her hairbrush and added it to her pack, along with a few spare packs of soaproot and mint sticks.

"There," she said in a satisfied tone.

Nixie gave a cat like stretch before saying, "*Come on, let's go downstairs and grab a bite to eat before we meet the others. We may as well leave with a full stomach.*"

As they went back downstairs, Marella double-checked in her mind what she had packed and what she thought they might need. She believed she had everything. If she had forgotten anything, well, by the time she needed it, it would be too late anyway.

* * *

Bradan and Orabel were both in the dining area. Orabel gave a couple of quacks towards Bradan when she first saw them and he turned around with a broad smile upon his face.

"Marella, I'm so glad you have the time for a quick bite to eat. It's lunchtime you're all meeting, isn't it?" he asked her, smiling at her nod. "Then you have time to eat this before you go. Consider it brunch, as I'm sure you've not really had anything so far." Bradan gestured towards a table close by and Marella sat down.

'This' happened to be a plate laden with food. It had sausages, eggs, bacon, mushrooms, and tomatoes. On a small plate next to it was some bread with butter oozing on it, confirming that the bread was still warm. There was a pot of tea on the table and a cup already filled, with steam curling across the top.

"Wow, Bradan, thank you so much," said Marella smiling at him. "This looks great."

Bradan leaned down towards her and whispered to her, "It was your mother's idea but don't tell her I told you so."

Marella cast her eyes towards the table before looking back at him. "I don't think that will be a problem," she said. "She isn't really speaking to me right now."

Bradan sighed and rubbed his hand down the front of his shirt. "I know; I heard," he said. "This is hard on her, Marella. She is torn between her feelings as Elder and as your mother."

Marella laid a hand upon his arm and tried to reassure him. "Don't worry, I do understand. I've had both Papa and Nixie explain it to me. I just wish I could tell Mama, but so far, Genna says she's avoiding me."

Bradan gave a small snort at Marella's words. "If she's avoiding you, then that's the mother in charge. You may see her before you leave. The Elder may step in by then," he winked at Marella. "Now eat up before this gets cold."

After Marella had finished her meal and washed it down with refreshing peppermint tea, she made her way out to the front of the Lodge where the trundle truck was being loaded. She could see a canvas, various blankets, pots, pans, and utensils in there, along with various non-perishable food items.

"This looks like a lot of things," she said to Bradan, who had followed her outside.

"It may do now, but it won't be long before these supplies are gone and you will have to reuse or recycle what you've already used into something else," he replied.

Marella nodded her head in agreement. It did seem a lot now but she was leaving for over a year. She wondered what, if anything, she would bring back with her.

Edlin came walking over to her as she inspected the truck. "Do you remember your Test Day?" asked Edlin.

"Of course I do," said Marella. "It's when my wish to be a Water Weaver was granted."

"I gave you a present then and I'm giving one to you now," said Edlin. He handed his packet to Marella, who held it with shaking hands. "Go on," he encouraged, "open it."

She unwrapped the parcel to find a travel mug. It was made out of leather and lined with pitch to make it waterproof. The leather was dyed a deep blue and had a triple spiral as its main design with the family markings making a border around the bottom, which had been burnt into the leather. Marella remembered the first travel mug that Edlin had made her. She had used it until it split and then she had put it into her memory box.

Her eyes filled with tears as she gazed at it. "Papa, it's wonderful. Thank you so much."

"You take care of it and make sure you bring it back, you hear me? In a year and a day I want to see you and your mug." Edlin's eyes were shining as he looked at his youngest daughter.

Marella nodded as she looked at both the travel mug and her father, before stepping forward and wrapping him in a warm embrace.

"I'm going to miss you, Papa," she said, "you and Mama both."

"We'll miss you too, but remember you're only a thought away. If ever you're in trouble, just holler to Torlan or Genna. We'll tell them to keep an ear out, as it were," he said to her.

With her father's arm around her, Marella continued to check what was in the truck so she knew what was there.

From the corner of her eye she could see someone approaching, so she turned slightly to see who it was. It was Jorja and Derwen, with Salali and Blasa coming behind them. Derwen had a parcel in his arms, which he held out towards her as Jorja spoke to them.

"Here is a going away present from Derwen and myself. It was going to be for your birthday, but you won't be here then. Luckily, we'd already sorted it, so you can take it with you."

Edlin removed his arm from around Marella's shoulders as she took the parcel from Derwen. She unwrapped it to find a warm travel cloak inside. The leather outer of the cloak was dyed a deep blue to match her new mug and also had the family markings burnt around the deep hood, along the front edges, and around the bottom. Marella noticed that interspersed with the family markings was the triple spiral again. The inside of the cloak was a beautiful silver-grey wool.

She held it up so she could see it all and smiled brightly. "Jorja,

Derwen, it is absolutely gorgeous. Thank you so much."

Jorja smiled back at Marella, but with a lump in her throat. Although Jorja and Marella weren't physically close, they had still been close enough in their villages they could pop round and see each other. Now Marella was going the Goddess knew where and Jorja didn't know if she would see her again. She gave herself a shake. Those sorts of thoughts were no good. Marella would see smiles as she left, not tears. Jorja was adamant about that.

Marella folded the cloak up carefully and packed it into the trundle truck to make sure it didn't get left behind. She put the travel mug into her leather backpack that she would carry. It wasn't a big pack and couldn't carry too much, but it meant she could keep smaller things close at hand she might need.

Derwen hugged Jorja tightly as she watched her sister pack to get ready to leave. He knew Jorja would find it hard, and wanted to help her so he thought hard on what might help. Blasa walked up behind him and gently nudged his leg.

"Honestly, Derwen, you are so dense sometimes. I think you've knocked your head more times than I have mine," he said to Derwen, with love in his tone and a twinkle in his eye.

Derwen shook his head slightly at Blasa as he continued to hug Jorja. *"And what do you want now?"* he asked. *"Can't you see I'm thinking?"*

Blasa gave a snort and replied, *"See it? I can feel it, and it is hard going! You're thinking too hard. What have you just done that Marella was involved in?"*

Derwen looked down at his hand and saw the shimmering silver swirl that had appeared during Marella's blessing of him and Jorja. *"That's it! Thanks Blasa, I know I'm a trial to you."*

"A trial alright," agreed Blasa, before walking off to stand nearby.

"Jorja," Derwen began, "I know how much you're going to miss Marella, so I've been thinking. We need something to keep you busy whilst Marella's away, and to give Marella something to look forward to upon her return."

Jorja looked at Derwen, wondering where he was going with this.

"So how about we plan for the marriage to take place when Marella gets back? I know it means us waiting for a year, but I also know you wouldn't be happy doing it without her" he continued.

Jorja looked at him, before placing her hand gently on his face. She could feel the stubble of the day's growth upon his cheeks. "I love you so much," she said to him. "Thank you for thinking of this."

"So, does that mean it's okay? We'll do it?" he asked.

"Yes," said Jorja, smiling. "Do you want to tell her or shall I?"

"You tell her, she's your sister," said Derwen, with an air of excitement.

"What are you two plotting?" asked Marella as she walked over to them.

"We're just plotting the wedding" replied Jorja.

"What?" exclaimed Marella.

"It's okay, don't worry," soothed Jorja. "Derwen just had the idea that we can plan the wedding whilst you're away so it's ready for when you get back. That way it keeps me distracted and you something to look forward to upon your return."

As Jorja had been speaking, a smile spread itself across Marella's face. By the time Jorja had finished speaking, her face was bright.

Marella threw her arms around Derwen and gave him a quick, hard hug. "What a wonderful idea, Derwen. You'll need all the help you can get though, keeping this one distracted." She smirked towards Jorja.

"What's all this about a wedding?" asked Edlin as he came to join them.

"Derwen has come up with an idea of distracting Jorja whilst I'm busy" said Marella.

"Whilst you're busy?" choked Jorja. "That's one way of putting it."

Marella put her arms around Jorja and they stood there for a moment, gently rocking in each other's arms. "I'll be fine," reassured Marella. "Like I've already been told by Papa, if I need anything I'm only a thought away and trust me, I'll shout!" Marella stepped back from Jorja after giving her an extra squeeze. "Come on, I need to go," she said brokenly.

She turned around and looked again in the trundle truck, taking the moment to get her composure back. When she looked back at her family, she saw Jorja wiping her eyes, with Derwen comforting her, and Edlin smiling at her with a knowing look in his eyes.

She checked once more, but couldn't say what she was seeing anymore. She looked around one last time to see if she could see her mother, but Riva was still nowhere to be found. She couldn't delay this any further.

She looked at Edlin, Jorja, and Derwen standing before her and knew it was a picture she would keep in her mind until she saw them again. She just wished Riva was also part of it, but she had made her decision when she disappeared.

"Papa, please let me know when Mama returns. I need to know she's okay," said Marella.

"I will, little one. She'll regret not being here but she's too hard-headed to give in right now," replied Edlin.

Marella took a deep breath and looked around those gathered in front of the Water Lodge. Along with Bradan and her family, there was now a collection of other people, both friends and strangers, all there to wish her well, but still no Riva.

Raising her voice slightly, she said to the crowd, "I'd like to thank you all for coming here and helping outfit me for this challenge. I promise you I shall do my best and will return in a year and a day, hopefully with all the artefacts to be restored."

With those words she moved in front of the trundle truck and started to pull it in the direction of the main square where she was meeting the others. She hadn't gone more than a couple of steps before Derwen and Edlin gently moved her aside and took one of the handles each.

"I will have to pull it myself soon enough," she told them, smiling.

"That is then, this is now," replied Edlin. "Let your old Papa help you this last time before you go."

So it was with a lump in her throat, and a sheen to her eyes, that she made her way to the main square with an entourage from the Water Lodge.

~ 9 ~

Upon arriving in the Main Square she could see Daren and Ula were already there. They too had a trundle truck packed full of items. As Marella came to a stop, Kai appeared with his trundle truck and Kenna sat proudly on top of it. Lani was the last to appear a couple of minutes later, looking flustered.

"I'm sorry I'm late," she said breathlessly, "I couldn't find something."

"No worries," said Kai. "I've only just arrived myself."

Lani looked grateful for his reassurance, and rested herself against the trundle truck for a moment, getting her breath back.

Finally they were all at the Main Square, all packed up and ready to go. They looked at one another, not knowing what to say or how to make a move. They all had friends and family with them. Marella noticed that Naida was there for Daren and cast her eyes downwards at the reminder of Riva's absence.

Then everyone was mingling and goodbyes were being said. Naida and Siorus came over to give Marella a goodbye hug as a few tears were shed.

"You take care now, you hear me?" said Siorus to Marella gruffly. He had always reminded her of a big bear.

Marella nodded at him as she was engulfed in his arms.

After Siorus, Naida swept Marella gently in her arms. "We will miss you, all of you. Look after each other," she said.

"We will," promised Marella.

Before long, everyone had said their goodbyes and they were ready to go. The four humans all turned towards their trundle trucks and made ready to leave. At the moment they had their hands on the long arms of their trucks, a blast of air blew around everyone. When the blast had stopped, the villagers were in for yet another surprise. In front of the four pairs, stood the Lord or Lady of their Element. They dropped down to one knee, showing respect for their Lord or Lady.

Lady Daire stepped towards Daren first. "Daren, Chosen of mine, you are going on this quest to retrieve the Shield of Earth, the *Tarian y Ddaear*. You will need to travel to the kingdom of the Gnomes and speak to their King, Ghobe. He can be greedy and narrow-minded, so be careful of how you speak with him.

We don't know who took the Shield," continued Daire, "so we can't give you much more information. However, to help you in case of danger, I can give you this. Please take my sword and use it in my name."

She held out a long sword that glinted dully in the midday light. It was grey, with a bluish-white sheen to it in certain lights. The cross guard was plain but the grip was wrapped with a brown and green metal thread. The pommel of the sword was decorated with serpentine and malachite stones. Just underneath the cross guard, on the rain guard, was the symbol of Earth. It was an equal armed cross with a green triangle at each end point.

"This sword is made of lead, a metal of the Earth. It is embellished with stones that represent earth and it has my symbol on it, which will confirm to any and all, that you are my Chosen. I wish you luck and give you my blessings," she said to Daren. "You will also have this scabbard to keep it in." The scabbard was made of a deep brown leather, with the symbol of Earth on it. With a fur lining for ease of drawing, the open end of the scabbard was protected by a metal ring. It would fit on his belt so that the sword hung by his side.

He stood up and took the sword from her, swinging it gently as he tested the balance. "Thank you, Lady Daire," he said to her in wonder. "You have given me a treasure beyond words."

"Use it well and in my name, that is all I ask," she replied to him before stepping back to the others.

Lord Adaryn then approached Lani. She looked up at him with concern plainly written on her face. He smiled to her before pulling her gently to her feet.

"My gift to you is one of the skies," he said. "I am giving you this crossbow made of Alder wood. I have prepared some bolts for you, which I have blessed." He handed her a quiver of crossbow bolts.

"I know you dislike violence, but I do not want you at a disadvantage. Use these sparingly, but do not be afraid to use them. You will need to go to the Sylphs and speak with their Queen, Paralda. She is fickle and selfish, and you will need to work to keep her attention. You need to find the *Plu y Gryphon*. It will not be easy."

Lani thanked him quietly as she looked at the crossbow and quiver. The crossbow gleamed warmly in the sunlight and embossed in the handle was the sigil of Air, three swirls going in a deosil direction. Lani could see that the string would be pulled back by a small lever, which was embedded in the side. This would give the string more tension than if she had to pull it back herself. The butt of the crossbow was decorated with fluorite and mica stones, both of which she knew corresponded with Air.

The quiver was made of leather and would attach to her belt. It was dyed a light sky blue with the sigil taking pride of place in the middle. She put it on her belt straight away, on her left hand side, so she could hold the bow in her right hand, and load it with her left. The bolts themselves were made of a shiny silver metal. She looked at Adaryn with a querying look on her face.

"They are made of aluminium," he said, "a light metal that flies true, but they are strong with my blessing. The quiver will never run out. Use them in my name."

Ethon moved forward to stand before Kai, who raised his head and smiled at him. Ethon laughed as he got closer to Kai.

"Here," he said, "you know what this is. Use it wisely - and coolly - in my name."

Kai took the sword from Ethon and looked down the length of it. It was the same length as Daren's, and similar in shape. The appearance, though, was different. The sword was made of steel and the grip was wrapped with red and yellow thread. The pommel had stones of Tiger's Eye and Bloodstone and the symbol of Fire, a triquetra of gold, was underneath the cross guard. The scabbard of Kai's sword was dyed a deep red, also with a fur lining and a metal ring, with the symbol of Fire etched into the leather.

"Thank you, sir," said Kai, admiringly. "I shall look after it and use it well."

"See that you do," said Ethon. "You will be going to the Salamanders and speaking with their Djinn. She is angry and jealous of anything, most of the time, so you will need to keep your cool. You need the Flame of Incandescence, also known as the *Fflam Eiriasedd,* but she won't give it up easily."

Lastly, it was Marella's turn. Erwyna approached her and bid her to rise. She gave her a long, sturdy wooden staff made of a number of branches all twined together. It had the triple spiral of Water pyrographed on it. The bottom twelve inches had been dipped into a rubbery substance, which would prevent the wood from splitting or slipping as Marella used it. There were two places along the top and bottom of the wood where the bark had been smoothed, then wrapped in silver thread to provide a strong grip. The top of the staff was embellished with silver, moonstones, and aquamarine crystals. There was also a pyrograph of the phases of the moon running along the length of the staff. A triple moon symbol lay on the opposite side of the Water symbol.

"Your staff was made by me," said Erwyna. "It is imbued with my essence and your determination. It is made of new and old willow branches so that it offers the wisdom of age, with the strength and flexibility of the young. Use it in my name."

Marella bowed her head at Erwyna as she held the staff in her hands. It felt warm and almost alive in her hands.

"You need to visit the Undines, Marella. There you will speak with Nixsa and retrieve the Cauldron. Marella, you must not fail. He is lazy at times, and can be overly sensitive, so you will need to practice tact and diplomacy."

"Once you have retrieved all four artefacts you must return to Charon as swiftly as you can. You only have a year left. By this time next year, the four artefacts must be here or the balance will be lost," finished Erwyna.

"Call on us if you need to, and we will help where we can," added Daire.

The four reverently placed their weapons on top of their trundle trucks, in a way that both protected them, but allowed easy access to them if necessary. Then they looked back towards the Lords and Ladies, who were watching them peacefully.

Marella looked towards her family for the last time and gave them a tremulous smile. With no more words necessary, she put her hands on the end of the arms of her trundle truck and started forward, pulling it with ease. Daren, Lani, and Kai all did the same and they headed off in the northern direction out of the Main Square. Earth was first and north, that much they knew.

There was silence in the Main Square as those remaining watched them go. Daren was the last one and he turned and waved at them all before he disappeared from sight.

Somebody coughed, a child laughed, but was quickly shushed, and nobody knew what to do.

The Lords and Ladies looked around at the people they had claimed for their own. Erwyna tried to reassure Edlin. "I will be with her in spirit, Edlin, son of mine. If she needs me, I will be there. I am confident in her and so should you be."

Edlin bowed his head to Erwyna as the tears flowed down his cheeks. He could safely show his emotions now that Marella was out of sight, knowing that it wouldn't upset her.

"I know," he said brokenly to Erwyna, "but I am her father and it is part of my job to worry about her."

"Tis true," replied Erwyna, with a smile on her face, "but you also need to give her room to grow. She will return to you, all of you," she said, including Riva, who had snuck unseen and unheard to the family group as Erwyna had spoken.

Edlin saw his wife and pulled her into his embrace. "I should be so angry with you right now," he said. "You weren't there when Marella needed you; you didn't even see her go."

Riva threw her shoulders back defiantly. "I did see her go. I saw her given the Staff of Water. I know that she will now be protected, I know that better than any of you."

"But Marella didn't see you," said Jorja to her mother in a quiet voice.

"No," said Riva, a strange tone in her voice, "but I will apologise to her when I see her again."

Riva clapped her hands a couple of times, drawing the attention of most of the crowd. "The four Chosen with their Partners have now gone. We must wait here and carry on as normal until they return."

With those words, she turned on her heel and departed the Main Square in the direction of the Water Lodge, leaving Edlin staring after her, with a mixture of amazement and disappointment written on his face.

Siorus and Naida joined Edlin as he stood there; looking in the direction Riva had gone.

"Don't take it personally," said Naida to him. "She needs time to adjust and is using her Elder duties as a cover. You know she loves Marella and how she is worried about her. Give her some time, she'll be okay."

Siorus clapped his big hand upon Edlin's shoulder and gave him wordless confirmation of Naida's words.

Edlin took a moment to himself before breathing deeply and standing tall. "Come on Jorja, Derwen," he said. "There's work to be done." With that, he too. set off towards the Water Lodge, with Jorja and Derwen exchanging glances before following behind him.

"Good luck, Marella," thought Salali to her. *"We await your return."*

~ 10 ~

They walked along a narrow path which wasn't yet wide enough for them to walk side-by-side, especially with their trundle trucks. Silence reigned supreme as they were each lost in their thoughts. Kai led the way, with Lani behind him. Marella walked slowly after her, with Daren taking the rear position. Shaw flew overhead whilst Ula, Kenna, and Nixie walked by the side of their Partners.

They followed the path as it headed northwards, all thinking about the families they had left behind, and what lay in front of them. None of them had any idea of what they were going to face.

They walked for just over an hour before Kai called them to a halt in a small clearing that was within a grove of apple trees.

"Come on, we'll take a quick break," he called back to the others, before manoeuvring his trundle truck into a better position. He sat on the ground and leaned back against the wheel of his truck. Going into his rucksack, he pulled out a flask of water and his travel mug.

Whilst Kai was doing that, the others pulled up with their trucks and moved them so that they formed a circle around them. They all copied Kai and pulled their travel mugs and drinks out of their rucksacks.

"I have elderflower cordial, if anyone wants some?" Lani offered.

"Yes, please," said Marella with a small smile. "I love elderflower."

Lani leaned over and tipped a small amount into Marella's mug, which was then topped up with fresh water. Lani did the same for herself, whilst Daren and Kai stuck with plain water.

They sat there for a moment before Lani spoke.

"This is it then," she said. "We've started our 'challenge' and we're already having a break?"

Daren laughed at her comment whilst Kai and Marella smiled.

"Yep, it certainly seems that way," said Kai in response.

"Well, for what it's worth, I for one, am glad for the rest," Lani said. "I'm not used to pulling a trundle truck behind me all the time. My arms and shoulders are aching." She rotated her shoulders as she spoke.

"I think we're all going to be a bit stiff this evening when we stop for the night," said Daren.

"I have some herbs we can brew into a tea which will help overnight," said Kai. "I've had to learn through experience," he said wryly.

"Think how fit and toned we'll all be at the end," said Marella.

They all laughed softly at her words.

"The end seems so far away," whispered Lani, her voice breaking.

The others stopped laughing as they realised Lani was upset, although she was trying her hardest not to show it. Marella moved so she sat next to

Lani and put her arm around Lani's shoulders.

"It will be alright, you know," she said to her. "We're here together; we can help each other. We'll make it."

"You don't know that for sure, so you can't say definitely," Lani replied.

Daren moved a bit closer to the girls. "No, we can't say that for sure," he answered her seriously, "but I do know we were all Chosen for one reason or another. We have each other, and we have our Partners. We are the Chosen of the Lords and Ladies. They have faith and confidence in us, and I have the same in them. Lani, try not to worry about things before they appear, let's enjoy what we can, when we can."

Lani leaned her head on Marella's shoulder as she listened to Daren. "You are so sure," she said. "How do you *know*?"

"I don't," Daren answered simply, "but I have to believe it or what are we doing this for? I'm not thinking about the bigger picture, what might or might not happen if we don't succeed. I'm staying with the here and now, with you three and our Partners. It's a beautiful day and I'm with my best friend, plus two others I have an amazing opportunity to get to know. I've been lucky enough to have met with Lady Daire, who has always been a bit of legend in Bridd." He paused for breath, but then seemed to run out of words, so he just sat and looked at Lani.

Lani pondered on his words for a moment before looking at him. "Ok, I know what you're saying and I can see why. I'll try to stop worrying about the what if's. I'm not giving any guarantees, mind you."

They all laughed softly at her words and Shaw gave a screech from where he had perched in a nearby tree.

"Do you think they're all okay at home?" Marella asked no one in particular.

"I'm sure they're all going about their normal work, pretending this day is nothing out of the ordinary," answered Daren, reaching over and giving her knee a gentle squeeze.

Marella nodded but didn't answer as she tried to swallow the lump that had appeared in her throat.

Kai cleared his throat and asked, "Where was your Mama, Marella?"

Daren shot him a look that told Kai he shouldn't have asked.

Marella's head was bent forwards and she studied her travel mug intently. For a moment, Kai didn't think she was going to answer him but then she lifted her head and looked at him. She cleared her throat and said, "She walked away not long after I returned to the Water Lodge. She didn't want me to come on the quest, said I had a choice."

It was Marella's turn to be comforted, this time by Lani and Daren, as Kai sat opposite her.

"Did you ever think about not coming?" Kai wanted to know.

"No," said Marella indignantly. "Erwyna Chose me, how could I refuse?"

"Some might," said Kai quietly. Daren glared at him. "Daren, I'm not trying to provoke anything here, honest." Kai spread his hands out in a placating gesture towards Daren. "Just think though – Lani is having doubts about the challenge, and Marella's Mama told her not to come, that there was a choice. Let's sort this now. Get it all out in the open, so it can't come out of hiding later on down the line and bite us in the butt. We're going to have to be honest with each other at all times, to come out on top of this challenge."

Kai took a drink from his mug before setting it down on the ground in front of him. Kenna walked over to him and sat down, silently showing her support for his words.

The others looked at Kai as he sat there calmly, waiting for their reactions. He could see the sheen of tears still in Lani's eyes. Daren looked irritated, and Marella had sparks flashing from her eyes. Kai sighed, it appeared he had upset her again.

"We are all here together," Kai continued, "four humans and four Partners. We need to balance each other out as much as we need to try to correct the balance of the Elements. I can be jealous and hot-headed, I know this, but I can also be enthusiastic and energetic. I am here to represent Fire in both positive and negative aspects. I don't want us all walking onwards with this challenge worrying about what ifs and maybes. We need to be strong for each other as there *will* be times of weakness for all of us. And we can't do if we are busy hiding things from each other.

He stopped speaking and looked around again. *"You are doing fine,"* said Kenna to him silently. *"You have the agreement of the Partners; they are just waiting for their humans to catch up."*

Kai felt better upon hearing Kenna's words. It was hard speaking up like this when he didn't really know any of them yet. He just knew it had to be done. Knowing he had the Partners' support meant more to him than he had thought it would. He relaxed back and had some more of his water, waiting for the others to speak.

It was Lani who spoke up first. "You are right, Kai. This challenge is going to be tricky enough as it is without infighting or hiding from each other. You are Fire, you've proved that." She gave him a wink, which startled him.

She turned around and faced Daren and Marella. "So here's the thing. Kai is Fire, I am Air, you two are Earth and Water. My bad points are that I can be fickle and inattentive, but I can also be diligent. Of course, communication should also be my thing, but Kai has beaten me to it just now," she finished with a smile. "So what about you, Daren, Marella? Name two bad points and then something to balance it out. Consider this our first 'Getting to Know Each Other' session."

Daren laughed at Lani's words and gave Kai a nod. Kai relaxed some more. If Daren was on his side, then it was only a matter of time before Marella came around. She wasn't stupid, but sometimes allowed her emotions to get the better of her.

"Ok, so I am Earth," said Daren. "My bad points are I can be materialistic and narrow-minded at times, however I can also be reliable and punctual. Your turn," he said, looking at Marella.

Marella sighed before she smiled and joined in. She knew this was necessary but hadn't exactly felt this was the right time. *"Would there ever be a right time though?"* she asked herself.

"No," came the answer from Nixie. Marella looked over and smiled in his direction. "I am Water, as such I can be overly sensitive and insecure."

Daren gave a snort at these words and coughed "No, surely not!" into his hand. This made the whole group laugh.

After punching his shoulder, Marella continued. "I can also be easy-going and compassionate," she finished.

"So now we all know two good and two bad points about each other," Lani said. "We will learn more as time moves on, but this is a good start."

They smiled at each other and sat back to relax for a moment. Lani and Marella finished their elderwater, and rinsed out their travel mugs using some of the water from Kai and Daren's flasks, before sitting still once more.

"Thank you everyone," said Lani quietly. "I... I just wanted to say it before we left here. I am in this with you. I'm sorry for wobbling so soon."

Kai leaned over and placed one of his hands over Lani's. "Don't worry about it," he told her gently. "I'm sure we'll all have our wobbles."

Kai leaned back against the tree trunk and closed his eyes. *"I hope you're not going to sleep,"* he heard Kenna say to him.

"Nope, just taking in the peace," he replied to her.

After a moment's silence, he opened his eyes and saw the others watching him. He could feel a slight flush to his face as he sat forward, before coming to his feet and straightening his clothes. No one said anything as they all stood up and started clearing away their things.

"Daren, have you heard of the Earth Portal?" asked Marella.

Daren glanced at Marella as he got ready to start pulling the truck again. He stood up and saw the others had stopped and were looking at him. He finished rearranging some of the items in his truck whilst he gathered his thoughts and memories. The others stayed quiet to give him the space he obviously needed.

"All I know is intertwined with the Gnomes too, so I'll share that as well. Okay, so here goes," he said. "There are various tribes of Gnomes, but the last I heard, the King resides with the Goedwig Gnomes. The Portal to get there is in the "north of the north, surrounded by green," but that's the only hint I've ever heard of. It's not much to go on, is it?"

"Various tribes?" questioned Kai. "Like…" he prompted.

"Well, there's the Goedwig tribe I've already mentioned," Daren said. "And then there's the Dwyn tribe, the Cartrefu tribe and the Gardd tribe. Apparently this King is originally from the Cartrefu tribe, until he became King, then he moved to his new home in the forest. There is another tribe I've heard of, the Dialedd, but all I ever heard about them was that they live for vengeance and revenge and are best avoided at all costs."

"If the Portal is in the 'north of the north', we might as well get moving," said Lani. "We're only about half an hour from the outskirts of Charon, and we need to keep going north."

In agreement, they all picked up the handles of their trucks and started on the path once more. By the time they arrived at the borders of Bridd, they had been walking for nearly two hours. They all huffed lightly as they walked the slight incline towards the village.

"I swear this has become steeper since I left," joked Daren.

Ula, who was walking next to him, just turned her head and looked at him. She didn't say a word, but her eyes were twinkling at him. He laughed at her and gave her head a quick stroke, before holding on again to his truck.

"Does anyone need to make a pit stop for any reason, before we carry on?" he asked with a grin on his face. "This is the last post of civilisation."

The others just looked at him and shook their heads at his antics.

"Come on, let's just keep on moving," said Marella with a hint of impatience. "We're supposed to be starting the challenge, and it just feels like we've gone for a bit of a stroll to visit your house."

She pulled at her truck and carried on walking, taking the lead towards the centre of the village. She hadn't gone far before someone shouted out her name. She turned her head around to see who it was, and saw Slade calling her. Slade was the Second of Earth and knew Marella well from her time spent with Daren.

"Hi Slade," she called back.

Daren lifted his hand up in a quick wave before carrying on pulling his truck. Lani and Kai just looked at each other and grinned. They found it amusing that here they were in Daren's village, but it was Marella who was greeted.

"I just wanted to let you know that Riva is back at Charon with your father. Torlan spoke to Awel," he told her.

"Okay, thanks Slade." Marella gave a sigh. She looked at her feet and just kept on moving forwards. Nixie ran next to her and bumped her leg with his body. She looked down at him as she walked. "I'm okay, Nixie, I am. This is her choice. I've made mine." She carried on walking, but her pace had slowed slightly and her shoulders now had a droop to them.

Having passed the message on, Slade walked alongside Daren. "Is there anything you need before you continue on?" he asked.

"I don't think so, not for me anyway. I'm sure the others are okay too; after all, we've only just left Charon. Ask us in three months' time and it might be a different story," Daren smiled.

"You know where you're going?" asked Slade.

"We know we need to find the Portal and it's in the 'north of the north and surrounded by green'," Daren recited.

Slade smiled at him, and said, "Yes, so helpful."

Daren grinned at him, and asked, "Can you narrow it down a bit?"

"Actually, yes I can," Slade answered. "The Portal is in a grove of trees and can only be used during the summer months when the trees are all in leaf. That's where the 'surrounded by green' bit comes in."

"Makes sense," murmurs Daren, thinking. "So it's in the north of the north, in the forest."

"The only other bit of information I have is the grove is 'of the three', but I don't know what that means," finished Slade.

"Okay, that's great. You've been a big help, Slade, thank you," said Daren. "We're going to carry on and see how far north we can get before nightfall, so we won't be staying here in Bridd tonight. Thanks again for your help."

"No worries, get Marella to give Awel a shout if you guys need anything and we'll help where we can," said Slade.

"Will do," replied Daren.

"Nice to sort of meet you Kai, Lani," said Slade, nodding to them both before walking off.

They all heard a cooing noise and looked up towards the sky. Flying next to Shaw was a ringneck dove with wings of brown and grey, a rich rose coloured head and breast and they could just about see the black neck ring as she rose and swooped around.

"That would be Awel presumably?" queried Lani.

"Yes, that's Awel," smiled Daren. "You know, some people might find it a bit strange to see a dove flying so closely to a hawk."

Lani chuckled at Daren's words. "You won't see that again unless we find another Partnered dove. None of the wild ones will come near him."

"I wonder why!" laughed Kai. "They don't want to end up being his supper."

The three of them laughed as they continued walking through the village towards the North Road. Marella was still in the lead with her head down. There were quite a lot of people around for the time of day and they all greeted Daren and Marella, wishing them all good luck, and gave assurances of help, should they be able to do so in any way.

* * *

They made their way out of the village and continued along the North Road, passing a few people along the way. The further away from the village they went, the less they saw. The fields of crops were fewer on this side of the village and trees made up more and more of the scenery.

There was still a track for them to follow, but it once again became a single track path, rather than somewhere they could walk side by side. Marella was in the lead, with Daren behind her, and Kai and Lani bringing up the rear. She hadn't spoken since Slade had given her the message.

"*Is she ok?*" Daren asked Ula.

"*She is hurting,*" came Ula's reply. "*She is trying to understand why her mother didn't want her to go, but can't get past the pain that decision caused. She is blocking us all out, even Nixie, although he is hounding at her to let him back in.*"

Daren quickened his pace slightly so he was right behind her. Nixie looked at him and said a quiet "*good luck*" as he dropped behind.

"Marella, talk to me," Daren said to her, as quietly as he could.

"There's nothing to talk about. We need to get as far north as we can, so we can find your grove," she said waspishly.

"There is something to talk about. Don't block us out. We need you and you need us. You're hurting Nixie by shutting him out. Come on, think! What did we talk about when we stopped? You need to open up and let us help." Daren tried to persuade her to talk.

"This isn't the time or the place, Daren, so just leave me alone," she snapped at him. "In case you had forgotten, we're on a time limit here and we have already stopped once, on a morning stroll that all of us have done a million times."

"We may have done it a million times, but separately, not together, and not pulling a trundle truck laden with items everyone thinks we will need" Daren responded, trying to remain calm.

"We still didn't have to stop for so long. We could have just had a drink of water and carried on. As it is, we'll be lucky to even be out of Bridd before nightfall." In her pain, Marella didn't care what she said or how she said it. There was a small part of her inside that knew she was being completely unfair, but she couldn't seem to rein in the part that allowed her mouth to run wild.

Daren slowly dropped back behind her and looked at Kai and Lani before shaking his head. Kai looked irritated, whereas Lani looked concerned. This was not a good start to the challenge.

* * *

They walked in silence for another hour or so, listening to the life in the woods surrounding them. The summer day was warm, but with the shade provided by the trees, they were cool enough. The Partners tried talking to their humans, but soon discovered a pall had settled over the small group.

Finally, as the sun lost some of the day's brightness, Daren and Kai spoke briefly to each other.

"Do you think we should stop and eat something soon?" asked Daren. "Lani is struggling a bit but she hasn't said anything."

"I think we should stop for the night. It's our first day and we're all going to be aching in the morning from pulling these trucks. An early night tonight with plenty of rest will help. Even Marella must see that. She's going to be aching too, once she allows herself to feel again." Kai responded.

"We'll keep an eye out for a clearing then, and we'll set up camp for the night. Luckily for us, it won't be dark for a while," said Daren.

Daren asked Ula to pass the message on to the other Partners so everyone knew what was going on. He knew the moment Lani received the message as her shoulders drooped in relief. It was the opposite reaction to Marella. Her back stiffened and she quickened her pace slightly, putting even more distance between herself and the others.

Nixie ran back towards Daren and jumped onboard his truck. He looked over at Daren and said *"I have given her the message, although she won't acknowledge it. She knows we need to stop. When we do, leave her alone. Don't try to make her talk as she will resist. Ignore her as nicely as possible and she will come round quicker. I've told the others too."*

Daren nodded his agreement to Nixie before he returned to Marella. Daren knew Nixie was correct with his assessment of Marella, but it still didn't stop him from wanting to speak with her. He could only imagine the pain she was in. He couldn't quite believe the actions of her mother himself. He'd seen some things in his time with Marella, where her mother had become more 'Elder' than parent, but he had never expected to see her mother neglect both her Elder duties and her parental ties too.

As Daren walked along, lost in his thoughts, he heard a screech and looked up. Hovering above them was Shaw. As soon as Daren saw it was Shaw, he turned his attention to Lani.

From the expression on her face, she was talking with him. Giving one more screech, Shaw circled once and flew off ahead. Lani turned her attention to Kai and Daren, who were both watching her, and said, "Shaw says there is a clearing about fifteen minutes away. There is also a stream nearby where we can fill our bottles."

Daren and Kai looked at each other and then back at Lani. "Another fifteen minutes then," said Kai looking towards Marella. She had stopped at the same time as the others, but hadn't turned around. With Kai's words, she started walking again. He huffed slightly at her, but then pulled his truck after her. Daren and Lani shared a glance, before Daren gestured for Lani to precede him. With a nod, she set off and they were on the move to the clearing.

When they arrived at the clearing, they set about getting it ready before the night came. They moved their trucks into the same positions as when they had stopped earlier in the day. Marella was with them, but still silent and distant. Daren looked at Nixie and thought *"still ignore?",* and hoped Nixie had heard him.

Nixie looked back at Daren and nodded his head, whilst confirming with his thoughts. *"Yes, still ignore her. She is coming around, but it is more because she is burying it deep within her, rather than letting it out."*

Daren sighed at Nixie's words, he had seen Marella react this way before, and it wasn't something she could just snap out of. It was almost like her body was functioning without her; too much pain and her mind shut down. All he could do was be there for her when she wanted to talk.

He turned to Ula and crouched down to stroke her ears. *"Ula my lovely, would you mind passing onto the others what Nixie has just said. I don't want them to give her a hard time. She is returning, little by little."*

Ula gave his face a lick from his chin to his forehead, making him laugh as he playfully scolded her, wiping his face on his sleeve. Ula said *"I have already done so. They do not know Marella as we do, so they simply cannot understand how much this has hurt her and her way of dealing with it. Lani is okay, but Kai is a bit irritated with her, so you may have to stay in the middle of them."*

Daren looked up at Kai and Lani and saw acceptance on Lani's face, and, as Ula had said, irritation on Kai's. He nodded to Lani and she gave him a small smile in return, before moving off to her truck to start unloading the things that she would need for the night.

Daren stood, with one hand on Ula's scruff, and said, "Shall we take a look around and see if we can find anything to eat, Kai?"

Kai looked at him for a moment without saying anything. His eyes flickered over to where Marella moved about and he started to shake his head. Kenna moved forward and deliberately placed one of her front paws on his foot. He looked down at her as she said, *"Don't be a fool, go with Daren."* As much as he wanted to stay at the clearing and call Marella out for being foolish, he didn't want to go against Kenna.

So he changed the shake of his head into a nod of agreement. "Sure, why not," he said aloud to Daren. "We won't be long, Lani," he said to her and received a wave in return.

* * *

As they walked off a way into the trees that surrounded the clearing, Kai saw Shaw was flying close by and he knew whatever happened now, Lani was also a part of it, and would hear what Daren had to say. Kai took a deep breath, but before he could say anything, Daren beat him to it.

"Look Kai, I know you are annoyed with Marella, but seriously, you just need to give her some space. It's not very often she gets like this. However when she does, it's because something has hurt her deeply, and usually something to do with her mother. They have a strange relationship and Marella always feels like she is lacking something in her mother's eyes. Trust me, I've seen this through the years, and nothing will make her come out any quicker. If you start on her, it will take longer as she will retreat even further into herself. She is not doing this deliberately; it is just her way of coping."

They carried on walking as Kai thought about what Daren had said. Daren walked beside him, content to let him speak now that Daren had explained as best he could.

Kai gave another sigh and stopped, leaning against a tree, and crossing his arms across his chest. "It's not that I don't believe you," he said, "it's just that I've never seen anyone react this way before. Where I come from, you talk about your problems before it reaches crisis point. I don't know what to do or say to Marella, but this silence is killing me. I just want to shout at her or shake her or something, just to get her to react."

Daren grinned at him and Kai looked at him in surprise; that was not the reaction he had been expecting.

"You think you're the only one that feels that, huh?" he questioned with a twinkle in his eye. "You'd be wrong. It frustrates me like you wouldn't believe, but I've had the… erm… pleasure of Nixie and Ula teaching me how to be more helpful. Trust me; you don't want to attempt that with Marella; not with Nixie around, or Ula for that matter."

Kai laughed at the wry look on Daren's face and asked, "You had to learn the hard way then?"

"Yep, I did," Daren chuckled. "I was convinced I could get through to her when Nixie couldn't, and I could make everything better. I was soon put in my place."

"Why is her relationship so strange then?" questioned Kai, running his hand through his hair. "With her mother, I mean."

"I don't really know," replied Daren. "When she was growing up, before the Test, her mother just didn't seem to have much time for her. It wasn't that she was neglected; my mother wouldn't have stood for that. It's just that if Jorja and Marella were together and both wanted to say something to Riva, then it would be Jorja to whom she would listen. When it was Marella's turn, something else would be more important."

Kai could hear the hurt Daren felt on behalf of Marella in his voice, and it made him stop and think about what that must have been like for her.

"Jorja realised what was happening and actually stopped going with her to their mother in the hope that Riva would listen to Marella. It was like Riva couldn't see Marella. Edlin was the one to whom Marella would go to, or even my mother. They both gave her the attention she needed. There was a time - only a short time - that Marella wouldn't speak to Jorja because of how Riva behaved, but she soon realised it wasn't Jorja's fault."

Daren paused and took a breath, looking around for Ula. She came and sat down next to him, giving him the reassurance he needed to continue.

"It wasn't always like that. Sometimes Riva would be there for Marella, and it would be obvious to everyone how she loved Marella; but most of the time, Marella was invisible to her mother. I thought it had changed when we went for our Test, as Riva had spent time with her that morning. However, once the furore calmed down about Marella only having Water, things went back to normal with Riva.

It was actually easier on Marella once she started her training with Murtagh. She had something else to concentrate on and she could focus on that, rather than trying to gain her mother's approval. I think she gave up on getting it at that point."

They both started walking again, towards the forest and away from the clearing with Ula and Kenna running ahead of them and Shaw flying overhead.

"By the time Marella returned to Ilyn, she was confident in her skills as a Water Weaver. She had trained hard and passed everything that had been given to her, but she still didn't get the approval she was looking for. It was almost like it was expected that Marella would pass everything, without having to work at it, although she did work, and she worked hard. Marella spent her time at her work and with the scribes in Charon, keeping records of what she had seen so they could be referenced in the future. As Riva is Elder of Water, she was always aware of Marella's visions, and what they could mean, but she never gave any indication to Marella that she was doing well."

Daren's voice raised in indignation as he continued, "It was my mother who gave congratulations to Marella on being the youngest, fully qualified Water Weaver that has been seen in generations. It was my mother who praised her when a vision came true. It was my mother who consoled her when a bad vision came to fruition, because something hadn't changed in time."

Daren looked at Kai as they walked and took a deep breath to calm himself. "Every time Jorja did well at something, we would all hear about it. It would be so easy for Marella and Jorja to not get on, considering how

Marella has always felt second best to Jorja, but they have managed to overcome that.

I can't imagine how hard it was on Marella when Riva told her not to come on this quest. When she had been Chosen by Erwyna herself, to have her mother tell her not to go and refuse to see her off, or even let her know she loved her, was proud of her… I just can't imagine it. But I do know Marella will need time to work through this. Just give her space and she will come round quicker. She needs our support now, not our condemnation."

They both stopped walking and looked around them. "We seem to have walked a fair way while you were talking," said Kai to Daren.

Daren looked at Kai and gave a huff of laughter. "Well, at least you listened."

"I did, and thank you for explaining it to me. Like you, I can't imagine how she must have felt with the way things were left between her and her mother. Also, growing up like that, I mean, I don't have any brothers or sisters but even so, I can't imagine being treated like that."

The two men stood there for a moment before Kai said, "You know, in Hufel, we always assumed Marella would be this big-headed, arrogant woman, who thought she could lord it over everyone. She's not what I expected."

"Arrogant? Marella?" Daren laughed. "You won't find anyone less arrogant, but it's not the first time she's been accused of that," he said as he remembered AuraLeigh from their Test.

Just as he was about to relay the tale of AuraLeigh to Kai, Ula came bounding up with a rabbit hanging from her jaws. Not to be outdone, Kenna ran by her side with another rabbit. Shaw screeched from where he sat on his branch, and preened his feathers.

Kai and Daren looked at each other and laughed as they saw that whilst they had been talking, their Partners had hunted down something for them to eat. They turned around and started to walk back towards the clearing.

"*Ask Daren to tell you about AuraLeigh on the way back,*" Kenna said. "*Lani is wondering where you are.*"

"How do you know about AuraLeigh?" questioned Daren, when Kai passed on Kenna's message. "You had already been Tested and Partnered by that time, so you weren't there."

Kai raised his shoulders into a shrug. "Don't look at me, I have no idea. I've never heard of AuraLeigh before."

"AuraLeigh was a girl from Bridd, who also thought Marella was arrogant. She claimed that Marella walked around Bridd as though she 'owned the place'. On the day of our Testing, after it was done and we were at the feast, AuraLeigh made the mistake of taunting Marella. Now it takes a lot to get Marella riled, but she won't back down if someone has a go at her either. Marella basically made AuraLeigh look like a spoilt little girl who was after attention. She spoke to her politely, but still made her feelings very clear, although she did create an enemy that day. AuraLeigh still won't speak to Marella, and goes out of her way to be difficult if she gets the opportunity."

"I would have loved to have seen that," admitted Kai as they walked together.

"Stick around and I'm sure you'll see it at some point," Daren laughed.

Ula and Kenna looked at their Partners, then at each other, rolling their eyes at how their Partners are behaving.

Daren chuckled as he nudged Kai, "I think we're in trouble again," he said.

Just then, Shaw took flight and went high into the sky. Kai watched him for a moment and said, "I think Lani has heard enough now, Shaw's going back."

Daren agreed with Kai, shading his eyes as he watched Shaw. "I wanted to be able to tell both of you, but didn't want to leave Marella by herself. I'm glad she sent Shaw with us. Marella will be okay, she always is. She will feel guilty though, and embarrassed."

Kai stepped over a fallen branch and agreed with Daren's assessment. "I can see that. If she's had to prove herself over and over, she will see this as a weakness. She'll just have to learn to trust us, won't she?" he asked.

"Marella doesn't trust very easily," Daren warned. "She holds only a few close to her, but if you make it to her inner circle you will have her loyalty for life."

"The same as she has yours," Kai said.

"She has my loyalty and my love," said Daren. Kai looked at him and Daren smiled. "In the same way a brother loves a sister," he added. "Our parents had a vague notion of something else, but we soon set them straight."

Kai laughed at Daren and said "I only wondered as you two are so close. It's like you understand each other instinctively at times."

"We are close but not in the way you think," said Daren. "I'm her big brother; she knows she can come to me with anything. I just have to remember to let her do it on her own terms or it takes longer."

With these words, silence overcame both of them and they finished the short walk back to the clearing with an air of satisfaction between them.

~ 11 ~

When Kai and Daren entered the clearing, they found Lani and Marella sat around a fire pit they dug and surrounded with stones. They had put some sticks in the ground and made them into a stand so a cooking pot could hang off them. They had also pulled a couple of old fallen tree trunks closer to the middle of the clearing and were using them as seats. They sat close together and Lani had her arm around Marella's shoulders, obviously comforting her.

"Is everything okay?" asked Daren, as he hurried towards them.

Marella sat up straight and gave Lani a tremulous smile. She wiped her face with her hands, looking childlike as she did so, before turning to Daren and smiling at him. "It's all good," she said to him. "I just needed some girlie time."

"Girlie time?" questioned Daren. "You've never needed that before. Does that mean… you're a girl?" he gasped, making the question sound outrageous, and everyone laughed.

"Yes, I'm a girl" replied Marella. "And I never needed it before, because you're not a girl."

"Obviously," Daren said, preening.

The others just laughed at their antics before Lani spoke up. "So, where are the rabbits?"

"How do you know we caught some rabbits?" asked Daren.

"You didn't," she replied. "Shaw saw Ula and Kenna do it"

"Ah, yes," said Daren, as he rubbed his face. "Here they are."

Ula and Kenna walked toward their Partners, still with the rabbits hanging from their jaws. When they were in front of Daren and Kai, they dropped the limp bodies to the ground. Kai reached down and picked up one of the rabbits. He looked from the rabbit in his hands to the girls, and said, "I'll just go and get this ready then, shall I?"

Lani put her hands on her hips and said, "Yes, that might be an idea."

Daren picked up his rabbit and followed Kai towards the direction of the stream. "I thought you were going to give it to them for a moment there," he said to him.

"I'm not that stupid," snorted Kai. "I want to live longer than today."

With a laugh, they looked at rabbits they were holding. "How do you fancy this today?" asked Daren, "spit-roasted or a stew?"

"Hmm, spit-roasted works for me," grinned Kai.

"Sounds good to me," agreed Daren. "Ula, would you mind asking the girls if they want spit-roast?"

Once they had the agreement of the girls, they started skinning the rabbits. They placed the carcasses on a couple of clean leaves. Daren retrieved his knife from his belt and proceeded to remove the heads, feet and guts from both rabbits. Kai picked them up from where Daren had placed them and, along with the heart, liver and other edible organs, offered them to Kenna and Ula.

"No thank you, Kai," said Kenna politely. *"We made sure we had something to eat before bringing you those."*

Kai laughed at her words before saying to Daren, "the cheeky pair don't want our cast offs, they've already eaten."

Daren grinned at Kai and asked, "Are you surprised?"

"I guess not," answered Kai before walking a short distance away and leaving them on a couple of animal trails. He had no doubt they would be cleared away in no time.

Whilst Kai was disposing of the parts, Daren had cleaned the rabbits in the stream and found some small sticks to hold the rear legs together, creating somewhere for the roasting sapling to go through.

Kai walked back and found a couple of saplings they could use. He pulled his knife out and stripped off the bark so it was smooth. Once that was done on both saplings, he passed them over to Daren, who slipped them through the rabbits.

After making sure that both they and their working area were all cleaned up, they made their way back to the clearing.

The fire wasn't lit in the pit yet as it wasn't cold. The girls, however, had collected enough firewood to not only cook their evening meal, but also last into the night.

Daren placed both saplings into the sticks that were over the fire pit and looked around him. The girls had been busy whilst they had been sorting out the rabbits. Both girls had taken their tarps out of the trucks and set them up in a simple 'storm shelter' which kept the tarp both underneath them and over them in a small triangle shape. There wasn't much room, but with the size of the tarp they had, there was enough for their clothing and sleep sacks. They had also filled a couple of the buckets with water.

Kai hunkered down next to the fire pit and, with a look of concentration upon his face, soon had a small fire burning. He stayed by the fire pit making sure the rabbits were kept turning and soon the smell of roasting rabbit wafted through the air.

Whilst he was with the fire, the others carried on bustling about the clearing, getting everything ready for the night. Daren set up Kai's tarp for him and they were soon sorted with the four tarps around the campfire in a rough diamond formation, but far enough away so no sparks would get on them.

"They certainly set us up well," murmured Lani as she looked in her truck. "No wonder my shoulders are aching. I think I've packed everything in here."

Daren grinned at her as he rummaged through his truck. "They certainly wanted to make sure we wouldn't want for anything at this stage," he agreed.

Before long, the camp was ready, but the rabbits were still cooking. Daren went over and sat on one of the logs next to Kai and they talked quietly as they tended the rabbits. Marella went off to find some greens from the nearby woods to add to their meal. Lani stayed in the clearing and spent most of the time rearranging her truck to make it easier for her to pull the following morning.

After an hour or so, the rabbits were done and Marella had returned with some wild Thyme for flavouring. She had also managed to find a patch of young, tender, Greater Plantain leaves which would add some nutrition to their meal.

With their plates at the ready, the rabbits were roughly divided between them, with the flavouring and greens added according to their individual tastes. They sat in agreeable silence as they all ate their hot meal.

In a short while, the food was all gone, and Daren leaned back against the tree trunk as he sat on the ground. "Thanks for doing the cooking, Kai. Those rabbits were delicious. I swear mine just melted in my mouth."

"No problem," replied Kai. "It's not as if I caught them, I just cooked them."

With his words, Daren looked over to Ula and Kenna. "My thanks to you two as well," he said, nodding his head in a mini-bow to them. "At least we won't go hungry so long as you are able to hunt."

"It depends if you deserve us to keep you supplied in food." Ula told him with a stern voice. *"We do this because we love you, not because it's our job. Just remember that."* With those words, she stood up and walked into the forest.

"Uh oh, what's going on?" asked Lani.

Daren stroked a hand over his face ruefully. "I have just been put in my place by Ula," he said. "I made the mistake of presuming she and Kenna would be hunting for us all the time."

"Oh Daren," sighed Lani, "you are so in tune with Ula most of the time, and then you go and say something stupid like that." She shook her head at him but her eyes were laughing.

Marella stood up from where she had been sat and searched in one of her small bags until she found a smaller bag containing different herbs. She also gathered their travel mugs and placed them near where she was working. She grabbed one of her loop-handled cooking pots and filled it from one of the buckets of water. She placed it on one of the saplings they had used for the rabbits. As the water started heating up, she placed a good sprinkling of chamomile flowers into the pot, then added some root of marshmallow. She left the pot over the fire, boiling the water for a short while before carefully lifting it and pouring the mixture into the four mugs.

While it was steaming, she passed one to each of them and they sat together, drinking their tea, full from a good meal.

It was in that post-meal glow that Marella sighed and looked at the rest of them. She could see Ula, Kenna, and Nixie curled up together, with Shaw perched in a branch above them. They hadn't eaten with their Partners, but Marella had no doubt they all had full stomachs.

She curled her hands around her travel mug and looked towards Daren. He was looking at her and raised an eyebrow when he saw her looking back. She gave him a slight smile before looking at Kai and Lani.

"I owe you guys an apology," she said, her voice regretful.

Kai just looked at her, whilst Lani gave her an encouraging look.

"It wasn't fair of me to shut you all out, and treat you the way I did. It's not an excuse, but at least Daren knew what I was like before this. You didn't, and I'm sorry you had to deal with my mood. It's just…" she stopped as she struggled to find the words.

"Marella, it's okay," she heard, from the one source she wasn't expecting. She looked over at Kai as he attempted to reassure her. "Daren took the time this afternoon to try and explain how things are for you. I don't understand all of it, and I'm sure Lani feels the same. I don't think even Daren can understand it all himself, but he at least was able to give me some idea of what you were going through."

Marella shot Daren a grateful glance, as once again he had come to her rescue. He gave her a look that told her she didn't have anything to worry about.

"I shouldn't have reacted that way though, and left you all to it. It's not very good when we're only on our first day of this, and I've already sunk into a bad mood," she said to the group.

"Don't worry about it. Seriously, it's okay," reassured Lani. "I wobbled today as well. I'm sure we'll all have something to deal with before this is over. At least we have ours out of the way."

Kai, Daren, and Marella all chuckled quietly at Lani's words. "You may well be right," said Kai to Lani.

"I'm going to spend some time Weaving each evening when we stop," said Marella. "I think it might help give us some idea of what's to come. Even if it doesn't, I can't see how it will hurt to do so."

"I think that's a great idea," said Lani. "Anything you can see that will help us has to be a good thing, right?" she said as she looked towards Kai and Daren.

"Right, a good thing" said Kai, as he laughed at Lani.

She gave him a glare that quickly changed into laughter, as Marella burst out in a fit of giggles. "Oh Lani," she said, "if only you could have seen your face then. I think Kai was too afraid of you to disagree."

Daren was holding his stomach, as he laughed with the rest of them.

"Oh yeah," he said sarcastically, "Lani's the quiet one, she's shy. That's why she looks as fierce as a mama bear protecting her cubs. Marella, you've just become Lani's cub."

At his words, he carried on laughing, holding his stomach even harder. For a few moments, hilarity ensued. No one could breathe properly, and Lani was wiping tears from her eyes by the time they all managed to calm down.

"Oh but I needed that," said Marella as a puff of air left her body.

"I think we all did," agreed Daren.

"Here, give me your plates and cups, if you've finished with them, and I'll go and wash them out," said Marella.

"I'll clean the pot," said Lani.

"I'll shake out the sleep sacks ready," said Kai.

"And I'll stay here and watch you all," said Daren. The others laughed at him, as everyone, including Daren, stood up to clear things away and get the camp settled for the night.

~ 12 ~

The animal Partners had all kept quiet, letting their humans get to know each other during the day. As they watched them bustle around, Shaw thought to Nixie, *"Is Marella going to be okay?"*

"She'll be fine," answered Nixie. *"She needed the time alone, which the others gave her. However, now she also knows they are there if she needs them. It's a good first step."*

Shaw bobbed his head in agreement as he fluffed up his wings to ensure the feathers lay properly.

"They've all done well considering what's been dropped on them," commented Ula to no one in particular.

"They do balance each other out nicely, don't they," stated Kenna happily.

"I think we should take advantage of the lull, and get some sleep whilst we can," said Shaw. *"I can't see it being like this every day."*

"No," agreed Nixie, *"I think we've been let in gently. I'm going to stay with Marella whilst she Weaves though. Sleep well my friends."*

~ 13 ~

Nixie watched as Kenna, Ula, and Shaw made their way towards their Partners. Daren gave Ula's head a quick stroke as he saw her near him. Kenna had her ears twitched by Kai, and Shaw preened himself as Lani ran a finger from his head down his back.

Nixie walked over to where Marella sat near the stream. She was staring into the water, but Nixie knew she wasn't seeing anything in particular. He bumped her hand with his head and waited for her to acknowledge him.

"I am lucky," he heard whispered into his mind. *"I've been such a fool today and yet the others have just accepted it and forgiven me. I'm so sorry for blocking you out again, Nixie. I don't know why you bother with me."*

He lifted his head up and nipped at Marella's hand. She moved it away and looked at him. Although the sun was beginning to set, he could see her face clearly as it gave her, and the surrounding area, a rosy hue. *"There's no need for that sort of nonsense,"* he said to her. *"I understand when you retreat. No one understands more. But I will not have this feeling of self-pity. You have family and friends who love you. You are Partnered with me, and you are the Chosen of Erwyna. Consider these things, and then tell me you feel sorry for yourself."*

Marella ran her hand over his head and down his back towards his strong tail. *"You're right as usual,"* she said. *"I don't know what I'd do without you."*

"You will never have to find out," reassured Nixie. *"Now, are you going to get some water for your chalice so you can Weave?"*

With those words from Nixie, she scooped some water up into her now clean cup, and carried it back towards her shelter. The others had all finished their jobs and were sat around the fire, talking quietly. They watched as she sat down in front of her tarp, and crossed her legs, getting as comfortable as she could on the hard ground.

She poured the water in the silver chalice and waited for a few moments so it would settle. She blocked out the noises from the others, the forest and the animals that inhabited it, and felt herself flowing inwards. Here she was able to see and hear clearly.

Her vision tunnelled until she could only see her silver chalice in front of her, although she could feel Nixie's presence both next to her and with her mentally. As she stared into the water, she saw a grove of trees with the moon in the sky. It was a full moon and cast enough light so she was able to identify the trees that were there. There was a shimmer in the centre of the grove and she saw the Portal.

She now knew what trees to look for to find the Portal, and was sure she would recognise it once she saw it in reality. As she felt herself floating to the surface, she felt the confidence and love Erwyna had for her, and heard her say, *"Little one, you are fine. You will continue on as you are and will be able to see things the others cannot. Use your visions to help you all. Work together and balance each other out. We have faith in you, but you need to put aside your worries about your mother. You will sort things out, however, it won't be until after this is over. This is more important than the two of you."*

Marella blinked and saw some time had passed since she had started Weaving. The fire had been built up, and there was another pot of water being boiled. From where she sat, she could smell the faint herby smell that told her it was skullcap, which would help soothe the nervous system and bring her body back down to ground.

She gave thanks to Erwyna for the vision and emptied her chalice, before wrapping it up carefully in its cloth and returning it to the truck. She unsteadily stood up, and walked over to the others, rubbing at her legs to get rid of the pins and needles that were there.

She smiled gratefully at Daren as he passed her a cup of tea, sipping it as she watched the steam furl and ribbon in the evening air. The others waited whilst she drank some of her drink.

"Okay, so this is what I know," she said, as she raised her head to look at them. "The moon was full and the trees I saw were still in their summer colours, so we either have a fortnight or a month and a half to find the grove." She stopped and took another sip of her drink. "I think I know now the grove being 'of the three' means the three sets of trees that make up the grove. I saw Ash, Dwarf Elm, and Hawthorn trees clustered together. The Portal wasn't there when I first looked at it, but then it sort of shimmered. I don't think the Portal is visible all the time."

"So, we have the grove of three, in the north of the north, when it is green," surmised Daren. "We know the three species of trees now, so we just need to keep heading north until Marella sees something that she recognises."

"Yes, simple when you put it like that," joked Kai.

Marella felt herself relaxing as she enjoyed the banter between the others, and let the tea do its job. Before long, she could feel her eyelids getting heavy, so it was no surprise when she heard Daren calling her a sleepyhead.

"Come on, love," he said to her. "You can't sleep there. Go on over to your tarp, and sort yourself out. We'll see you in the morning."

Marella looked at him sleepily and couldn't think of a reason why she should stay up. Lani also stood up and came to her. "I'm going to bed as well," she said. "We'll leave the boys to it."

With those words, Lani led Marella towards the simple shelters, where they went their separate ways to get ready for sleep. Once Marella had finished, she changed the direction of her sleep sack, so her head was near the opening. She lay down on her stomach, and put her head on her crossed arms. From that position, she could still see the fire, and hear the murmur of Daren and Kai as they spoke. She gave a glance to her left and saw that Lani was lying in pretty much the same position. She gave her a sleepy smile before resting her head on her arms again.

She felt Nixie curl up beside her. As she lay there in the world of not quite slumber, she thought she felt a hand pass gently over her head in a caress, but by the time she thought of opening her eyes, it was too late and no one was there. The fire was banked down, and Daren and Kai were also in their beds. She slipped softly into sleep, wondering what tomorrow would bring.

~ 14 ~

The days fell into an easy rhythm as they continued their journey northwards. They pulled their trundle trucks behind them, making good progress. The aches and pains of the journey were forgotten as their muscles and joints became accustomed to the walking and the trucks.

They continued to feast on fresh meat most nights; they had enough hunters in their group to ensure that if it was available, it would be served. They all had herb knowledge, and were pleased to share with each other, so they all tried a new tea at some point in the week following, although they each had their favourites that they would return to. With Nixie among them, they always managed to find fresh water.

The scenery changed as the vegetation became sparser, and travellers passing their way became fewer in number. Still they walked onwards, searching for the grove of Marella's visions. She continued to Weave every night, but nothing new was to be seen. Marella took this as a good sign they were heading in the right direction.

Bit by bit, they became comfortable with each other, sharing snippets of their past. The favourite time for this was after they had eaten their evening meal, and Marella had Woven. This was the time to relax and enjoy each other's company.

They had been travelling for just over a week, and had stopped for the night. They had eaten and Marella was preparing her silver chalice. She poured in some water and relaxed herself. She felt herself folding inwards and followed the vision.

An archway was in front of her and she could see the lush, green leaves on the trees on the other side. It looked like a summer's day, with the sun shining brightly on the path and trees. On this side of the arch though, it appeared dusty, with the wind whipping up bits of dry earth. The full moon was shining and lit the way to the Portal.

She swam towards the surface of her consciousness and gradually felt her senses return. She took a deep breath in and the familiar scent of skullcap greeted her. This gave her a small smile as Daren always made sure there was a cup ready for her return. She opened her eyes, not rushing this process, and after a moment, she felt able to move, so unfolded her legs, swaying slightly as she stood to return her chalice to the truck.

The others were waiting for her by the fire, all sipping their own hot drinks. After carefully placing her chalice back in the truck, she made her way over to them, before sitting down on the ground.

"Here you go, Marella," said Lani as she handed her a cup of skullcap.

"Thanks Lani," replied Marella. "I've seen some more information, so I think we're getting close."

The others leaned forward at her words. This was what they wanted to hear. As they waited for Marella to collect her thoughts whilst she had a sip of her drink, the Partners all appeared and made their way to the fire too.

"I've seen the Portal… or at least what I think is the Portal," she started. "It's like it's built into a wall, an archway through the wall. There seems to be a time difference though as it was night-time on one side, and bright sunlight on the other."

Lani nodded at Marella as she stopped to take a drink. "I've heard before that time runs differently through the portals," she said matter-of-factly.

Kai looked at Lani in surprise, both eyebrows rising. "When have you talked about portals? And who were you speaking to?" he asked with a querying note in his voice.

Lani blushed and looked down at her cup before answering Kai. "It's one of the things we were taught by Bronwyn at Alaw," she said. "I thought everyone knew that."

Kai and Daren looked at each other in surprise before they laughed softly. "No, Lani," said Daren gently. "We weren't taught anything about portals. You are the one with the information here."

Lani shrank back into herself when she realised they were all watching her. Her shyness was easing because of the amount of time they all spent together, but she still disliked being the centre of attention.

Marella gave her an encouraging smile and asked, "Please, Lani. Will you share what you know? We only have my visions to go on so far, and that's okay for seeing it, but apart from that we're blind."

With Daren and Kai also looking at her, Lani took a steadying breath before leaning forwards slightly with her elbows on her knees.

"The portals can be as big or as small as they want to be. No one knows who controls the portals – when they appear, what size, shape, appearance or anything like that. They can be in the middle of nowhere, or the centre of a village. Some move, some remain in the same place." She stopped and took another sip of her drink.

"I think we are going to the main four Portals, the big ones of each Element. If we are meeting with the King or Queen of that Element, it makes sense that we use the front door, if you like, rather than a side entrance. I'm hoping this means we will see them sooner rather than later once we are through the Portal, because, like I said, one of the things we were taught is that time runs differently there. We may have had a year and a day when we started this challenge, but there's no saying we will have the same amount of time left when we return from each Portal."

Kai let out a soft whistle at Lani's words whilst Daren leaned back against a tree stump. Marella sat, going through what Lani had just said.

"So we could spend a whole year in there…" started Kai.

"And what? Be back out the same day?" finished Daren.

"Yes," answered Lani. "Or it could work the opposite way around, which would be the worst situation for us."

"Is there any way of knowing how the time works once we are through the Portal?" asked Marella.

Ula stood up and barked to draw everyone's attention. She nodded at them all before sitting back down again and licking her front paw, which made them all laugh.

Daren gave her a quick squeeze before saying aloud "Do you want to say that again for me, Ula? And this time I'll translate for everyone," he said with a smile at his Partner.

Ula looked at him with her eyes twinkling with the love she held for him. "*I was simply answering Marella,*" she said. "*Yes, there is a way of knowing how the time is working when we are through the Portal. Every Partner will still know what the time is HERE even when we are THERE.*"

Daren saw Marella looking relieved, and knew Ula had spoken to her at the same time. It was Daren who repeated Ula's words to Kai and Lani though. "So as long as we can contact our Partners, we'll know how much time we've spent or have left," he concluded.

"That's a big relief. They never mentioned that part in training," Lani said wryly.

Daren laughed at her words. "They probably don't know," he said. "I get the feeling we're all learning as we go along here."

Kai and Marella nodded in agreement before they all lapsed into a comfortable silence. The night was slightly cooler than it had been, so they were all grateful for the fire in front of them.

"How do you think they all are back at home?" asked Lani quietly into the silence.

Kai glanced at Marella, but turned away before she could see him. He turned towards Lani and gave her what he hoped was a reassuring smile. "I'm sure they're all okay," he said. "Probably wondering what we're up to."

"Have you heard anything from anyone?" asked Daren softly to Marella.

"I've had a quick message from Torlan saying Papa was missing me, and Salali says that Jorja says to hurry up as she wants to marry Derwen," answered Marella, with a smile quirking her lips.

"Nothing from your Mama though?" asked Kai.

"No Kai," huffed Marella, "Nothing from my Mama." After a moment, Marella let out a sigh. "I'm sorry, Kai. I shouldn't have snapped at you like that. I know I won't hear from her until this is over. Not only do I know her, but Lady Erwyna also told me this isn't the time or the place to sort this out. I'm only expecting to hear from her if I have to contact her as Elder of Water."

"I'm sorry too, Marella," said Kai. "I didn't mean anything by that, I just…"

"I know," she sighed. "You'd have thought I would have heard something by now." She shook herself and straightened her shoulders. "Still, we don't have time to think or worry about that. We've an Earth Portal to find, and the moon is nearly full. If we don't find it soon, we'll have to wait a month."

The others knew by her brisk tone of voice she was not prepared to discuss it any further that evening so they let the subject drop.

"I've been thinking…" said Kai, grinning when he saw the wary looks on their faces.

"What?" asked Daren, wondering what Kai was going to say next.

"We need to find the Portal, right?" asked Kai.

They all nodded whilst looking at him. Kenna was sat beside him with her tongue lolling from the side of her mouth, looking for all intents and purposes that she was laughing at them.

"Well, we're on a time limit and we know, or think, that we're in approximately the right place, correct?" he asked.

"By the Earth, just get on with it, will you," said Daren exasperatedly.

Kai laughed at Daren's impatience and held his hands up in surrender. "Okay, okay. Look, my idea is to ask our gorgeous Partners over here, if they wouldn't mind scouting the area. They can move faster on wings or four feet than we can, and it could save us a huge amount of time."

A short silence followed his words before Daren spoke up. "You know, that's not such a bad idea. It just might work."

"Thanks for the vote of confidence," laughed Kai. "Seriously though, I'm sure Kenna won't mind so long as I ask nicely," he said, looking over at where she sat, "but do you think the others will help?"

"*We are in this together,*" said Shaw to Lani in his deep voice, whilst the others just heard him screech as he bobbed up and down on top of the truck where he had been resting.

"*It's about time,*" said Ula to Daren. "*I was getting bored.*" Daren snorted at her words, knowing she was only teasing.

"*You only need ask, you know I will help in any way I can,*" reassured Nixie to Marella.

"It looks like that's agreement all round then," said Daren with a smile. "Thanks everyone."

Kenna gave a small yip from where she was sat and continued to look at Kai. Marella knew she wasn't actually saying or thinking anything to him, so she shrugged her shoulders when Lani looked at her.

Suddenly Kai burst out laughing. It boomed throughout the clearing and scared a bird out of a nearby tree. The others looked at Kai before looking at Kenna. Slowly, a smile passed over Marella's face. She looked at Daren and Lani and explained, "Kai only said that he was sure Kenna wouldn't mind, so long as he asked nicely. He hasn't yet asked her, nicely or not. We have; but not him."

Daren and Lani smiled as they realised Kenna was waiting to be asked. She was sat back on her haunches, her red fur shining by the firelight. Kai walked over to where she sat and sank down onto one knee before her.

"Oh Kenna, queen of my heart, from the depths of my soul I ask you this," he said dramatically, holding his clasped hands in front of his heart. "Please, would you do me the great honour of scouting for this wretched band of travellers on paws so swift?"

The others couldn't contain their laughter at Kai's antics, and the sound of their laughter filled the evening air.

Kenna stood up and ambled towards Kai, who was still on bended knee. She walked around him, Kai watching her from the corner of his eyes where possible, until she stood in front. All of a sudden, she jumped towards his chest, which knocked him off balance, and he landed in a heap on the floor. Kenna made herself comfortable on his chest, and brought her face down towards his so that their noses almost touched.

'NOW that you have asked, I will do,' she told him, with a teasing note in her voice.

"She says yes," Kai shouted out loud, making the others jump.

Daren walked over to him as Kenna jumped off his chest. He held his hand out and helped Kai to his feet. "You are a fool, Kai," he said to him. "When will you remember to ask first, and not just presume?"

Kai laughed with Daren. "Like you're one to talk. I don't know, I'll remember someday, but it's a good job Kenna loves me and puts up with me. I'm sure I drive her to distraction."

"You drive us all to distraction," muttered Marella beneath her breath.

Lani looked at her quizzically, but Marella just gave her a smile and shrugged it off. How could she explain there was something about Kai that seemed to rub her the wrong way, when she didn't understand it herself? She was putting in a huge effort to get along with everyone equally, but found herself wanting to bite back when Kai said something to her, even when he was being nice. Actually, that wasn't all true, she admitted to herself. Lani was so easy to get along with and was just like a younger sister. Daren was just Daren, and they had been together for so long it was as easy as breathing. The only one she was having problems with was Kai who really hadn't done anything wrong. Marella didn't understand it, didn't have the time for it, and so kept on shoving it to the back of her mind.

They all started to bed the camp down for the night. It wasn't long before everything was put away and ready for the morning. Lani and Marella lay in their shelters with their heads out, like they did most nights. Marella rolled onto her back and stared up at the sky. From where she lay, she could see the moon, shining against the starlit sky.

"Goodnight all, I hope you are well, I miss you," she whispered, and the wind gently took her words away. She rolled onto her side and pulled her head inside the tent before snuggling down to sleep.

~ 15 ~

The following morning, they woke up and made breakfast. They sat in a circle on some stones they were using as seats. The conversation was sparse as no one talked much in the mornings.

"We need to find the Portal soon," blurted out Daren. The others looked at him, but didn't speak. "We can't wait for next month, and the full moon is in two night's time."

"Do you know something that we don't?" asked Lani quietly, as she sipped her drink.

"I just know we need to find it soon. I think Lady Daire came to me last night, but I can't remember much about it. I just have this feeling we need to find it," replied Daren.

"I'm not going to argue against feelings," said Marella, whilst Kai also nodded his agreement.

They mentally called to their Partners, who were also busy having their breakfasts. When they had finished, they came to the circle where they were sat.

"I've just said to the others, we need to find the Portal and soon. We can't wait until next month. We've got to find it now. And that means we are going to need your help," Daren spoke to all four Partners. "I think Lady Daire visited me last night, but I can't remember what it was about. I just know we need to find the Portal."

Nixie stood up and arched his back into a big stretch, almost like a cat. He shook his body and then waited. Shaw shook all his feathers up before smoothing them back down. He extended his wings and bobbed up and down before closing his wings and waiting. Kenna also stretched out, but she was almost like a dog as she stretched out her front paws in a move that looked like a bow. Ula just stood and shook herself from nose to tail, before giving a soft bark at Daren.

"We're all ready. Tell us which way you want us to go," she said to him.

Daren looked at her in surprise. "Why do you need me to tell you where to go?" he asked. "Surely you guys are better than me at scouting."

Ula gave him what looked like a lopsided grin. *"Honestly Daren, you'd forget your head if it wasn't screwed on,"* she said to him, causing Marella to snort with laughter. *"You are the Chosen of Earth, handpicked by Lady Daire herself, and we are looking for the Chief Portal of Earth to take us to the very heart of the Element itself, and you ask why? Do I need to explain any further?"*

"No, I guess not, not when you put it like that," mumbled Daren.

"Trust in yourself, Daren," said Marella. "Open your senses and your heart. You will surely feel something that will tell our Partners which general direction to head in."

Daren got himself comfortable on the stone and closed his eyes. Whilst he was searching inside himself, Marella explained to Kai and Lani what Ula had said. "We will need to be more in touch with our Element, if we are to move forward."

Lani and Kai nodded their agreement to her words, whilst closely watching Daren. Suddenly he opened his eyes and pointed. "It is somewhere over in that direction," he said.

Ula barked, Kenna yipped, Nixie chattered, and Shaw gave a screech before they set off in the direction Daren had shown.

Daren still sat on the stone whilst the others packed away their things, putting them in the trundle trucks, ready to move once they had a better idea of which way to go. After a moment, Daren gave himself a shake and stood up before moving to put his things away, although Kai had already started. "Thanks Kai, I'll finish now," Daren said to him.

Marella walked up and asked for his travel flask so that she could go and fill it with water. He gave it to her and watched as she walked over to Lani. He realised that Kai was watching him, watching her. He looked at Kai and raised an eyebrow in question.

"You watch her a lot," said Kai, "are you sure you're only friends?"

"Definitely friends, but more like my sister," Daren replied. "Why are you so interested anyway?"

"I'm not interested," said Kai quickly. "It's just seeing you watch her all the time, makes a man wonder if the stories are true, that's all."

"Oh please don't tell me you believe those," scoffed Daren. "Marella and I knew long ago we were never going to be more than what we are. We're happy with that, our parents are happy with that, it's only the gossips in the villages that keep trying to make more of it than there is."

Kai's face flushed a little as he heard Daren's words. He had listened to the stories himself, only because no one seemed to have a relationship quite like Daren and Marella's that was purely friendship. Only now, he found himself getting irritated at the thought of something going on. *"Or perhaps it's because Marella that irritates me,"* he thought to himself. *"She's so prickly, I just can't be bothered."*

"Perhaps you're interested because you don't want it to be true," said Daren suggestively. "Are you interested in Marella?"

"Don't be ridiculous," said Kai shortly. "We've only just started this quest and we certainly don't have time for any nonsense like that. We need to work together to get this sorted and get back to Charon. Besides, Marella's too prickly for me. I'd need someone calmer."

"Is that so?" asked a voice from behind him and he groaned silently as he realised Marella stood behind him. He turned around to look at her and saw the stormy look in her eyes.

"I just meant that…" he started.

"I don't care what you meant," Marella snapped at him, "too prickly am I? Well I do apologise," she added sarcastically. "How about we get this quest finished so you can return to Hufel, I can return to Ilyn, and then you won't have to deal with me at all."

With those words, she threw his travel flask at him, before turning around and walking off, hurt in every line of her back as she went.

"I'm so sorry," apologised Daren. "I didn't see her coming back."

Kai rubbed his hand over his face. "It's fine, I'm sure I would have done something to upset her soon enough anyway," he said. "I'll just keep out of her way for the time being until she calms down."

By this time, everyone had everything packed away, and Marella had filled all their travel flasks with fresh water to see them through the day. After walking away from Kai she went to a stone near where she had parked her trundle truck, and sat there with her arms wrapped around her knees.

Lani went over to her. "Are you okay?" she asked.

Marella turned her head so that she could see Lani. "I'm fine," she said but added nothing further.

"I'm sure Kai didn't mean it," Lani started, but was interrupted by Marella.

"I don't care if he meant it or not," she said. "I just want to get this quest over and done with."

Lani shook her head at Marella's words. It was obvious from her reaction that she did indeed care about what Kai had said. She sat with her in silence until Marella spoke again.

"I just wish we could find the Portal. I'm fed up with wandering and wondering. I feel like we should be *doing* now."

"I know what you mean," agreed Lani. "I'm sure with our Partners out looking they will find something soon enough."

"Yes but will they?" questioned Marella. "If the Portal only shows at certain times; how will they find it unless they are there at exactly the right time? And if they are there at the right time, then we won't be unless we're all together. This waiting is what is getting to me."

Just then, Shaw landed on the ground in front of them. He bobbed his head to Lani and Marella. *"We are not looking for the Portal"* he explained. *"We are all searching for your grove of three. Nixie has given us the picture of it from your vision so we all know what we are looking for. I think I may have seen something, but Ula was going for a closer look before returning here. We need to wait for Nixie and Kenna to see what they have found too."*

"Nixie, how are you doing? Ula and Shaw think they may have found something," Marella queried.

"We're on our way back now, there's no grove in the direction we went," answered Nixie.

"Kenna and Nixie are on their way back," said Marella, "they haven't found the grove."

Lani looked disappointed but said, "Then let's hope that Ula and Shaw have found it."

Within a few moments, Nixie and Kenna had returned, and sat by their Partners as they waited for Ula's return. It wasn't long before she appeared in the campsite, puffing slightly.

Daren put some water in a bowl and placed it on the ground so Ula could have a drink. She sent her thanks before gratefully slurping it down.

"I think Shaw and I have found the right place. When I looked there is the grove of three, and it is surrounded by green. The full moon is due, so if we move there today, we will be ready in case it shows tonight. It won't take too long to get there. There should even be time for you to have a nap, in case it does show."

Daren looked around and saw the acknowledgment on everyone's faces of their Partners passing on Ula's message. Marella stood up and extended a hand to help Lani to her feet.

"What are we waiting for, then?" she asked. "If you are ready, Shaw, Ula, please show us the way." With those words, Marella walked to her trundle truck and got ready to go with Lani right behind her.

Ula had finished her drink and was ready, with Shaw in the air, before Marella had even finished speaking. Without a word, they left the campsite, with Marella and Lani hot on their heels. Kai and Daren looked at each other, and shrugged their shoulders.

"I guess that means we're going now," said Kai.

"Looks that way," replied Daren. "Come on, or they'll leave us behind."

* * *

The day passed rapidly as they made their way to the site Shaw and Ula had found. Marella found herself looking around as she walked, in case any of it seemed familiar.

As they walked, they noticed the land was covered with Ash, Dwarf Elm and Hawthorn trees. This could definitely be the 'grove of three' they were looking for. It only took the morning hours to walk there. It would have been quicker without their trucks, but as they had only just started, none of them wanted to leave them behind.

Just as Ula and Shaw told them they had arrived, Marella looked around. "This is it," she confirmed. "This is the place I saw."

The others were happy they had made progress at last, and set up their camp. As it was nearing lunchtime, they had a light snack before discussing what they would do later on.

"I think Ula's suggestion of a nap was a good one," said Lani. "We are presuming the Portal will open tonight, and from Marella's vision, it is daytime on the other side. We don't know what time of day though, so it might be early morning. We're also meeting King Ghobe, so we need to be sharp."

Daren agreed with her. "I think it's a good idea. We have no idea if they even know we are coming, and what sort of welcome, if any, we will receive."

"Perhaps we should rest at different times though," suggested Kai. "I know Marella's vision said it was dark here but who's to say that's the first time it appears. They also might have lookouts and I for one don't want to be caught unawares."

"I'm going to Weave again before I rest," said Marella. "I just want to see if anything different comes through."

"Well, why don't you and Lani take the first rest," suggested Kai to Daren. "I'll sit with Marella whilst she Weaves and then when you two wake up, we can take our rest."

Marella looked uncomfortable with Kai's suggestion but didn't say anything. Daren looked at her and raised an eyebrow in question. Marella gave him a slight nod to say that she was okay with this. Kai watched the exchange between them, a slight look of frustration on his face.

"*Kai, don't take on so,*" said Kenna, moving to his side.

"*Why does Daren feel the need to check with Marella that she's okay to be with me?*" he asked, a bit grumpily. "*It's not like I've ever hurt her, nor would I.*"

"*I know that,*" said Kenna, laughing at his tone. "*But you have to see it from their view. They are as close, if not closer, than siblings. Daren has always looked out for Marella, and this journey so far has been the hardest for her. You left with the blessing of your family and with excitement in your heart. Marella left with a major part of her family not wanting her to go and fear in her heart instead. And then there's you.*"

"*What do you mean 'and then there's me'?*" asked Kai.

"*You and Marella are opposites. She is all Water and although you have Earth as well, Fire is your dominant element. Marella has never had dealings with a dominant Fire before. Even when she had her training in Hufel, Aine never had anyone there that was as dominant as you in Fire. She doesn't know what to make of you. And you aren't making it easy with your big mouth,*" she finished with a twinkle in her eyes.

"*I'm not annoying her deliberately,*" said Kai, "*I don't know what to make of her! One minute, she's in control and seems balanced and then the next it's like she's wallowing, throwing a 'poor me pity party'. It drives me crazy.*"

"*Don't you realise that you're the only one it affects though?*" questioned Kenna. "*Daren and Lani don't seem bothered by it at all. So why should you be affected, hmm?*" Kenna gave him a knowing look before walking off to bump noses with Ula.

Kai sat and thought about what Kenna had said. It was true Daren and Lani didn't seem bothered, so why did it bother him? He had thought it was because Daren was used to her, but he knew Lani and Marella hadn't met until this all started.

Kai jumped as Daren nudged his shoulder. "Kai - Lani and I are going for a rest. We've thrashed out the details whilst you and Kenna were talking. Ula and Shaw are going to wake us in a couple of hours so you and Marella can rest."

Kai looked around and saw Lani was getting into her tent, but Marella was nowhere to be seen. "Where's Marella?" he asked.

"She's gone to the water with Nixie. I think she needs some time alone. She'll be back soon though, I'm sure, and then she'll be Weaving. I don't think she'll bother you."

Kai looked at Daren, a strange look upon his face. "What do you mean? She doesn't bother me."

"Of course not; just like you don't bother her," laughed Daren. "Keep the fire burning, will you? I'm sure Marella will need a cup of skullcap when she's finished."

"I'll sort that out," promised Kai. "You go and rest. See you in a couple of hours."

Daren walked off and went inside his tent with Ula padding up behind him, settling herself down in front of the tent flaps. Kai could see Shaw resting in a nearby tree. Kenna was curled up in front of the fire and he knew Nixie was with Marella.

She really was a conundrum, he thought to himself. Hot, cold, emotional, placid; he never knew what he was going to get when she opened her mouth.

"*At least you'll never be bored,*" said Kenna sleepily. "*Now stop thinking so loudly and let me sleep.*"

Kai didn't know what to make of her remark so let it go. He pulled out a book from his trundle truck and made himself comfortable. There was no need to make the skullcap this early. He would start it when Marella started Weaving.

* * *

After an hour or so, Marella and Nixie came back. Kai looked up from his book as she entered the clearing. He could tell just by looking at her she felt more balanced, more relaxed. Spending time by the water had obviously soothed her, and it made Kai realise just how connected to her Element she was. He watched her as she retrieved her silver chalice out of the trundle truck and unwrapped it, before pouring some water into it from her flask. She did all of this without looking in Kai's direction and he found himself wanting her to acknowledge him.

Marella moved closer to the fire and sat on the floor, leaning against one of the trunks they had pulled to the fire as a seat. She crossed her legs and settled herself down so she was comfortable. She looked over at Kai and he was surprised to see how vulnerable she looked.

"I'm going to Weave now," she said quietly, not wanting to disturb Daren or Lani.

Kai nodded his head at her. "I'll have a cup of skullcap ready for when you're finished."

Marella bowed her head in acknowledgment, "Thank you."

Kai put his book aside and watched as Marella entered the light trance needed for her to Weave. He hadn't really seen her do this before as he had always been busy doing other things, or just hadn't bothered looking. This time though, he was intrigued. He also wanted to make sure she wasn't disturbed. He didn't know for sure, but didn't think it would be a good idea.

Nixie sat beside her with a paw on one of her legs. He turned his head and looked at Kai, before speaking to him.

"Kai, you must be patient with Marella. She is doing the best she can under difficult circumstances. You are in touch with your parents through Kenna at least once a week. The only one who reaches for Marella is Edlin. Even Jorja is too busy with her Earth duties. She doesn't know how to act with you, and that makes her irritable. She will take it out on you simply because she doesn't know how else to act around you."

Kai listened to Nixie as he spoke. *"Marella is so different from any of the girls I know, we seem to clash every time one of us speaks. I don't want it to be like this, but I seem to irritate her just by being here."*

"Well your attitude at the start didn't help, now did it?" reminded Nixie wryly and watched a look of embarrassment wash over Kai's face.

"No, I guess it didn't," said Kai. *"I will try my best to be a friend for Marella and hopefully we can work out whatever the problem is between us,"* he promised Nixie.

"That's all we ask," responded Nixie, with Kenna raising her head, and nodding in Kai's direction.

"So it's both of you, is it?" laughed Kai, *"ganging up on me, eh?"*

"Not just you, we've been speaking to Marella too," reassured Kenna.

Kai turned his head back towards Marella and watched her for a moment. She was deep within her trance now and he could see her eyes moving beneath her eyelids. He took the opportunity to really look at her. He could see how pale her skin looked, which only emphasised the bruised shadows beneath her eyes. She had been slim when they first met, but even he could tell she had lost weight within the short amount of time they had all been together, even though they ate well due to their Life Partners.

Kai was surprised by the surge of protectiveness that went through him as he looked at her. He didn't want to fight or argue with her anymore, he wanted to help look after her, to be her friend like Daren was. Nixie sent a wave of warmth in Kai's direction.

"That's a good place to start," he told Kai.

Kai didn't understand what Nixie meant by 'start', but he was going to do everything in his power to become Marella's friend.

"She'll be coming out of her trance soon," said Nixie. *"Now might be a good time to start the skullcap."*

Kai dusted himself off before approaching the fire and getting some water on to boil. He got the skullcap leaves and placed them in a couple of travel mugs, one for him and one for Marella.

By the time the tea was ready to drink; Marella had come out of her trance and tidied away her things. She made her way to the fire and took the drink from Kai gratefully. She sipped it slowly and Kai made no attempt to talk. He let Marella have the silence she needed.

She had nearly finished her drink before she spoke, and even then it was quietly. "We are in the right place and the Portal should open tonight. As we go through the Portal, there will be three paths in front of us. Daren has to choose one and lead us forward. We are there to support him only, he must take the lead. This is his Element and he is the Chosen."

Marella took another small sip and then placed her drink on the ground next to where she sat. "Do you know anything about King Ghobe?" she asked Kai.

He shook his head. "No, nothing. To be fair, I didn't really know anything about any of the Elementals before starting this challenge. I've been reading one of the books I brought with me though, and it's starting to explain about different tribes within the Elements. Nothing so far about anyone specific though."

As Kai was speaking, Daren and Lani joined them. Kai looked up in surprise. "Is it time for you to get up already? That time passed quickly," he said.

Lani smiled at him, "It did indeed, although I feel like I could sleep for days, rather than hours. I still miss my bed."

The others chuckled at her words as it was indeed true. They had all the comforts they could have, but they were still sleeping on the ground.

"What were you saying about King Ghobe?" asked Lani.

"I was asking if Kai knew anything about him," replied Marella, filling Daren and Lani in with the small amount they had missed.

"So I'm to lead then," mused Daren. "Just what does that mean, I wonder?"

"It means we are there to advise only, but all talks with King Ghobe must be done with you as the mouthpiece," said Marella.

"So do any of us know anything about King Ghobe?" asked Lani. "I know I was only given sparse information about the portals, and almost nothing about the Elementals that reside there."

They all looked at Daren, but he shook his head. "The only thing I know is what Lady Daire told me when she gave me Her sword – greedy and narrow-minded."

Marella shrugged her shoulders. "I can only tell you what I've been shown, but they're not all like that, and not all the time either. They can be wise and reliable, persevering with something until they get a result. It appears though, that King Ghobe has been king for a long time, and now his mannerisms are more on the 'bad' side than good. He originally came from the Cartrefu tribe, which we might know as House or Home Gnomes. When he was chosen as King, he moved to the Goedwig tribe in the forest.

His 'house' is quite big as he feels he deserves as King. It is actually three trees, the house itself, with a hidden entrance from another tree, and then a third is the supply room, with grains, beans, potatoes and everything else the Gnomes may need during the winter," explained Marella.

"So he does at least care about the other Gnomes and makes sure they have enough to eat," said Lani, feeling hopeful.

"Sorry Lani, but no, not really. You see, the other Gnomes may fill the supply room but King Ghobe makes sure he has first pick during the cold season, warm season, any season," answered Marella.

"Well, he just sounds delightful," muttered Lani, "I can't wait for this."

"There is one way to make our reception easier," said Marella. "Do any of you have any stones with you, in particular green ones like malachite, jade, or peridot?"

Lani looked downhearted as she shook her head. "I didn't think to bring anything like that with me," she said.

"I brought some stones, but not green ones," said Kai, looking despondent.

"It's all right," chirped Daren, looking very happy with himself. "I've got some. I put some in my bag, although I had no idea why. I guess this is the reason."

He went over to his truck and pulled out a rucksack. From out of that, he pulled out a small drawstring bag made of leather. He opened the neck of the bag and tipped the contents into his hand. There were six or seven stones, of various shapes and sizes, but they were all three of the stones Marella had just named.

"That's excellent, Daren," said Marella with a smile. "We may make it through this first test yet. That's all I have though. I'm hoping to get more from my Weaves as we get closer." She paused as a though occurred to her, "I hope I *can* Weave, I hadn't thought of that. What if I can't Weave when I'm through a Portal?" Marella's breath started to come faster at the thought.

Lani reached over and put her arm around Marella. "Don't panic or stress just yet," she said. "Wait until we get there."

The others laughed at the look of shock on Marella's face, following Lani's words.

Lani looked around at them calmly. "I don't suppose any of you have thought about this, but Marella has a point. She may not be able to Weave in the Earth portal. Kai, you and I may not be able to use our gifts either. It may only be Daren who can. It's something we will have to check when we get there."

The look of shock on Marella's face was soon mirrored on Kai and Daren. Lani was right, none of them had thought about that. They were going to the very heart of the Earth Elemental, so it stood to reason the gifts of Water, Air, and Fire wouldn't work there.

Daren put the stones away, now knowing why he had brought them. As he turned away from his truck and moved back towards the fire, he said, "Marella, Kai, it's time you went for your rest. We will wake you in a couple of hours."

Marella turned to him abruptly, "How can you just send me off to bed after what Lani has just said?" she questioned. "This is a big thing, Daren. It's with the help of my Weaves we've been able to get this far. What if I can't Weave? How will we know what to do? By the Waters, Daren, don't you get it? We'll be blind once we're through there if I can't."

The fire made a sudden popping noise which drew everybody's attention to it. A spark flew out of the fire and hovered above it. As they watched, the spark enlarged and became flames, forming into the shape of Ena, the phoenix. She floated down towards the ground and rested on one of the stone seats around the fire.

"Now what's with all the tension?" she asked. "You haven't even made it through the Portal and you're all stressed out."

Marella waved her hands around ineffectively, "Ena, Lani has just said I might not be able to Weave whilst in the Earth Portal. Is this true?"

Ena bowed her head in affirmation. "Yes, it is. Daren is the only one who will be able to use his gifts – Earth to Earth. The rest of you will still be needed though, and you won't be blind, Marella. You have each other, and you have your Partners. Don't make the mistake of thinking it's all about you," she finished sternly.

Marella crossed her arms across her stomach in a protective motion. Lani once again proved herself to be the comforter, as she spoke to Ena whilst simultaneously reassuring Marella.

"We all know we are in this together, Ena, but Marella's Weaves have proven to be indispensable to us, in our search for the Earth Portal. How are we supposed to go forward without them?"

Ena raised her wings and straightened them out before folding them closed again. "So young, so full of knowledge... so stupid most of the time," Ena said sarcastically as she sighed.

"Now hold on, Ena, there's no need for that," exclaimed Daren in protest. "Yes, we're young, but we're the ones who have been Chosen by our Lords and Ladies. We have a job to do and we will do it. Forgive us some nerves as we prepare for our first task, but we have no experience with which to equate this. We feel like we are on our own, and we don't know what we're supposed to do."

To everyone's surprise, Ena raised her head back, and laughed. Daren looked around at the others in surprise at her reaction.

"Excellent, Daren," said Ena, "You are stepping up nicely as the leader of the Earth quarter. You are protective of each other, but you still aren't relying on your Partners as you should. None of them were upset, but you didn't take any cues from them."

They all looked a bit shamefaced at Ena's reminder. It was true that they had been the ones making the decisions first and only really asking their Partners if there was something they wanted them to do, like scouting for the Portal.

Nixie nudged Marella's hand with his nose. *"It's okay,"* he reassured her. *"Ena is just reminding you we are all in this together. Think though, how hard would this journey have been so far without our help?"*

Marella looked at Nixie and poured all the love and respect she had for him through their connection. He sent the same back and Marella knew they were okay. However, she was going to pass on his words to the others as he was correct.

"Nixie has just asked me a question, which I think we all need to hear," she said to the others. Ena turned her head to look at Marella, but didn't say a word. She nodded her head to Nixie, in what Marella thought was an approving manner.

"Go ahead Marella," urged Daren.

"Nixie asked if I realised how hard this journey would have been so far without the help of our Partners." She looked around at them all. "He has a point – think about it. With Nixie's help, we have found fresh water every time we have made camp. Ula, Kenna, and Shaw have all helped bring fresh meat to our 'table' every night. They went out looking for the Portal, and found it quicker than we could have done. They will be the ones that are aware of any time differences once we go through the Portal..." she stopped to breathe.

"There is something else you will need to know too, about your Partner's abilities," said Ena. "Once you are through the Portal, any of the Portals, your Partners will always see true, and may also be able to share their vision with you. You need to start paying attention to them and trusting them more."

They all stood there, looking from one to another. One by one, they all looked back at Ena. She nodded her head, satisfied she had made them understand. She couldn't say any more but she wanted them to be prepared. There was, however, one more thing she could prompt them to do.

"One last question before I go," she said to them. "Have any of you practiced yet with the gifts given to you by your Lords and Ladies?"

Lani was the first one that answered. "No, I haven't," she admitted, biting her lip.

"Nor I," said Marella, who then looked at Daren and Kai. They in turn looked at each other and shook their heads. "We haven't either."

"You were given these gifts for a reason, not just to look pretty," Ena scolded them. "Don't you think it's about time you started to take this seriously? You need to know how to use them – swords, staff and bow. Whether you like it or not, your lives may depend on them. This is the calm before the storm, so use this time to prepare yourselves. I don't know when I will be able to return, but I'm sincerely hoping to see a better bonded group when I do." With those words, Ena flew up towards the sky, disappearing in the afternoon sunlight.

Silence remained behind her until Marella broke it by saying to no one in particular "I'm going to get some rest, I'll see you later." With that, she walked off to her tent and went inside. Nixie followed her, but stayed outside the tent flaps, where he curled up into a ball and was asleep within seconds.

Kai looked at Lani and Daren, "I'm going too. See you in a bit." He went over to his tent and disappeared inside. Kenna was right beside him but, just like Nixie, opted to stay outside the tent.

Daren and Lani dropped down onto a couple of the stones and Daren started to poke the fire with a stick. He ran a hand through his hair in frustration, making Lani smile as the ends stuck up in every direction.

He glanced over to her and stopped when he saw her smiling. "What?" he asked.

"Nothing, it's just your hair," she said with a smile in her voice.

"Oh," he said, before smoothing it down.

Laughing at him, Lani stood up and moved over to her truck. She searched in there for a couple of minutes before lifting out a package and bringing it back to the fire. Daren watched her as Lani unwrapped her crossbow from its protective leather cloth. Once it was unwrapped, she placed it on her knees and looked at it. She ran her fingers gently over the embossed sigil of Air on the handle. She picked it up so she could look at the different parts more closely, before placing it back on her knee. She reached down and pulled up the small quiver which was full of small, silvery bolts. She took one out of the quiver and held it in the palm of her hand. It felt so fragile and lightweight; she couldn't imagine it causing any damage, although Lord Adaryn had said otherwise.

She gave a sigh before putting the bolt back in the quiver, and looked at Daren, who sat there watching her. "We're going to have to practice, you know. Ena wouldn't have told us to unless she's worried about what's coming."

Daren gave a quiet snort, "Yes," he said "because this isn't challenging enough now, is it? Of course, we're going to have to practice, with weapons none of us have used before. I don't know why I thought this was easy," he finished sarcastically.

Daren watched as a flush bloomed in Lani's cheeks. "I was only saying," she said defensively.

Daren ran his hand through his hair again. "I know, I know, I'm just so frustrated with all of this. I feel like we're getting warnings about this and that, but nothing is happening. It's like we're stuck in limbo."

"Be thankful for the quiet," said Lani. "I get the feeling that things are going to start happening soon."

Daren nodded at her words. He settled back down and just stared at the small flames that were flickering gently.

* * *

The hours passed as Daren and Lani kept themselves busy. Lani now seemed to be fascinated with her bow, and kept looking at it and her bolts. Daren, however, seemed to be avoiding his sword and looked anywhere but where it was kept. He did spend some time reading through one of his books, although Lani couldn't see the title of it so wasn't sure if it was actually research or just reading.

Marella and Kai woke up at different times and came out of their tents to join the others. Marella sat with Lani and looked at her crossbow with interest. "It's beautiful," she said to Lani, who nodded in agreement.

"I know. I keep looking at it, thinking how deadly it must be, but all I can see is the beauty of the wood, the workmanship, the sigil," replied Lani.

"So when are you going to practice? *How* are you going to practice?" asked Marella.

"I don't know for sure, I'm going to ask Shaw because I don't want to hurt anyone or anything before I have to," answered Lani.

Marella nodded her head, "That's sounds like a plan," she said. "I'm going to have to find a practice partner though. There's not much I can do by myself."

Lani laughed at her. "Good luck with that," she said, "I don't know if the boys will want to play with you". Lani gave a wink and another laugh as she finished speaking, which made Marella laugh too.

It was at that moment Daren walked over with a cup of peppermint tea for them both. "What's tickled you two?" he asked, handing them their cups.

"Nothing much," giggled Marella, "We were just talking about practicing, and I said that I would need someone to practice with."

"And I said I didn't think you or Kai would volunteer," finished Lani innocently, which set Marella off giggling again.

"Hmmm," said Daren, looking from one to the other, "I think there's more to it than that, but I'll leave you be," he said, before going back to the fire and talking with Kai, who looked over his shoulder at the girls.

This set them off into fits of laughter again as they watched Daren and Kai try to figure out just what was so funny.

"Come on," said Marella, pulling Lani to her feet, "let's go get something to eat whilst we still can. It won't be long before it starts getting dark, then we'll be through the Portal... hopefully."

They all sat together around the fire, enjoying their meal, washing it down with some chamomile tea. Their Partners had eaten by themselves, but now rejoined the group.

"Daren, have you any sort of plan for once we're through the Portal?" asked Kai.

Daren gave a small cough, and put his plate down on the ground in front of him before answering. "Not really," he admitted. "My plan mainly consists of getting through the Portal, finding King Ghobe, doing what I need to get the Shield, and trying to leave as swiftly as possible."

Ula raised her head and looked at him before dropping her head back onto her paws again.

Daren scratched his head as he looked from Ula to the others. "Yeah, that's as good as it gets."

"Well, it's a plan of sorts," said Marella encouragingly.

Daren sent her a quick smile before looking over her shoulder. "Well," he said, "I guess the best plans are those made on the hop." He got to his feet and brushed his trousers down. The others watched him before Marella felt a brush of *something* across her back. She turned slowly to see the Portal appear behind her.

Marella, Kai, and Lani all stood and moved next to Daren so that they were looking towards the Portal. The Partners all stood close by. Night had descended by then and everywhere was dark. The insects and animals that only come out at night were starting to make their presence known.

Daren squared his shoulders and took a deep breath. He looked at Ula, who had placed herself on his right hand side. She gave his hand a lick before moving her head underneath his hand. He gave a quick fondle of her ears as he asked, "*Are you ready, my love?*"

"*We're all with you all the way. We can do this,*" she replied and he felt her love coming through loud and clear.

~ 16 ~

Daren paused before moving at a steady pace towards the Portal. A couple of steps in front of it, he stopped and looked behind him. The others had moved with their trundle trucks and were right behind him, Partners by their sides. Kai nodded his head in encouragement, Lani smiled at him, and Marella gave him a wink, followed by a blown kiss. Daren felt a sense of peace infuse him as he looked towards the Portal. They were all here together, the time for waiting was over, the time of the Earth Portal was *now*. With these thoughts, and the rest of the group right behind them, Daren and Ula took their first steps through the Portal.

As they crossed through, Daren felt a faint tingling on his skin, but that was it. *"I was expecting something a bit more exciting than a tingle,"* he said to Ula. She just laughed in his mind and said, *"I'm sure we'll have all the excitement we can cope with soon enough."*

He looked over his shoulder ensuring that the others had safely made it through. They stood behind him, looking around, before returning their attention to Daren. It was daylight here, which made it easier to see their surroundings, but it took a moment for them to readjust their thoughts. After all, they had left in the pitch-dark, and now it appeared to be around midday.

As per Marella's Weave, there were three paths in front of them. One went off to either side, whilst the third twisted in front of them.

"So, now what?" asked Marella.

"Now we walk… again," smiled Daren.

"Do you know where we are going?" asked Lani, shifting her grip upon the handles of her truck.

"I'm thinking… that way," pointed Daren. The others looked over and saw what Daren had already seen – the right hand path was bordered by the biggest Fly Agaric mushrooms any of them had seen.

"I'd say that's a pretty safe bet," muttered Kai as Daren laughed.

So they set off in the direction Daren had pointed out, looking around them as they walked, both because of the sheer size and variety of plants, trees, and fungi they were surrounded by, but also because they didn't want to get any surprises from the Gnomes they knew would be around.

They had walked for just over an hour when Ula said to Daren, *"The sun is rising in the grove we have just left. It is a new day."*

Daren stopped and looked at her. *"I knew the time ran differently, but I never thought it would be that quick. We've only been here an hour."*

Ula nodded her head. *"Don't forget though, time is not a straight line. It doesn't flow smoothly. It make take an hour here now to see a new day there, but then it might take a day here for an hour there. It isn't consistent over here either. There's no way that you can make a comparison between how much times passes here for there. Do you understand?"*

Daren scrubbed his hand over his face. *"Yes, I understand. How are we supposed to keep track of the time…"* He stopped and dropped his hand back down before turning to face Ula fully. *"We're not supposed to, are we?"* he questioned.

"No, you're not," answered Ula. *"Your job here is to undertake the task King Ghobe will give you and succeed. You cannot afford to become distracted from that by the passing of time. We will tell you if the time issue becomes urgent."*

Daren looked at the others who also appeared to be in deep discussions with their Partners. *"Is everyone having the same conversation?"* he asked Ula.

"Yes, we thought it was the right time to let you all know how it would work," replied Ula. *"This is your time, but you will need the help and support of the others. This isn't going to be easy you know."*

Daren gave a quiet laugh, *"I'm not expecting it to be. We've had it simple enough so far. I'm just waiting to see what happens before I start worrying about things I can't control."*

"You are not alone, just remember that," reminded Ula.

"I haven't been alone since the day we met," replied Daren. *"You are my everything."*

Ula responded by sending a wave of love through their bond, which immediately made Daren feel better; it always did.

Daren looked around to see if the others had finished and saw they were looking at him too. "Have you all finished?" he asked them with a smile.

"Yes, we've had our orders," replied Kai, smiling with the others. "We now know we are to ignore time, unless our Partners say otherwise. We are to back you and support you in every way possible, and get out of here as soon as we can," he finished with a laugh.

"It's not just about backing and supporting me though," said Daren seriously, "we are in this together and none of us know what is going to happen. We are without Marella's visions now, and none of your gifts will work here either. We need to help each other. Only by doing so is there a chance we will come out of this unscathed."

"Gifts?" scoffed Lani and the others looked at her in surprise. They had never heard that tone in her voice before. "I don't have any gifts. I have Shaw and my crossbow from Lord Adaryn, that's all I have."

"Lani, you are gifted," said Marella, as her time to reassure Lani came. "Shaw and the crossbow are amazing; however, you are also gifted in Air. You wouldn't be here otherwise. Just be patient and trust in yourself."

Lani gave a small huff and didn't acknowledge Marella's words. Marella looked at the others, but they just looked back at her. Although

Lani was the quiet one, she had always been there, and had seemed quite confident in herself even if she was the youngest. The fact she thought she didn't have any gifts was something for them to think about and help her with. Everyone had a gift, they were connected to the Elements, and they could all do something. Perhaps Lani just needed to find out what it was.

"Come on," said Daren, picking up the handles of his truck again. "We need to keep moving."

They others grabbed their trucks and continued walking along the pathway. They were quiet as they walked, lost in their thoughts.

"Ula, is that true? What Lani thinks? Does she not have a gift?" asked Daren.

"She is right, Daren. Lani doesn't have a gift yet and it is something she will need to work through on her own. Lani is not weak and is here because she is Lord Adaryn's Chosen one, but as of yet, she can't manipulate Air."

Daren was silent as he pondered Ula's words. He knew he could make plants grow quickly. After all, it's what he had been doing when Lady Daire had brought him to her. He wasn't sure what Marella and Kai could do. Were Marella's Weavings classed as a gift? It wasn't anything they had really spoken about.

Just then, Kenna gave a small yip, and Kai's head turned left and right as he looked around. "We've got company," he said.

They continued walking forwards, but slowed their pace and became more watchful of their surroundings.

Shaw gave a screech from overhead and Lani said, "There is a clearing up ahead, and a force gathered there. Whether it's to welcome or warn, Shaw can't be sure."

Daren nodded at Lani and Shaw's words. He turned his head slightly so his words would flow behind, rather than in front of them. "Let's take this as a welcome. We'll go in politely, but keep your guards up. We don't know yet what we're dealing with and I don't want us to be taken unaware."

The others nodded and adjusted their clothing, generally making sure that they would be presentable. Kai was feeling a bit disgruntled with himself, because even after Ena's warning, he hadn't retrieved his sword out of the truck and it was now too late. He didn't want to make any sudden moves when he was sure that they were now being watched every step of the way.

He looked at Lani and she smiled, looking down towards her waist. He followed her eyes and saw she had the quiver set on her belt. He looked behind her and there, tucked away but still in plain sight, was her crossbow. Kai relaxed slightly, knowing one of them had at least prepared. He looked towards Marella and saw that her staff lay on top of the truck, also in plain sight. He chuckled to himself; the girls were prepared even if he wasn't. He made a mental note to ensure he was better equipped in the future.

They made it to the clearing before stopping. There, all around the edges in every direction were the Gnomes. Kai thought they looked like small children, apart from the beards that all the males seemed to have. They stood straight and each of them held a spear in their hand. None of them spoke, just stood there looking straight ahead.

A Gnome, standing directly ahead of Daren in the centre, took a step forward and in a voice deeper than they expected, greeted them.

"Welcome to Naear. King Ghobe extends his greetings to the Chosen of Daire, and his companions. He looks forward to meeting you and he offers you guest stay privileges." With those words, he took a step back and rejoined the wall of Gnomes.

They looked at each other before Daren took a step forward. "Thank you for your greeting on behalf of King Ghobe. We look forward to meeting with him." Daren gave a slight bow towards the Gnome who had spoken, then returned to his place in front of his truck.

"If you would please follow us, we will escort you to King Ghobe. He is expecting you." With those words, the Gnome turned on his heel and walked away, obviously expecting them to follow.

Daren looked around and saw the other Gnomes were watching them carefully, holding onto their spears in a way which told him they knew how to use them. He cocked his head towards the Gnome who was walking away, "Come on," he said, "we need to go."

He picked up his truck and moved forward with Marella on his heels. Lani followed right behind Marella, as Kai came in last, keeping his eyes on the Gnomes filing in behind him.

"This doesn't so much feel like an escort as a guard," he thought to Kenna.

"That's because it is a guard," replied Kenna. *"Just keep your calm and let Daren take the lead."*

They walked for about half an hour in the same direction. Marella could see every so often, Daren would try to engage the Gnome leading them in a further conversation, but to no avail. After a while, Daren stopped trying and just concentrated on walking.

Before long they had reached an area which looked the same as the rest of the forest upon first glance. As Marella looked more closely, she saw they were actually in the village and the trees were houses. As they stood in the centre of a clearing, more Gnomes came into view.

Marella noticed immediately they all wore similar clothing in shades of green and brown, perfect for blending into their surroundings. They were all the height of young children, but were obviously older. As she looked around, she couldn't see any that looked to be around her age. Apart from their height and clothing, there didn't seem to be any other connecting factor.

They stood in the centre of the clearing, not saying a word to each other, their senses on alert. The Gnomes were murmuring amongst themselves, but quieted down when movement appeared from the back of the gathered crowd.

A Gnome was pushing through, coming towards Daren and the others. He stopped when he reached Daren, before reaching up and grasping Daren's hand.

"Welcome, welcome, Chosen of Daire. We are honoured to have you here," he said.

"Thank you," replied Daren, wanting to look at the others, but not daring to take his eyes off the strange Gnome in front of him.

"My apologies," the Gnome cried, "I haven't introduced myself yet. Oh I am so forgetful at times. I am King Ghobe and I am so happy you are here. We have prepared a place for you to stay and we want you to be as comfortable as possible."

King Ghobe's voice was quite high-pitched and Daren couldn't help but compare it with the deep voice of the guard that had spoken to them originally.

"Thank you, King Ghobe," said Daren. "I look forward to seeing our accommodations. However, we are here on quite urgent business on behalf of Lady Daire. Is there somewhere that we could speak?"

"By the Earth, you're an impatient young man, aren't you?" squeaked King Ghobe. "There's plenty of time for that. You need to freshen up first. Alana will show you were to go."

"But…" Daren tried to continue but King Ghobe was already looking around the clearing, waving his arms in the air.

"Alana, Alana, where are you? Alana, I need you. Come here. Oh there you are," he said in relief. "Alana my dearest, please show the Chosen of Daire and his companions to their accommodations. They will need to freshen up and rest, then we can all sit down together and discuss what Lady Daire needs. You'll be there for that, won't you, Alana? You'll come and enjoy some food with me, won't you Alana?"

Marella resisted the urge to laugh, but with his high-pitched voice and the fact she didn't think he'd taken a breath since he'd started talking, it was quite hard. She didn't dare look sideways, because she knew Lani would also be finding this funny.

Marella looked in the opposite direction of where Lani stood, and saw who she presumed to be Alana, pushing her way through the crowd. Alana was a friendly looking Gnome, with long, chestnut brown hair in two plaits. She was wearing a long brown skirt with a green shirt. There was a gorgeous deep green leather belt around her waist, and what looked like wooden clogs on her feet.

"If you'd all please follow me," she said with dignity, before turning around and leading the way out of the clearing. Daren looked at the others before picking up his truck and pulling it after Alana. Ula followed behind

Daren and gave a small bark to the others. The Partners followed after Daren, walking closely by their companions. The rest of the crowd just stood there and watched them leave. Daren looked over his shoulder just before the clearing went out of sight and saw King Ghobe standing there, rubbing his hands together, looking completely different from the high-pitched, excitable Gnome they had just met.

~ 17 ~

They followed Alana to a set of three trees standing marginally off to one side. Alana showed them where to put their trucks, and then led them inside. Daren and Kai had to duck their heads slightly to get through the door, but Marella and Lani were okay.

When they entered, they saw they were inside the main room of the 'house'. It was small for them, seeing as it was the trunk of the tree, however it was tastefully furnished and the wood seemed to glow with warmth.

"The kitchen is through here and there is also a bathroom, but it is only very small, the bedrooms are up these stairs," she told them. "I'm afraid there are only two bedrooms so you will have to share." She looked at each of them in turn.

"Thank you, Alana," answered Daren. "What time should we be ready to meet King Ghobe?"

Alana gave him a steady look and thought for a while before answering. "King Ghobe will keep you waiting for a while," she finally replied. "He doesn't rush anything and with the reason you are here, he will take his time. Don't react to this, it is all done deliberately."

"Wait, you already know why we are here?" asked Daren in surprise.

"Yes, Chosen."

"My name is Daren," he said distractedly. "Was it Lady Daire who told you we were coming?"

"No, Chosen. The one who met with King Ghobe is not trying to help you, but to hinder. I don't know who it was, but King Ghobe knew the eight of you were coming, and that you need the Shield of Earth. He will not give it up easily. Do not trust him."

"Why are you telling us this?" queried Kai. "Surely your loyalty belongs to King Ghobe?"

"You would think so, wouldn't you, Chosen of Fire?" answered Alana. "King Ghobe never introduced me properly. I am Alana, Priestess of Daire. It is She that I serve, so I will help you as much as I am able." She gave a small bob of her head in Daren's direction.

"I am honoured to meet you, Alana, Priestess of Daire," replied Daren formally. She gave him a small smile in return.

"I will leave you now and let you get settled. I would expect you will be here for at least a fortnight, so expect a longer stay than you envisioned. I would not unpack everything though as you might need to leave suddenly," finished Alana.

Lani's head shot round at Alana's words. She had been busy looking at the pictures on the walls whilst Alana spoke to Daren. "What do you mean,

Alana?" asked Lani. "Are we safe here?"

Alana bobbed her head and gave Lani and reassuring smile. "Yes, Chosen of Air, you are safe here... for now. I am trying to give King Ghobe the prompts to help you, but I don't know who it was that spoke to him about your arrival. Whoever it is wants you to fail. You must be prepared for anything and everything. I will help you in every way I can."

With that, she turned on her heel and left, closing the door quietly behind her; leaving the companions and Partners in silence.

* * *

"She knew who we were," murmured Marella, wrapping her arms around her waist.

Daren looked at Marella and cocked his head. "Of course she did, she knew we were coming, Marella. She is a Priestess of Daire."

"No, I mean, she knew *who* we are," Marella said and tried to explain further. "Kai asked why she told us these things, and she called him Chosen of Fire. Lani asked if we were safe, and she was called Chosen of Air." Marella shrugged her shoulders as she looked at Daren. "She knew, but we didn't tell her."

"Perhaps Lady Daire told her," suggested Lani.

"She might just be guessing," said Kai dubiously. "We are sort of dressed for our Elements."

Marella thought of what they said. "Perhaps Lady Daire did tell her, and perhaps she did guess, but can we be sure we can trust her? There seems to be an extra player in this now. Who was it that met with King Ghobe, and why don't they want us to succeed? Don't they realise what is at stake if we fail?"

Ula gave a small bark that got their attention. She moved until she was in the middle of the room and made sure she had their attention before she did anything else.

"We are here for one reason and that is to get the Shield of Earth. It is here, I can feel it. That means it has become a little easier because we won't have to make it. Alana can be trusted. She is a Priestess of Daire; as such I can see her soul. She is pure and only wants to help. She knows who you are, because Lady Daire has spoken with her prior to our arrival. We are going to need her help if we wish to be successful. Keep your guards up but don't distrust everyone. For each one who wants us to fail, there are two more who want to help us succeed."

A loaded silence filled the air following Ula's words. Daren cleared his throat and said, "erm, Ula said that..." before being interrupted by Lani.

"Daren, we heard Ula. All of us," she looked at him with wonder in her eyes. "I've never heard anyone else's Partner before."

Ula gave a huff of laughter before moving over to Lani and licking her hand. *"It saves time and we are all in this together,"* she replied to Lani.

"It saves time?" laughed Daren. "Hold on a minute, Ula. What did you mean, you can see her soul?"

"You caught that then?" huffed Ula. *"You think you are the only Chosen of Daire? Think again my love. You were Chosen, but you keep on forgetting you are Partnered, you all do,"* she said looking around the room. *"You are one half of this Partnership and you have your gifts. I am the other half and I have my own. We have received the ability to see who is also a friend to our Lord and Lady, and what they really think."*

"So you mean once someone claims to be a friend or Priestess you will know if they are telling the truth?" questioned Lani.

"That is right, gentle one," replied Ula.

"Wow," said Kai on a drawn out breath. He looked at Kenna with wonder in his eyes. "What do you see? I mean, how do you know if someone is a friend?"

"Nothing yet, fy Cariad," answered Kenna, *"We haven't met anyone who is a friend to Lord Ethon yet."*

"Which I guess is understandable being as we're in the Earth quarter," said Kai, laughing at himself.

"So we have to wait until we go through our Portals to receive the gifts?" questioned Lani.

"Not necessarily," replied Shaw. *"The gifts will be given when circumstances require it. The Portal is the last time that you will get them."*

"So I have to wait then," said Lani in a frustrated tone.

"We all do, Lani," Marella tried to comfort her. "Look at it this way; if it goes the way of the Wheel, you're next in line. We'll be going to the Air Portal next."

Nixie jumped onto Ula's back and gave out a sharp yip to get everyone's attention. *"Lani, you need to stop worrying about the gifts. You were Chosen for what is in your heart and soul. We need to concentrate on what we need to do here, rather than what gift is given and when. Why do you think we haven't mentioned this before? You humans are too easily side-tracked."*

A shocked Lani looked at Nixie, then at Marella, before returning her gaze to Nixie.

"That was a bit harsh, Nixie," said Daren in Lani's defence but Ula turned her head to look at him and her golden eyes seemed to glow.

"That was not harsh, heart of mine. It is what needed to be said. We have been on this journey together for how many nights now? And every step of the way you forget we are all in this together. Eight are needed to bring balance back, not four. There is balance everywhere – even between humans and Partners. To send four humans by themselves would not bring back balance. You need us; you're just not accepting it yet.

We are here for the Shield. We have just found out someone is trying to work against us. We already know time runs in a different way here, and yet all you are bothered about right now is when you will receive your gifts, and what they are. This is a greedy and selfish attitude that I will be no part of.

We are going to go out for a while and leave you four alone. We want to look around and see where things are. I suggest you take Alana's advice and get settled. King Ghobe won't see you today."

With those words, Ula walked out of the room, Nixie jumping off her back as she did so. Kenna followed them and Shaw flew out the doorway.

"That told us," said Daren in the silence.

"They're right, you know," said Marella. "Since we started, we've been making the decisions by ourselves and not even bothering to ask them their opinions. We've basically given them the roles of providing fresh meat and water for us. Until the other night when we asked them to scout for us and weren't we so clever, coming up with that?" she continued scornfully. "I'm surprised they haven't said anything sooner. How could we treat them this way?"

Instead of answering her, Kai moved away towards his truck. "I'm going to sort a few things out upstairs," he said. He took a bag and a few loose items from his truck and went up the stairs. He got to the top, looked at the rooms on the left and right, before moving into the one on the right.

* * *

Daren, Lani, and Marella all drifted apart once Kai had gone to the room he would be sharing with Daren. They were all deep in their own thoughts, pondering what their Partners had said. Marella wandered into the kitchen area and started boiling some water to make a herbal tea to help clear her mind.

She made three more mugs before picking up hers and one other, leaving two on the table. "There's a cup of tea on the table for you," she muttered as she walked past Daren and Lani, carrying the mugs in her hand towards the stairs.

She quietly went upstairs and nudged the right door open with her foot, grateful Kai hadn't latched it shut. She entered the room and looked around for him, seeing him lying on the bed he had chosen, with his arms crossed behind his head and his legs crossed at the ankles.

He looked over at her as she entered. She raised both hands and said "I've made you a tea. It's lemon balm. I thought it might..." before trailing off and just looking at him.

Kai just lay there for a moment, looking at her. Of all the people he expected to walk through the door, he didn't think it would have been her.

Marella started to fidget uncomfortably as Kai said nothing. She looked around the room and saw that although it was sparse, it had all they needed. There were two single beds for Kai and Daren, a table and chair with a jug and washbasin on it, a blanket box at the bottom of both beds and a wardrobe tucked behind the door.

Finally, Kai lifted himself onto one elbow and said, "Thank you, you can put it down here please," indicating a small table set between the beds.

Marella walked over and carefully placed the mug on the table, being sure that she didn't spill any of it. "I thought it might help all of us," said Marella.

"Take a seat, if you want," Kai replied, nodding towards the other bed with his head.

"Thank you," said Marella before sinking onto it. The bed was soft, far softer than the ground they had been sleeping on. She sat there and looked at Kai, waiting patiently for him to speak.

After a moment's silence during which Kai continue to stare at her before he asked a question. "Why you?"

"Pardon me?" replied Marella, looking confused.

"Why did you come up here? Why not Daren or Lani?" he said.

Marella felt a spear of hurt run through her at his words, and it must have shown on her face, because Kai sat up and swung his legs over the side of the bed. He ran his hand through his hair as he sat forward, his knees almost touching hers.

"I don't mean it in a bad way," he tried to explain. "I am sharing this room with Daren, so it makes sense for him to come up. I am closer to Lani than I am to you, simply because of our Elements, so I would have expected that. But you? We irritate each other, sparks fly whenever we are together, so why would you come up here? Especially with a drink to try and help? I don't get it," he finished, looking up to meet her eyes.

"I don't know," replied Marella. "I was making a drink, thinking about what Nixie and the others had said. The next feeling I had is I needed to come up here, that you needed me." She spluttered to a stop, took a breath and then continued, speaking faster than before "I mean, not that you needed me, but that you needed someone. It's just that I was making a drink and the timing was right and I thought you'd like one."

Kai leaned forward and gently placed his hands around hers. "You were right though, I did need you. I need to talk to you and I know you will give me the truth, your honest opinion, not what you think I want to hear. You don't care if it's going to hurt or not, you'll just give it to me straight."

As Marella looked at him, she could see a twinkle of humour in his eyes and knew he was teasing her. "You're wrong, you know," she said, leaving her hands in his. "I do care if it hurts, but I'm also not afraid to say something if it needs saying. I would sooner take a painful truth over a soothing lie any day."

Kai gave her hands a squeeze before moving to get his mug. He took in a deep breath in as the aroma teased his nostrils. "I love lemon balm; it's one of my favourite teas."

"Stop trying to change the subject, Kai," said Marella. "Why did you need me? What truth are you looking for?"

Kai took a sip before putting it back on the table. He faced her fully before saying, "I want your intuition. I need to know your feelings on this."

Marella looked at him, studying his face. His dark brown eyes were serious and his auburn hair looked ruffled, as though he had shoved his hands through it more than once. His lips, usually pulled into a smirk, were in a straight line as he asked for her help.

"What do you mean by 'this'?" she asked, eventually breaking the silence.

"Being here in the Earth quarter. I feel… off. I can't describe it any better than that, but I just don't feel right. Like something is wrong. I don't like it," he said.

"You realise I'm not the best person to ask though, right?" questioned Marella. At his look, she tried to explain further.

"It's about the Elements and where we fit in," she said. "Daren is Chosen in the Earth Quarter, he is at his strongest. Lani is Air and Earth's natural opposite, so I'm guessing she is feeling very weak and insecure right now. She's probably wondering what she is doing here and how she can help. I think that's what Lani was saying downstairs, about the gifts. It's not that Lani is being greedy or anything like that, it's just that she feels helpless."

Kai nodded at her words and gestured for her to continue.

"You are more closely allied to Air than you are to Earth, so I think that's where your feelings come into it. If we were in 'our' world then I don't think you'd feel this way. But we're not, we're here and that means until we leave, you're going to feel this way."

"What about you?" asked Kai.

"I'm Earth's natural partner, we work well together. That means, although I feel slightly off balance, I still feel that everything is going the right way, how it's meant to be. Daren and I have worked and played together for years, I know his strengths and capabilities, the same as he knows mine. I have every confidence in him and know he will do the best he can in any given situation. Just remember, whilst you feel insecure, Daren is feeling the most confident he has ever been. He is strong here; he is the Leader of the Earth Quarter."

Kai looked at her as she finished and Marella rubbed at her nose, embarrassed.

"You've really thought about this," he said, approval in his voice.

"No she hasn't," said Daren's voice, startling them both. Marella turned her head and saw that Daren and Lani were stood in the doorway with their drinks in hand.

Marella gave them both a slight smile, wondering how much they had heard and if she had upset Lani. They both entered the room and sat down on the beds next to Marella and Kai, who gave Lani's shoulder a small bump as she sat next to him.

"What did you mean, Daren? Why hasn't Marella thought about this? It certainly sounded like she had to me," said Kai, looking over at Daren to see what emotion was written on his face. He was expecting to see a hint of jealousy or something similar to account for his words, but instead all he could see was love and approval shining from Daren's eyes as he looked towards Marella.

Daren slipped his arm around Marella's shoulders and pulled her into a one-armed hug. Marella dipped her head down and rested it upon Daren's shoulder. It surprised Kai as he realised he was the one feeling jealous of Daren.

"Marella hasn't thought about what she's just said to you, because that isn't what she does. She was thinking when she was downstairs, but it was about what Nixie and Ula had said," explained Daren as he looked at Kai.

"The best words, and usually the most truthful, are the ones she doesn't think about. These are the ones that come straight from her intuition, the ones that don't have thought behind them. Thoughts just confuse her," laughed Daren, shifting as Marella tried to elbow him in the ribs.

The others grinned at his words, whilst Marella tried to act as though she was offended. The effect was spoilt by the grin that broke through and lit up her whole face.

Kai's breath caught in his throat as he looked at her and he coughed, trying to turn his thoughts away from Marella and back to the problem at hand.

"Why did you say that you weren't the best person to ask? It sounds to me like I asked exactly the right person," said Kai to her.

"All I meant is that you are Fire and allied to Air. Air is about communication, so I simply thought you would have preferred to hear Lani's explanation about it, which would give you more information and facts, rather than from me, the Element you clash with most," said Marella, looking across at him.

"Marella, Marella, Marella," said Daren in a sing-song voice, sighing and shaking his head. "Sometimes, it's the ones we clash with most that we need."

At this, Marella did shove her elbow in his ribs, making sure she didn't miss.

"Ooph," spluttered Daren, clutching at his side.

"Sorry, my lovely," she said insincerely, "did I get you?" She gave him a big, false smile and turned away.

"That does it," shouted Daren, "you're going down".

To the amazement of Kai and Lani who were still wrapped up in a serious conversation, Daren suddenly threw Marella back on the bed and started to tickle her stomach and ribs. Marella squealed at him to let her go, whilst writhing about on the bed trying to escape.

Whilst Kai and Lani sat there, watching them with their mouths slightly open in shock, Daren and Marella continued to tickle and play fight with each other. After a short while, Marella's breaths were coming in wheezing gasps and Daren had stopped his taunts and teasing, mainly because he couldn't breathe, talk, and laugh, at the same time.

Finally, Daren let her go and they both sat on the bed, panting heavily and trying to stop laughing. Marella raised her hand to her hair which was now sticking out in all directions.

"You goof," she said to him, grinning. "What did you do that for?"

"You deserved it," said Daren. "You elbowed me."

"You deserved that," retorted Marella, her voice rising as she spoke.

"Whoa, whoa, whoa," cried out Lani, her hands raised up in front of her. "Don't start again, please!"

Daren and Marella looked over at the other bed, as if realising Kai and Lani were still there. They looked at the expressions on their faces and, just like the siblings they thought they were, burst into peals of laughter at the same time.

Both Kai and Lani tried to keep a serious face, but it was difficult with the contagious laughter filling the room. Before long, all four of them were laughing and clutching at their stomachs.

"Stop, stop," gasped Marella. "My stomach hurts, my cheeks hurt, I can't breathe."

This made them laugh even more, although they were slowly calming down.

"By the Flames, you two really are like little kids, aren't you," said Kai, shaking his head in amazement.

"How are we supposed to keep them in line?" asked Lani, trying desperately to keep a straight face.

"I'm not even going to try," said Kai, pretending to go all haughty on them.

This just made Daren and Marella laugh as they both sat on the bed.

"We've years on you two," said Marella, nodding her head towards Kai and Lani, "although I'm sure it won't take you long to catch up."

Daren grinned at her words before putting his arm in front of Marella and pushing it, and her, backwards on the bed.

Marella gave a yelp as she went back and heard the laughter from the others.

~ 18 ~

Once they had calmed down, Lani and Marella went to their own room to sort out their things. Lani heaved her backpack onto the bed closest to the door with a humph. Marella, turning around so that she could see, laughed at Lani's face.

"You look slightly red there, Lani. Do you need some help?" questioned Marella.

"No, I'm fine," replied Lani, a little breathlessly.

"What do you have in there?" asked Marella, looking at the backpack curiously.

"A little bit of everything, I think," said Lani grumpily. "I've left this in the truck since we started as everything I needed, I already had at hand. I think this is what my mother packed for me. I figured now was a good time to sort it out."

"Good idea," agreed Marella. "I'd repack it with the essentials and keep it hidden. Alana did say we might be leaving in a hurry, so make sure you have everything you need."

"Have you done yours yet?" asked Lani. "I don't know what to put in mine."

"I'm keeping it as light as possible," replied Marella. "My Weaving chalice, a change of clothes, my cloak, utensils, travel mug, and a book."

"A book?" laughed Lani. "That's not essential."

"It is," insisted Marella. "It's the one my father gave me and gives information about the quarters and who lives there."

"If you say so," grinned Lani and carried on with her own unpacking and sorting out.

Kai and Daren had stayed in their room after the girls left, but were doing the same thing.

"Come on Kai, you can help me sort out my truck. I need some help carrying this inside," said Daren.

"Oh come on," groaned Kai. "You're not doing it all right now, are you?"

"Yep, the sooner it's done, the sooner we can prepare, come on lazy," answered Daren. He held his hand out, and Kai grasped it before pulling himself up from the bed, where he had only just sat down.

They went downstairs and pulled Daren's truck near to the door before they started unloading it. As they carried armfuls of gear into the house, Kai asked, "Why are we doing this now, Daren? Is there something you're not saying?"

Daren gave a slight nod to his head and in a louder voice said "Stop grumbling Kai, I need to get this sorted before I can meet with King Ghobe, and you said you would help."

Kai raised his eyes to Daren's and saw him flick his glance over to the side where the trees and bushes started to encircle them. Suddenly understanding what Daren might be saying, Kai grumbled loudly back at him.

"Okay, okay, I'm coming. I said I would help but honestly, you've more junk in here than the girls. Yeesh!"

"We heard that," came a shout from inside and Kai grinned widely. Daren looked at him and they both started laughing as they continued backwards and forwards from the truck to the house.

After ten minutes or so, they had cleared Daren's truck. He pushed it into one of the three tree trunks they had been allocated and said "Come on Kai, we're on a roll. Let's sort the others out, then it's all done."

Kai grumbled and groaned but helped Daren with the other three trucks. As he walked past him with his arms laden with items, he muttered, "You are going to explain this to us when we're done, you know."

Daren just smiled and nodded his head before moving off to get some more.

The girls were surprised to see what Kai and Daren were doing but joined in with the spirit of it by sorting their things into different piles.

By the time Daren and Kai had finished the other three trucks, there were a number of piles on the floor in the living room.

Marella stood in the middle with her hands on her hips, surveying the piles around her. "That's all the camping equipment," she said, pointing to each in turn. "That's all related to food and drink. This is all our personal bits."

"Thanks love," said Daren. "We'll need to sort this out amongst ourselves, so we repack the trucks with what we need and in the order we think we'll need it. Keep anything personal you don't want to lose in your backpacks."

"We've already done ours," said Lani to him. "We've stashed them under our beds."

"Excellent," nodded Daren. "I don't want anything left in these trucks we will need or are personal to us."

"You think they're going to be searched, don't you?" questioned Kai. "That's why we've done all this."

"Yes, I do. It's not just what Alana said, but a feeling I've been getting over the past few days. It was urgent we arrived here when we did, and we've done so, but the fun isn't over yet." He smirked at them all. "We've arrived in the middle of a hornet's nest, and the only one we can trust so far is Alana."

"But they know now we've brought everything inside. Won't they think we've sorted it out and taken out anything personal?" asked Kai.

"They might guess, but I think not. Everyone, so far, seems quite honest, everyone that is apart from Ghobe. He definitely has a hidden side and I don't know yet who else can see it. We're being watched, so I need all of you to be careful at all times. You need to keep your guard up and watch what you say." Daren looked around at the others with a very serious look on his face.

"Alana has already said King Ghobe will keep us waiting and I'm sure he will. I think he's playing power games and will do everything he can to make us feel insignificant. Whatever you do, do *not* react. You can't let him see it is working, even if it is."

He paused and considered his next words. "Marella, you need to watch your emotions. Keep them under control. I don't want anyone complaining you've upset them, or rocked the boat." He looked at Marella's face as he spoke. He could see thunderclouds gathering as she heard his words, but then her face cleared, and she nodded acknowledgment to him.

"Lani, I know you feel unsure, Marella's already explained why, but you need to control yourself. Draw strength from us or Shaw if you need to, but you cannot appear weak. Ghobe is looking for the weak link, and whilst we're here, you're it. He won't hesitate to try and use you."

Lani looked like she was going to cry, but shook herself, and nodded emphatically at Daren.

Finally, he turned to Kai. "You are also off-balance, I know; but I need you to be here, to be committed to this one hundred percent. I might need your sword-arm, I have no idea what Ghobe is going to throw our way, but it won't be easy."

Kai stood up and extended his arm to Daren, who grasped it in a warrior's friendship hold. "My sword is yours and I am with you all the way. I have less strength here than you, but what I have is yours whenever you need it."

Marella and Lani both stood up at the same time and went over to Daren and Kai, and placed their arms around their waists. They stood there, in a group hug, for a few moments. No one said anything, they just rested on each other and let silence rule.

Silently, their Partners entered the room. They had kept out of the way, not because they needed the space from their humans, but because they knew the humans needed to work things out. This quest, whilst not physically hard at the moment, was taking a toll in other ways and it needed sorting before they could move on.

Nixie made the first move and joined the group hug by weaving himself through Marella's legs. Shaw flew and landed on Lani's shoulder before spreading his wings so he touched the back of Lani's head with one and Daren with the other. Ula came up and pushed her way in between

Daren and Marella, whilst on Marella's other side, Kenna stood on her hind legs, resting her front paws on Kai's thigh.

A sense of completeness filled the group. They all felt like everything, or every one, had slotted into place and they knew, in that secret place in their hearts, they were stronger together.

* * *

The moment was disrupted by a knock to the front door. Everyone pulled back and Marella and Lani hastily gathered items from one of the piles and ran upstairs with them. Daren straightened his clothing, just trying to give them a few extra moments. Kai took some more items and moved them into the kitchen area.

Daren slowly walked to the door before opening it. There, on the doorstep with a big smile on her face, stood Alana. She was carrying a big jug with tea towel placed over the top. Daren gestured for her to enter and she made her way past him into the living area.

"It's okay, Marella… Lani," she called. "It's just me. I've brought you over some lemonade."

Kai came out of the kitchen and Marella and Lani made their way back down the stairs.

"Well done, all of you," said Alana proudly.

"Huh?" grunted Daren, eloquently.

"You have worked out, and overcome, the first obstacle," answered Alana.

She looked at them all before gesturing for them to sit down. Alana sat in one of the straight-back, single chairs by the fireplace, whilst Daren and Lani sat on the plump sofa. Marella took the other chair, and Kai perched on one of the arms with his arm resting along the back.

"The one thing no one could warn you about was how each of you would react to being in a Quarter. This is something so incredibly personal and related to you. More insecurity would have been caused, if this had been mentioned to you before, so we needed to see how you would react before we could say anything," she said.

Everyone just looked at her, so she took a deep breath and tried to explain further.

"Lani, you have been insecure since you came through the Portal. It steadily got worse, and culminated in your outburst about the gifts. Am I right?"

Lani chewed on her lip and nodded shamefacedly. Daren put his arm around her shoulders and gave her a quick squeeze.

"There is nothing to be ashamed of, Lani. It is because of who you are. Air is the natural opposite of Earth and you are part Air and part Fire, there is nothing of Earth in you, in a proactive manner. If you were Air and Earth, you wouldn't have been so affected. Like young Kai here, he is part Fire, part Earth. He feels the same as you, but in much smaller quantities. Marella feels only slightly different because she is Water. She doesn't have a secondary Element, but Water is Earth's ally so there isn't that much resistance for her."

Lani nodded her head as she understood Alana's words. "Thank you, Alana," she said. "I didn't like feeling like that. I felt out of control. I feel a bit better now, but still not like myself."

"The original wave of the Element is calming down; you just need time to adjust. You will be okay, but you won't feel yourself until you are back in your own world. None of you are meant to be surrounded by just one Element, even you, Marella," said Alana.

"What does this mean for Marella then?" asked Kai, looking down at Marella's head with a worried look on his face.

Daren and Lani both looked up at Marella who sat there, not acknowledging his words, but instead concentrating on her folded hands.

Alana looked at Kai and Marella and gave a reassuring smile. "It means, Chosen of Fire, that when you cross the Fire Portal, Marella will be of no use to anyone until the first wave has passed. You will all need to care for her and take heed of anything she might say or do. Although she might just be mumbling nonsense, Marella might also feel something relevant to your quest on an instinctive level."

"So I'm just going to be bumbling wreck then?" questioned Marella, with a slightly bitter tone to her voice. "Great, something else to add to the list."

"List?" questioned Lani.

"Marella made a list when she was younger," explained Daren to the others, "on the list was everything that set her apart by only having one Element. Mostly it was things her mother would say to her."

"Marella, you are doing something that only these other three will ever understand. Even your Partner cannot fully comprehend, because the Elemental Wave affects the Partners differently. No one else has travelled from your world to the Quarters before. Just remember who you are, what your gifts are, and you will be fine. The others will protect and care for you; just the same as you all do now, on a daily basis.

You have all figured out you are strongest together. When all eight of you are linked, you will be nigh on impossible to defeat. Imagine the link you have with your own Partner. Now imagine that with the other six in your group. You've already been doing this, although I don't believe any of you have realised."

Alana stopped to let her words sink in. The others sat there in a stunned silence.

"Alana, none of us have even thought about linking. I don't know about them, but I didn't even know it was possible," said Daren to her.

"Pish, Daren," scoffed Alana. "Use your head. You are leader in this Quarter."

Daren went red, as the others gaped at Alana.

"Come on," said Alana to him, "tell me why I've told you to use your head. Think about linking. Think it through."

The others were silent whilst Daren thought about Alana. He heard a faint whisper in his head but didn't think it was Ula talking to him. He looked at Alana. "Marella," was all he said.

Alana nodded and sat back in the chair, a pleased look upon her face.

Marella was looking between Daren and Alana, waiting for an explanation.

"Of course," cried Kai, snapping his fingers.

Marella and Lani both looked at him, Lani patiently, Marella not so much.

"Would one of you please mind explaining," she said a bit harshly. "You may get it, but Lani and I still don't understand."

"Marella, speak to me," said Shaw.

"What is it, Shaw? What have I done wrong now?" asked Marella, feeling overwhelmed by her emotions. *"I am so fed up right now. Just when I think I have my balance back, I get hit with something else. I feel so in the dark."*

Shaw sympathised with Marella, as she had indeed been hardest hit with this quest so far. However, he wasn't her Partner, so he could also see that she would wallow in her self-pity if left alone.

"Enough with the theatrics, Marella. Stop feeling sorry for yourself and think!" said Shaw with a bite to his 'voice'.

Marella felt hurt by his words, and turned to Lani to complain about him. When she saw Lani's face, however, she stopped. Lani was almost convulsing with laughter and was struggling to catch her breath.

When she saw Marella looking, she struggled to gain control. Daren and Kai still said nothing but, just like Alana, sat with smiles on their faces.

"So you think it's funny too, do you?" asked Marella, fed up with the whole scene.

"No, Marella, I don't but you don't have to be upset. There is too much stimuli for you to see clearly. Listen to Shaw. Calm your emotions and think. Use your head, not your heart, and you will see the answer for yourself," said Lani in her quiet voice.

"Great, now you're saying I feel sorry for myself," snapped Marella.

"What do you mean?" asked Daren, trying hard to control his laughter.

"Shaw just said I needed to stop feeling sorry for myself and…" she paused and thought about what she had just said, "… think."

She looked around at the others. Alana still hadn't said anything, but hadn't stopped smiling either. Daren and Lani were still trying to control their laughter, whilst Kai looked like he wanted to laugh, but was making a serious attempt at not upsetting her further.

"Shaw said," said Marella. "That's it, isn't it? The linking, I mean. I link with the other Partners when we speak."

"Yes, Marella, that's it exactly. Shaw is the one who spoke to you, because Lani was the only one who didn't understand. Through speaking with you, Shaw left his link with Lani open so she could hear him too. Because you were speaking on an 'open path', Lani could also hear your response which is what helped her to see the answer. Ula has already spoken to Lani using an open path, but she didn't realise what was happening, and so accepted it without question."

"Open paths, linking," muttered Kai. "It's a whole new language."

"Not a whole new language, Kai, but something you never would have learned if the necessity hadn't been there. For years, the only link required was between one Partner and one Human, but times are changing and with the artefacts stolen and the eight of you together, you must learn to speak with each other if possible."

"So did you know twenty odd years ago this was going to happen?" questioned Lani, looking over at Marella.

Alana understood where Lani was leading with her question. "No, Lani. Marella came as a shock to most of us. I think Erwyna was the only one not surprised. However, the birth of Marella gave the rest of us a 'heads up' if you like. We knew for a person to have been born with only one Element and the ability to link to various Partners, times were changing and we needed to be on our guards."

"That didn't work though, did it?" asked Daren.

"No it didn't, Daren, you're quite right. We became complacent the older Marella became. With no danger to be seen, we became lax, and that is when the thief took advantage of us and stole the artefacts," said Alana.

Everyone sat in silence for a moment before Daren slapped his hands down onto his knees, making Lani jump.

"So," he said abruptly, "what do we do now? I presume Ghobe won't be seeing us today. We need to get the Shield back. Is there anything we can do to hurry Ghobe up?"

"You can start by calling him King Ghobe" said Alana, displeasure on her face. "He may not be a very good King, but he is still King of the Gnomes, and you should show your respect."

"Okay, King Ghobe," said Daren. "But we still need to find the Shield."

"You do and you will, but you must remember King Ghobe is having you watched at all times. I would imagine he will choose soldiers that he knows are loyal to him. You were right in thinking your trucks would be searched, and have done well in emptying them. You won't know when though, so don't put anything back in there you don't want discovered."

Alana continued "I think it will be five days before King Ghobe will see you, so use the time wisely and practice with your weapons. You must become proficient with them, if you aren't already."

"Sorry for interrupting you, Alana," said Kai, "but why five days?"

"Five is a number associated with the Earth Element; it is one of our sacred numbers. King Ghobe might not be too happy you are here, but he does know you are here at the bequest of Lady Daire, so he won't be too obvious in the things he does," replied Alana.

Alana finished her lemonade before standing up. "I need to leave you now, but remember what I said. Do not react to anything and don't let your guards down. This won't be an easy stay, however it is necessary. Look after each other and use each other's strengths. I will come and see you again when I can."

The others rose as she said goodbye. They stood and looked at each other before Daren said, "Okay, then. So we have a rough idea of what's happening. Time to play the game."

With those words, he set about sorting out his things, so that they were in some semblance of order for the oncoming days.

~ 19 ~

The days that followed quickly fell into a routine. There was nothing they could do apart from practice with their weapons. Daren overcame his reluctance to practice with his sword, as Marella tried Weaving to no avail. Lani took to taking walks with Shaw, whilst Daren and Kai started to practice daily, and could be seen, and heard, sword-fighting in front of the house.

It was the third day, and Marella was sat at the front of the house, resting her back against the wall as she watched Daren and Kai who were taunting each other.

"Come on, Kai, show me what you've got," said Daren, standing there holding his sword out in Kai's direction.

"More than you," replied Kai with a smile as he walked towards Daren.

"We'll see about that, shall we?" grinned Daren before moving into his first position.

Kai matched him and then, to some unseen signal, they moved forward and their swords clashed, the noise ringing around the clearing.

When they had first started practicing, Marella had been afraid for them as they were using 'real' swords, not wooden practice ones. She soon realised they knew exactly what they were doing and her fears had subsided. Now, after three days, she sat there reading her book at the same time. She was still trying to find out more about the Elementals and what might help them in their quest.

Marella raised her head when she heard the taunts and teasing between the two of them peter off. Looking up, she saw Daren and Kai had stopped practicing and were facing her direction. Standing just to one side and watching her, was the guard that had greeted them when they arrived through the Portal.

"Why aren't you practicing?" the guard asked her without preamble.

"No one will practice with me," answered Marella, cocking her head to one side as she looked at him.

"You should still be practicing," he said, "even if no one will do it with you. You should get used to moving with your staff so it becomes part of you. Every moment you are separate, you are at a disadvantage."

Marella stared at him for a moment with her mouth slightly open. She saw a sparkle enter his deep brown eyes and then a smile crossed his craggy face.

"Go and fetch your staff, I'll practice with you,"

Before he could change his mind, Marella jumped up and ran inside the house to retrieve her staff. Within seconds, she was back and standing in front of him.

Kai and Daren both came over to her. "Are you sure you're okay with this?" questioned Daren.

"I'm sure," said Marella, her face lit up with anticipation.

"Okay then," said Daren. He sat down where Marella had been and Kai dropped next to him.

"She's going to get hurt," worried Kai.

"No she won't," replied Daren. "This is what she needs. We should have practiced with her."

"I'm going to call Lani back," said Kai. "Marella might need her afterwards."

Kai gave a mental call to Kenna and told her what was happening. *"You really should have more faith,"* replied Kenna, laughing. *"But don't worry, I'll get Lani."*

Kai looked over to where Marella and the guard were standing. He was giving her some basic instructions on how to hold her staff before they started. Kai saw her adjust her hands and nod her head. She stepped back into a large circle that had been drawn in the dirt.

"Before you start," called Kai, "do you think we could know your name?"

The guard turned to him and with a short huff of laughter said, "Of course, Chosen. My name is Carrick, and I am a friend of Alana's."

Kai nodded his head towards him. "Thank you Carrick. I am usually known as Kai, not Chosen," he said with a grin on his face.

"Pleasure to meet you, Kai, but for now, I have an engagement with this young woman here," said Carrick.

Daren and Kai watched as Carrick and Marella made themselves ready. Marella had taken off her jacket, so was just in her navy blue trousers and a loose white shirt. Carrick was dressed in brown trousers with a lighter brown shirt over the top and cinched in with a brown leather belt.

"Are you ready, Marella?" Carrick asked her.

"I am," she replied.

"We will start by just touching staffs – no fighting yet," he told her.

"Okay."

"Just follow my lead," said Carrick as he moved towards the centre of the circle.

Marella did just that and moved with him, almost like his shadow. Carrick started by moving his staff into different positions, with Marella copying him. They did this for a few minutes before Marella asked Carrick when they were going to start.

Carrick grinned at her and said, "We have started, little one. You need to be able to move your staff without hesitation, for it to become part of you and for the strength to grow in your arms and legs, so they don't tremble at a most inopportune time. This will help to warm up your muscles, so that when we start fighting, you don't hurt yourself."

"But I won't have time to warm up if we are fighting for real," protested Marella.

"No you won't," agreed Carrick, "but hopefully, you will have enough muscle tone and memory, it won't hurt so much afterwards for you. Now quiet and concentrate. I'm going to get faster, try to keep up."

With those words, Carrick started moving his staff into different positions, faster and faster until his body and staff flowed as one and it was impossible to tell where one move finished and the next one began.

Daren and Kai watched in amazement as Carrick moved and Marella followed. Although she was slightly behind him in speed, she matched him perfectly for the moves.

"Has she ever fought with a staff before?" Kai asked Daren in a hushed voice.

"Never, that I know of," confirmed Daren, also speaking quietly. "I've never seen her move like this before."

"It is part of the blessing of being Erwyna's Initiate," said Nixie.

Both Daren and Kai started with surprise as they realised the Partners were with them, and also watching Marella.

"What do you mean, Nixie?" asked Kai. *"Marella can do this with no training because of Lady Erwyna?"*

"Not all of it," replied Nixie. *"Most of it is Marella's innate ability to move and use the staff, but she has had a helping hand by Erwyna, yes."*

"You and Daren are both able to fight with your swords because you've played with them from the time you were little boys," said Ula. *"But when you were given your swords by Daire and Ethon, you too were blessed with a little more skill, a little more speed. You just haven't noticed it because it's something you've done for a while."*

"So Lani was also blessed by Lord Adaryn?" questioned Daren.

"She was indeed," replied Shaw proudly, entering the conversation for the first time. *"She has been blessed with farsight and accuracy. You should see her aim now, it's fantastic. Of course, she doesn't realise it's anything out of the ordinary because she's never shot a crossbow before or been with anyone who has."*

Daren and Kai looked at Shaw and then over towards Lani who was carefully making her way over to them, trying not to disturb Marella's concentration.

"I think we should tell her," said Daren.

"Go on then," said Kai with a smile.

Lani dropped to the ground next to Daren and handed them both a mug of water she had brought with her.

"She's amazing," said Lani, with wonder in her voice. "Look at her move!"

"We've just been discussing this," said Daren, gesturing towards the

Partners and Kai.

Lani looked at him with interest. "So you've linked AND used an open path? Alana will be impressed;" she smiled, "so what was said?"

"Apparently we were all blessed by the Lords and Ladies of our Element when we became Chosen," said Daren. "Kai and I have been blessed with a little bit more skill and speed, Marella has been blessed with grace and ability, and you, Lani-sweeting, have been blessed with farsight and accuracy, according to Shaw. He's very proud of you," finished Daren.

Lani's mouth dropped open in surprise. "I never knew… I never realised," she stuttered.

"I don't think any of us would have realised if it hadn't been for us seeing Marella move like this and knowing none of us have practiced with her," said Kai, smiling.

He leaned back against the wall and continued to watch Marella flow as one with her staff.

After a few more moments, Carrick began to slow down. As they both became easier to see, the others could see Carrick's face was red, his breaths coming rapidly. Marella was glowing; her face alight.

"That was amazing!" she exclaimed, once they had stopped. "I've never felt like that before. Thank you Carrick!" She bounded over to his side of the circle and gave him a kiss on the cheek which managed to make him go even redder.

"Now, yes, well then," he mumbled "You did very well for your first time, Marella, but I don't want you getting over-confident. You will need to practice this every day. I'll know if you don't," he warned.

"No, yes, I know, I will," said Marella happily, her words all jumbling together.

She looked over towards Daren and bounced on her toes. "Did you see?" she asked excitedly, "Did you see me move?"

Daren laughed at her and reassured her he had seen. "By the Earth, Marella, you're reacting like you're a child again," he laughed.

Marella reacted by sticking her tongue out at him, her laughter filled the clearing. "I don't care," she said. "That was just… I don't have words. Carrick, can we try fighting with them now, just for a short while?" she begged.

Carrick looked over at her and couldn't help but smile at her enthusiasm. "You're going to regret this later," he warned her. "Your muscles will go stiff and you'll be in pain. Are you sure you want to continue?"

"YES!" exclaimed Marella. "I don't know why, but I need to do this. Please, Carrick, just for a few minutes."

"Okay then," sighed Carrick. "Follow me again and we'll see what you've got."

The others laughed at Marella's enthusiasm and Carrick's resignation, before settling back down to enjoy the show.

They started slowly, with Carrick explaining as they went along, but before long he stopped speaking and concentrated on trying to get his hits in against Marella.

Marella moved around the circle, defending every hit from Carrick, a look of concentration on her face. The hits and whacks of their staffs grew louder as they both put more effort into it. The hits were coming thick and fast now, echoing around the clearing as both Marella and Carrick fought each other.

"Someone's going to get hurt," cried Lani. "We need to stop this."

Shaw flew over to her and landed on her shoulder, placing his wing around the back of her head. Ula moved over to her right side and sat down on her haunches, making sure her body touched Lani. Kenna moved to the left and copied Ula whilst Nixie curled up in front of Lani. Lani was now surrounded by the Partners and she looked at them in amazement.

"I should stop worrying then, I take it," she laughed.

The Partners shifted slightly, but kept their focus on Marella.

"This is unbelievable," whispered Daren.

"I know," agreed Kai, also whispering.

Suddenly, there was a loud thwack and Carrick's staff went flying out of the circle. Everyone jumped and watched as Carrick and Marella abruptly stopped, Marella's staff laying across Carrick's shoulder, into the groove where his neck and shoulder met.

Both Marella and Carrick were breathing heavily. Marella slowly moved her staff from Carrick and placed the tip on the ground, leaning onto it with her two hands at the top, her head resting on them.

Carrick raised his head to look at her whilst the others held their breaths. "You disarmed me," he said to her, in wonder. "No one has ever done that and you say you've never practiced before today. If you hadn't controlled that last hit, you would have broken my neck."

Lani gasped in shock at Carrick's words before looking at Marella.

A look of shame crossed Marella's face. "I'm so sorry, Carrick. I didn't mean to get carried away. I was just enjoying myself… I guess too much. I didn't mean to hurt you. Please forgive me."

Carrick crossed the circle before Marella could utter another word. His head only came up to her stomach but he put his arms around her legs and hugged her tightly. She let go of her staff, reached down and clasped him just as firmly, before letting go as he stepped back.

"Do not ever apologise for being good with the staff, Marella," he said. "It was a pleasure to fight with you and trust me, I wasn't holding back towards the end. I have every confidence you will be more than capable of protecting yourself with your staff, no matter who or what you are up

against. You are Goddess-Blessed to fight like that and it was an honour…
my honour."

Carrick bent over and placed his hands on his knees, laughing slightly
as he caught his breath. "I am the best with the staff," he said "which is
why Alana chose me to help you. No one has ever beaten me the way you
did and in such a short amount of time. I think it will be me asking for your
help with the staff in the future, not me helping you."

Carrick stood up and pulled at his shirt which had stuck to his back. "I
need to go now and freshen up before I go on duty. Thank you Marella,
and I look forward to practicing with you again," he said, before walking
away from them, giving a friendly wave to them all as he went.

Daren came up to Marella, lifting her in the air and swinging her
around.

"By all the Elements, Marella, you were magnificent," he laughed.

Marella threw her head back and laughed with joy. "It did feel good,"
she admitted.

"Well done, Marella," exclaimed Lani. "That was wonderful to watch,
although remind me not to offer to go against you" she chuckled, wryly.

"I'll do it," offered Kai to Marella. She looked at him whilst Daren and
Lani spoke excitedly to each other. She cocked her head as she considered
his words.

"I'll help you practice," he explained. "If you want to, that is. If you
need me, I'll help you."

Marella grabbed Kai and gave him a squeeze, enjoying the feel of him.
"Thank you, Kai," she smiled. "You know, I might just take you up on that.
I hope you don't regret saying this."

Kai's arms came around Marella and he returned the hug. "I won't
regret it," he promised, looking down into her blue eyes.

Marella's breath caught in her throat, and she coughed before moving
out of his arms. Her face was flushed and she was breathing faster than
when she had been fighting with Carrick. She raised her hand to her hair
and brushed wisps of it back off her face with a hand that trembled. "I
must look a mess," she said, a hint of nervousness in her voice, "I think I'll
go and take a bath."

She stepped away from him, still looking at him, before turning around
abruptly and heading toward the house.

Kai watched her go, before being jolted out of his reverie by a clap to
his shoulder. "Put your tongue away or we might have issues," joked Daren.

Kai gave Daren a sideways glance, before watching Marella as she
retreated to the house, casting one look over her shoulder before
disappearing through the doorway.

Once she was out of sight, Kai turned and faced Daren. Daren was
stood with his arms folded across his chest, a serious look upon his face.

Kai shrugged his shoulders and lifted his hands in the air before him. "What?" he asked.

"I was joking until I saw the look on your face," replied Daren. "What is going on with you and Marella? You go from not wanting anything to do with her, 'too high maintenance' or something like that to now you're watching her like you're dying of thirst, and she's a tall, cool glass of water." Daren stopped and took a breath, giving Kai time to answer.

"I don't really know," admitted Kai. "She intrigues me, I can't figure her out."

"There is no one else like Marella," said Daren. "She is one of a kind. If you hurt her, Kai…" Daren trailed off. He liked Kai and now considered him a friend. He didn't want to threaten him, but he also knew that he couldn't bear it if Marella was hurt.

Kai slapped his arm around Daren's shoulders and together they walked away from the house. "I don't want to hurt her, Daren. I understand what you're saying and what you're not saying. Watch over us, see for yourself. I just want to get to know her. I almost feel protective of her, and yet I've no idea why, really," finished Kai, feeling puzzled about his feelings.

Daren grinned at him as they continued walking into the woods surrounding their house. "I understand - that's how I've felt about Marella all my life."

Kai looked at him sharply and Daren gave out a bark of laughter, sounding for a moment like his Partner.

"Protective," clarified Daren, still laughing. "How many times do I have to tell you, I love her as a brother, nothing else. Look, I don't want to stand in your way, but have you thought this through? We're at the start of a quest, we still have no idea what's going to happen, and we still have a year to be together. If things don't work out with you and Marella, will you be able to carry on as normal?"

"I know, I know," said Kai, "I don't want to do anything that might jeopardise us all, but I also don't want to ignore what I'm feeling either. I guess what I'm saying is, I just want to get to know her; be her friend. If something comes from that, so be it. If not, then we are friends and nothing more."

"I think that's the best idea," said Daren in agreement. "That must be why you're the eldest," he joked.

Kai laughed at Daren, "hmm, so what's the reason you're the joker of the pack then?" he asked.

Daren just grinned and spread his hands in front of him.

Camaraderie restored and intentions understood, they both turned around and went back to the house for a drink.

~ 20 ~

The next day passed without event. Marella had some aches and pains, but had soaked in a bath the previous evening and rubbed down her body with a lotion packed with herbs, so wasn't as sore as she had expected to be.

Kai and Daren spent time sparring with each other again, whilst Lani went into the woods to her practice area and shot at her targets. Marella loosened herself up by practicing again with her staff.

They stopped for lunch and all met up in the kitchen where the smells of roasting meat filled the air.

"Mmmm," sniffed Lani. "That smells delicious."

"Roast pork for our evening meal," said Daren, smiling. "I'm looking forward to this already."

"So what's for lunch then?" questioned Kai.

"Salad, cold meat, bread - make your own," said Marella.

They all bustled around the kitchen, getting their food and drinks ready. Just as they were about to sit down and eat, there was a knock on the door.

"I'll go," said Daren as he made his way to the front door.

The others craned their heads to see and hear who it was. Standing at the door was an unfamiliar looking official, if the gold chain around his neck was anything to go by.

"I am here by order of King Ghobe. He requests your presence tomorrow to speak with you about the Shield of Daire." His words sounded haughty and he somehow managed to give the appearance of looking down his nose at Daren, even though Daren was twice the height of him.

Daren gave a small bow, "Thank you for the information, we will all be there."

"I was told to only request your presence," said the official, looking uncertain.

"That may be so," replied Daren, "but the eight of us were sent on this together, so we will all be there."

"Hmm, yes, well, I will inform his majesty and see what he has to say," humphed the little man before turning away and making his way across the clearing.

Daren watched him leave before turning around and closing the door. The others waited until he had retaken his seat before speaking.

"Do you think that was wise?" asked Marella, with a look of concern on her face.

"Until I know anything further from Alana, or Lady Daire herself, then yes, I think it was the right thing to do," came Daren's reply. He chewed on his sandwich before placing it on his plate and looking at the others.

"Listen to me; we know Ghobe is greedy and narrow-minded. Lady Daire has told us that already. We can now add power-plays to the list. That's what this has all been about and to be honest, we can't be completely sure of his loyalty to Lady Daire either. If he's met with someone prior to our arrival, like Alana said, then we have to tread carefully." Daren took a sip of his drink to moisten his throat and continued.

"This is another game of his – to separate us, so I see him on his terms. We already know we are stronger together; we've figured that out. We were Chosen by the Lords and Ladies to do this together, we have come this far together. I am not going to leave you behind for a meeting that is the only reason we came here.

Tomorrow morning I want us all there, properly dressed, and carrying the gifts given to us. Ghobe won't like it, but this is official business and we need to be prepared. I don't know what he's going to do; however, I do know it won't be good. He's kept us here cooling our heels until it suits him.

I suggest we rest for today, do whatever you want, but stay close. We have no idea what tomorrow will bring, or even if we'll be sleeping here tomorrow night. I'm feeling on edge and I don't think it's all my own emotion."

Daren stopped and looked at the others who had sat there in silence whilst he was talking. They had carried on eating and Marella swallowed her mouthful before answering him.

"Okay, so I get why we all need to be there. Why don't you think your feelings are all your own?" she asked him.

"Marella, you've known me long enough, you know I've done things that I've been incredibly nervous about."

Marella nodded her head in agreement and gestured for him to continue.

"The thing is, I know what I feel like when I'm nervous, and this is not it."

Lani looked at him with a question in her eyes. Daren smiled at her, so she took a breath and said to the group "Do you think it might be Lady Daire sending you a message?" Once she had asked her question, she looked down at the table and muttered "stupid question" to herself.

"Lani, stop it," said Kai. "It's not a stupid question and you have every right to ask it. No one here is going to laugh at you."

Lani looked at Kai gratefully, and then looked at Marella and Daren, who were both looking at her with smiles.

"Actually, Lani, I think you might be right," said Daren. "Or maybe it's Ula's feelings as well, but they don't feel like hers either. All I know is they're not all my own, and the feelings are getting stronger the longer we're here."

Silence reigned at the table for a few moments as they finished off their meals. Kai finished his drink before banging his mug on the table as he set it down, making Lani jump.

He grinned at her, "Sorry, Lani," he said.

She gave a soft laugh in response before finishing off her drink as well.

"I think it's my turn to clear up so off you pop, everyone. Do what you want to," said Marella to the others before standing up and taking her plate and mug to the kitchen sink to start washing up.

Lani placed her plate and mug on the counter next to Marella before saying a quick, "See you later," to everyone, and getting ready to go out. Once she was out the door, Marella watched her walk towards the woods with Shaw circling overhead.

Daren also came and placed his dirty pots on the counter. "Thanks love," he said, giving her a quick peck on the cheek, "I'm going for a walk with Ula." He walked off and before he had gone more than a few steps outside, Ula came bounding up to him, jumping up at him like she was a cub once more. Marella heard his laughter and Ula's yips and barks before they too headed off into the woods, albeit in a different direction from Lani.

Marella jumped again as Kai came up behind her and placed his plate and cup down. "Relax, Marella. It's only me," he said, laughing.

"Yes, right, I know," said Marella, feeling flustered.

"Do you want me to help?" asked Kai, enjoying the sight of her being slightly ruffled.

"No, it's fine," replied Marella. "You go and spend some time with Kenna. I'm going to Nixie as soon as I'm done, just for a while."

"If you're sure," said Kai, before edging towards the door.

"I'm sure," said Marella, with a smile. "Off you go, see you later."

Kai turned around and left the house and, just as with Daren, before he had gone far, Kenna was there wrapping herself around his legs, more like a cat than a fox.

Before he disappeared from sight though, Kai turned around and waved at Marella. She lifted a sudsy hand and waved back. She watched him enter the woods and gave a sigh.

"*What's the sigh for, little one?*" asked Nixie.

"*I don't really know,*" said Marella, giving a little laugh at herself.

"*Well come on then, finish up. I can hear the water calling us. We've time for a quick swim.*" Marella saw Nixie scamper outside, and watched as he stood on his back legs, watching her.

When he saw she was watching him, rather than finishing the dirty pots, he gave a bark. Marella jumped again, and quickly finished clearing up, before running upstairs and changing into her swimsuit. She threw her trousers and a loose shirt back on, grabbed her boots and a towel, before running downstairs.

She stopped only long enough to latch the door before taking off after Nixie, laughing as she went, the sound echoing through the trees.

~ 21 ~

The following morning, everyone was up with the sun. They stood together outside, watching the sun rise over the trees. It cast a soft, golden glow on the woods, bathing everything with light. The air was fresh and crisp, caressing their skin.

Lani gave a sigh of satisfaction before turning away from it. "Right then, I dibs the bathroom first!" With a laugh, she raced back inside and towards the stairs before anyone else could comment.

"Sneaky woman," laughed Daren. "She's quiet, but you have to keep your eyes on her."

"Hmm, I know another one like," agreed Kai, looking at Marella.

Marella looked at them, a look of innocence upon her face. "I have no idea what either of you mean." Then she laughed, gave them both a quick hug. "If Lani's in the bathroom, I'm going to the lake. I'll bathe there and be back in plenty of time."

"Make sure that you are," said Daren, seriously. "I want us to be together when we see Ghobe."

"King Ghobe," chided Marella, "Don't worry, Nixie will be with me. I just need to swim before this meeting. Who knows when I'll have chance again?"

"Let her go," said Kai. "The longer you keep her here, the more chance of her being late. She needs this."

Marella gave Kai a grateful look, thankful he understood that she needed to be immersed within her Element one more time.

"Okay, okay, off you go," said Daren, laughing. "Nixie, please don't let her get lost in the water," he said out loud.

"The cheek of you, talking to my Partner like that," said Marella, grabbing a towel and heading towards the door.

"Don't worry Daren, I'll have her back in time," said Nixie. *"Kai is right though, she needs the water right now."*

With a jaunty wave and a spring in her step, Marella soon disappeared into the woods.

"Do you think she'll be alright there by herself?" worried Daren.

"She's been alright up to now. Marella can take care of herself," reassured Kai. "Come on, we still need to get ready. I'm sure King Ghobe will keep us on our toes today."

Before long, Kai and Daren were dressed and ready to go. They were both in black trousers and white shirts, with a surcoat that emphasised who they were. They were knee-length, but Daren's was green velvet, with the Earth symbol embroidered with golden thread. Kai's was a red-orange velvet with his Fire icon embroidered in gold thread. They both had their scabbards buckled around their waists in preparation, although neither of them had the swords inside.

They stood in the kitchen, leaning against the counters as they sipped a hot tea, the aroma of peppermint permeating the house.

As Kai looked through the kitchen window, he saw Marella returning. "Here's Marella," he said, whilst blowing the steam from his hot drink and taking a careful sip.

Marella skipped through the doorway, with wet tendrils of her hair caressing her shoulders. "I feel better," she said. "Is one of those for me?"

She took Daren's drink out of his hands and took a swallow, gasping as the heat hit her tongue.

"Ouch, that's hot," she exclaimed.

"Serves you right for stealing mine," laughed Daren before grunting, as she poked him in the ribs.

"Go and get dressed, I'll make you one and shout when it's ready," said Kai.

"Thank you, Kai," she said, smiling at him. "I won't be long," before running up the stairs.

"You know, you're supposed to be on my side with her," chuckled Daren.

"There are no sides, but you're the one who wanted everyone ready," smirked Kai. "There's no time for your usual shenanigans!"

Daren spluttered at Kai's choice of words. "Shenanigans?" he laughed. "I didn't know anyone used that." Still laughing at Kai, he took his drink into the living room and made himself comfortable on one of the couches.

* * *

Marella tapped on the door before opening it and slipping inside. Nixie was curled up in the middle of her bed. Her gaze went from him to where Lani was just finishing getting ready.

"Lani, you look beautiful," breathed Marella.

Lani was stunning in a long, silvery-grey dress that shimmered as she moved. It was square cut across the neckline, and the sleeves tapered down to points, which were held in place by small, silver rings on Lani's middle fingers. It was fitted at the top but flared out softly from her hips. Around her waist was a deep golden girdle to which she had attached her quiver of bolts. The bow itself was slung over her back, using the silver strap that came with it. Completing her outfit was a simple pair of grey, leather moccasins.

Her long, golden hair was left loose and it floated around her head as though in its own private breeze. The sides were joined together in a plait, which flowed down the middle of her back.

Lani blushed prettily at Marella's words. "Thank you Marella," she said. "Daren said we needed to dress properly and this is my ceremonial dress. I figured this was the most proper thing I have and also shows I am Air.

"It's perfect," agreed Marella. She laughed with Lani whilst getting her own dress out of the wardrobe. "I have complained to Nixie ever since we left about bringing a dress with me, but now it appears I need it."

"You'll listen to me at some point, I have every confidence in you," smart-mouthed Nixie.

Lani just laughed and then shrugged her shoulders at Marella's glance. "I heard," she said. "It was on an open path."

Marella smiled, "You know, this is so nice. I always felt like a freak, being able to hear the other Partners when no one else could."

"You're not alone now, you have all of us," said Lani before apologising to Nixie, following his snort. "I'm sorry, Nixie, I know she has always had you."

"Don't you worry about him," laughed Marella, "he's just laying it on thick to get your attention." She went over to him and ran her hand from his head to his tail. He preened from her attention and then butted her hand.

"Come on you, it's time to get ready. Why am I always the one telling you to hurry up?" grumbled Nixie, good-naturedly.

"Because you only have to stand up and you're ready," teased Marella. "Hush now, and let me start."

Marella pulled her blue dress out of the wardrobe and put it on the bed. She grabbed her shoes and girdle, and placed them ready. She changed out of her trousers and shirt, shivering slightly as a morning breeze came through the open window. She quickly picked up her dress and threw it over her head, wriggling her body until it fell down in soft folds around her ankles.

Marella straightened her shoulders and ran her hands down the bodice, smoothing out a couple of wrinkles. She placed her girdle around her waist, making sure the silver links weren't twisted and it fell down the middle of her dress. She bent down and slipped her feet into black leather pumps.

"There, what do you think?" she asked Lani.

Lani grinned at her, "I love your hair," she said with a wink.

Marella gasped, "By the Waters, I'd forgotten about that."

Lani laughed at her. "Come and sit down, I'll do it for you."

Marella pulled the chair from the small table that was on one side of the room, and placed it in the centre, where she sat down carefully, not wanting to crease her dress.

Lani used a wide-toothed comb and gently started combing through Marella's wet hair.

"What do you think will happen today?" asked Lani, concentrating on combing.

"I honestly don't know, Lani," said Marella. "Daren told me King Ghobe was putting on a show when we first met him. It will be interesting to see if he does the same today. I think we all need to be vigilant; keep our eyes and ears open."

There was a fluttering of wings and Marella saw Shaw land on the windowsill before hopping through the opening.

"There is a large force of armed guards gathering near King Ghobe's residence this morning," he told them both.

"Yep, we definitely need to be careful," stated Marella.

Lani finished combing through the wet hair before styling it for Marella, leaving the rest to dry naturally. She pulled a section back from each side of Marella's forehead before twisting it round and round until it formed a rope-like strand. She pulled both sides together at the back of Marella's head, and secured them with a small piece of blue ribbon. Lani did the same again but this time pulled the sections from lower down on the side of Marella's head, just near the top of her ears. She twisted and then pulled them together at the back. Grabbing the loose bit of the first section, she secured both strands from the sides to it with a silver ribbon, leaving the ends to sit loosely amidst the rest of Marella's hair.

Lani passed Marella a hand mirror, which was on the table. Marella looked at her reflection and saw her hair looked very stylish but simple. With the twists Lani had done, Marella was hopeful her hair wouldn't stand out on end like it usually did.

"Thank you, Lani, it looks wonderful," she said, running her hand down the back.

"Come on, let's go downstairs. I'm guessing we'll be called for soon if there is a force gathering," said Lani.

* * *

Together they walked down the stairs, being careful not to trip over the hems of their dresses. As they walked towards the kitchen, Kai turned around with a cup of peppermint tea in his hand.

"Here you go, Marella, as promised," he said.

She took the cup out of his hand and placed it on the table. She spread her hands and did a twirl.

"What do you think?" she asked, "Will this do?"

"Works for me," replied Kai with a twinkle in his eyes as he looked at her. "You look gorgeous."

Marella gave a small grunt at his words, although she was pleased with what he had said. "I'm not trying to look gorgeous, Kai, as you know. Do you think I will look presentable for King Ghobe? Daren? What do you think?"

Kai laughed at Marella, pleased he had gotten a rise out of her again. He looked over at Daren who hadn't answered Marella.

Daren was holding a cup of peppermint out towards Lani, but he hadn't said anything. He was staring at her, mouth agape. Lani was blushing under his scrutiny, but also didn't speak.

"Daren," said Marella, sharply.

He jumped and spilt the drink, breaking the spell between him and Lani.

"Ouch!" he exclaimed. "Marella, what did you do that for? This drink is hot."

Marella laughed at him. "Do you want to give Lani her drink before it gets cold?" she questioned.

Daren looked down and realised he was still holding Lani's drink. "I'm sorry, Lani, here's a tea for you."

Lani took the cup from him and wrapped both hands around it as though she was cold.

Marella went to Daren and mock-whispered to him, "You might want to wipe your mouth, love. You have a bit of drool in the corner." She grinned at him wickedly before moving back towards the table.

Daren moved his hand to his mouth before realising Marella was teasing him. A faint flush of colour appeared on his cheeks. He gave Lani one more look before looking at Marella.

"You know I don't like you very much, don't you?" he asked Marella, the words completely at odds with the loving tone in his voice.

"Yep, I know," replied Marella, grinning at him. "Anyway, as much as I am loving this, we need to get back to business. I asked Kai his opinion and just got rubbish so I'm asking you, as our esteemed Leader of the Earth Quarter, will we pass for the meeting with King Ghobe?"

Kai laughed and Daren grinned at Marella. Daren made a point of looking Marella up and down and even twirled his finger around, in a gesture to make Marella turn, which she did.

"Hmmm, I guess you'll do. Your hair looks great though," he said.

Marella curtsied in reply, laughing as she did. "Why thank you, kind sir," she said. She stood back up and picked up her drink, leaning against the table as she drank. "Have you got the stones for King Ghobe?" she asked him as she drank.

Daren patted his trouser pocket. "I've got them in here, although part of me is loathed to give them to him."

"*It won't make any difference,*" said Ula, "*but at least you are showing him courtesy. Who knows? He may act the same way.*"

"Shaw said a large force is near King Ghobe," said Lani to no one in particular.

This short statement had a sobering effect in the warm kitchen. Smiles slowly disappeared as they each considered what the next few hours might bring.

~ 22 ~

There was a knock on the door; a sharp rapping noise. Everyone looked at each other before Daren went to open it. Stood outside was the same little man from the day before and he still looked as grumpy as ever.

"I am here to escort you to King Ghobe," he said in his nasally voice. "Please follow me."

"Certainly," replied Daren, respectfully. "Come on everyone," he said to the others, watching the official as he realised they were coming with them.

Kai picked up both swords, passing Daren his as he walked past him. Daren gave him a nod of thanks and put his sword carefully within the scabbard. Lani followed Kai, looking regal and graceful as she glided forward. Marella was the last one out, closing the front door behind her. She stood tall and unafraid as she looked at the group of guards who were there as 'escorts'. She carried her staff with her, and looked every inch the Chosen of Water.

They followed the official as he walked away from their house. The Chosen were able to walk at a statelier pace, considering their legs were longer than his, whilst still remaining close to him. The four Partners all walked next their Chosen, with the exception of Shaw who was flying near Lani.

"May I ask your name, sir?" Lani asked the official.

He looked at her in surprise. "My name? Why would you want to know my name?" he asked.

"In Awel Ysgafyn, where I come from, it is only considered polite to know the name of someone who is doing you a service," Lani replied. "I would just like to know your name, so I am able to thank you for escorting us to see King Ghobe."

There was nothing the official could do with Lani's statement, apart from give her his name. It was phrased in such a way as to be the most inoffensive it could be.

He gave her a sideways look before stopping in front of her and giving a small bow. "My name is Logan, Chosen of Air, and it is a pleasure to meet you officially."

Lani gave him a smile which lit up her whole face and made her light blue eyes sparkle. "It is a pleasure to meet you too, Logan, and thank you for your company. My name is Lani, if you would prefer to use that instead of Chosen."

Logan gave a small nod before scurrying ahead of them, but they could all see that he was happy with their exchange.

"*Lani has made herself a friend,*" said Ula to Daren as they continued to walk along.

"Why do you say that?" queried Daren. He had been pleased to see Lani interact with him, but didn't think it was anything out of the ordinary. Logan would have had to have a heart of stone not to respond to her.

"King Ghobe is very officious, but he doesn't treat the members of his court with much respect. Logan never offered his name simply because he didn't think we would be interested. Now that Lani has asked him, it has made him feel appreciated. This is something worth remembering. A little respect can go a long way when none is expected." Ula gave a slight wag of her tail and Daren stroked her head as they walked along.

"You see straight to the heart again, my love," whispered Daren inside his mind. Ula didn't reply but gave his hand a small lick.

They were nearing the centre of Naear where King Ghobe had his residence. The eight of them were surrounded by guards with Logan leading the procession. They could see faces looking out of windows as they passed by, but no one seemed to be outside.

"Where is everyone?" whispered Marella to no one in particular.

"I don't know, but I don't like this," replied Kai in a soft voice. "Be prepared for anything."

Marella gave her shoulders a roll and held onto her staff more securely. Lani brushed her hand over the quiver of bolts at her waist and looked at Shaw as he flew overhead.

They reached the clearing at the heart of Naear and saw King Ghobe sat on a big wooden chair. It was engraved with ivy, trees, and leaves. King Ghobe watched them approach.

Logan gave a bow towards King Ghobe. "My Lord, may I present the eight Chosen?"

Daren and Ula took a step forward. Daren bowed at the waist towards King Ghobe, whilst Ula bent forward so one of her front legs was stretched out and the other was bent.

"My Lord," said Daren in greeting and waited for King Ghobe's response.

He sat on his chair, looking at the eight of them, not speaking. The guards started to fidget, but a look from Logan stopped them moving. Marella, Kai and Lani, remembering Daren's words about King Ghobe liking power plays, didn't speak or move, but just kept looking at him.

Before long, King Ghobe gave a smile to Daren that was anything but pleasant. "What can I do for you, Chosen of Earth?" he said, with a snide tone to his voice.

"We are here at the bequest of Lady Daire, Lady of Earth. She has asked us to retrieve the *Tarian y Ddaear* and said you may be able to help us. I have also brought you a gift from Bridd," Daren spoke calmly and concisely as he handed over a small green pouch to one of King Ghobe's guards.

King Ghobe took the bag from the guard and emptied it into his hand. He stroked the stones as he spoke. "Hmm, yes, the *Tarian y Ddaear*. This seems to be very popular at the moment." He looked at Daren with a sly look in his eyes. "I may be able to help you, but first you will have to help me."

"What is it you need help with, my Lord?" questioned Daren, keeping the tension from his body, as he wondered what King Ghobe was going to come up with.

"Alana, come here please," called King Ghobe. In the silence of the clearing, Alana's progress towards King Ghobe was evident. She walked to the front of his chair and gave a curtsey.

"How may I assist you, my Lord?" she asked with a quiet, yet powerful, voice.

"The Chosen here are after the *Tarian y Ddaear* and they seem to think that I can help. I have decided I will, but first they must help me." King Ghobe gave her a quick explanation. "I have decided you and Carrick will accompany them to Esgyrn Forge, where they will be able to retrieve the shield."

"Ersgyrn Forge?" questioned Alana, alarm in her voice. "But that's where..."

"That's where you need to go," interrupted King Ghobe smoothly. "I have been told once you get there, and lay Lady Daire's sword in the flames of the forge, the shield will be yours. Of course, it may not be that easy, but I'm sure you'll manage."

Alana gave a quick jerk of her head to show she understood, before turning around to look at Daren and the others. There was worry evident in her face, but Daren also knew now was not the time to question it. There was something off about King Ghobe and he knew it wasn't going to be easy reaching this Esgyrn Forge. Better they speak about it in private rather than giving King Ghobe a show, he thought.

"Thank you for your assistance in this matter, King Ghobe. I am sure Lady Daire appreciates all your efforts on our behalf," said Daren.

A quick flicker of uncertainty crossed King Ghobe's face. He pasted on a smile and bent his head in acknowledgment of Daren's words. "Thank you for the gift, much appreciated. You may go and prepare for your journey now. It might be best if you leave straight away," he said, making it clear this was not a suggestion, but rather a command.

"I will go and prepare my things and meet you at the house," said Alana. Carrick gave them a nod from across the clearing where he stood, a strange look on his face.

"By your leave, then," said Daren before turning around and walking towards the back of the clearing, in the direction where they were staying.

No one said a word as they followed Daren and Ula, walking swiftly, but without haste.

* * *

When they arrived back at the house, they all went to their rooms to change out of their formal wear and into their travelling clothes. Marella retrieved her backpack from underneath the bed and double-checked the contents; Lani did the same. Within moments, they were ready and headed back down the stairs to meet with the others.

Daren and Kai appeared moments later, and set their backpacks down on the floor near the front door.

"I'm making a drink," said Lani. "I know he said we need to go now, but we can have something to eat and drink first, surely."

"We have to wait for Alana and Carrick anyway," said Daren. "I wouldn't mind an orange tea, if you're making."

Marella sat down in one of the sofas. "So," she started, "what was King Ghobe playing at then, Daren?"

Lani stood against the doorframe of the kitchen, listening, whilst Kai and Daren sat down. Daren sat next to Marella and turned, so that he was facing both her and Lani.

"I don't know for sure," he admitted "but there were some things he said and didn't say that have intrigued me. We need to speak to Alana and Carrick first to make sure, but I do know this isn't going to be easy. Alana was worried when he mentioned Esgyrn Forge."

"He did say the *Tarian y Ddaear* was popular at the moment. I wonder if it has anything to do with the 'person' who told him we were coming," pondered Lani from the doorway.

"Okay, so what do we know?" asked Kai. "One, we have to go to a Forge Alana is worried about. Two, we need to lay your sword in the flames of the forge – I'm not sure about that one, Daren."

"Three, we need to leave today," added Marella.

Lani moved from the doorway and started bustling around in the kitchen. Even though it was only mid-morning, the others could hear her getting plates and food sorted.

"Do you need any help?" called Kai through to her.

"No, I'm fine. Carry on talking, I can still hear you," replied Lani.

Ula, Nixie, and Kenna walked in together and sat down. It appeared they had been having their own discussion. Marella looked around as she couldn't see Shaw, but just then, he landed on the windowsill.

The Partners sat quietly whilst Lani was moving around and it wasn't long before Lani carried through a tray of drinks. Kai went to the kitchen and came back with another tray of sandwiches and cut carrots, cucumber, and peppers. They helped themselves to what they wanted and sat there, eating quickly.

Ula gave a small yip which got everyone's attention. *"I'm going to speak on an open path so we can all hear,"* she said. *"We have been talking with some of the other animals that live here. Esgyrn Forge is a bad place according to them. There is something there that frightens ALL of the animals, not just the timid ones."*

"Oh well, that's just peachy," snorted Marella. "Sorry, Ula, I didn't mean your information."

Ula gave her an open-mouthed smile, *"I know, Marella. We knew this wasn't going to be easy."*

"The good news is Esgyrn Forge isn't far from here, just over a day's walk," said Nixie.

"We will need to find a place to camp tonight and then we can be there early in the morning if we leave soon," said Kenna.

"Alana and Carrick are here," said Shaw from the window.

There was a rap on the door and then it opened. Alana poked her around the door. "It's only Carrick and I," she called.

"Come on through," said Daren. "We're in the living room."

As Carrick and Alana went through to the living room, the others made room so they had a place to sit.

"Help yourself to some sandwiches and nibbles," said Lani. "We thought it a good idea to refresh ourselves before making a start."

"Plus it gives you time to explain what has you so worried, Alana," said Daren, looking over at her.

A small grimace passed over Alana's face as she helped herself to a sandwich. She leaned back in her chair and looked over at Carrick who was looking stony-faced.

"It has long been said Esgyrn Forge is… well… haunted is the wrong word," she trailed off as she tried to put her thoughts together.

Carrick leaned forwards and put his elbows on his knees. "Esgyrn Forge is under the 'protection' of a rogue Elemental," he said, gruffly. "No one goes near the place, and all the animals run from it. No one has been able to get there for nearly two years. It used to be one of the sacred places, the water was pure, and the earth was fertile. We had a blacksmith who would make marvellous items with metal from Lady Daire, but no longer."

Silence greeted his words as the others thought of what he had said.

"Hold on a moment," said Kai, looking at Carrick. "You say a rogue Elemental? I thought you guys were the Elementals here? Are you saying it's a rogue Gnome – or something else?"

"It's something else," answered Alana. "We are the Guardians of the Element, the Elementals are quite different and each Quarter has their own. Ours are usually very tall, some over eight feet tall and can look like a group of rocks, or tree roots, or anything that is natural to the Earth Element."

144

"And this is what is at Esgyrn Forge?" double-checked Kai.

"Yes, I'm afraid so," replied Carrick. He pushed himself up and said to the group "Come on, sitting around here talking about it won't help us. We need to be making a move."

They all stood up and put their plates and cups back on the tray which Daren then carried through to the kitchen. Marella rinsed them off before leaving them to drain on the side. They grabbed their backpacks, made sure they had everything they needed, and closed the door behind them.

~ 23 ~

"So, which direction?" asked Kai, as he adjusted his backpack to make it more comfortable.

"Follow me," said Carrick and led them off down one of the little dirt tracks that surrounded them.

Marella and Lani dropped back so that they could walk and talk with Alana. They chatted about inconsequential things as they walked along behind Carrick and the others. Their Partners were all over the place, running in front and behind whilst all the time, Shaw flew overhead sounding his cry occasionally. The day was beautiful and the sun shone through the trees. Marella could smell the earth as they walked along and see the flowers in full bloom, dancing in the sunshine.

"What are you thinking about?" asked Lani, as the conversation between herself and Alana came to natural halt.

"Just the heat of Gorffennaf and how it would be at home; the things that are normally happening, and how much time Nixie and I would spend at the lake. I miss it," replied Marella.

"What? Being at home or being by the lake?" asked Lani astutely.

Marella gave out a bark of laughter that echoed through the trees. "You're good," she said to Lani, still chuckling. "I am missing the lake, and the time spent there with Nixie. I miss my Papa and his hugs." She drifted into silence as she got lost in her thoughts.

"You don't miss your mother?" asked Alana gently.

Lani made a sharp gesture with her hand to Alana, but the question had already been asked. Marella shifted her backpack across her shoulders and took a moment before answering.

"I do miss my mother," she said, "but my relationship with her is complicated, more complicated than with my Papa."

Alana reached over and patted her hand. "Sometimes, if something is worth having, then it's the hardest thing to achieve," she said. "I'm sure you and your mother will work things out."

"Let's hope so," muttered Marella.

"Come on, you three," called Carrick, "step up the pace or it will take forever to get there."

"Alright, alright, we're coming," Alana shouted back. "Yeesh, he gets so uptight at times."

Marella and Lani laughed with her as they quickened their pace to catch up with the men.

They continued walking at a steady pace for the rest of the day, making only brief stops. They didn't feel the need to stop for lunch as they had eaten before they left their house. Sunlight filled the air and it was a warm and lazy day. Although they didn't know what they would face at Esgyrn Forge, they were all relaxed.

"This may sound strange," started Lani as she walked along, "but I feel more at ease now than I have during the whole time we were settled in a house."

"That is hardly surprising," answered Carrick. "You were on edge there because you didn't know what King Ghobe had planned and felt like you needed to be forever on your guard. The only one I saw relax was Marella when she was beating me with her staff," he laughed.

All the others joined in his laughter, including Marella. "I'm sorry about that," she said, smiling at him.

"No you're not and you shouldn't be. The time may come when you need to be able to use that staff as something more than just a walking aid," said Carrick. "Have the rest of you been practicing as well?" he asked.

"We've been sparring together," said Kai, gesturing to himself and Daren whilst Carrick nodded in approval.

"That's good, but I'll have a go with you too. You will become complacent if you only spar with each other. Then when someone does something you're not used to, it will shock you. You need to be able to react to the unexpected, without any hesitation," said Carrick.

He turned to Lani. "And you, have you been practicing with your bow?"

She nodded her head proudly at him. "I have and I never miss a shot," she declared.

Carrick smiled at her words and at the pride that suffused her body. "We'll take an early rest stop today, we're not far away, so it won't matter and this is important. We can have a tryout and see what we're dealing with."

Carrick nodded to himself, looking pleased whilst the others looked warily at each other. They were sure they would be aching in places they had forgotten about by tonight.

Alana chuckled at the looks on their faces as she continued to follow Carrick towards their destination.

After another hour or so, Carrick called a halt to their journey. "This is a good place to stay," he said, looking around. "The grass is still green, the birds are still singing, and there is water nearby. There is life yet in this place."

The rest looked around and started to set up camp so they wouldn't have to do it later when they were sore.

* * *

For the rest of the day, they were put through their paces by Carrick, whilst Alana sat on a rock nearby and watched them. Carrick made a target for Lani which he kept moving farther and farther away until it was just a speck in the distance, but Lani managed to hit it every time. For Kai and Daren, he had them spar with each other whilst barking out corrections to their stances, to their moves, and what they should have done. He also gave Marella a good workout. Although she did manage to beat him again, it was a close call.

After they had washed up in the stream that was gurgling nearby, they returned to the clearing to the delicious smell of roasting fowl. Alana had picked some fresh salad greens from the forest nearby and had seasoned the bird with herbs and spices she carried with her. They all sat down and ate their tea contentedly.

"Alana, Carrick, can I ask you something?" asked Marella once they had all finished and tidied away their things. They were resting around a small fire as the evening descended upon them.

Carrick looked over to Marella. "Of course you can, little one," he said.

A lump appeared in Marella's throat as he called her by the nickname her father used. She swallowed to get rid of it, but not before Daren shot her a glance that said he had caught the reference.

"Why do you think that King Ghobe sent you and Alana with us?" she asked, carrying on as though nothing had occurred.

Carrick snorted at her question whilst Alana looked thoughtful. "Because he wanted us out of the way," said Carrick strongly. "He is up to something, with someone who is working against Lady Daire, and we are his strongest opposition. If something happens to us when we're with you, then you get the blame and we're not around to bother him anymore. Two birds; one stone."

Alana agreed with him. "That's true, but also, if we're not there, then he believes those who are loyal to us and to Lady Daire, will be without leadership and more easily enfolded back into his plans and schemes."

"Great," clipped Kai. "Just great. So he sends you off with us on a fool's mission, but we get the blame if something happens to you? Just wonderful."

"Oh stop grumping, lad," said Carrick. "Do you think that Alana and I plan to have something happen to us? The same could be said to any of you *or* your Partners. There is no guarantee you will come out of this unscathed, even if you are the Chosen of the Lords and Ladies. The quicker you accept and prepare for that possibility, the better off you will all be."

Shaw flew down at that moment and landed on Lani's shoulder. He rubbed his head against her cheek and she gently stroked his feathers. "I hadn't thought about anything happening to Shaw," she said to no one in particular. "How will I carry on if something does?"

Alana plopped down next to Lani and bumped her shoulder. "No one is planning on getting hurt, Lani," she said. "However, if it happens, you carry on."

Lani looked at her with hurt swimming in her large grey-blue eyes. "This is Shaw we're talking about, Alana. He's part of me."

"And he always will be, even if he isn't with you physically. Your Partner is a gift from your Lord and is just as much a 'Chosen' as you are. Your Lords and Ladies have plans for all of you," she said, looking at the group as a whole. "If the worst does indeed happen, and you lose your Partner, you carry on. You grieve, but complete the task you have been given. Your Partner will always be with you in your heart, even if they are not by your side. Their spirit will always remain, and you know they will be looked after by their Lord or Lady."

Nixie bumped Marella with his head, and she threw her arms around him, holding him tight. "I don't know how I would carry on without you," she whispered to him.

"*I feel the same way, but that is a risk we understood when we undertook this task,*" replied Nixie. "*You would carry on, the same as I would have to if anything happened to you.*"

Marella could feel the tears leaking from her eyes as she contemplated a time without Nixie. She held him close and could feel his body quaking against her as the emotions pounded into him too. The emotions were vibrant in the air. They were all taking comfort in being physically close to their Partners. Marella looked over at Alana and Carrick and saw they were watching the Chosen with looks of sympathy on their faces.

Marella took charge of her emotions and tried to stay strong. She gave Ula a mental nudge. "*Ula, we need to carry on. We can't let this overwhelm us or we may as well give in now. Daren needs to say something. If he doesn't, we will all be low as we try to sleep tonight.*"

Marella felt reassurance from Ula before she responded. "*I'm giving him a moment, Marella. It's the first time the idea has occurred to him and he's not as used to dealing with his emotions like you are. They all need a bit of time. He will respond soon, don't you worry.*"

Marella carried on holding Nixie, but also looked around at the others in the clearing. Before long, she could see they were working to come out of the funk. Their Partners were showing physical signs of love and reassurance to their humans – Shaw was rubbing his face on Lani's cheek, Kenna was stood on her hind legs with her paws on Kai's shoulders, and Ula was sat in front of Daren, leaning into him as he had his arms wrapped around her.

Daren removed his hands from around Ula and gave himself a quick shake. Ula licked his face before walking around the back of him and standing by his side, facing the others. Daren raised himself until he was kneeling, resting his backside on the heels of his boots. His hands rested on his thighs as he waited for everyone's attention.

Marella and Nixie looked at him and he gave them a wry, crooked grin that lifted Marella's heart. He wasn't about to become downhearted over this, she realised.

Kai and Kenna were the next ones to focus. Kai coughed before straightening his shoulders and looking around. Kenna looked at Ula and gave a small yip of acknowledgement. Kai looked at Daren and Marella felt like she could see the strength of Kai being replenished. The connection between Kai and Daren was almost tangible and it took Marella's breath away. Kai turned his head and looked at her. She couldn't make out what was in those chocolate brown eyes, but it gave her a warm glow inside. She gave Kai a small smile and turned away, looking over to Lani and Shaw.

Lani had tears running down her face, which were making Shaw's head wet as he rubbed against her cheek. She was stroking his back and Marella could see her hand trembling. However, as Marella watched, Lani lifted her head and looked across at her. She gave Marella a tremulous smile which grew steadier and more confident the longer she smiled. She put her shoulders back and straightened her spine. Lani looked over at Kai and Daren and nodded to them. Shaw shook his wings and gave such a screech of defiance Marella was sure Lani would be temporarily hard of hearing.

Alana and Carrick were watching the eight of them, a look of pride on their faces. Alana smiled at them as they looked towards her.

"I can make no guarantees to you," she said. "Even the Lords and Ladies can't see what will happen, but know this. You are not now, and never will be, alone. You will have the strength of the Elements behind you and, more importantly, the eight of you are bound together. Like the separate weaves on a rope, you are stronger together. You will help each, and be there for each other, with something even stronger than a familial bond. I was intending to give this to you later, but it feels like the right time now."

She handed each of them a small acorn. Daren looked down at it, rocking it in his palm. "What do we do with these?" he asked.

"If ever you need me, no matter which Quarter you are in or wherever you may be, cover this with earth and say my name. I will try my best to get to you or to assist you in whatever it is you need."

"Thank you, Alana," said Daren, "you have given us a great gift."

Carrick also stepped to them and gave out a small present. "This is the same as Alana's, but will call to me. Use it wisely," he said, his voice solemn and deep.

Into each of their hands, he dropped a hazelnut. Marella curled her hand around the acorn and hazelnut before putting them into her waist pouch. "Thank you both," she said to them, hearing the others murmur their thanks at the same time.

"Come on," said Daren. "I think it's time we hit the hay. Who knows what's going to happen tomorrow and I, for one, feel shattered. Marella, how you cope with emotions all the time, I'll never know," he said with a smile.

The others all agreed with him as, two by two, they made their way to where they were sleeping. Marella had no doubts all Partners and humans would be as close to each other as her and Nixie were.

She lay there, trying to relax her body, whilst listening to the night sounds of the forest. She could feel Nixie's body close to hers and the gentle reassurance of his bond. Slowly, her eyes drifted shut and she passed into the realms of sleep, dreaming of acorns and hazelnuts.

~ 24 ~

The birds chirping with the dawn chorus woke Marella up from a deep sleep. She took a deep breath of the clean, fresh air down into her lungs before expelling it. She couldn't hear anyone up and about and by the feel of Nixie lying next to her, he wasn't awake yet either.

She edged away from him, knowing he would feel her anyway, but know that she was okay. She stood up and pulled her wash bag out of her rucksack. She tiptoed towards the water so she could freshen up.

After she had finished her morning ablutions, she sat on a rock facing the water. She let the sounds of the water flow over her, bringing a feeling of peace inside her. The gurgling of the water calmed her nerves and reassured her on a deep, internal level.

Marella heard footsteps behind her and, just for a moment, resented the intrusion into her world. She gave herself a telling off for reacting that way. She looked over her shoulder so that she could see who it was.

"Good morning, Marella," said Kai, his deep voice husky due to the early morning.

"Good morning, Kai," she answered with a smile. "I'm surprised to see you awake so early."

He grunted slightly in acknowledgement before dropping down onto the rock next to her. She looked at him, but he was focused on the water passing them by.

"Sounds good, doesn't it," she said.

"Yeah," he said, "reassuring, almost."

"And do you need reassurance this morning?" she asked.

"I do," he said, looking down towards the ground. "Last night hit me hard. I hadn't ever thought of being without Kenna, and I don't know what I'd do without her. Then there's today. We don't know who or what we're up against, but King Ghobe not only doesn't expect us to succeed, he also has us down as his scapegoats if anything happens to Alana or Carrick. So, yeah, I need some reassurance."

By the time he had finished, his voice was raised with annoyance. Marella could feel the tension rolling off him in waves and could see it in the tightness of his shoulders. She put a reassuring hand onto his forearm and squeezed it. He looked down at her hand on his arm, then looked at her. She smiled.

"Kai, this is but the first hurdle," she said gently. "The Lords and Ladies have more faith in us than you do right now. Alana and Carrick are well able to look after themselves; after all, they've been doing it under King Ghobe's nose all this time. We are all here together and we're not completely helpless you know!"

"But we don't know what's there," Kai protested.

"You don't know everything that's going to happen in the next half hour," said Marella in retort, "so how is this any different?"

"I don't usually have to worry about people I care about being hurt in the next half hour, that's how it's different," said Kai, snappily.

"You could though, if you really thought about it," said Marella. She gave his arm a shake. "You could worry about everyone, all the time, but it wouldn't do you any good. You'd just end up a nervous wreck."

She inhaled deeply, letting her senses be filled by the water. She opened her eyes and looked at him, seeing the anguish on his face. Marella leaned towards him and gently put her hands on either side of his face, cupping his cheeks.

"The cares of tomorrow must wait until this day is done," she said. "Let's sort out this rogue Elemental first, and then you can worry about the next Quarter." She gave him a quick wink, then, surprising them both, she brushed her lips over his.

"I'm going to get breakfast started," she said before hurrying back to the campsite, leaving Kai sitting there, his fingertips touching his lips. A slow smile started to spread across his face as he felt his tension easing. He would be okay today, he decided, he wasn't going to let anything happen to him or Kenna. He already had reasons to carry on and stop worrying, but now there was something else. He wanted to find out more about the intriguing girl who touched his senses. The one Chosen of Water.

* * *

By the time Kai returned to the campsite, everyone was up and bustling with action. Daren was shaking out everyone's bedding before it was rolled up and put across the top of their rucksacks. Lani and Marella were both by the campfire, sorting out a cooked breakfast and steaming mugs of tea. Alana was nowhere to be seen, but Carrick was sharpening one of his daggers on a whetstone.

The four Partners were sat together at one side of the clearing, watching the movement of everyone else. Their stillness was more noticeable, amidst the hustle and bustle of the campsite.

"Is everything okay with you guys?" Kai asked on a broad path, so that they could all hear him if they wanted to.

"We're fine, there's no need for us all to be rushing around," answered Kenna with a tilt of her head.

"Rushing around like fools?" said Kai to her wryly, hearing the unspoken words.

"I never said that," replied Kenna mischievously.

Kai gave a bark of laughter that drew the attention of the others. He nodded his head in the direction of the Partners and explained, "I was just asking Kenna if they were all right, as they were sat so still. According to her 'there's no need for us all to be rushing around'."

"Like fools?" queried Daren.

"That's what I said," laughed Kai. Everyone chuckled at this small interaction as they carried on making their preparations to go.

Within a short amount of time, everyone was ready. Everything was packed away and the clearing looked the same as when they had arrived. However, Alana still had not returned, so they couldn't go anywhere.

"Carrick, do you know where Alana has gone? Will she be long?" asked Daren with a hint of impatience.

"I'm here, you can stop your worrying now, lad," came Alana's voice. They turned in the direction of her voice to see her limping into the clearing.

"Alana," cried Lani and ran to her side, helping her walk to the others.

"I'm all right, Lani, don't fret," reassured Alana. "I just twisted my ankle, that's all. Just give me a couple of minutes to strap it up and I'll be fine."

"How did you do it?"

"Where have you been?"

Marella and Daren asked their questions of Alana at the same time. Alana looked at them and gave a chuckle.

"You two really should be siblings," she said, still chuckling to herself. "I was stupid and tripped over a tree root," she said, answering Marella first. Then she looked at Daren. "I was talking with some of the other Elementals, trying to find out some more information about the rogue."

This statement made everyone shut up and move closer.

"Did you find anything out?" questioned Kai.

"Nothing really of any use," complained Alana. "It's big and the others are afraid of it. The animals won't go near Esgyrn Forge anymore. They say it's been tainted."

"Tainted?" repeated Lani. "That doesn't sound good."

"Hmm? No, no it doesn't," said Alana distractedly as she searched through her bag for a bandage.

"We're ready to go whenever you are," said Daren.

"Yes, okay, I won't be long," she said, finally finding the bandage in her bag. "Lani, dear, would you go and put this in the water for me please?"

Lani ran off with the bandage and soon came back with it wet. "I've wrung it out," she said. "I didn't think you'd want it dripping."

"No, that's fine, thank you," said Alana, taking the bandage from Lani. She proceeded to wrap it around her ankle until it was completely bound up. She stood up and gingerly placed her weight on her ankle. She breathed a sigh of relief and smiled at the others. "It's okay," she said. "I'm fine."

She shut her rucksack and swung it onto her back. "Come on then, let's go."

With that, Carrick turned around and started to lead them out of the clearing, with Daren coming up last. He gave the clearing one last look over his shoulder before catching up with the others, ready for whatever the day would bring.

~ 25 ~

They walked at a steady pace, not rushing for the sake of Alana's ankle. She had a rough walking staff to aid her, as she had found it harder than expected. Conversation was muted as they headed towards Esgyrn Forge, all wondering what to expect.

Within an hour, Marella noticed the surrounding areas were changing. Instead of a healthy, vibrant green, the grass was starting to dry up and go brown. The bushes and trees lost their look of growth, looking spindly and undernourished instead. She caught sight of Daren as she looked around in sorrow. He looked haggard and exhausted.

"Daren, what's the matter? Are you okay?" she asked him, moving over to his side and draping his arm around her shoulders.

Daren gave her a quick squeeze. "I'm fine, Marella," he rasped, his voice sounding croaky. He gave a cough to clear his throat before trying again. "I'm fine. I just need to make it to the Forge."

"What's the matter with you? You were fine when we left camp this morning," she asked again.

"It is the rogue Elemental affecting him," said Alana. She stopped Daren from walking and pulled him down so she could look him in the eyes. She squinted at him, moving his face so she could see better. Finally, she nodded and fumbled in her waist pouch.

"Here, take these, they will help," she said, pouring some seeds into Daren's hand.

"What are they?" asked Daren as he raised his hand up so he could see them.

"Sunflower seeds," explained Alana. "Until we reach the rogue Elemental, you need to eat one of these every time you start to feel weak. You would be best to eat two or three before we actually engage the rogue. They hold the power of the earth and the sun which will help combat the rogue's plague on the land."

"Why am I affected and not you?" questioned Daren. "Not that I want you to feel like this but…" he trailed off.

Alana just smiled at him. "You, dearest Daren, are the Chosen. I am a Priestess - the same but different. You are attuned to Lady Daire as you are Her Chosen, but you are connected to the Earth; so if the earth is hurting, so will you. I am attuned to Earth as a Gnome, but my connection is to Lady Daire. Does this make sense?"

Daren nodded his head whilst slowly chewing on a sunflower seed. "If I am strongest here though, it must be me that fights the rogue, yes?"

"No," said Alana, "you are here as part of a whole. You must all fight the rogue to the best of your capabilities. This may be your Quarter, but you can't do it alone, Chosen or not. However, the rogue is attacking you through your connection to the land. If it was a natural sickness, then the sunflower seeds wouldn't help you. As I can already see them making you feel better, I know that it is the rogue causing this. By giving you the sunflower seeds, I can fight in my own way, bringing the balance back to you."

"Thank you, Alana," said Daren, "I appreciate your help."

After reassuring Marella he was going to be okay and storing his sunflower seeds in a small pouch, he continued walking towards Esgyrn Forge, a place that he could feel was wrong in his very bones.

* * *

Before long, the scenery had changed to a dull and lifeless brown. The birdsong had stopped and Marella couldn't hear any other animals around them.

"*Nixie, have the animals all gone?*" she asked him.

"*They have, they won't return until the rogue has gone. Then life will return to Esgyrn Forge, as it was meant to be,*" replied Nixie.

The pace of their walking slowed down as the companions started to take notice of what was going on around them, not wanting to be caught unaware. Marella, muscles quivering with tension, held her staff at the ready. Carrick loosened his sword, with Kai and Daren following suit. Lani swung her crossbow from across her shoulder and walked forward, holding it in readiness.

They all carried on walking towards the Forge, their awareness on high alert. Marella kept looking around her. She was also hearing the updates that were coming from their Partners.

"There's the Forge," breathed Daren, his voice barely above a whisper.

"Daren, you must lay your sword onto the Forge," said Alana.

Daren nodded his head to show he had heard her before moving silently along the path. As he moved, he poured some more sunflower seeds out of the pouch, swiftly put some into his mouth and started chewing.

Suddenly, from the very earth beneath their feet, erupted the rogue. Marella gasped as she had her first look at the Elemental that had driven life away from the sacred place of Lady Daire.

He was very tall, over nine feet in height, and his body was made out of terracotta clay. Marella could see sticks, stones, sand, and rocks made up his body, giving it a very 'lumpy' look. His arms were huge and grew bigger as they went down towards his club-like fists.

He roared at them, bringing his hands up to beat upon his chest. "You *dare* to enter my Forge?" he shouted. "This is my Forge, you don't belong here. Now GO!"

As he shouted 'GO', he leaned forwards and the companions were struggling to stay upright as they were bombarded by a force of wind, pebbles, and clods of earth.

"Daren, quickly, raise a shield," gasped Alana, falling backwards as she struggled with the force of the attack.

Carrick, pulling Lani with him, had dropped to the ground, making them as small a target as possible. He covered her with his cloak in an attempt to stop some of the smaller stones from damaging her body.

Kai and Marella were stood together, appearing as if they were in an embrace. Kai had his arms around her waist and Marella had her head tucked into his shoulder, with her arms pulled in tight between them.

The Partners were all safe - Shaw was flying overhead, away from the force of the wind, whilst the others had made a break for some spindly trees that were off to the side, still swaying in the wind, but out of the direct line of fire.

Daren dropped to one knee and slammed both hands into the earth. He then raised both hands up to join together over the top of his head. As his hands joined, an opaque shield appeared between the companions and the Elemental. Marella lifted her head to see the attack was still happening. It was, but instead of it coming towards them, Daren's shield was deflecting it to the sides.

She pulled out of Kai's arms and moved towards Daren's left hand side, holding her staff in a fighting stance.

Kai pulled his sword out of its scabbard and raised it to his lips, before whispering the name of Lord Ethon. He then moved to Daren's back and put his hand on Daren's right shoulder.

Carrick and Alana also readied themselves while Lani loaded her crossbow and made sure she could access her pouch of quivers without any difficulty.

"Ready?" asked Daren, his voice shaking with strain.

"We're ready," confirmed Marella for all of them.

"*Ready, beloved?*" Daren thought to Ula.

"*We're all ready, Daren. Let go of the shield,*" said Ula.

With those words, Daren dropped his hands to his sides and swiftly stood up as the shield dropped. Before it had gone completely, everyone was moving to attack.

Marella darted forward, running behind the Elemental, and gave him a massive thwack to the back of his knee. He stumbled but quickly recovered, sweeping his arm behind him to try and knock her out of the way. Marella ducked but felt the wind as his arm passed where her head had been.

Lani was like a sylph – quicker than the eye could see, darting around the rogue, shooting her bolts out with accuracy, but with little noticeable effect.

Kai and Carrick were hacking at the Elemental, as they tried to cause some sort of damage.

As Daren headed towards the thick of the action, Alana pulled him back. "Let your companions keep you safe for now," she said. "You must lay your sword in the Forge, or we will never defeat him. Now go." With a shove, she pushed Daren towards the wooden building in the middle of the clearing.

She then reached into her pocket and pulled out three horse chestnut seeds, still inside their prickly pods. She shouted at the others to duck and then threw them at the Elemental as hard as she could. The first one stuck in his leg, the spines on the pod making it difficult for the Elemental to dislodge it. The second landed on his shoulder and the third was on his arm.

As the others moved away and ducked down towards the ground, Alana stood tall as her earth bombs detonated, ripping out chunks of clay and making the first real dent in the Elemental.

He roared in anger, or maybe it was surprise, Marella couldn't tell the difference, but she could see he was very angry. They all moved in to attack once more while Alana pulled out various seeds and stones from her pouch, cantillating as she did so.

Out of the corner of Marella's eye, she saw Daren dart past, intent on reaching the Forge. He ducked inside the door and raced to the centre of the large, open room. Right in the middle was the biggest anvil Daren had ever seen. He reached down to his scabbard and pulled out the Sword of Daire. He placed it on the anvil and took a step back, wondering what would happen next.

As Marella continued to fight the Elemental with her staff, she also tried to keep a close eye on Daren. She could see him through the doorway, staring at his sword which wasn't doing anything.

"Daren," shouted Alana, over the noise of the fight. "Call Her name! You need to use the sword in Her name so call Her."

A look of enlightenment spread over Daren's face and he nodded sharply to show he understood. Marella watched his head bow down and could just about make out the movement of his lips as he called to Lady Daire.

As she watched, the Forge lit up with a verdant light. Daren's sword was enclosed with green fire. Marella thought she could hear words but wasn't sure, as the Elemental had started to fight even harder the moment the Forge lit up.

Suddenly, Marella heard Nixie in her mind. *"Marella, use the staff. Use it now so Daren can return to the fight."*

"Use the staff?" she panted, as she continued to hit the Elemental. *"Use*

it how?"

"With the staff, you can control water. It's your gift! Lady Erwyna thinks it wise that you use it now. Call the water, Marella."

Marella gritted her teeth as she stepped back out of the Elemental's immediate range. She held the staff in front of her with both hands and straightened her arms.

"WATER!" she shouted and then her jaw dropped in amazement as a torrent of water appeared from the top of the staff, and shot past the elemental, catching only the side of him.

She readjusted her grip on the staff and held it vertically. She braced her legs and called for water once again. This time the direction of the water hit the Elemental right in the midriff.

"Marella, how are you doing that?" questioned Lani, breathlessly.

"I'll explain later. Daren needs to join us, NOW!" she said, urgently.

At those words, Daren ran from the Forge, his sword still burning with green flames.

"Kai, come to me," he shouted as he ran towards Marella.

Daren stopped and faced the Elemental. "Lani, on my left," he instructed. Without a word, Lani moved.

"Kai, on Lani's left, quickly now," said Daren, watching as Kai moved to Lani and gave her a small smile.

"Marella, you're last, hurry, come on."

Marella moved to left of Kai, still holding her staff in front of her. The Elemental was stubbornly trying to fight the water attack and hadn't realised what the others had done.

As Marella stood next to Kai, she transferred the staff into her left hand. With her right, she held onto Kai. He in turn held Lani who then placed her hand on Daren's shoulder. In the same order, their Partners moved into position in front of them, ensuring that some part of their body was touching their human.

"It's coming, brace yourselves," warned Daren as he held onto his sword tightly.

The water had stopped from Marella's staff, but they could all feel a buzzing through their veins. The intensely burning flames of Daren's sword became brighter, until the companions were unable to look directly at it.

Then, with a boom that shook the ground, a beam of beautiful green light shot from the sword, straight into the chest of the Elemental. He bent over at the waist, trying to avoid the beam, and roared with agony as the light went straight through him.

The light continued to burn and the feeling of being connected to the earth, that flowed through their veins, became stronger.

The Elemental started to shake and moan. He roared his displeasure until he finally stood up and raised his face to the sky. The companions distinctly heard his cry of "Lady Daire, help me," before he exploded in a shower of earth.

* * *

In the silence that followed, the companions stood there, processing what had just happened.

"Is everyone okay?" asked Daren into the quiet.

"We're fine," said Kai, "but where are Alana and Carrick?"

"We're here; don't worry," they heard from behind them. As they turned, they saw Alana and Carrick standing up as they moved from behind the tree where they had taken shelter.

"As soon as Daren called Lani to him, I knew what was going to happen," said Alana. "So I pulled Carrick with me, and we got out of the way of the power that was flowing."

"Damn, that was strong," said Carrick in his gruff voice, shaking his head as bits of soil fell to the ground.

"Is it done now?" questioned Lani, looking around her.

"It is, life will soon return here," said Daren, looking down at his sword which had returned to its original appearance. He looked around, checking on his friends, before putting his sword into his scabbard. He pulled out a brown, hessian pouch that had a piece of string woven through the neck in a tie.

"I need to collect the earth that was part of the Elemental" he said to the others, before moving over to where it had exploded.

"Won't it just fall through the holes?" queried Marella as she walked by his side to help.

"No, look," said Daren and he opened the neck of the pouch so Marella could see inside to the finest green silk lining she had ever seen.

"Wow," she breathed. "That's gorgeous."

"It is," agreed Daren. "The Lady Daire is giving our rogue a resting place where he will remain dormant for a long time. If we don't place him in here, he will return and cause havoc all too soon."

With all of them helping, the dirt was scooped up and placed carefully inside the pouch. As the last handful went in, Daren gave it a little shake to make sure all the dirt was inside before pulling the tie closed. As it pulled shut, there was a brief flash of green light and the top of the pouch sealed itself.

"Alana, I think you're supposed to have this," said Daren as he gave her the pouch.

"Thank you, Daren. I will take care of him," replied Alana.

"So now what?" said Kai. "I thought once we fought the Elemental, the shield would be ours. Isn't that what King Ghobe said? I don't see it anywhere."

Daren laughed at Kai. "Do you even know what you're looking for?" he questioned.

Kai rubbed his face, looking a tad embarrassed. "Well, no, I guess not," he said.

"The Shield isn't here," said Daren. "King Ghobe has it back in Naear, hidden. He wasn't expecting us to return, so didn't worry about us finding out it wasn't here."

"How do you…" started Lani before stopping herself. "In the Forge, you were talking to Lady Daire, weren't you?"

"Yes, I was," said Daren. "I know where the Shield is in the same way I knew how to defeat the Elemental. The pure power of Earth was channelled through Her sword to overload the Elemental, but we also put the power of our own Elements in there too so that the rogue will balance himself out. Even when he does reform, he won't be the same Elemental he was before."

"You mean he'll come back," said Lani with alarm in her eyes.

"Not for a long time," reassured Daren. "Come on, let's have some lunch."

"Lunch?" choked Lani, as she gasped with laughter.

"It is nearly lunchtime," said Daren. "I don't think it will matter if we have it early. We have been busy this morning."

As the clearing resounded with the companions' laughter, birdsong could faintly be heard from nearby trees.

~ 26 ~

It was decided over lunch they would return to Naear as quickly as possible, before King Ghobe could hide the Shield again.

"I don't think it will matter now," said Daren. "It's like I can feel it, so I don't think he'll be able to hide it where I can't find it."

"Even so, let's not take the chance," said Carrick. "Your quest isn't over yet, youngling. You still have three more Quarters to go."

"True, very true," said Daren, nodding his head, "but at least my part is coming to a close"

"Is that relief I can hear in your voice?" said Lani, looking at him with questions in her eyes.

"I think so, yes," answered Daren. "It's nice to be part of a team, but I don't know if I'm cut out for this leadership lark."

"You did fine," reassured Alana. "You've set a good example for the others."

"There's a first time for everything," said Marella, jokingly and punched Daren in the arm.

"Yep, crisis is over. They're back to normal," grinned Kai, laughing at Marella and Daren.

They travelled back to where they had broken camp earlier that morning just as dusk settled around them. The time had gone quicker than they had expected, so they made haste in setting up their sleeping arrangements for the night.

There was some small talk around the campfire, but everyone seemed tired and they were quick to retire for the evening, all promising they would be up and out early the next day.

* * *

True to their words, the camp broke at first light and they began the march back to Naear. Alana still carried her walking staff, but seemed like she needed it less and less.

Just before they entered the boundaries of Naear, Daren spoke to Alana. "I just wanted to say thank you for the sunflower seeds you gave me yesterday, and to return the rest of them to you."

"There's no need to thank me," said Alana "and keep them with you. I think you might need them again."

"Oh," said Daren, looking down to the pouch. "I sort of hoped I wouldn't need them."

"You've been in your strongest element, affected only by the rogue. You still have to travel to your natural opposite and that is where these may help. I don't know for sure but I can't see how they would hurt."

"Right," agreed Daren, tucking the pouch safely in his back pack. "Air, our next Quarter."

"Yes, that's the one," laughed Alana. "Let's get you safely out of this Quarter first though, eh?!"

Carrick called the group to a halt and they stood in a circle, waiting to hear what he had to say.

"Once we cross the boundaries, King Ghobe will know we have returned. He will only have a small opportunity to hide the Shield, however, there will be an opportunity. I would suggest you keep your senses sharp. He wasn't expecting any of us to return; indeed he was hoping we wouldn't. He hasn't been straight with you so far, so I wouldn't expect it now. Take care, keep sharp, and mind your manners! Don't let him ruin your quest at this stage," said Carrick sternly as Alana nodded in agreement next to him.

"To be honest, and please don't be offended by this, but I'm ready to leave the Earth Quarter now," said Lani quietly.

"That's not surprising," said Alana. "This is your weakest Element, however, I have to say, I think you've done amazingly well. Not only were you able to cope with the wave when it first broke over you, but you've also trained hard, fought an Elemental, and become part of the Elements yourself. For an Air person in the Earth Quarter, I would give yourself a pat on the back."

Lani blushed at Alana's words and gave a whispered thank you as they continued along their way.

After a couple of minutes, Daren stopped and shook himself. Carrick grinned at him. "Got the shivers there, lad?" he said.

"Tingles more like," replied Daren. "I can't remember feeling like that when we left."

"Oh, they were there alright, but you're more in tune with your Element now. I'm guessing it won't ever leave you, either. Now concentrate on that Shield and let's get you back home."

Daren nodded to Carrick before they continued walking at a swift pace. Although no one had known they would be returning, especially on what day, they nevertheless soon gained a following as they headed towards the heart of Naear and King Ghobe's throne.

King Ghobe was sat in his chair as the group approached him. Without even thinking about it, Daren was at the front with Kai and Carrick on one side and Alana, Lani and Marella on the other.

They approached King Ghobe and Daren bowed his head towards him in a show of respect. "We have fought with the rogue Elemental of Esgyrn Forge and were victorious. Life has already begun to return to the area."

King Ghobe looked concerned as he listened to Daren. "Yes, but did you find the Shield?" he asked. "That is what you went for, after all."

"That is exactly what we went for, as that is where you told us it would be," replied Daren. "I have since been informed that the Shield is not, and never was, at Esgyrn Forge but instead, has been here all along."

"And just who told you that?" sneered King Ghobe. "Alana, I presume? Not that she would know anything."

"No, it wasn't Alana," answered Daren calmly. "In fact, I know right now, the Shield is hidden inside the trunk of the tree that stands at the back of your home."

"What? But, how?" spluttered King Ghobe before trying to take his words back. "I mean to say, how would you possibly have a connection to something that isn't here?"

"It is here," said Daren, "and I am more than willing to go with you now, to retrieve it."

King Ghobe looked like he wanted to protest, but a shout went through the crowd that had gathered.

"Take them," came one shout.

"Show them that it isn't here," said another.

"You wouldn't do such a thing," came another.

In fact, so many shouts filled the clearing that the individual words soon became indistinguishable from each other.

King Ghobe stood, raised his hand, and silence began to fall. "I will go now with the Chosen of Earth and his companions, to look at where he says the Shield is. Once we have done so and proven it is not there, I think it might be best if they leave the Earth Quarter at their earliest convenience."

Daren acknowledged his words with a bob of his head. "As soon as we have the Shield, we will be more than happy to take our leave."

King Ghobe looked unhappy at Daren's choice of words, but he had committed himself now so stepped forward, prepared to lead the way.

The crowd moved with them as they followed the King to the tree behind his home. He made a point of encircling the tree to show Daren there wasn't anything there.

"See, Chosen? There is nothing here but the tree. The *Tarian y Ddaear* is not here." King Ghobe raised his voice in triumph, and the crowd cheered, supporting their King.

"There may be nothing here for you, King Ghobe, but there is certainly something here for me." With those words, Daren simply pushed his hand through the trunk of the tree. Those that could see what he had just done gasped in surprise, and whispers soon became louder as the event was passed backwards through the crowd.

Marella watched King Ghobe and saw a look of despair cross his face, as he realised he had been found out. He pulled together his confidence, putting on a brave face, determined to undermine Daren in whatever way he could.

Daren withdrew his hand from the tree, his fingers tightly furled around something hidden in the palm of his hand.

"Surely you don't expect me to believe you hold the Shield in your hand?" scoffed King Ghobe, raising a few chuckles amongst some of the Gnomes in the crowd.

"You may not believe it, but it's true," stated Daren. He held his hand out and there, in the middle of his palm, was a miniature shield of green and gold. It had the same pattern on it as on Daren's sword and was embossed around the edges.

"That is the *Tarian y Ddaear*?" laughed King Ghobe. "Why, it wouldn't shield the Earth against anything. Trickery, I tell you, sheer trickery."

Without saying a word, Daren lifted the shield and held it high. As he did so, the shield began to grow until it was full-size, and glowing in the light. He looked over at King Ghobe who was also looking green now, a sickly, pasty green which told of his guilt.

The crowd soon started muttering and now the shouts were against King Ghobe.

"Guards," he called. "Take these Chosen inside the Detention Tree. I will need to speak with them regarding the theft of *Tarian y Ddaear*."

"The theft of it?" repeated Marella, unable to keep the indignation out of her voice.

"Yes," said King Ghobe, his voice getting higher and more indignant, as he thought of things to say. "The only way for the Chosen to have known it was there is if he put it there himself. He was trying to steal it, take it by trickery. Guards!"

No guard came towards them and the muttering became louder. Alana pushed her way to the front of the group and spoke directly to King Ghobe.

"You are the one who has resorted to trickery. You sent Carrick and I off on this mission, knowing it was already here and safe, but hoping we would perish in the process. I'm not sorry to say you were mistaken, and not only have we returned, but we are stronger than before."

"But you are still my subjects," cried King Ghobe, "you have to do as I say."

"No longer are you King of the Gnomes, Ghobe," came a melodious voice from the back of the crowd. The crowd parted as Lady Daire made her way gracefully to the front.

"My Lady," said Daren as he sank to one knee, everyone else quickly following his example, apart from King Ghobe.

"What do you mean, I am no longer King of the Gnomes?" demanded Ghobe.

"I think you forget to whom you are speaking, Ghobe," admonished Lady Daire. "I am Lady of the Land and as such, I am entitled to have whomever ruling my Quarter as I desire. I have left the decision to the Gnomes in the past, but it appears they have made a mistake with you. You are no longer King. You may return to the Cartefru tribe, if they will have you."

Ghobe spluttered incomprehensibly as he was led away by a couple of the very same guards he had called over to detain Daren.

Lady Daire turned to face the crowd. "It is not often I force a decision to be made, I much prefer you all to have, and use, your own free will. However, Ghobe was dealing with an enemy of mine and working against my Chosen. This is not acceptable."

The crowd all managed to look ashamed at her words. Then one young voice piped up. "Lady Daire, I understand what you have done and why, but what will become of us without a King?"

Lady Daire smiled and the Gnomes relaxed. "There will be a King; a King who rules in my name and is pure of heart. From now on, I will be here to see each King or Queen before they start ruling to ensure their loyalty. If there is any treason in their heart, they will not be King of the Gnomes."

The Gnomes started muttering again and looked at each other and their neighbour.

"Carrick, please step forward," called Lady Daire softly.

Carrick stepped forward and dropped back down to one knee. "My Lady," he said, "how may I be of assistance?"

"You may be of assistance by ruling the Gnomes in my stead," she replied, as a look of shock crossed his face and his jaw fell open.

"But, but…" he said.

"You have treated every Chosen here, whether human or animal, with respect and care. You have trained the Chosen of Water when no one else would. You ensured the safety of those in your care whilst on a quest that was nothing to do with you. You are my choice for King of the Gnomes."

"But surely, Alana…" he carried on protesting.

"Alana is my Priestess, and as such, cannot be Queen. She will, however, be ruler by your side. Heed her words because she speaks with my voice."

With those words, Lady Daire looked over at Alana. "You have done so well, my child. I am so very pleased with you and yours. Rule wisely by Carrick's side. Work to find out who else has been working against us and deal with them accordingly."

Alana bowed her head and murmured "My Lady," in response.

"Daren, Chosen of Mine, please stand. Ula, join your human," she called.

Ula stepped forward and stood by Daren's right hand side. Daren looked at Lady Daire, waiting patiently for her to speak.

"You have both been wonderful," she said to them. "You have led your companions through the Earth Quarter and found the *Tarian y Ddaear*. Hold it above your heart and I will transport it to Bridd where it will await your arrival back in Charon."

Daren started to lift the shield but then hesitated.

"What is it, Daren? Speak freely," said Lady Daire.

"Will it be safe? I mean, we've only just found it and it's one of the things we need. How will it be safe until we return to Charon?" he asked.

"Ever worrying, aren't you?" Lady Daire smiled at him. "*Tarian y Ddaear* will be safe inside a monolith in the town square of Bridd. To everyone else, it will only look like an engraving of the shield, but they will all know you have been successful. Do it now."

Without any hesitation this time, Daren raised the shield towards his heart and held it there. With a flash of green light, it disappeared and Daren lowered his arms.

"It is done," sighed Lady Daire. "Well done, all of you. I think it is time you head back to your world, time is indeed moving on and it is Lughnasadh tomorrow."

Marella gasped, "Lughnasadh? But I thought that was still ages away."

"Time moves differently, little one," replied Lady Daire. "Take today and this evening; spend it with King Carrick and High Priestess Alana, but tomorrow you must journey onwards to the Air Portal."

Lady Daire looked around the clearing at the bent heads of her Gnomes, at her newly appointed, bemused looking, King Carrick, and her proud High Priestess Alana, and knew things were going to settle down in the Earth Quarter now. Her enemy had been thwarted this time, but Lady Daire wondered if they had already been to the Air Quarter? This was something she would speak with Lord Adaryn about.

"Fare thee well, all of you," she said. "For hearth and home, you have my blessing. For you and yours, you have my blessing." With those words, she faded from sight.

Everyone was silent for a moment before the talking started. Everyone was talking about the visit Lady Daire had paid; no one said anything about ex-King Ghobe.

Carrick looked at the others and smiled, still a bit befuddled about what had just happened. "Come home with me," he said. "I have a bottle of fermented raspberries I can hear calling my name and I'd be honoured to share it with you."

"That's all well and good, King Carrick," said Alana, putting a slight emphasis on his title, "But what about your loyal subjects?"

"Erm, everyone can go home and take today as a holiday," announced

King Carrick to the crowd.

The crowd cheered and quickly dispersed, heading home to share the news there was a new King of the Gnomes, appointed by Lady Daire herself, to any who hadn't been there.

The Chosen companions and Alana followed Carrick back to his home. It wasn't as grand as King Ghobe's had been, but it suited Carrick perfectly.

"Will you move into King Ghobe's house?" asked Lani as she looked around.

"I don't want to. Will I have to, Alana?" he asked her.

"I don't see why. King Ghobe had to be given a home as he came from a different tribe. You've always had your home here, so here I think you should stay," answered Alana.

Everyone found a place to sit and relaxed for what felt like the first time in weeks.

"Lughnasadh tomorrow," said Marella quietly. "Time really is moving on."

"It is," agreed Carrick "and you still have a long way to go. You can count on help from the Earth Quarter though, from here on in." He walked around the group, handing out wooden cups and filling it with raspberry juice.

Kai took a sip from his and started coughing and had to wipe his eyes. "This is unlike any raspberry juice I've ever tasted," he laughed.

"This is fermented raspberries," explained Alana "and it has a very high alcohol content, so I'd be careful if I were you. You don't want a hangover as you make your way back to the Earth Portal tomorrow."

Everyone laughed as Kai took another sip, a careful one this time, now that he knew what to expect. A light tea was quickly made and shared amongst everyone and the time passed comfortably as the evening fell and they all retired.

~ 27 ~

At first light, Marella awoke, unsure for a moment where she was. She looked around the room and felt the warmth of Nixie by her feet. Lying across the room was Lani, snoring gently. Shaw was sat on the windowsill, his head still tucked under his wing.

Marella lay there for a moment, thinking back over the events of yesterday. "Well, that's Earth done," she thought, "and today is Lughnasadh."

Lughnasadh was the Festival of Fruits, or the First Harvest; and was the time to celebrate the first of the three harvest celebrations. Marella wondered if all the decorations were up in the villages and what they looked like this year. She remembered last year, the colours chosen were deep orange and a golden yellow. Marella felt a wash of homesickness flow over her as she thought back to how beautiful Ilyn had looked.

She stirred, sitting upright. It was no good lying abed, they had places to go. She nudged Nixie with her foot.

"*It's time to wake up, my lovely,*" she thought to him.

Nixie snuggled further into the bed and tried to ignore her.

"*Come on, lazybones. If I have to get up then so can you.*" Marella threw the covers on top of Nixie, knowing he would wriggle out from underneath them in moments.

A muffled snort of laughter came from Lani's bed and Marella turned to look at her, raising one eyebrow in question.

"You really know all the tricks with your Partner, don't you?" Lani giggled.

"We've been together for a while now," grinned Marella. "I'm sure you know tricks to get Shaw moving too."

Lani chuckled at Marella, "I do, but throwing the covers over him isn't one of them." Lani dragged herself out of bed and went over to the washbasin so she could wash away the sleep. Getting her hands wet, she turned and flicked water in Shaw's direction. "This is, though."

With a screech and a dirty look, Shaw shook down his feathers to get rid of the water droplets before flying out of the open window, leaving the girls' laughter behind.

The smell of bacon and eggs permeated the air as the girls got ready, making them hasten in order to go and have something to eat.

When they arrived downstairs, Kai and Daren were already sat around the table as Carrick bustled around cooking bacon, eggs, sausages, and mushrooms.

"Wow, thanks Carrick," said Marella as she sat at the kitchen table, nodding her thanks to Kai who passed her a peppermint tea.

"At least you'll leave the Earth Quarter with a full belly," he said, slapping at his own stomach.

"Shouldn't someone be doing your cooking for you, now you're King?" asked Lani, subtly prodding at Carrick.

Carrick turn a ruddy shade of red before blowing out his breath, and shaking his wooden spoon at Lani. "Now don't you start with me, young lady," he said, sternly before a grin broke across his face at the laughter of the others.

"I have to get used to this King business," he continued, still laughing. "What am I supposed to do? By the Earth, what was Lady Daire thinking when she appointed me?"

"I'm guessing she was thinking you're strong and wise, have discipline, already proven how loyal you are, and you work well with Alana," said Kai, ticking off each point on his fingers, much to the delight of the others.

"There, that told you," said Lani before stuffing a piece of sausage in her mouth.

Carrick just looked at Kai, open-mouthed in surprise. "Well, I, er, erm, I don't know what to say," he blustered.

Daren just laughed at Carrick. "I'd give up now. I would say Lady Daire knew exactly what she was doing."

"I think you'll make a magnificent King," said Marella. "Feel free to call on us anytime you want."

Carrick gave a tender smile to all of the companions. "Thank you, all of you. I feel honoured to have spent this time with you and your amazing Partners. You will always be welcome here in the Earth Quarter."

"And that goes from me as well," said Alana as she entered the kitchen, smiling as she did so.

"We're going to miss you," said Marella, looking fondly at the pair.

"We will miss you too, but your time here – for now - is done and it's time to move on. You don't want to keep Lord Adaryn waiting, now do you?" laughed Alana.

"True enough," agreed Daren. "So, what's the plan?" he asked, looking around.

"For a start, I intend to finish my breakfast," said Marella, winking at Daren.

"Right, thanks for that, Marella," he said, laughing at her. "So, anyone else? Anyone have any *good* ideas?"

"I actually think Marella's idea is a good one," said Kai, defending Marella. "We need to finish our breakfast before moving out. We're back on travel rations after this until we reach the Air Quarter."

"And sleeping on the ground," said Lani, grumpily, which just made everyone laugh.

"You'll be back in a bed in no time," said Carrick. "I'm sorry we can't get you any closer to the Air Portal, but we have to remain a certain distance from each to ensure Elements are balanced."

"We will certainly accompany you to our Portal though," added Alana. "No need for us to leave each other just yet."

"That would be great, thank you both," said Daren.

"Come on now, eat your food. We still need to get sorted out," said Carrick to no one in particular before sitting down and digging into his own breakfast.

* * *

It was only a short while later when everyone had eaten all they could, had plenty to drink, and had packed all their belongings. Marella was sat by the small stream, saying goodbye, when she felt Carrick behind her.

"Come on, little one, it's time to go," he said to her.

"I know but I'm really going to miss this place… and you" she said, looking up at him. "You've been just like my Papa."

"And you have been like my daughter," he smiled "but now you have to continue your quest to return to your real Papa. You have the steadfastness of the Earth behind you now. The rest will fly by. Come now, I have a gift to give each of you." And with that he pulled her to her feet before leading the way back to the others.

When they reached the clearing, everyone was ready to go. When they saw Marella returning, they started to put their backpacks on.

"Wait a moment, before you do that, we have a gift for you," said Alana to them. "Today is Lughnasadh and you will be missing your villages' celebrations. You won't really have much of one yourself, being on the road. So I've packed a small feast for you all, to remember us by, when you have your own Lughnasadh festival on the road.

Alana handed Daren a bundle of food which was all wrapped up in cloth which he placed into his trundle truck, underneath the waterproof cover.

"Thank you Alana, Carrick," he said as the others nodded their heads in thanks.

"I've also made a little something for each of you, to remember your time in the Earth Quarter," said Carrick, before handing each of them a small, wrapped present, tied with string.

The companions all looked at each other before carefully unwrapping Carrick's presents. Daren was the first to reach the present inside and he held up the miniature carving Carrick had made for him. It was a perfect replica of himself and Ula standing side by side.

"Wow, Carrick," he said, his eyes shining, "this is amazing. Thank you so much, I love it."

Kai had finished unwrapping his and opened it to see his carving of him and Kenna. He was sat cross-legged on the ground and Kenna was on her back paws, with her front paws resting on his shoulders. He coughed to get rid of the lump that had appeared in his throat before he was able to speak. "Thank you Carrick, I will treasure this always."

Lani's eyes were already very bright as she saw what Daren and Kai had received. With trembling fingers she lifted her carving out so everyone could see. There was Lani, perfect in every detail; right down to the crossbow hung over her shoulder. And on her other shoulder, with one wing outspread around the back of Lani's head, was Shaw.

She lifted her eyes, which were now leaking tears onto her cheeks, to Carrick. "Thank you so much," she whispered, holding the carving carefully.

Everyone turned to Marella and she took a deep breath before retrieving her carving from the wrapping. She lifted it out and let out a small yelp. There, in the palm of her hand was herself in fighting stance with her staff. Nixie was by her side and looked ready to take on anyone and anything.

She looked at Carrick but was unable to speak past the tears clogging her throat. He just coughed a bit gruffly before smiling at her, his own eyes suspiciously bright.

"How did you manage to get these done so quickly?" asked Daren, still looking at his own carving.

"I've been working on them for a while," said Carrick, "but it's amazing how it can go when you have the blessing of Lady Daire," he finished with a wink.

Marella moved over to Carrick and dropped to her knees before him. She pulled him into a hug which he gladly returned. "Thank you for everything," she said to him, before kissing him on the cheek.

Carrick raised his hand and lightly caressed her cheek. "It's been a pleasure and an honour," he said, looking at all of them. He gently pulled himself free of Marella's arms. "Come child, it's time to go."

At the same moment, everyone started to move about. They all made sure their gifts were tucked away safely in their backpacks, and that their trundle trucks were ready to go. After they finished their preparations, the companions looked at Daren. He smiled back at them, "Right then, let's go."

Carrick took the lead, with Alana by his side. Daren followed them, with Lani, Kai, and Marella all coming along behind.

"*Are you okay, little one?*" questioned Nixie to Marella, from his perch on top of the trundle truck.

"*I'm fine,*" she replied, "*just a bit sad to be leaving Carrick and Alana, that's all.*"

"You're leaving them physically only, remember that," said Nixie. *"They will always be in your heart, the same as you will always be in theirs. Nothing lasts forever, but it isn't gone forever either. The wheel turns and life moves on. People will come and go in your life; however, for those that are true, a part of them will always remain with you."*

Marella acknowledged his words by sending a flow of love towards him. He was so wise at times; she didn't know how he always managed to find the right words to soothe her soul.

* * *

It took them a while to reach the Portal because none of them felt like rushing. They took a slow amble through the forest, making light conversation as they did. However, all too soon they arrived.

There was time for one last round of hugs, goodbyes, and tears before Carrick made the announcement they should go. "It is time for us to say goodbye for now, but know we will come when you call us. Thank you for helping us bring balance back to the Earth Quarter and we wish you well as you move on."

"Thank you for all your help and wisdom, we couldn't have done it without you," said Daren on behalf of the companions.

"Sure you would," smiled Alana, "you're the Chosen, it just might have been more difficult, that is all."

Her words made everyone chuckle, so it was with light hearts they crossed the Earth Portal and returned to Wraidd Elfennol at the same place where they had originally come from.

~ 28 ~

After they had crossed through the Portal and their feet were planted on the soil of Wraidd Elfennol, they took a moment to get their bearings.

Lani looked back at the Portal, but couldn't see Carrick or Alana. "Do you think they've gone already?" she asked sadly.

"No, I think they're still there, but we can't see them because of the magic involved," replied Daren, readjusting his belt. "Come on, let's move. We can walk for a good way today before setting up camp. Lani, do you know where the Air Portal is located?"

Lani shook her head, her blonde hair flying loose as she did so. "No, not really, I'm hoping for some inspiration as we travel," she laughed.

The others grinned at her as they readied themselves to start on their march, once more searching for an elusive Portal.

"Nixie, I know Carrick and Alana said that it was Lughnasadh, but did they mean there, here, or both?" Marella questioned.

"It is Lughnasadh here, little one," answered Nixie. *"It is the beginning of the month of Awst."*

"We didn't lose too much time in the Earth Quarter then?"

"No, not much, it may be different for each Quarter though, remember."

Marella nodded her head as she marched along, lost in her thoughts.

They walked for some days before Lani thought she recognised some of the landmarks surrounding them. Lani took a deep breath in, lifting her nose into the air, for the smells of the woods she was familiar with. She looked around her, trying to find her bearings so they would know which direction to move in.

"Shaw, would you mind going high for me? I don't recognise where we are," she asked him.

With a small screech, Shaw flew high into the sky, catching the updrafts with ease. The companions watched him hover above them as his head turned this way and that. Instead of just telling Lani which way to go, he drifted down to earth and landed on Lani's shoulder. The others crowded in so they might all hear.

Shaw rubbed his head over Lani's cheek as she spoke to him, trying to find out what was wrong.

"Shaw, answer me, my love" she said aloud. "Where are we? What have you seen that upsets you so? Answer me so I may help you."

Visibly upset, Shaw huddled in closer to Lani, seeking reassurance. Lani looked around helplessly at the others. Marella came forward and stroked her finger down Shaw's head and back.

"Shaw, you are upsetting Lani by not answering her. What is it you saw up there? We need to know," she said to him on a path that also included Nixie and

Lani.

"Come on, Shaw. You can do this. Whatever it is can't be that bad. We're all here and we can deal with it together," encouraged Nixie.

"Please Shaw," begged Lani, her mental voice tremulous.

Shaw turned his head from where he had tucked it into Lani's body and looked at Nixie. *"It's broken,"* he said, *"it's all broken"*.

Marella and Lani looked at each other, confused. Nixie looked at Shaw and then to Marella. *"I think we'd better head off in that direction,"* he said. *"I feel this is something we should all see, although going from Shaw's reaction, it's not going to be good."*

* * *

They set off with Kai and Daren taking turns helping with Lani's trundle truck, whilst she spent time comforting Shaw.

After a while, Shaw started speaking to Lani, using a path the others could hear. *"Everywhere is broken, Lani. The tree where I cracked my shell, where I learnt to fly, my family's home. It's gone, broken. It's not there. I couldn't see it."*

Everyone looked at each other, what could Shaw mean? It hastened their steps as they tried to rush onwards to find out what had happened.

They arrived at the outskirts of a village and a scene of destruction greeted them. Buildings had been toppled over or collapsed. Great fissures were in the roads and pathways. A layer of dust coated everything and caught in their throats as they surveyed the area.

"What on earth…?" gasped Daren.

Ula gave a bark and looked back at him.

"I think you have it spot on, Daren," said Kai, quietly. "I think this was Earth shaking up. The Elements must be really out of balance for this to happen."

The others looked around, wondering at the strength of Earth it would have taken to cause this much damage.

"Look, there are some people," cried Lani, running towards them and leaving her companions behind.

They all ran after her, with their trucks bouncing along behind, as she headed towards what looked like had been the main part of the village.

"I know this village," exclaimed Lani, panting as she ran. "This is one of the outlying villages of Alaw, called Cwmwl."

They came to an abrupt halt in front of a small group. The people there were covered in the same fine layer of dust that covered the buildings and looked full of despair.

"What's happened here?" asked Lani to the one closest to her.

"The ground underneath my feet started to rumble, way down deep. It sounded like a thunderstorm, loud claps of thunder, but there wasn't a cloud in the sky. We all ran outside and saw the buildings rippling and the ground heaving and rolling. Everyone was running around, screaming. It didn't last long, only a few minutes, but this is what we've been left with," explained one of the men, whilst the others nodded in agreement.

"Has help been sent? Can we help in any way?" asked Daren.

"Alaw have been sending food and water for us, whilst we've been busy trying to put everything back to rights. It's just taking time," said another man.

"You can't really help, but thank you for the offer," said one of the women of the group. "If you're who I think you are, then the four of you are needed by all the Elements, not just our village."

Shaw gave a screech from up high and the woman raised her head to look at him. "My apologies, hawk. The eight of you are needed."

"That is Shaw and he accepts your apology," said Lani. "If we are not needed here, then we will continue on our way. Like you say, we need to reach the Air Portal. Do any of you know where it is?"

The group murmured amongst themselves before shaking their heads. "If I were you, I'd stop by the main Air Lodge on your way. Elder Erion may be able to help you."

"Thank you, that's where we're heading now," said Lani. "Take care and good luck."

Walking carefully through the devastation, they picked their way through the rubble, making small detours where necessary, to reach the other side of the village.

All were lost in their thoughts as they continued walking. "The whole area is damaged," said Kai.

"Yes, it will take a while to put things right there. I wonder if anyone from Bridd is helping them, I forgot to ask," said Daren.

There is a party from Bridd arriving tomorrow which includes builders and earth shifters, as well as Gardeners. Cwmwl will soon be restored, although the trees and surroundings will take a bit longer. New ones will be encouraged to grow by the Gardeners, but it will still take time," said Ula on a broad path.

"Come on everyone, let's keep moving. We should make it to Alaw in a couple of days, if we keep up a good pace. Let's go and then we can speak with Elder Erion directly," suggested Lani.

"We'll follow your lead, we're in your Quarter now," said Daren with a smile.

Lani straightened her shoulders and took one last look behind her at the village in the distance. "Let's do this," she said and, with an air of determination, started to pull her trundle truck in the direction of Alaw.

* * *

For two days they kept walking at a steady pace, only stopping for short breaks or overnight stays. The conversation was sparse amongst the companions as they preferred to keep their breath for walking. Messages were flying to and from the Partners as they tried to get information on events that had occurred during their time in the Earth Quarter.

Using a broad path once more, Shaw told everyone what he had heard. *"The earthquake was centred here, which is why Cwmwl was hardest hit, but it seems ripples were felt all over the island. Everyone is reporting some sort of damage, but most of it is being dealt with by the villages themselves. Charon has become the place where all coordination is taking place, although Messengers from all over Wraidd Elfennol are helping out as much as they can."*

"What are Messengers?" asked Kai. "I've heard of them, but I'm never sure what it is exactly that they do."

"There are two types of Messengers," explained Lani. "First you have the physical ones, who are runners. They run from village to village, carrying a pouch that you put your note in and you pay them to take it for you. Then you have the Silent Messengers. These are based in the Air Lodges in the five main villages and they can send messages to each other mentally. It's a quicker way to send messages, but is harder work for the Messenger. And usually, you still need the runners anyway, to reach the outlying villages."

She took a breath and then carried on. "I was training to be a Silent Messenger myself. I still have a year of training to finish though. Who knows what will happen now."

"I'm sure you'll be okay," reassured Marella. "I know you're missing the training now, but surely that's something you can return to. After all, you're doing this as Lord Adaryn's Chosen, so he obviously sees something in you."

"Let's hope so," muttered Lani.

Daren nudged her with his shoulder as they continued to walk. "I agree with Marella. You have Lord Adaryn's backing as His Chosen. You'll be able to do what you want after this." He grinned at her and she grudgingly smiled back. It was hard to be petulant when Daren was around.

~ 29 ~

Before long, they had arrived in Alaw. As they entered from the North side of the village, people would stop and greet Lani. She would smile shyly at them all, while Shaw screeched his greetings from on high.

"Whereabouts will your family be?" asked Marella, as they walked along one of the main paths towards the Air Lodge at the centre of Alaw.

"I'm hoping they will be here," replied Lani, "but we don't actually live in Alaw itself. We live in one of the smaller villages, called Awel Ysgafn. I know Shaw has spoken with Cari, my mother's Partner, to say we are here."

"Do you think they'll be able to get here before we have to leave again?" asked Kai.

"I certainly hope so, but I'm not counting on it. They know what I'm doing and they will understand if I don't see them. It's not like we're here on holiday," said Lani. "Look, there's the Air Lodge."

The others looked over to where Lani was pointing. Alaw's Air Lodge looked similar to the other Lodges, a roundhouse with a pointed thatched roof. The support beams of the entrance way were covered in carvings, similar to those Marella had seen on the Water Lodge in Charon.

As they approached the Lodge, Erion came out of the door. A smile lit up his face as he saw them and he held his hands out in greeting. "I am so pleased to see you. Come in, come in and refresh yourselves," he said in his modulated voice.

They parked their trundle trucks next to the Lodge and made their way inside. Marella looked around in interest, but the layout of the Lodge was the same as the Lodge she had been in. The difference lay in the woods used and the carvings and colours on the walls.

Erion noticed her looking about and smiled at her. "Not much of a difference is there, Marella?" he asked.

She shook her head, still looking around. "No, not really. I guess I thought it would be completely different."

"It was done this way intentionally," Erion explained. "All the Lodges are built in the same way, so we all know what goes where, no matter where we are. The differences occur in how each Lodge is decorated. Here, the wood we have used is Alder and Birch as both of these woods hold a special place in Lord Adaryn's heart. The colours we use are pastel shades of yellow, blue and grey. This way, it becomes the Air Lodge you see before you."

"And the carvings?" queried Marella, "What animals do you have in those?"

Erion gave a small chuckle. "I thought you'd be interested in those. Your mother told me how you were fascinated with the Water carvings at

Charon."

Marella felt uncomfortable with the mention of her mother. The others, knowing how she felt, directed the conversation away from that.

"So what animals are carved here then?" asked Kai, giving Marella a sympathetic look as he tried to distract Erion.

"We have badgers, bulls, and squirrels on the Earth Lodge in Charon," said Daren to Kai, taking up the baton of distraction.

Erion chuckled, but let the focus move away from Marella. "Here in Alaw, the most common carvings are birds. We have the red-shouldered Hawk, like our friend Shaw up there. We also have owls, falcons, magpies, and even bats. They are all representative of Air."

Lani gave a shudder, "I'm so glad that Shaw wasn't a bat."

"*You would have loved me even if I was, heart of mine,*" Shaw thought to her.

Erion led them through the dining area where he busied himself getting cups and saucers, jugs of water, and biscuits to put on the table before them.

"You would have loved Shaw even if he had been a bat, Lani," said Erion, looking at her when she laughed.

"That's what he's just told me," she explained.

Erion gave a smile as he carried a tray of cups to the table. "I thought he might. Never shy in giving his opinion, is our Shaw."

"Actually, I thought he was the quiet one, just like Lani," said Marella in surprise.

"If he's been quiet, it's only because he's happy with the way things are going," said Erion. "Lani will tell you he can be quite vocal if he's upset over something."

Lani nodded in agreement. "He has been rather quiet so far. Not to worry though, he's perfectly okay."

They all sat down and helped themselves each to a large glass of fresh water. Taking a plate, Daren helped himself to some of the freshly baked biscuits, still warm to the touch. He took a deep breath in, smelling their rich, buttery aroma which intoxicated his senses.

"Watch out everyone, Daren's going to inhale them all," joked Kai, grabbing a biscuit and taking a bite out of it.

Everyone laughed, including Daren. "I can't help it," he said, "they smell so good."

"They do indeed," agreed Erion. "We shall have to thank Taren for them."

"Taren is Second," explained Lani before anyone could ask. "She is Partnered with Vail"

"What kind of bird is Vail?" asked Daren, still sniffing appreciatively over the biscuits.

Erion laughed. "Vail isn't a bird, Vail is a dog. You see, Taren is strong in both Air and Earth, so her Partner is appropriate for her."

Just then, a handsome mongrel trotted into the room. His fur was short and bristly, a beautiful, rich caramel colour, from the tip of his nose to start of his tail. The rest of his tail though, was as black as night.

"Speaking of Vail, here he is. Taren must be close behind as well," said Erion, nodding his head to Vail.

"Greetings to the Chosen of the Lords and Ladies. The Partners of Air all send their blessings to you." Vail spoke on the broad path so they could all hear. The companions all bowed their heads in acknowledgement whilst the Partners each made their own greetings.

"If you will follow me, I will show you to where you can rest and refresh yourselves before your journey starts again." With those words, he turned around and left the room, the rest of the Partners following him.

"Come now, your Partners will be well looked after. Take your repast, this will tide you over until the evening meal," encouraged Erion.

A tall, willowy woman gracefully entered the room, almost seeming to float instead of walk. Her voice was low and melodious as she introduced herself. "Hello, Chosen. I am Taren. If you need anything whilst you are here, please let me know."

Lani stood up and went over to Taren where they embraced. Taren kissed the top of Lani's head before lifting Lani's chin up with a finger so she could look into her eyes. "How are you, my lovely?" she asked Lani. "I hope the Earth Quarter was kind to you."

Lani smiled and reassured Taren. "It was hard at first, especially when the wave hit me. I had no idea about that but everyone helped me. We made some fantastic friends whilst we were there."

Taren gave a small laugh before putting her arm around Lani's shoulders. "Only you could go off on a life-changing quest and come back talking about the friends you have made."

Lani blushed and looked down at the floor.

Daren rose to his feet and approached them. He held his hand out to Taren. "Hello, Taren," he said. "I am Daren, Chosen of Earth. Lani has proven herself to be both loyal and capable on our quest, and can now call the King of the Gnomes and their High Priestess, a friend. I wouldn't call that insignificant. I am proud to know Lani and am more than happy to follow her lead."

Marella and Kai looked at each other, open-mouthed, following Daren's statement. Lani looked at him in wonder and Taren just smiled. "You are quite right, Chosen of Earth. Having friends and people you can rely on is most important, especially on a quest such as this. Please accept my apologies, Lani, Daren."

Daren nodded his head before returning to his seat and picking up one of the biscuits he had discarded. He wouldn't look at Marella or Kai, instead concentrating on his plate.

Lani squeezed Taren's hands, "Of course you're forgiven." She turned to the others and introduced Taren to them. "This is my aunt Taren; she's my mother's sister. She has helped me so much in the past."

Marella saw a faint pink flush spread across Daren's face and neck as he heard that Taren was related to Lani. Nevertheless, he raised his head and looked at Taren. "Merry meet, Taren," he said, with a wry grin on his face.

Taren laughed and returned the greeting. "Do not feel embarrassed about standing up for my niece, Daren, even if you did mistake the meaning behind my words. I am pleased to find out Lani has such good friends with her."

Everyone laughed and the atmosphere relaxed as Lani sat back down, pulling Taren into a chair next to her.

"We have called for a meeting this evening with the other Elders so we can all keep up to date with what has happened. This way, we can fill you in on what's happening as well. Is that agreeable with you?" Erion asked Daren.

Daren chuckled as he replied to him. "It's fine with me, but it is Lani you must speak to. We are in her Element now, and as such, she is the leader of our group."

Erion started at Daren's words and looked at Lani who blushed but raised her chin defiantly. Erion smiled when he saw this and nodded to himself. "Very well then – Lani, is the meeting agreeable with you?" he asked.

Lani looked at the others, lingering on Marella. Daren and Kai both nodded and carried on eating.

"Marella?" questioned Lani, in her soft voice, "Is that okay with you?"

Marella raised her eyes and looked at Lani. She shrugged her shoulders, trying to appear casual. "It's fine, Lani. We need to have this meeting."

Lani bit her lip before answering Erion. "That will be fine, Erion. What time do you need us there and where do you want us to stay in the meantime?"

"You are more than welcome to use the guest rooms here, unless there is somewhere else you'd rather go?" asked Erion. "And the meeting has been set for sunset."

"We will stay here then, for now," said Lani, "and we'll see you at the meeting."

At that, Erion stood up. "As much as I would love to stay and talk with you, there are things I must attend to. Take your ease and make yourselves comfortable. I look forward to seeing you all later this evening." He left the room with a cheery wave.

"What about you, Taren?" asked Lani. "Are you able to stay for a while?"

"I am at your disposal, Lani-love," said Taren with a smile.

"Excellent," smiled Lani. "Please fill me in on what's been happening since we all left."

Everyone listened to Taren as she explained how the weather had become unpredictable. "The Earth Gardeners have their work cut out for them as they try to ensure the crops aren't damaged and we will have enough food for the winter," she said. "Everyone from every village is helping as we never know what's going to happen next. The earthquake that hit Cwmwl came as a huge surprise."

"But what about the Weavers?" questioned Marella. "Surely they have had some warning of what's going to happen?"

"Oh, they have, Marella. All of the Weavers are constantly scrying in their chalices, trying to find answers to what is going to happen next and where, but the waters are murky. To hear them talk, it's almost as if someone is deliberating obstructing their efforts. They are not a happy bunch of people right now."

"Oh," said Marella, slumping back in her chair.

"Marella, why don't you try?" suggested Kai in a soft voice.

Marella looked at him questioningly. "What good will that do, if all the Weavers can't see anything? I won't be able to see anything either."

"Don't be so sure," said Kai. "After all, you do have a slight advantage. You're the Chosen of Water, as well as a Weaver, and you only have the one Element which makes you stronger in it."

Lani nodded in agreement with Kai's words. "It's worth a go, Marella, surely?" she encouraged.

Marella looked at Daren to see what he thought and could see clearly from the look on his face he too thought it was a good idea.

"Ok, I'll try," she said before looking at Taren. "Is there somewhere I can go where there is free-flowing water?"

"Of course, there's a small stream just behind this Lodge. Is that enough?" asked Taren.

"Yes, it's not the amount of water I need, but the essence which helps me – the sounds, the feel, it's all part of it," explained Marella. "I may as well try now," she said. "It's as good a time as any."

She stood up to get her silver chalice out of her backpack and headed towards the back door. She heard a chair scraping along the floor and looked back, expecting to see Daren, but instead, it was Kai who was standing up.

"I'll come with you and make sure you don't fall in," he laughed.

"You don't have to…" started Marella, before stopping when she saw Daren shaking his head. She cocked her head to one side as she looked at him. "What's the matter, Daren. You know I'll be fine."

"I know you will but I'd also prefer it if you allowed Kai to go with you. Who knows how deep you'll be going with this one and Nixie isn't here. Please Marella."

Marella nodded before looking at Kai. "Thank you, Kai, I'd appreciate your company."

Kai grinned wryly as they both walked towards the door. "Like you had any choice," he laughed. "Daren knows how to get you to agree to anything."

Marella smiled, "That's his advantage of growing up with me. He knows what to say to make me listen, even if I don't want to."

"Is it so hard, me being here with you?" asked Kai, somewhat regretfully.

Marella wondered at his tone as she answered him. "It's not hard at all, I like spending time with you. It's just that I won't be very good company whilst I'm under, and most people don't want to be around someone who's not answering them."

"I'm not most people, Marella," said Kai. "I enjoy spending time with you and I wouldn't have come if I didn't want to."

She smiled at him. "Thank you Kai."

* * *

They found the stream and Marella located a spot where she could rest. "I suggest you get comfortable too, I don't know how long I'll be."

Kai nodded and looked around for a spot where he could keep an eye on Marella, but not be too close so he disturbed her, and sat down. He watched her get some water in her chalice, her lips moving silently as she did so, before settling down and becoming still.

He watched her for a while before shifting as one of his legs started to go numb. Marella didn't move, but sat there, staring into the chalice. After a while, Daren brought him out a cup of tea. "She still there?" he asked Kai.

"Yes, she's not moved much at all since she went under," Kai answered.

"She won't move much at all, but she will be stiff and wobbly when she comes out," warned Daren. "Do you want me to sit with her?"

"No, I'm fine," said Kai. "I'll stay with her."

Daren smiled to himself. "Okay Kai, that's fine. I'll send some more food and drink out for you both in a while."

Kai nodded to Daren, not really listening to him as he kept his focus upon Marella.

Time went by and still she didn't come out. Kai passed the time by thinking back over all the things that had happened to him and Kenna so far. None of it was what he had thought when he found out he had been Chosen. He grinned to himself. It's a wonder they all treated him so fairly considering what a jerk he had been when they first met.

Kai jumped as he felt a paw land on his knee and he looked down to find Nixie sat there.

"You were a jerk, but we knew you had a good heart." Nixie laughed, making Kai laugh too.

"Is she alright, Nixie? She's been gone a long time. I'm starting to worry." Kai asked the otter.

"She's fine; she's with Lady Erwyna right now. She has found out something she needs to tell everyone, but Lady Erwyna has kept her there whilst she breaks some news to her."

"What is it? Is Marella okay? Is her family alright?" asked Kai abruptly. He knelt down so that his face was more level with Nixie's. *"What's going on, Nixie. Tell me, please."* He felt like he was begging the otter to tell him more, but couldn't stand the thought that Marella was hurting.

Nixie reassured the distraught man. *"Kai, calm down. Marella will be fine, no one is hurt."* Once Kai has resumed his seat and had calmed down somewhat, Nixie began again.

"Lady Erwyna has kept Marella behind because She wanted to tell her that her mother will not be coming to the meeting tonight. Erwyna didn't feel it was something Marella should find out when Bradan walks through the door instead of Riva."

Kai took a quick breath in, shocked by Nixie's words. *"But it's a meeting of the Elders,"* he said, his words dazed. *"How can Riva not be there? Not only as Marella's mother, but as Elder of Water, surely she would need to be there. I don't understand."* Kai dropped his head into his hands.

"Marella has already been told she won't see her mother until the end of this quest," explained Nixie, *"so it won't come as a big surprise to her. She will still be hurt by it though, and will try to hide it by pretending she doesn't care."*

"But why, why won't she come? Has it been forbidden?" asked Kai, desperately trying to understand the reasoning behind it.

"According to Riva's Partner, Genna, Riva thinks it will be too big a distraction for Marella to see her, now considering how things were left."

"You mean with how Riva refused to even see her daughter leave, on a quest given to her by the Lords and Ladies of the Elements? One that she was Chosen for from the moment she was born? How would that be a distraction for her?" said Kai bitterly.

"Exactly, Genna actually thinks Riva is the one too afraid to face Marella right now, and has told Riva this but to no avail. Riva isn't the one coming here tonight, Bradan is."

"Poor Marella," thought Kai. Nixie jumped up and put his paws on Kai's shoulders, looking at him.

"Don't you dare feel sorry for her, Kai," said Nixie sternly. *"She won't thank you for it. Be there for her but don't pity her."*

Kai nodded his agreement to Nixie. *"I understand what you're saying, Nixie, but I still find it incredible her mother won't be here. After everything Daren's told me, I still thought she'd take the first opportunity that presented itself, but I guess I was wrong."*

"Daren and Lani already know too, Ula and Shaw have told them," said Nixie, *"so everyone should act normally when Marella comes back. She'll be out soon, so Daren should be bringing out a cup of tea for her any moment. Ah, here he is now,"* said Nixie, before moving to sit by Kai's side.

Sure enough, Daren was walking towards Kai holding two steaming mugs of tea, the scent of which wafted towards Kai.

"I have this for her, she should be back soon according to Ula," said Daren as he passed Kai the other mug. "Have you heard…" he trailed off.

"Yes, I have. Nixie has just told me. I can't believe it though."

"This is just like Riva. She has done this so many times as Marella was growing up. Honestly, I know she loves Marella, but she has a damn funny way of showing it," said Daren angrily.

"Nixie said Erwyna was keeping her behind so She could tell her Herself," said Kai.

"Well, that might make it a bit easier, but expect Marella to act as she is absolutely fine. I'm sure she won't be, however, she doesn't expect anyone to look beyond the mask she wears." Daren sighed loudly. "I'm going back inside. If she sees me here, she'll know we've been talking about her. See you shortly."

Daren walked away, his head drooping as thoughts for his best friend ran through his mind.

Kai sipped his drink, waiting for signs Marella was coming back from her Weaving. It wasn't long before she started to twitch, then shift where she sat, before raising her head and looking around. She stretched her body where she sat, lifting her arms upward, and moving her head from side to side to get rid of any kinks.

Kai slowly approached her. She still jumped upon seeing him, but it quickly changed into a smile when she saw the mug in his hands.

"I guess you had help knowing I'd be back soon," she smiled as she gratefully accepted the hot drink.

"Yes, Nixie told me and Daren brought it out," said Kai.

Marella blew over the top of the mug and looked at Kai, hiding her expression behind the mug. "Did Nixie tell you anything else?" she asked.

"Yes, he told me you were with Erwyna, and that I should stop worrying," said Kai, deliberating making no mention of anything else.

"You were worried about me?" said Marella.

"You were gone a long time so yes, I was starting to worry. Oh, I know you're more than capable, but I'm still allowed to worry" said Kai defensively.

"I'm not complaining," reassured Marella. "It's just… well, usually, no one is really there to worry."

"Well there should be," humphed Kai. "You shouldn't be doing this sort of thing when you're by yourself. There should be someone there to help you afterwards."

"Like by bringing me a hot drink?" asked Marella, laughing. "Kai, are you offering?"

Kai laughed too as he realised how stupid he sounded. "Yes, just like that," he agreed. "Look, I know you've been doing this for years by yourself, but I'd like to sit with you when you Weave, if that's alright? Just whilst we're on the quest. I really don't like the thought of you by yourself."

Marella looked thoughtful as she continued to sip her drink before draining it down to the dregs. "I think I'd like that," she said, smiling up at him.

Kai held his hands out to her and she slipped hers inside as he pulled her to her feet. She swayed as she stood and he grasped her waist. She put her hands on the top of his arms as she steadied herself.

"I guess I was gone for a while, then," she mused, before trying to take a step back. Kai tightened his hands on her waist so she couldn't move. She looked at him, an unspoken question upon her face.

Kai bent forward and kissed her forehead before resting his head on hers. "Welcome back Marella," he whispered, before stepping back and releasing her.

Marella touched her forehead where he had kissed her and smiled at him. "It's good to be back," she answered.

Kai bent down and picked up the mug she had left lying on the ground. "Come on, let's go inside and you can tell everyone what you saw."

Together, in comfortable silence, they walked back to the Air Lodge. Nixie trailed behind them, smiling to himself and very happy with the way things were turning out.

"*It's going well so far,*" thought Nixie, and felt a warm rush of acknowledgement from Kenna.

~ 30 ~

The rest of the day passed quickly and the Elders were soon being welcomed to the Air Lodge. Bradan had approached Marella as soon as he had arrived, taking her to one side where he had spoken to her. They shared a hug before rejoining the others, with Marella acting as though everything was normal.

The companions had decided Daren should be the one to explain everything as he had been the Leader of that part of the quest. As he stood there, sharing what had happened with the Elders; Kai reached over and touched the back of Marella's hand with a finger.

She looked over at him, cocking an eyebrow in question. "Are you okay?" Kai whispered softly.

Marella looked at him thoughtfully. "You know, I am fine." She laughed at the look of disbelief on his face. "No, I really am. I know you think I'm hiding it but I'm really not. I think I knew from the moment we left I wouldn't see her until this is over." She rubbed at her cheek while continuing, "I'm not anticipating seeing her until this is finished."

Kai said nothing but continued to look at her. "You know you have my support, don't you?" he asked, not wanting to disturb Daren.

Marella grasped his hand and squeezed it gratefully. "I do know and it means more to me than you realise. I have more support now than I have ever had," she said quietly.

They both sat there, listening to Daren finish their story, content with each other's company.

"And so we were escorted back to the Portal by the new King of the Gnomes and his High Priestess. They pass on their greetings to the Elders and also say if they are ever needed in any way, we just need to contact them," finished Daren, before sitting down and taking a sip of his drink.

"That's quite a tale," said Kegan, Elder of Fire.

"I assure you every word is true," replied Daren with quiet dignity.

"I'm not disputing that, young Chosen," said Kegan. "I'm just saying that it was quite an adventure and you've only just started."

"Yes we have, but we are ready to continue and will face whatever is thrown at us, together," said Lani, startling everyone. She stood up and faced them all.

"We have completed the first part of our quest and we have managed to retrieve the *Tarian y Ddaear*, but that doesn't mean we can relax. We are now on our way to the second part of our challenge, where we need to get the *Plu y Gryphon*. To do this, we need to find the Air Portal, travel through, and meet with Queen Paralda. Lord Adaryn has already said this will be difficult, just like everything else we are expecting to deal with.

We have taken time out of our travels to meet with you and bring you up to date with what has happened so far. Now I tell you, we will be leaving on the morrow, to try and find the Air Portal. We do not have time to waste and I, for one, do not want to spend this evening rehashing what has happened.

If you have any information that you think is relevant, and would like to share with us, then the timing is right. If you do not have anything, then please excuse us as we need to make preparations for our departure."

Lani stood with her hands on her hips as the silence in the room took on an awed feel. Daren, Kai, and Marella were all beaming with pride at how she had taken charge of the meeting. The Elders all looked stunned whilst Bradan was trying to hide his smile behind his hand.

"Now, see here, young lady," blustered Kegan, but Lani interrupted him.

"My apologies, Elder Kegan, if you think I have been rude. That was not my intention. I am not sorry though, for saying what needed to be said. I am presently the Leader of our group as we are in the Air Quarter. I also know my companions support me in what I say."

Marella stepped up and stood beside Lani, with Daren and Kai standing slightly behind them. It was at that time the Partners also made their feelings clear by joining the Chosen and presenting a united front to the Elders.

"We all know the meetings held between Elders can go on for some time. Time we do not have. Lughnasadh has already been and gone and we still have three more items to retrieve, and possible time delays," continued Lani. "So I say again, if you have information to share, please do so."

Lani looked around at the Elders, gauging their reactions to her words. Erion had a small smile on his face and he gave her a wink of approval. Bradan was smiling by this point and gave her a thumbs up. Demi had a sour look on her face and Lani could tell she disapproved of Lani's actions. Kegan had gone bright red in the face, matching his hair colour.

Demi stood up and faced the people in the room. "Whilst I may not approve of Lani's words or attitude, I do agree they need to be able to move on to their next quest," she said. "Daren, I would just like to inform you that a monolith is now in the Town Square at Bridd with an engraving of a shield and your names on there. I'm presuming that is a means for us all to know if you were successful or not."

Daren smiled at his Elder, "that's correct, Elder Demi. Lady Daire said she would be raising a monolith so the villages and everyone who goes there can see we were successful and also know what stage we are at."

Demi sat down, rearranging her skirts as she did so. Erion looked around and seeing no one else prepared to speak, stood up. He bowed his head to Lani before raising it and asking a question of her. "Lani, I know you know what you need to retrieve and who you need to speak with, but do you know where you need to go?"

Lani shook her head, "No, Elder Erion, I'm afraid we don't, which is one of the reasons why we don't have time to spare."

There was some grumbling at that point from the Elders before Bradan stood up and addressed Marella. "Didn't you say that you Wove to find the Earth Portal? Won't that help with this situation?"

Marella smiled at him as he sat back down. "I did Weave, yes," she confirmed, "but we were also told by Slade roughly where to look. He had a rhyme that once we deciphered; we knew we were in the right direction. Then it was just a case of looking and walking."

Lani spoke up once Marella had finished. "Slade told us it was in the 'North of the North' which made sense as it was the Earth Portal we were looking for and the corresponding direction of Earth is north. We are going to head east, away from the villages, as a starting point. I am hoping Marella will be able to confirm this once we are closer to our destination."

Erion nodded his head at her words, "Yes, that makes sense and is as good a starting point as any. Is there anything you will need to restock before you leave?"

Lani looked at the others who all shook their heads. "No thank you, Elder Erion. We were lucky enough to be well provided for by the Gnomes, so we aren't really running short of anything yet."

"Very well, at least let me provide you with some bundles of fresh food. You'll be on your own until you reach the Air Portal," said Erion.

"My thanks," said Lani, seconded by the others.

"Now, if there is nothing else, we would like to take our leave for the night," requested Lani.

Erion looked around the room and didn't see any dispute over the companions leaving.

"Goodnight then, Chosen. Sleep well and I shall see you in the morning before you leave," said Erion and they left the room.

* * *

"That went well," said Daren with a grin once they reached the stairs and started to climb them.

"Lani, you minx you," laughed Marella. "What happened in there? You surprised me."

Lani blushed and laughed at Marella. "Well, you said I was the Leader of this part. I figured it was time to show it."

"You certainly showed them," said Kai, chuckling. "Well done you, I'm proud of you."

Shaw wooshed silently past Lani's head before landing on a spindle at the top of the stairs. *"You need to get used to commanding meetings that way, dear heart, if you are meeting Queen Paralda as the Leader and Chosen of Air."*

"True, very true," acknowledged Lani.

At the top of the stairs, they split up and went to their separate rooms in order to prepare their things for leaving the next morning.

Marella checked her backpack before flopping down on the bed, her blue leather travel mug in her hands. She rubbed her fingers over the embossed designs and looked over to Nixie.

"Do you think they're all okay?" she asked him.

"I know if there was a problem, you'd be contacted," Nixie tried to reassure her.

"Hmm, that's not quite what I asked and you know it," said Marella.

Nixie curled around on the bed, getting comfortable for the night. *"If there was something, Bradan would have told you. I'm sure everyone is fine but missing you. Come on now, settle down. We have a walk in the morning so rest up."*

With those words, it appeared Nixie fell asleep instantly, his body relaxing into even breaths as he rested.

Marella replaced the mug into her backpack, and undressed for bed. She climbed beneath the covers, trying hard to still her mind even as her body relaxed. She could faintly smell the fresh flowers that had been placed in her room and hear the murmurs of other voices in the Lodge. As she lay there, falling slowly to sleep, she thought of Kai and his request to sit with her as she Wove. A smile curled her lips and she fell into a deep and dreamless sleep.

~ 31 ~

Early next morning, the companions were up with the sun. They moved around the Lodge, preparing their breakfasts and making sure they had everything packed and ready to go. They were sat in the kitchen, drinking a steaming mug of elderberry tea and talking about where they thought the Portal might be; when Erion came in to greet them.

"Good morning, Chosen. I hope you all slept well last night?" he queried.

"Very well, thank you," replied Lani with a smile. "I'm sure we'll all miss your beds when we're on the ground tonight."

Marella chuckled at Lani's words, knowing it was Lani who hated sleeping on the floor more than any of the others.

"I've arranged for some fresh food to be wrapped up and placed on top of your trundle trucks," Erion said to each of them. "When are you planning on leaving?"

"Round about now," said Lani. "As we are unsure where the Portal is, we need to get going so we have as long as possible to find it. As of now, we still have time, but we don't know how it will go on the other side."

"Ah, yes, I've heard about that," said Erion. "So it is true then? Time flows differently in the Quarters?"

"Yes, it's true. We didn't lose much time in the Earth Quarter, but there is no guarantee we won't lose months in one of them. So for each one, we need to make sure that we're not lollygagging."

"I wish you well then, and know that if you need anything, if I or any of us can be of any further assistance, please let me know," said Erion.

"We will," promised Lani.

They finished their last minute preparations and met outside. They readied their trundle trucks, said their goodbyes and Lani called out "Are we all ready?"

At the chorus of agreements, screeches, barks, and yips raised in reply, she grinned, her eyes twinkling in the morning light. "Well let's go then."

Lani started to move forwards, heading for the Eastern path out of the Alaw. She turned to look back just before they rounded a corner, and waved to Erion and Taren who were stood together, waving goodbye.

"I'm sorry you didn't have time to see your family," said Daren.

"It's fine, Daren, but thank you for saying so. It was probably for the best anyway. Taren will tell my mother I was there and I'm fine. If I had seen her, I would have burst into tears and that wouldn't have done me any good for my 'in charge' persona I was showing," she laughed.

"You are stronger than you realise," said Daren, "you need to have more confidence in yourself. We have and Lord Adaryn has, or he wouldn't have Chosen you."

Lani flushed and looked down and away from Daren. "Well, erm, thank you for saying," she stuttered.

Kai and Marella, walking behind them, shared a smile at their interaction, but didn't say anything.

* * *

They walked at a steady pace for the rest of the week, only stopping for light lunches before continuing on their way, changing positions so they all had a chance to speak with each other, when the path wasn't wide enough for them to all walk together. They set their camp up as late as possible and dismantled it as early as they could. They passed through villages where everyone seemed pleased to see them. They didn't see any further damage like they had at Cwmwl.

Seeing one village reminded Kai of the damage he had witnessed. "Do you know how things are going in Cwmwl?" he asked Lani.

Lani flashed him a smile as she continued to walk. "It's recovering well now. Most of the buildings are now rebuilt, with some adjustments. The Gardeners have been busy replanting and encouraging new growth, so it doesn't look so desolate now. Every Element has sent people out to help. Shaw's birth tree is still gone, but he lives with me now anyway. I think it was the shock of it that upset him the most."

Kai nodded his head, "I'm glad they're all okay. It's a lot of work for everyone. I wish we could have helped in some way."

"But we are helping, Kai, don't you see? The earthquake was caused by an imbalance in the Elements. We're trying to right that balance. So we may not be physically there rebuilding houses, but we are doing what we can to help, not just the people of Cwmwl, but everyone who calls Wraidd Elfennol their home."

"You are wise beyond your years when you believe in yourself," said Kai, smiling down at her like a proud older brother.

She laughed at him and took a deep breath, looking around her as they walked. "Isn't it beautiful here?" she asked, looking across at the Birch and Aspen trees that grew in plentiful supply. "I can't believe we're halfway through Awst and will be heading into Medi soon. The leaves will start changing soon. That's my favourite time of year."

"Yes, it does look beautiful when they turn, but it will mean colder nights for us," said Kai practically.

"Oh hush," she said, slapping at his arm. "Leave me with my dreamy notions will you!"

* * *

"We need to stop," called Nixie to everyone on their broad path.

Lani looked around to see what might be the problem and saw Marella had dropped to the ground. She left her trundle truck and raced back to where Marella was lying.

Daren sat down and pulled Marella into his arms, trying to make her comfortable. "What's the matter with her? Why didn't she say anything? Why didn't you say anything?" asked Kai sharply.

"We were fine," replied Daren, a bit defensively. "We were just walking and talking about where the Portal might be, when her eyes glazed over and she fell to the floor."

"Stop arguing, this isn't the time," barked Nixie. He climbed onto Marella's lap and placed his paws on her head. The others watched in silence as Nixie's body twitched whilst Marella's lay in perfect stillness.

"Daren, raise the shield in a circle around us," said Ula, urgency in her voice.

Daren looked around to find Ula standing guard, with Kenna by her side. "But what about Marella?" he asked, "I can't just leave her on the ground."

Kai moved forward. "I'll take her, you do your thing – and quickly."

Daren placed Marella into Kai's arms, then drew a circle in the dirt, enclosing them. "Lani, please call Shaw down. I don't want him out of the shield. Quickly, please."

Within seconds Shaw was on Lani's shoulder. By now, Ula and Kenna were visibly shaking, their bodies taut. The hackles were raised on Ula's shoulders and Kenna's fur was standing on end.

Daren dropped to one knee, clapped his hands together with a deep booming noise, and slowly raised them high into the air, joining them together over his head. As he did so, a radiant shield rose into the air and enclosed them.

Daren lowered his arms and shook them out. "That should hold us for a while," he said. "Now, does someone want to explain what is going on?" he asked exasperatedly.

"Marella is under attack," said Kenna to them all.

Kai looked at his Partner, disbelief on his face. "What do you mean, under attack?"

"What part of 'under attack' do you not understand, Kai?" asked Kenna abruptly.

Kai looked down at Marella in his arms and tightened his grip. "How can we help?" he queried. "There must be something we can do. How do we fight this?"

"Fight is what you must do, however, it won't be on the earthly plane, but a mental one," explained Shaw.

Everyone looked at him as he told them what to do. *"Remember how you all joined to fight the Elemental? Do the same, now, quickly."*

Everyone moved into position so that they were all joined, Kai holding Marella's right hand whilst Daren grasped her left. Their Partners made their own, smaller circle in the middle.

"Clear your minds and concentrate on Marella," said Shaw. He waited until he saw they were ready. *"Now, follow me."*

Kai opened his eyes to see they were still in their circle, but were now in a desolate wasteland, devoid of any life. He looked down and saw that, although the Partners were in their circle, Marella had vanished.

"Where's Marella gone?" he asked, raising his voice to compete against the wind rising around them.

Everyone looked around before Nixie yipped to get their attention. *"There she is, come on, we need to help her."*

The wind continued to get stronger as they made their way over to where Marella lay. Before they could reach her, her body was lifted into the air, and she was swept inside a vortex. Her hair and clothes were being pulled in every direction; however, Marella was still, her head lolling forwards.

"Now what?" thought Kai as he looked up to Marella.

"What do we do now?" asked Daren, echoing Kai's thoughts.

"We need to get her out of there," replied Ula.

"But how?" questioned Lani. "How do we get her out of the vortex?"

"Lani, you can get her out. The gift from Lord Adaryn was the ability to control wind storms. Think of slowing the vortex down, carefully, so that Marella drops slowly to the ground. You should be able to stop it spinning."

Lani gasped, "Shaw, I can't do that. What if I can't do it? What if I hurt Marella? Isn't there another way?"

Nixie bumped into Lani's legs, knocking her and making her stumble. *"You can do this, Lani; you just need to trust yourself. If you can't, then trust Lord Adaryn. We NEED to get Marella down and you're the only one who can help her here."*

Lani looked at Kai and Daren, who both gave her encouraging smiles. "You can do this," said Daren.

"Let's get Marella back," said Kai.

Lani squared her shoulders and took in a deep breath. *"I don't know what I'm doing,"* she said despairingly to Shaw on a private band.

Shaw landed on her shoulder and rubbed her cheek with his head. *"I am with you, Lani, always. We'll do this together. Now, raise your hands and concentrate on slowing that air down."*

Lani raised her hands towards the vortex and in her mind saw the air was slowing. She felt a weight on her mind, a headache starting between her eyes. "It's not slowing down," she cried.

"Concentrate," encouraged Kenna.

Focusing her will even more, she saw in her mind's eye Marella gently being lowered to the ground, the air swirling slower and slower around her.

"It's working," she heard Ula say to her.

Lani felt her arms start to tremble, her breath coming fast. She concentrated on the vortex and Marella, willing them with every part of her, to comply with her wishes.

"Daren, Kai, come over here and help Lani. She needs your strength," she heard Shaw say faintly.

She felt two hands on her shoulders and felt a rush of strength and determination run through her. Her arms steadied and her focus sharpened. She could now see the vortex was indeed slowing down and Marella was nearing the ground.

After a few heart stopping moments, Marella was finally back on land, and the vortex had dispersed.

"Well done, Lani, you did it," praised Kai as he gathered Marella back into his arms.

"How do we get back though?" asked Daren to Shaw.

"The same way we arrived here," Shaw replied, *"follow me."*

With a rush of displaced air, they disappeared from the wasteland, opening their eyes to see they were back in the forest clearing, Daren's shield still glimmering around them.

"Did we really go anywhere?" asked Daren as he looked around. "Is it safe to bring the shield down now?"

"Yes, beloved, you can drop it now," answered Ula, giving his hand a lick.

"In answer to your question, yes we really went somewhere. That was a province of Air," said Kenna.

"Marella," said Kai, stroking her hair from her face, "come back to us, you're safe now."

"I'll get some water," said Lani, hearing the gurgle of a stream nearby.

"I'll get a fire going. I think we need to have a rest before we go any further," said Daren to Kai, who nodded in agreement.

* * *

As Lani and Daren bustled around them, their Partners helping where they could, Kai stayed on the ground with Marella in his arms. He murmured to her, asking her to come back to him, telling her she was out of harm's way, that they missed her. Marella twitched, but showed no signs of waking. Kai carried on with his low encouragements as he watched Lani and Daren set up camp around him.

"Nixie, why won't she wake?" he asked the otter, who had stayed by Marella's side.

"She's scared. She'll be able to tell us when she wakes who attacked her but only

when she feels secure," answered Nixie. *"Keep on talking to her; I know she can hear you. I'll keep trying to reach her through our bond."*

By now, the camp was set. Lani had some water boiling over the campfire. She grated some ginger into a teapot and filled it with boiling water. She left it to steep before returning to Marella. Daren was sat on the ground, next to Kai, holding Marella's hand.

"Nixie says she is scared and that's why she won't wake up. We need to talk to her so she knows we're here," Kai explained.

Lani went to Marella's trundle truck and pulled some of the waterproof bedding out of the truck, before putting it down on a bed of rushes she had sorted at the same time as the water, near to the fire. She pulled out Marella's pillow and placed it on the bed. She put some blankets on the top to make it as comfortable as she could before turning to Kai.

"Lie her down on her bed, Kai. You'll go numb if you stay like that much longer, and this will give her a chance to move if she needs to."

Kai looked like he was prepared to argue when Daren gave him a smile. "Come on, Kai, we're not saying you have to leave her, but this will help you both."

Daren and Lani both moved away, giving Kai some space. Reluctantly, he lifted Marella's body gently onto the pallet Lani had made. He made sure she was comfortable before stretching out the kinks sitting on the ground had given him. He didn't want to admit it, but they had been right to move Marella.

He returned to Marella's side, holding her hand and continued to whisper reassurances to her. She began to move, thrashing her head from side to side. Nixie came over and climbed onto the pallet with her, lying on her legs. She seemed to calm down to some extent, but it wasn't long before she started to move about again.

"Daren, Lani, come here, I need you," called Kai. They both came over to see what was happening.

"She just started doing this. I'm afraid she's going to hurt herself," said Kai, worry evident in his face.

"Kai, you have done what you can. You need to let us help now," said Kenna.

Kai looked at Kenna who sent reassurance to him through their bond. *"That is how we can help her, Kai, with the bond. Move back and let us help Marella."*

Kai nodded before letting go of Marella's hand. Rising to stand with Daren and Lani, he watched their Partners work on bringing Marella back.

Ula moved to stand near Marella's head whilst Kenna moved to her position at Marella's feet. Shaw flew down and landed near Marella's left hand as Nixie moved from Marella's legs to her right hand side.

As the companions watched their Partners, they could hear a faint subsonic hum in the air, more like a vibration on their skin. As Marella twitched, the humming became louder until Kai thought it felt like static on his arms, making the hairs stand up.

"Can you see this?" whispered Daren to the others. "They're glowing."

As Kai looked at the Partners, he could see what Daren meant. There was indeed a faint glow about each of their Partners. A golden sunshine yellow shone from Shaw whilst a burnt orange came from Kenna, matching her fur. Nixie was a deep blue whilst Ula had a luxuriant shade of green staining her white fur.

The colours glowed brighter, moving towards Marella and wrapping her in beams of coloured light. As the light enclosed her, Marella seemed to relax into it, stopping her thrashing. After a few moments, the light began to fade and the Partners stepped back, apart from Nixie who went forward and stood near Marella's head.

The companions watched in wonder as the light came from their Partners, but now they wondered what would happen next. Almost in answer to their question, Marella murmured a name. In reply to her unheard whisper, Nixie moved and touched his nose to her face, letting her know without words he was nearby. He turned his head and looked to Daren. *"She's asking for you, Daren. Come closer and take her hand."*

Daren watched a fleeting look of hurt cross over Kai's face before he could stop it. "Go on then, Daren," said Kai, abruptly. "You heard Nixie, she's asking for you."

Kai waved Daren towards Marella before turning on his heel and leaving the clearing.

Daren, who had started to move to Marella, stopped and watched him go, feeling torn.

"Stay with Marella, I'll go to Kai," said Kenna to him, moving away to follow Kai.

Daren crossed to Marella's side and took her hand in his. "Marella, come back now. You've been gone long enough."

With her eyelids fluttering as though they were held down with a heavy weight, Marella opened her eyes. She gave a small cry as she saw Daren next to her and tried to raise herself.

Daren pulled on her body until she was sat upright, then embraced her, showing her how worried he had been.

"What's been going on?" whispered Marella, her voice sounding scratchy.

"We'll tell you later," said Daren, passing over the mug of tea from Lani, "first, drink this ginger tea Lani has made for you. It will help you to recover."

"Where's Kai?" asked Marella, looking around the clearing, but not seeing him.

"Just drink your drink. We'll explain everything," said Daren.

"I'll go and find him," said Lani reassuringly, before turning on her heel and heading out in the direction Kai had taken.

Marella could feel strength returning to her limbs and mind. She continued to sip her tea, trying to recall what had happened. She could remember talking to Daren about the Air Portal but then… nothing. It was all blank, yet she knew there was something she needed to tell them.

"Don't worry yourself about that," said Nixie. *"It will come back to you in time. Your body and mind needs to recover from the attack."*

"Attack, what attack?" asked Marella, still sipping her drink.

"We don't know who is behind it, but someone attacked you mentally. Your body was being held in a vortex on an Air wasteland. Lani was able to use the gift to control air given to her by Lord Adaryn and broke the vortex, bringing you back. Everyone was worried about you, however, Kai is the one who refused to let you go," said Nixie, bringing her up to date with what had happened.

"Kai? He's not here now, where did he go?" questioned Marella.

"It may have something to do with Daren's name being the first one past your lips when you woke up. Kenna says he is taking a minute to get his equilibrium back."

"Oh no," groaned Marella. *"I never meant to hurt him. I didn't even know what I was doing."*

"And he realises that. Don't worry, Marella. Kai is returning now and we can all discuss what happened. We're staying here tonight." With that, Nixie moved away to where Ula and Kenna were sat under the watchful eyes of Shaw who was perched in a nearby tree.

Kai and Lani walked back into the clearing and Kai immediately looked over to where Marella was sat. She smiled at him to reassure him she was okay. He helped himself a mug of tea before he came and sat down, Lani next to him.

"I just wanted to say thank you to all of you," said Marella, her voice breaking. She coughed to clear her throat and tried again. "Nixie tells me you saved me from an attack I can't remember."

"You certainly gave us all a scare, Marella," said Lani. "Can you remember anything?"

Marella shook her head. "No, I remember talking to Daren about the Air Portal, then nothing."

"Perhaps if we tell you what happened with us it might trigger some sort of response within you," suggested Lani. At Marella's nod, Lani started explaining what happened from the moment Marella had collapsed. At the conclusion of Lani's explanation, Marella sat there; digesting everything she had been told.

"I know something happened," she said. "I know I need to tell you all something. I just can't remember what it is. I'm so sorry."

"There's no need to apologise. What we need to do is figure out why and how you were attacked," said Lani.

Daren and Kai agreed. "We can't protect ourselves against something that we didn't even know could happen," said Daren.

"Well, we know now," said Marella with a grin, "so I guess some good came out of it."

Daren snorted, "Only you could find the silver lining in that," he said before pulling her into a rough hug. "Don't you ever do that to me again, you hear me? You scared the living whatevers out of me!"

"I'll try not to," reassured Marella, returning his embrace. She straightened up and spoke to the group as a whole. "Now, I know you're not going to like this idea, but I think it's time I Wove. I need to see if there is anything there that might help us."

She raised her hands against the protests that followed, "I am used to Weaving in all conditions, it's what I've been trained to do. I need to do this. I'll do it anyway, whether you approve or not."

"You may as well give in now, you know she'll just do it anyway," said Kai, the first thing he had really said since they had sat down. "Besides, I said that I'd sit with her when she Wove."

Marella looked at him gratefully. She hadn't been sure he would still do so after the recent event.

Daren and Lani looked at each other before agreeing. "I'll get some food ready for afterwards," said Daren.

"Be careful, Marella," admonished Lani.

"I will be," she said. Marella struggled to get up, but Kai was there to help her. "Thank you," she mumbled to him as she wobbled her way over to retrieve her silver chalice out of the backpack, which rested on top of the trundle truck.

* * *

She walked to the stream, taking her time to assess her surroundings. The birds were singing and it didn't feel ominous in any way. She found a spot where she would be comfortable and put some water in the chalice before sitting down.

Marella looked around and saw Kai was sitting a short distance away, leaning against a tree.

"Before I Weave, I just wanted to thank you for looking after me before," she said to him. She watched as a look of discomfort passed across his face.

"It's absolutely fine," he said, "I would have done it for anyone."

Marella felt an irrational stab of jealousy at the thought of him caring for Lani in such a manner, before remembering that after all he had done for her, it was Daren's name she had called. She could understand now why he had left the clearing.

She grinned at him and he quirked an eyebrow at the mischievous expression on her face. "So I didn't get any special treatment then? Should I be sad?" she asked him cheekily.

"Nope," he said, popping the p in the word. "Nothing special at all, you just keep on wishing, Marella."

"Maybe I will," she said before winking at him.

He gaped at her actions before shuffling against the tree. "You're not here to flirt," he said. "You have a Weave to attend to. So hop to it." He smiled at her and Marella started her Weave, knowing things were once again normal between them.

Marella was under for some time, with Kai keeping a watchful eye on her. Nixie and Kenna both kept him company. He recognised the signs of Marella starting to come back so asked Kenna to go back to the clearing to ask Lani or Daren to get a mug of skullcap ready for her.

As she collected her things, she seemed thoughtful. Kai didn't question her, rather letting her have the space she seemed to need. They returned to the clearing, the silence pleasant between them.

"Everything go okay?" asked Daren as they rejoined the others.

"Everything was fine," answered Kai before taking a seat with the others.

"Did you learn anything?" asked Lani from where she sat.

Marella plonked herself down next to her. "I did, I learnt a few things, but not all of which I am allowed to share right now. I will tell you what I can."

Daren cocked his head at her words. "Not allowed?" he said. "Who says that?"

"The Lady Erwyna, that's who," she said with a smile. "Would you go against the words of Lady Daire?"

Daren smiled abashedly. "No, I guess I wouldn't," he admitted.

Marella snorted at him. "You know you wouldn't, so just accept what I can say."

The others settled down to listen to what she could tell them.

"First of all, we are heading in the right direction for the Portal. I've been given a clue which I hope will mean something to you, Lani." Marella took a breath and then recited from memory. "Come and go but always there, can you hear our whispers on the wind?"

She looked at Lani who was repeating the words to herself. Lani raised her head to look at the others. "I think maybe I do understand it," she said. "It may have something to do with the Aspen trees, one of Lord Adaryn's favourites. The sound of the wind blowing through their leaves sometimes sounds like whispering. It is one of the oldest trees here on Wraidd Elfennol. It is also the first to re-grow after a forest fire. Perhaps that is what the 'Come and go but always here' part refers to. I can't be sure though, I'm sorry."

"Not a problem, we'll figure it out. At least we know we're heading in the right direction," said Daren.

Marella nodded in agreement before continuing. "I was also getting flashes of yellow and grey but, once again, I'm not sure what it means."

"That I do know," said Lani. "Yellow and Grey are the colours of Air; they're Lord Adaryn's colours. It makes sense we would see them for the Air Portal."

"The last thing I can tell you is, whoever is working against us has paid a visit to Queen Paralda." Marella ignored the gasps that followed her statement and continued. "Queen Paralda has sent them away without assisting them in any way, but Lady Erwyna warns she may do the same to us. It appears that she is not taking any 'sides' at this point, so we may have difficulty trying to get the *Plu y Gryphon*."

"Do you think there's any way of getting the Feather without going through Queen Paralda?" queried Kai.

"Probably not, if it's anything like the Earth Quarter, she will know the moment we set foot through the Portal," replied Marella.

"Just a thought," laughed Kai, as Daren shook his head with a smile upon his face.

"So what happens now?" asked Daren to no one in particular.

"Now we rest as tomorrow we walk," answered Lani. "We know we're going in the right direction, so we do now as we did for Earth. We walk, Marella Weaves, we hope luck smiles on us, and we find it before too much time has gone by."

The others, agreeing with her sentiment, settled themselves down to a restful evening, good food, and conversation… for in the morning, they would walk.

~ 32 ~

For the next two weeks of Awst and the first two weeks of Medi, the companions walked and searched for the Air Portal. They covered parts of Wraidd Elfennol Lani had never seen before.

"Do you think we've crossed the Portal already and we just don't know it?" she asked one day, stopping her truck for a quick rest.

"I don't think so," said Daren. "I'm sure we would have known if we'd passed through it."

Lani rubbed her hands, trying to get the feeling back into them. "I can always hope," she grumbled.

Kai laughed at her whilst he rubbed his own hands. "I must admit, I'll be glad to find the Air Portal. I'm also very glad we didn't have this much trouble with the Earth one, or we would have been really fed up."

"Come on, don't get despondent now," said Marella. "We're getting close to it, I'm sure."

"How do you know?" asked Daren in exasperation. "Every time you Weave, you get the same thing - yellow and grey, come and go - and yet we're no closer."

"I just know and you will too," said Marella, smirking.

Kai grinned at the two of them "Don't you two ever stop sniping at each other?"

Lani laughed with him as Daren and Marella turned to look at him with matching indignant looks on their faces, before they also started laughing.

"Are we going to stop here for the night?" asked Marella, once she had stopped laughing, looking around the woods. "There is water nearby, I can hear it."

The others looked at Lani who shrugged her shoulders. "We may as well. Here is as good a place as any when you're wandering aimlessly."

They set up camp, each going about their own jobs in order to get sorted as quickly as possible. Daren and Ula decided to go hunting for some fresh meat, the bundles they'd been given by Elder Erion long gone.

"I'll make you a deal, Daren. You get the meat and I'll get some fresh greens to go with it," said Lani, smiling.

"It's a deal. Would you please, please, PLEASE look for some Lamb's Quarter," he begged. "It feels like a lifetime since I've had any."

"I'll see what I can do," replied Lani as she collected her basket to put the greens inside. With a whistle to Shaw, Lani left the camp with Daren and Ula hot on her heels.

"Looks like we'll be eating well tonight," said Kai, rubbing his stomach. "I can't see those four coming back without something."

Marella laughed distractedly as she picked up her silver chalice. Kai cocked an eyebrow at her. "You're going to Weave?"

Marella nodded. "Yes, I know we're close, Kai. I can just feel it. Trust your emotions, I've been told, so I am."

"Fair enough, I'll be here waiting for when you return," he said.

Marella flushed as a fleeting thought went through her mind, of how nice it would be if he was waiting for her in a different context. She blinked and thrust the thought far away. This was definitely not the time for anything like that.

She walked to the side of the fast-flowing river, smelling the freshness of the water and letting it permeate her senses. She could feel the spray on her face and could already see dots of water splashing her trousers.

She sank gracefully to the ground, setting herself up for the Weave. "See you soon," she whispered to Kai before dropping into her trance.

* * *

Kai and Kenna sat nearby, watching Marella in case she needed them. *"Are you alright, Kai? You seem a bit distracted,"* said Kenna.

"I'm fine, fy cariad. Just thinking, that's all."

"What about? Talk to me." Kenna lay herself down on the ground and crossed her front paws, looking steadily at Kai.

"I'm thinking about what happened in the Earth Quarter. I'm wondering what will happen in the Air Quarter. I'm panicking about the Fire Quarter. I'm terrified of entering the Water Quarter and facing my opposite Element. I'm thankful for the friends I've made, and I'm also wishing for more than I can have right now."

Kenna perked her head up and looked at him, a foxy smile on her face. *"Nothing to worry about then?"* she laughed through their bond.

Kai gave a snort of laughter as he plucked a piece of grass and started to chew on the end of it. *"No, love; nothing to worry about."*

"The Earth Quarter is done. You have made some good friends there, and they will always be with you should you need them. The Air Quarter we cannot predict, but will face it together. You have no reason to fear the Fire Quarter. That is OUR Element and it WILL be a success. The Water Quarter will be hard, no doubt about it, but you have those friends you're thankful for, who will help you. As for the last one, wishing never hurt anyone. If it gives you something to hope for, to aspire to, then wish away. If it is meant to be, the timing will present itself. You just have to be patient," was Kenna's practical response.

Kai breathed deeply of the fresh air surrounding him whilst he considered Kenna's words. He wished he could turn off his fears in such an easy manner, although he did understand what she meant.

"Why don't you relax? Try doing what Marella's doing, it might make you feel better."

"What? Weave?" came Kai's shocked reply. *"I can't do that."*

"No, foolish boy. Relax into the water; let the sound of it surround you. Feel the water on your face, see it rushing by. Taste the drops on your tongue. Relax."

Kai followed Kenna's instructions and soon found himself mesmerised by the flow of the water past him. He could smell the freshness, and the sound of it was music to his ears. He understood now why Marella always seemed so refreshed after spending time near moving water.

"I can't wait to show her the beach at Hufel," he thought drowsily to Kenna.

"I thought you were supposed to be watching me, not the other way around." Marella's laughing voice snapped Kai back to awareness of his surroundings. He quickly stood up and dusted himself down.

"Marella, I'm so sorry," he said. "I was just, just, erm…"

Marella just laughed at him and slipped her arm through his before they both started walking back towards the camp.

"I was just teasing you; I've told you before I'm fine when I Weave. It was nice to see you relaxing."

"I understand how you feel about water now, in a small way at least," he said. "I felt like I could lose myself in there and let my cares float away. It felt wonderful."

"I'm sure we all feel the same way about our Elements, but I do love mine for that. No matter how I'm feeling, whether I'm upset, angry or just low, I know being near running water will make me feel better." Marella smiled.

"I don't know about that for my Element," laughed Kai. "Fire usually does the opposite for me. It heightens my emotions, emphasises them, and I feel like I need to do things faster, quicker, immediately."

"When you think of Fire, what do you think about?" asked Marella curiously.

Kai looked at her questioningly. "What do you mean?"

"I mean, do you think of Fire as a campfire, a bonfire, a forest fire? What sort of Fire goes through your mind when the word 'fire' is used?"

"I've never really thought about it." Kai chewed his lip thoughtfully. "I guess, when I think of Fire, I think of a bonfire, burning brightly against a night sky."

"That's certainly fiery," agreed Marella. "That wouldn't calm me down at all. Okay, so how about this? Next time you want to calm yourself, within your own Element, don't think of a bonfire. Think of a single candle flame, or the softly burning hearth fire, providing warmth and comfort."

Kai thought about Marella's idea. "You know, that just might work. I've never really thought of Fire as anything but fast burning, exciting, and wild."

Together they returned to the camp, chatting about different kinds of

Fire and Water, to find Lani had already returned, and was getting the campfire ready to start cooking.

* * *

"Hello, you two," she smiled. "A good Weave?" she asked Marella.

"Yes, it was. I'll tell you all about it once we've eaten. Where's Daren?"

"He's on his way back. Ula brought down a wild boar, so we'll have plenty to eat tonight plus extra to pack away with us. I found some Lamb's Quarter and Chickweed we can add to it."

"Sounds delicious," sighed Marella, appreciatively. "What do you want me to do to help?"

"You can go and wash the greens, if you don't mind? They're in the basket over there."

"That's fine. I'll do them now, Nixie is now in the water anyway." With that, Marella went back the way she had just come, to wash the greens and spend some time with her Partner.

When she returned from the river with a dripping Nixie by her side, the smell of roasting pork filled the woods.

"By the Waters, I love that smell," she said, taking in a deep breath.

Lani and Kai smiled at her whilst Daren laughed. "There's nothing quite like it," he agreed. "So Lani tells me you had a good Weave, are you going to share?"

"I'll tell you after we've eaten, as I'm sure you already know." She smirked at him, knowing how impatient he would be.

Daren just groaned at her, then turned away, going back to the campfire where the boar was spit-roasting.

"*You can be very wicked when you want to be, you know,*" laughed Ula.

Marella just looked at her with an innocent smile on her face, before moving to sit down on one of the upturned logs. "*It won't hurt him to wait,*" laughed Marella.

It wasn't long before the meat was cooked and they sat down to a delicious meal of roasted boar with fresh greens, and some Elderflower cordial to drink. After they were finished, they sat together feeling replete.

Marella straightened up and cleared her throat. The others looked at her and Daren shifted into a sitting position from the reclining state he'd been in.

"So," she said, slapping her hands on her knees, "I guess I should tell you what I saw so we can figure it out."

"Well, only if you're ready," said Daren sarcastically, throwing some grass in Marella's direction.

She laughed as she batted it away. "Stop that or I won't tell you."

Daren just grinned at her and gestured for her to continue.

"We are heading in the right direction, and we're now heading into the right time as well," Marella said. The others looked at her.

"It's the 'yellow and grey' part I've been seeing," Marella explained. "The grey is some sort of rock. We need to find a hill covered with this rock and the Portal is at the top of the hill. It looks like three arches and is covered with lichen and algae. The yellow is the colour of the Aspen leaves in Hydref. There will be water nearby, but we may not see it, as it may be underground. Even so, the rock will have shakeholes caused by the water."

"They could have told us before. We could have spent longer in Alaw," said Daren grumpily.

"Hush now, Daren. Everything for a reason, you know that. Listen to the rest of what Marella has to say or you won't learn anything, and you'll be complaining that you don't know anything."

Daren accepted his rebuke from Ula with a grimace in her direction. Marella just grinned at him and continued, "We need to be careful around the shakeholes as they can easily crumble."

"I think it might be limestone you're talking about," said Lani as she thought about her knowledge of stones and minerals. "That's grey and is usually covered with lichen. It won't be too hard to find, especially if Shaw helps us to look," she finished, throwing her Partner a loving glance.

"The other thing isn't so good," Marella sighed. "I know Nixie told you I would be able to tell you who had attacked me when I woke but I can't. I've woven, I've meditated, and I've even asked Lady Erwyna to look through my mind to see if She could find anything – there's not, nothing solid anyway. Lady Erwyna thinks someone is using a shield to hide behind, which isn't good because it means they know what they're doing!"

"Okay, so we can deal with the not-so-bad news, because at least we know we're going in the right direction." Kai tried to reassure her.

"There is something," she muttered, "but it's really not helpful."

"Tell us anyway, Marella," encouraged Lani. "You never know, it might help."

"I saw three colours, the same colours our Partners glowed when bringing me back. Yes, Lady Erwyna has shown me that," she said in response to Daren's silent question.

"What colours, Marella?" asked Kai, looking around at the others.

Marella dropped her face to her knees and wrapped her arms around her legs. "I saw green, yellow, and red" she said sadly.

"Earth, Air, and Fire," said Kai.

"So the only Element that didn't attack you was your own," stated Daren.

"It certainly looks that way," she agreed.

There was a moment's silence as they tried to understand what this could mean. Where all three Elements involved in this? But they had already been to the Earth Quarter, Carrick and Alana couldn't have been more helpful. Marella's head spun as she tried to understand what was going on.

"Well, there's nothing we can do about it now. We don't really have much to go on, sorry Marella, and what we do know is just confusing us more. Let's put it to one side and deal with it when we have more information," said Lani pragmatically.

Everyone agreed with Lani and decided to think on it when they could. The rest of the evening passed with tales by the campfire and easy laughter. They went to bed, filled with renewed purpose that at last they knew what they were looking for.

~ 33 ~

Early next morning, they packed up camp and set off whilst the sun was still making its way above the tree line. Shaw was flying high, using his superior eyesight to try and find the grey hill.

As they walked along, Marella looked at the trees surrounding them. "It really is turning yellow," she said. With the silvery white of the trunks and the leaves changing colour, it really was a sight to behold.

"They will change from their summery green to deep reds and bright golds," said Lani as she looked around. "They're one of my favourite trees. Sometimes, when I've been out walking through the woods near my home, it appears like a path drenched in gold. I can't use the right words to describe it, to give it justice. It's simply stunning."

"I think you're describing it just right," said Marella, smiling at her friend.

Just then, Shaw flew down and landed on Lani's trundle truck with a screech. Lani stopped pulling and turned to face him.

"What is it, lovely? Have you found the hill?" she asked.

Shaw bobbed his head whilst replying in her mind. *"I have, we should be at the base of the hill by this evening, if nothing delays us."*

"Woohoo!" Lani cried, giving a little happy dance.

The others grinned at her antics whilst Shaw just sat there, watching his Partner.

"Good news, then?" asked Daren, a great big grin on his face at Lani's happiness.

"Yes, sorry," she gasped, slightly out of breath following her impromptu dance. "Shaw says so long as nothing gets in our way, by this evening we should be at the bottom of the hill. Come on, let's go."

With that, and with a skip in her step, Lani grabbed the handles of her trundle truck and started walking briskly onwards. Shaw launched himself into the sky with his characteristic screech.

After glancing at each other with smiles on their faces, the others followed Lani, feeling a purpose once more in their steps.

* * *

They walked for the rest of the day, keeping a steady pace, and only stopping for short breaks before moving on. So it was with some relief they came to a stop shortly before sunset, with the hill directly in front of them.

Marella looked at the rock ahead. Sure enough, it was grey in colour with a path winding upwards. There were also outcroppings of rocks Ula was enjoying bounding over. Marella smiled at the fun Ula appeared to be having.

The others looked at Marella for guidance before doing anything else. "What do you think, Marella?" asked Lani. "Is this the right place? Does it match your Weavings?"

Marella took note of what she could see, comparing it to what she could remember from her Weave. A sense of rightness started to make itself known within her and a smile broke free. "I think it is," she said. "I think we've found it."

Daren and Kai gave a whoop of joy, giving each other a high five, whilst Lani just laughed at them.

"Let's get the camp set up and something to eat" said Lani. "Then we can figure out what to do next."

They set up camp, moving at ease amongst each other, like a choreographed dance. Ula came back with a couple of rabbits for the pot that had been too slow getting away from her. Before long, the tents were up, the rabbits were cooking, and water for hot drinks was bubbling away. As they waited for the rabbits to finish cooking, they talked amongst themselves.

"So we go up tomorrow to try and find the Portal then?" asked Kai.

"We can go up and have a look, but I don't think we'll find it," replied Lani.

"Why not? What are we doing here if we won't find the Portal?" asked Daren in surprise.

Lani looked at him, intellect shining through her eyes. "Daren, how much do you know about the Elements and their correspondences?" she asked.

"Not much, really," he muttered.

"I didn't think so, and no, it wasn't a criticism," smiled Lani. "This is part of what we were taught as part of our training for Silent Messengers. It is easier to send messages to each Element at the time of day which corresponds to them. I don't know why."

The others looked interested so Lani continued. "Do you remember what time of day it was when we crossed the Earth Portal?" she asked, looking at them all.

Kai shook his head and Marella chewed on her lip thoughtfully. "It was dark," she said.

Lani nodded. "Yes, it was dark. The nocturnal animals and insects were about when the Portal first showed up. Now, the time I've always been told for Earth was the middle of the night, but the Portal arrived once full darkness had set in."

"So what's the time for Air?" asked Kai.

"Dawn, the arrival of the sun marks the time when Air is at its strongest. That is when I think the Portal will arrive."

"And that is why you're not expecting us to find it," concluded Daren. "Well, why don't we get up there early so we are there?"

"You want to go clambering over rocks, in the dark, on something that we don't yet know is true?" asked Lani incredulously.

"I see no reason to doubt you," said Daren firmly.

Lani smiled, but shook her head. "No, I don't think it's a good idea. We have no idea what's up there. Yes, there's a path here, but we don't know how long it goes on for. There are the shakeholes to consider as well, remember? Marella has already warned us of them."

Lani took a breath and considered the options. Daren, Kai, and Marella kept silent. Lani was their leader now and they would follow her lead. She came to a conclusion and stated resolutely "No, we will go up in the morning. If we can find a plateau or something where we can set up camp, we will do so. Then we will be ready when the Portal shows itself."

"Makes sense to me," said Kai, giving Lani his support.

"Then it's decided," said Marella. "Let's get some sleep because we're rock climbing tomorrow."

There was laughter, but also agreement from the others as the fire was bedded down for the night. Marella gave a small shiver as she went into her tent, thankful they had packed sturdier ones from Alaw. She didn't think the tarps would have worked for much longer. It wouldn't be long before they'd need the fire to stay lit all night. She snuggled into her sleep sack with Nixie curled up close to her.

"Goodnight my gorgeous," she said to him sleepily.

"Goodnight little one," he replied, curling up even tighter before falling into a deep sleep.

Marella stroked his back for a short while before stopping. She didn't want to disturb his sleep. She rolled over onto her side, pulled the sleep sack up around her ears, and drifted off into a sleep filled with golden leaves

.

~ 34 ~

It was early next morning when Marella awoke, but she could already hear sounds of movement outside her tent. She stretched, feeling the kinks ease in her body. Looking around, she saw Nixie had already left the tent. She dressed before easing out. She sorted out her morning ablutions before returning to the camp and speaking to the others.

"There's a chill in the air this morning, don't you think?" she said to Daren as she leaned up to kiss his cheek.

"Certainly is, but then again, it is mid-Medi. The leaves are turning, there's a nip in the air, Hydref is certainly here."

Marella looked around, "Where's Kai and Lani?" she asked.

"I don't know where Kai is, but Lani has gone climbing," replied Daren. "She wanted to have a quick look around before we all left."

Marella shrugged her shoulders as she helped herself to some of the hot oatmeal bubbling over the campfire. "I'm sure she'll be back soon then," she said before sitting near the fire, tucking into her breakfast with relish.

Just as she finished her bowl, she heard the light-hearted sound of Nixie and Kenna playing together. They rolled each other over into the dirt, both trying to gain the upper hand. Marella laughed as she watched them.

She felt a hand on her shoulder and she tipped her head up to see Kai standing there, laughing at them too. She covered his hand with hers and gave it a small squeeze. "Good morning sleepyhead," she said with a smile.

Kai squeezed her shoulder in return before grabbing a bowl for himself, and sitting down next to her. "I wasn't asleep," he said before spooning a portion of oatmeal into his mouth. His eyes watered as the heat hit his tongue and he sucked in a quick, deep breath to try and cool his mouth.

Marella took pity on him and got a cup of water for him. She laughed as she handed it to him. "Here you go, but it does serve you right for trying to eat too quickly."

"You're a heartless woman," Kai said, gulping down the cold water.

"If I was, I wouldn't have got the cup, now would I?" Marella chuckled. "So if you weren't asleep, where were you?"

"We were scouting around," Kai answered, eating quickly. "Kenna told me last night she had found a cave in the rocks she thought would be big enough to put our trundle trucks in. We can't go rock climbing pulling those things."

"Ahh, I see," Marella said. "So you went to check it out. Is it big enough? Will they all fit?"

"They should do. I think we pack what we can, store the trucks, and cover the entrance. That's the best we can do until we get back. It's pretty desolate here; we're days from the nearest village, so I can't see anyone just happening along to find them."

"Works for me," agreed Marella. "I'll start going through my things now while we wait for Lani to return."

With that, she stood up and rinsed out her bowl and spoon before returning to her tent and the trundle truck and started organising what she was going to take with her.

It didn't take long before she had everything sorted. She really didn't need to take much with her as they had no idea what they would face. She couldn't take everything as she couldn't carry it all. So in the end, she took a change of travel clothing, her formal robes, eating and drinking equipment, plus her book about the Lord and Ladies that went everywhere with her.

She decided she would wear her travel cloak as it would keep her warm and dry and could double up as a blanket if needed. She would also carry her staff, she could use it as a walking aid if needed, but in all honesty, Marella just wanted it to be close by her.

She ducked out of the tent and then proceeded to dismantle it and pack it away neatly in her truck so everything was ready to go. As she did so, she saw Kai and Daren were doing the same.

"Has Lani returned?" she called to them as she packed.

"No, not yet, but Ula says she is on her way," answered Daren, swiftly folding his tent over until it became a small bundle.

It didn't take them long to sort out their own tents and they packed as much of Lani's as they could without invading her privacy.

Lani entered the campsite and smiled when she saw the bustle of activity in front of her. "Thanks everyone," she said as she sorted out what she needed to take. "Kai has told you about the cave, I presume?" She grabbed a hot drink before the campfire was extinguished, passing other cups around as well.

They nodded in agreement as they stood there, holding their cups and blowing across them as the wind picked up and started to whip across the clearing.

"There is a sort of path that ambles up to the top, so we can either follow the path, or take the direct route of climbing over the rocks. I would recommend the path if only to ensure none of us are injured before we reach the Portal."

She took a sip of her drink before continuing. "There is a plateau at the top large enough for us to spend the evening, but not big enough for the tents, so we're going to have to leave them here. The weather is different at the top too. It's gone misty up there and the rocks are wet."

"Sounds like fun," said Kai, dryly, to the amusement of the others.

"Completely," added Daren.

Lani finished her drink and threw the dregs onto the ground where they were soaked up by the earth. She rinsed her cup out and placed it in her backpack, which she then hoisted onto her shoulders. She checked her bow and quiver, gave the clearing a glance, then went to her trundle truck, prepared to go.

The others followed suit and they followed Kai to the cave Kenna had found. Once they had packed their trucks into the small enclosure and double checked they had everything they required, they left the space and Kai proceeded to lay some branches in front of the cave.

"Here, let me help," said Daren and raised his hands out in front of him. A faint green glow encircled his hands and the branches Kai had just placed started to grow over the entrance. By the time Daren had finished, they covered the cave and were indistinguishable from vegetation that had been there for years.

"That should do it," said Daren, brushing his hands together smugly.

"So long as we can find it when we're finished," jibed Marella. She laughed at Daren's disgruntled look. Marella put on her cloak, shouldered her backpack, and picked up her staff. She turned to face Lani who was doing the same. Daren and Kai took up their own equipment and they stood looking at each other.

"Ready to go climbing?" Lani asked with a smile.

As one, they turned and headed up the path, taking care of loose rocks and stones that tumbled down as they walked.

* * *

It didn't take them long to reach the top, although they did have to be careful due to the shakeholes and loose shale beneath their feet. They scrambled their way to the top, laughing breathlessly at the ease in which their Partners made it.

Marella shivered within her cloak and pulled it closer around her as she looked around. Although Lani had told them it was misty, Marella still found herself to be surprised when seeing it for herself. She had assumed because it was the Air Portal, it would be dry and probably breezy. Instead she saw that the water had turned the stone a dark grey colour and it was easy to see the lichen growing there. She stepped around a puddle of water and walked to Lani's side.

"So, we're here, what do you want us to do whilst we wait?" she asked.

"I don't really know," murmured Lani. "I never really thought past getting up here so that we were ready." She gave Marella a despairing look, "What should I do?"

"I think the first thing we need to do is sort out some sort of shelter and a fire, otherwise we're all going to be very wet before long," said

Marella in a quiet voice.

Lani started looking around her, but couldn't see any sticks or branches they could use. "Daren, Kai, are there any branches over there?" she called to them as they explored the other side of the plateau.

"There's nothing here but rock and water," answered Daren.

Daren and Kai walked over to where the girls were standing. "We need to get a shelter raised and a fire started," said Lani, smiling at Marella in thanks.

"It appears we were a bit hasty coming up here so soon this morning," she continued. "We don't have anything here that will help, so I can't see anything else but to go back down and get some supplies."

"Sounds like a plan to me," agreed Kai. "We can't stay up here without going mouldy."

They dropped their backpacks in a pile as they went back down the rocks to the woods below. Daren and Kai gathered some larger branches as supports for their shelter whilst Lani and Marella concentrated on getting brush, leaf, and grass coverings to place over the supports. Marella also collected some ferns to place on the floor to provide a covering against the cold, hard rock. Carrying their unwieldy bundles back up the slick rocks proved to be a bit tricky, but they all made it back to the top without any mishaps.

Kai and Daren locked some of the forked branches together to form a freestanding tripod. They then placed the other branches around it to make a frame whilst Marella and Lani laid the foliage on top to make a vegetation layer, which would help keep them both dry and warm, making sure to leave a smoke hole at the top and a doorway so they could get in and out easily.

Kai gathered some of the firewood and built a small fire within their shelter that was protected from the mist. It wouldn't be enough to keep them warm but it would provide enough heat so they could at least have hot drinks throughout the day.

It was a long, damp, and dreary day they spent huddled in their shelter. With all the Partners and their Companions cramped in there, the temperature soon rose. Their food was cold meat, bread, and cheese because none of them wanted to go back down the rocks again for anymore firewood, which they would need if they wanted to cook food.

"If the Portal doesn't show in the morning, then we'll have to go back down again anyway," said Lani.

"It will show, I'm sure," reassured Daren.

"I hope so," Lani muttered as she stroked Shaw's feathers.

They spent an uncomfortable night within their shelter, so it was with relief when Lani told them they should get out.

Marella rose stiffly and left the shelter, stretching as she did so. She rolled her shoulders to try and ease the kinks knotted there and noticed everyone else was doing the same. In spite of herself, she smiled as she looked at them.

They all stood there together, shivering in the moist early morning air, their Partners by their sides, when the air on the other side of the plateau started to glisten. They looked at each other and started moving towards the iridescent haze, stopping a short distance away.

Before their eyes, the Air Portal slowly flickered into reality. There now stood a solid triple archway that looked like it was made out of the same stone as they stood upon, whereas only moments before had been nothing.

None of them could see anything through the Portal, as the mist on their side of the Portal seemed to be permeating the other side as well.

Whilst the companions stood there, looking at the Portal, Shaw took flight, screeching into the air. *"Come on,"* he said to them. *"Who knows how long this Portal will stay here. It's what we came for, so let's move."*

Lani gave a small burst of laughter at Shaw's words. "Come on then, it looks like we've had our marching orders."

With the sound of their laughter filling the misty, damp area of the plateau, the companions and their Partners stepped through the Air Portal and disappeared from sight, leaving only an echo behind.

~ 35 ~

Once through the Portal, the mist dissipated until it was gone. They stood together, taking note of their surroundings before making any move to go forwards.

The Aspen trees Lani so admired were in full bloom on this side of the Portal, deep reds and burnished golds rather than the bright yellows they had left behind.

Looking at them, Lani inhaled deeply. "If we wanted physical confirmation that time runs in a different way through the Portals, we now have it," she said, pointing to the trees.

Marella looked in the given direction and saw the difference in the colours. "By the Waters," she breathed.

"It's certainly clear here," murmured Daren as he shook some of the sunflower seeds from the pouch, before he popped one into his mouth.

"Look, we can't just stand here. We need to find Queen Paralda and, if it's anything like the Earth Quarter, we're probably being watched right now. Daren, prepare yourself for the wave. Do you still have the seeds from Alana? I hope they will help," said Lani.

"I've just taken one in preparation," said Daren.

"I suggest we start moving then," said Kai, laughing.

"That's a plan," agreed Lani. "Come on then, there only appears to be the one path so far." Lani led them down the solitary path, they hoped, would take them to the place Queen Paralda called home.

They had walked all day and hadn't come closer to seeing anyone, although the feeling of being watched had affected them all at some point. Suddenly, Lani stopped and groaned. The others went to her in concern, Marella placing her arm around Lani's waist.

"What's the matter, Lani?" Daren asked.

"I've just realised something I should have remembered before we even stepped through the Portal," she moaned.

"What is it? Are you okay?" asked Marella.

"Yes, I'm fine;" said Lani, standing upright, "but we won't find the Air village on the ground. We've been looking in the wrong place." Marella and Kai looked at each other in confusion.

Shaw came down and landed on Lani's shoulder, giving a small chirrup to gain her attention. Once Lani was looking at him, Shaw spoke. "*You may have forgotten, Lani, but I hadn't. Whilst you've been looking to the ground, I've been checking the skies. We haven't gone past it and we are headed in the right direction.*"

Lani slapped a hand over her face and scrubbed it for a moment. When she had finished, she looked at the others ruefully. "OK, so what I realised is I've been leading you onwards thinking the village would be just like Naear. Then I remembered what I had been taught about Awyr, which is the name of the place of residence of Queen Paralda." She stopped and took a breath, still looking at the others.

"It isn't on the ground," she said contritely. "We've been looking in the wrong place. Luckily, Shaw had my back and we are at least going in the right direction and can now look in the right place."

"It isn't on the ground? Then how are we supposed to get there?" asked Daren, a bit snippily.

Kai looked at Daren and moved to stand a bit closer to him. "How are you feeling, my friend? Has the wave hit you?"

Daren glanced at Kai before looking at Lani. "My apologies, Lani, I don't know why I said that."

Lani smiled at him, "Don't worry about it Daren. You've lasted longer than I did before making any comments."

Daren bobbed his head before looking back to Kai. "I tell you now, this natural opposite business is not much fun. My respect and admiration for Lani has risen beyond all belief."

"Thank you… I think," grinned Lani whilst Marella and Kai chuckled at Daren's unusual lack of tact.

"You can laugh," Daren grumbled "but you two still have to deal with it."

"And we'll all get through each one because we are stronger together," said Lani as she linked her arm through Daren's.

"You can say that," Daren still grumbled, "You've already been through yours."

"And you're going through yours now. Marella and Kai still have theirs to go through, so stop grumbling and work through it," said Lani, cutting through his self-pity. "Now, we are literally going to go onwards and upwards to find Queen Paralda. If you need a rest, Daren, please say. Don't be a martyr and suffer in silence."

With that, they continued walking onwards in search of Awyr. They spent the rest of the day without sight of the village and had a night spent under the stars before resuming their trek the next morning.

* * *

Daren was still grumbling about the village not being on the ground when they stopped for a drink by a fast-flowing stream mid-morning.

"By the Waters, if I moan as much as Daren when we're in the Fire Quarter, someone please gag me," said Marella, only half joking.

Daren shot her a filthy look in response and opened his mouth to answer when Lani interrupted.

"Marella, please don't mock when you haven't yet gone through it.

You don't know how horrible it makes you feel. You are not yourself until the effects of the wave wear off. Don't forget, we were told it is easier if you have that Element as part of you. Daren is Earth and Water, as well as being the natural opposite to Air, so this is hard. A little bit of patience, if you will."

Marella looked shame-faced at Lani's response and apologised to Daren immediately. Kai sat back on his heels and looked thoughtfully at Lani. She became self-conscious and rubbed her cheek.

"What?" she eventually asked when Kai didn't say anything.

"Nothing, I'm just impressed with you," said Kai, smiling. "You've become really comfortable in your role as leader. I just hope you remember to act this way when we return to Wraidd Elfennol."

Lani smiled. "It's easier to be leader when I'm here with all of you," she said. "Everyone just treats me differently when I'm back home."

"Then don't let them," said Kai. "You are a strong person, you've proven that. Don't let them fit you back into their box at the end of this challenge. It would be a travesty against everything we've done."

"That's a bit strong, don't you think?" said Lani.

"Not at all. You were Chosen by Lord Adaryn, you are leading us in the Air Quarter where we will meet the Queen of the Sylphs. We will find the *Plu y Gryphon* and a monolith will be raised in Alaw. To go back to timid and self-doubting Lani would go against that."

"You really believe all that?" asked Lani with wonder in her voice.

"If I didn't, I wouldn't follow you" said Kai, grinning. "Have a little faith in yourself. If Lord Adaryn Chose you, that's good enough for me."

Marella and Daren were both quiet during their exchange, but nodded in agreement with Kai's words. Lani looked at them with love shining in her eyes. "I don't know how to thank you for the faith you've shown in me, but I will, somehow."

"Maybe you can show some of that faith and follow me," said a voice from behind them. "Queen Paralda is waiting and she doesn't have much patience."

Lani turned her head to see who had come to them, with nary a warning from any of their Partners.

* * *

Standing before them was a pale and delicate looking woman, with long light blue hair that seemed to move of its own accord. Complex blue and grey markings appeared to move and flow underneath her skin. The clothing she wore was a simple pair of trousers and a shirt, much like Marella and Lani's, but hers were the colours of sky blue and light grey.

"My name is Aria and I am one of Queen Paralda's handmaidens. If you would like to follow me, I will take you to her now." Her voice was breathy and melodious. She waited as the others glanced at each other. Their Partners made it easy for them by moving towards Aria.

"How will we get to your village?" asked Lani, courteously.

"Just come with me," said Aria, giving them no answer at all.

They moved over to where Aria stood and once they were all there, she turned her back and started to walk away. With a quick glance at each other, they followed behind her.

Once they had walked a short distance, Aria turned her head and spoke over her shoulder at them. "Please don't be alarmed."

"Alarmed? Alarmed by what?" asked Daren. Before he could get an answer the wind picked up around them, swirling like a dervish yet still strangely calm in the centre.

"Just stay together in the eye and you will be fine," reassured Aria, standing still. The companions crowded around her, unsure of what was happening.

"You asked how you would get to Awyr, Chosen of Air? This is how you get to Awyr," stated Aria proudly.

Marella tried to look out beyond the spinning plumes of air but it just made her dizzy. She shut her eyes to try and regain her balance. Nixie put his paw onto her foot for some physical reassurance whilst he spoke in her mind. *It is all for show, Marella. Just remember that. Queen Paralda may be the Queen of the Sylphs, but she still answers to Lord Adaryn. She seeks to impress, to intimidate. Be calm.*

With Nixie's love surrounding her, Marella felt her heart slow its rapid beating to a stronger, steadier pace. She could see the others taking reassurances from their Partners too as they stood within a tornado going to Awyr.

It only took moments for them to arrive, but it felt like a lot longer. When the rotating winds died down and dissipated, Marella took a deep breath in.

"That was… unusual," she said to the others, trying not to be disrespectful.

Aria turned her head, her light blue hair floating in the breeze, and smiled. "It takes some getting used to, but you all did very well. None of you have become ill, which is always a good thing."

"Are people usually ill when they travel by tornado?" asked Lani, a thin note of sarcasm in her voice. "How surprising."

Aria grinned at Lani, the first real look the companions had seen. "I'll take you to see Queen Paralda. I think she's going to love you."

The companions glanced at each other once more before following Aria.

* * *

They entered a covered walkway which led through to an aromatic herb garden. It was filled with lavender, anise, and lemongrass, the scents filling the air. In the centre stood a slim lady with long black hair, wearing a long, white, loose fitting dress. She had her eyes closed and her arms were held out. Around her wrists and enclosing her hands, the companions could see the gyrating swirls of air she carelessly controlled.

Aria led them in a small way before bringing them to a halt. "It is probably best you wait here until she has finished."

"Paralda," shouted Aria. "I have brought your guests to you."

Queen Paralda gave no indication she had heard Aria, but the winds blowing around her hands sped up, turning faster and faster, before she flipped her hand towards the sky and the spun strands of air shot out, creating a sonic boom in the sky that echoed around them. She brushed her hands together, a small smile on her face, as she turned to greet the Companions.

"Welcome to Awyr, Chosen of our Lords and Ladies," she said, as she held her arms open wide. "I have been awaiting your arrival with anticipation."

Lani took a step forward and bobbed her head towards the Queen of the Sylphs. "Greetings to you, Queen Paralda. I am Lani, Chosen of Air, and current leader of our group. This is Marella, Chosen of Water; Daren, Chosen of Earth, and Kai, Chosen of Fire. Our Partners are Shaw, Nixie, Ula, and Kenna."

As Lani made the introductions everyone, including the Partners, all bobbed their heads towards Queen Paralda.

"How nice, such lovely manners, my child," said Queen Paralda once Lani had finished. "Come, follow me and we shall have some refreshments."

As one, they followed the queen towards a grotto where they could see a table had been laid out with drinks and food. Paralda gestured with her hand, "Please help yourselves to anything." She then sat down and watched them.

Lani helped herself to a lemongrass tea and sat down. Marella opted for an anise tea and sat down on Lani's left. Kai and Daren both helped themselves to some food before taking their places.

Once they had settled down, Paralda smoothed out the skirts of her white dress before folding her hands into her lap, a benign smile upon her face.

"So, I understand you are here for the *Plu y Gryphon*, is that correct?"

"Yes it is, your majesty," answered Lani.

"Oh please, we'll have none that. We're all friends here," laughed

Queen Paralda.

Lani swallowed another mouthful of her tea. "Yes, Queen Paralda, Lord Adaryn has told us that is what we seek." Lani tried again.

"Well he would be the one to know," she said. "And did he tell you where to find it?"

"No he didn't, only that we needed to come to the Air Quarter and seek you out."

"And so you have, dear one, and so you have. The question is now what do you do?"

"Now I am hoping you will be able to give me some idea on where I might find the *Plu y Gryphon,* or indeed, even help us with this challenge as the King of the Gnomes and his High Priestess helped us when we were in the Earth Quarter." Lani answered Queen Paralda's question with a thread of steel making its way into her voice.

The queen gave a tinkling laugh that somehow just seemed slightly off to Marella. She looked over at Lani and saw a flicker in her eyes that said Lani had heard it too.

"If I help you though, it won't really be your achievement, now will it?" The queen said.

"If you give us information that helps us, then I'm sure Lord Adaryn would be pleased. However, the achievement of finding and collecting the *Plu y Gryphon* will be ours, unless of course, you intend to come with us," said Lani, returning the verbal sparring.

Queen Paralda gave another one of those false, tinkling laughs and waved her hand in front of her. "Me? Come with you? Why, the very thought. Whoever would look after my kingdom if I was gallivanting around with you? Honestly, child, who do you take me for?"

Lani placed her cup back on the table and sat straight. "My lady, I am very aware of who you are, and I don't take you for a fool, so please give me the courtesy of doing the same. I am here at Lord Adaryn's request, not for social pleasure. If there is no information or assistance you can give us with regards to finding the *Plu y Gryphon,* then we will take our leave and continue the search alone."

The false smile dropped from the queen's face and a look of spite crossed it, flashing out of sight as she tried to control herself.

"My, you do think highly of yourself, now don't you?" she murmured, her fingernails scraping lightly on her chin. "Could you drop Lord Adaryn's name anymore, I wonder."

"I will use Lord Adaryn's name as often as it takes for us to make progress with this challenge. If that is the only way to do things here in the Air Quarter, then that is the way I shall proceed."

Another light laughter joined their grotto, breaking the tension that had filled it. Aria walked back into sight, clapping her hands lightly. "Oh well done, Lani, well done indeed."

The companions looked at each other in confusion.

"There aren't many who will stand up to my sister, they usually end up cowering before her. There is hidden strength in you, youngling." Aria bowed her head towards Lani in appreciation.

Paralda fluffed up her skirts in annoyance and brought the conversation back to herself. "Be that as it may, it doesn't explain how, or indeed even why, we should help the Chosen."

"We should help because our Lord has requested it," replied Aria. "And as for how, that's the easy part. All they need to do is find Hynafol and ask him for a feather."

A sneaky smile crossed Paralda's face and she started to nod as she considered. "Yes, I guess you're correct, Aria," she said slowly. "We should help, and it's such an easy thing."

She clapped her hands together, the noise echoing around the grotto. "You will stay and rest here tonight, whilst I make arrangements for you to travel onwards to meet with Hynafol. He lives high in the mountains though, so it will take you some time to get there. I will help where I can." She nodded decisively to herself. "Yes, that's what we'll do. And Lord Adaryn will know that we have helped, yes," she muttered.

She looked up as though realising they were still there. "Oh, go on, follow Aria, please do. She'll show you where you can stay today."

With that, Paralda stood and swiftly exited the grotto, her skirts swishing around her as she walked away.

The companions looked at each other in bewilderment and put down their cups. They stood up and turned towards Aria who was watching them in amusement. "Don't worry about her, it will be okay," she tried to reassure them before leading them down a different path towards where they would stay.

* * *

Aria led them to a house that looked very similar to any they would find in their own villages. She smiled as she bade them to enter. "We've made it as close to your homes as possible so you will be comfortable. Please, take your rest. Hynafol isn't known for staying in one place, so finding him won't be that easy on the mountains. Not that we have found, anyway."

"Why are you helping us?" asked Lani, grabbing Aria's arm before she could leave.

"Like I explained to Paralda, because it's the right thing to do. That doesn't mean it will be easy though, and there is nothing I can do about that." She gently disengaged Lani's hand from her arm and walked away.

The companions looked at each other before Lani shrugged and threw her backpack onto the floor. "Well, if rest is what we should do, then rest I will. I'm going to take today to have a bath and relax, because it sounds like it's going to get a whole lot harder from here on in."

"It doesn't appear we can do much more anyway," said Marella as she sat down on one of the couches. "We haven't been given leave to walk around, we don't know anyone, and we don't even know who Hynafol is."

Marella felt a slight movement near her and turned her head, to see Ena standing on the stairs, her feathers glowing with gentle flames.

"Ena," cried Lani. "I'm so pleased to see you."

Ena bobbed her head towards Lani in acknowledgement. "You are being sent into the mountains to seek Hynafol. He is the one who will help you with the *Ply y Gryphon,* but not in the way you are thinking. Hynafol is a gryphon, an ancient and wise soul. If he deems you worthy, then he may just give you one of his feathers."

"A gryphon?" said Kai in wonder. "I didn't know they were real."

"Just like phoenixes aren't real?" sniffed Ena in disdain. "You should know better by now, Chosen of Fire."

Kai looked down at his shoes as he realised the truth in Ena's words.

"Is there anything we can do to find him quickly?" asked Lani.

"Not really. Hynafol knows you are coming, however, before he will help you, he needs to know you are strong enough. The *Ply y Gryphon* may represent Air, but it carries a weight all of its own."

"So the journey is the challenge, not the destination," said Lani. "I'm sure there's a saying about that."

Marella smiled wryly at Lani's statement, knowing which phrase she meant.

"It won't be easy, and it will be cold, that much I can tell you now," said Ena. "I will make sure Paralda sets you up with tents and the right equipment, but I wouldn't expect anything else from her. She will do the bare minimum, but doesn't want to be involved."

"How can she not be involved?" said Marella. "If the Elements are out of balance, then everyone will be affected, doesn't she see that? Or does she think she will be safe here in the Air Quarter so it doesn't matter."

"That's precisely what she thinks, Chosen of Water. She feels safe here in Awyr and doesn't consider the possibility of anything hurting her or her people. For however she may appear to you, she does care for her sylphs."

"Well that sucks," grumbled Marella.

"Be that as it may, you still have your jobs to do. So rest today, eat plenty, bathe, and relax. For tomorrow you set out to find Hynafol." With that, Ena shimmered out of sight, her flames casting off small sparks before disappearing completely from view.

Lani slapped her hands together and turned towards the stairs. "I'm off for a bath, try not to be too loud," she said with a small chuckle before running up the stairway.

Marella wandered into the kitchen to see what food and drinks were there. She made herself busy by brewing a pot of tea and making some sandwiches. She carried it all through to the living area on a tray she had found. When she walked back in, Daren and Kai were talking together whilst Ula and Kenna lay near the hearth.

Daren smiled at her as he saw the tray and made a space on a nearby table so she could put it down. Then, they helped themselves to the food Marella had made, although Daren also added some of his sunflower seeds as well.

They ate together in comfortable silence and quickly cleared the big plate. "It's alright," said Marella, "I've made a separate plate for Lani, and covered them over to keep them fresh."

"So what are we going to do today?" asked Kai, looking at them both.

"Nixie is already out having a look around, but I don't expect him to find anything. Queen Paralda seems stringent on what we can, and can't, see."

"You think she's hiding things from us?" asked Daren.

Marella nodded emphatically whilst finishing her last piece of sandwich. "Most definitely, think about it. What exactly have we seen since we arrived? What people? What houses? This is Awyr, but what is it, exactly?"

The questions Marella raised were valid ones, and the men realised they hadn't really looked any deeper than the surface.

"So what do we do?" asked Daren. "Do we go outside and try to find out more, when we haven't been invited to do so? Or do we stay inside, relax, and hope for the best?"

"I'm going for stay inside and relax" said Marella. "Nixie is having a look, however like I said, I'm not expecting much. Ena has been here and she hasn't given us anything to worry about apart from the fact it is going to be hard going, and cold, when we leave here. So I'm going for a bath after Lani, and then I'm going to curl up with my book and relax all afternoon. I'll try to go to bed early tonight so we can have an early start tomorrow. I can't wait to meet Hynafol."

"You're confident we will find him then?" asked Kai, leaning back in his chair.

"Of course we'll find him. He already knows we're coming, so it will just be when it's the right time for him."

"Marella," Lani called from upstairs. "The bathroom is free, it's all yours."

Marella tossed a smile over her shoulder as she made her way to the stairs. "Catch you later, boys. I can hear a bath calling my name." With that she bounced up the stairs, her laughter trailing after her.

Daren and Kai shared a glance before laughing. "She's very confident, isn't she?" asked Kai.

"Not always, but she hides it well." Daren smiled fondly. "She is right in this though, I think. What's the point of looking for trouble? I'm sure we'll find it soon enough as it is."

"A day of relaxing it is then," agreed Kai. He wandered off to the kitchen, "I wonder what other food they have?"

Daren laughed as he retrieved his sword and held it up to the light, glinting softly. This is how he would relax; spending some time looking after the sword Lady Daire had given him. He would make sure it was sharp and prepared for the challenges he was sure lay straight ahead.

They had a very relaxing day, followed by a sumptuous evening meal. They spent some time together and their friendship became even stronger. The companions retired early to bed, as they had received a message saying Queen Paralda would see them early in the morning.

~ 36 ~

At sunrise, they were ready to meet the Queen, although Kenna had taken some persuading to move. They were still laughing about her lack of enthusiasm as they left the house to see Aria waiting for them outside.

"Good morning Chosen," she said cheerfully. "I hope everyone slept well?"

"Some better than others," laughed Kai, nudging Kenna with his leg. Kenna just raised her nose into the air and moved away from him, which made him laugh even harder.

"If you'd come this way," gestured Aria, smiling at the group. She led them along a path with Whistling Thorn trees dotted along the way. They were in full bloom and the dense clusters of yellow and cream-coloured flowers filled the air with their strong fragrance.

Queen Paralda was sat in the same grotto as yesterday. She looked calm and composed as she watched the companions head her way. "I hope you are well rested?" she enquired, the companions murmuring their affirmations.

"I have sorted out a pack for each of you. I've put everything in there I think you will need, but you will obviously have to fend for yourselves once the food has run out. I suggest you try to find Hynafol as soon as possible, the weather is turning where you are going."

Lani stepped forward and bowed her head towards Queen Paralda in a gesture of gratitude. "Our thanks, my lady. By your leave, we will set out before long in order that we may cover as much distance towards Hynafol as we can."

Queen Paralda acknowledged Lani's words with a gracious smile. "Of course, you may leave whenever you wish. You'll need all the time you can to find him."

"Thank you again for the packs and I hope we will see you again soon, with the *Plu y Gryphon* in our possession." With those words, Lani turned on her heel and made her way over to the packs, the others following behind.

Aria was waiting for them and indicated to each of them which was their pack. Aria looked behind them and smiled towards Queen Paralda. "I will just take them to the edge of Awyr, to make sure they are going in the right direction," she called.

Paralda nodded her head whilst looking at her fingers, making it abundantly clear they were no longer her concern. The companions put the travel packs onto their shoulders and followed Aria, glad to be moving away from Paralda.

They walked in silence for a few moments before Aria began speaking to them in a low voice. "Paralda has been visited by someone, I don't know who, who wanted her to delay you until you wouldn't be able to reach the rest of the Quarters before your year and a day had expired," she said.

"She has refused to do this, but has also said that she won't help you in any way. She is breaking her word by telling you it is Hynafol you need to seek, and by giving you these packs, so please don't think badly of her.

She is walking a fine line as we think there may be a traitor amongst us, who is reporting everything that happens. I just hope this isn't reported as I don't know what the comeback might be."

Lani looked concerned at Aria's words. "We didn't mean to cause any trouble by coming here," she said.

Aria smiled reassuringly at her. "We know that. We know you were sent on this challenge by Lord Adaryn, or you probably would never have visited. But once you were here, it is only right you appear before the Queen of the Quarter that you're in. It's what you did in Earth and what you will do in Fire and Water."

Aria looked around to see if there was anyone else on the path with them, but could see no one.

"Listen to me and heed me well. Follow this path onwards, it will lead you to a mountain range called Mynydd o Sibrydion. If you stay on the path, you will see three mountains, a smaller one shielded either side by a larger one. Head towards the smaller one. That is where Hynafol was seen last. More than that, I cannot say."

"Thank you, for everything," said Lani, holding Aria's hand gratefully. "You've helped us more than I thought you would."

"One last thing, beware the whispers on the wind. They're not always friendly voices, and the advice cannot always be trusted. Use your intellect and intuition." Aria stopped walking and watched as the companions walked past her, heading towards the range. "I wish you well, Chosen of the Elements," whispered her voice after them. "May Lord Adaryn keep you close during this time."

* * *

They walked for most of the day, only stopping briefly for rest and provisions, before continuing on their way. They talked about the information Aria had given them, and what they should do.

"It's definite now," said Marella as they walked along. "There is someone out there who doesn't want us to succeed. The questions are who and why?"

"I agree," said Lani. "King Ghobe was turned, Queen Paralda approached. What will we find when we're in the Fire Quarter, I wonder."

"We'll find out when we get there," said Kai. "You never know, there might not be anything," he finished, hopefully.

Daren just snorted. "Keep on dreaming, Fire man," he said. "I don't think we'll be that lucky."

By the time they stopped for the night, Awyr was but a memory in their minds, having long since passed from sight. The nights were closing in as the seasons changed, and Marella wasn't looking forward to spending the nights in the mountains, as it would get dark even quicker there.

They emptied their packs properly for the first time since they had picked them up and found Queen Paralda had not only made sure they had fresh provisions, but had also packed two tents for them. They were only simple triangular-framed tents, but they were big enough for two and would also help to keep the heat in. They were waterproofed on the outside, with a thick cotton twill on the inside.

They placed the tents next to each other and started a fire going. They prepared a hot soup to eat with the fresh bread they had found in their packs. They sat around the fire, feeling content with full bellies.

"How long do you think it will take us to get to the range?" asked Marella, yawning widely and stretching her arms above her head.

"I would think a couple of days," said Daren. "It looks closer than it is, I'm sure."

Marella hunkered down under her thick cloak and held onto her drink. "I've decided, I like the cold a lot more when I'm not out in it."

Kai smiled at her, "It's a good job I'm here then, isn't it? I can keep you warm." Kai stuttered as he realised how his words could be taken. "I mean, I can keep you all warm, with my Fire. I mean…" He stopped as the others erupted into peals of laughter before smiling ruefully at them.

"You knew what I meant," he said, rubbing his chin.

"Yes, we did, dear one, but that was irresistible," laughed Lani.

Kai just smiled and shook his head at them before he stretched out his body and stood up. "I'm going to bed. I'll see you lot in the morning."

He made his way to the tent he and Daren were sharing and held the flap open for Kenna. Once she was inside, he closed it behind him. The others chuckled for a few more minutes at seeing Kai get ruffled, then one by one they too disappeared into their tents.

It wasn't long before their campsite was quiet except for faint rumbles coming from Ula. A shadow passed over them and pulled at the tents before disappearing as the wind that blew gently over the clearing.

"Stay safe my friends," came the faint sound of Aria's voice. Marella smiled in her sleep and turned over, snuggling down into her sleep sack.

~ 37 ~

For the next week, they slowly made progress towards the mountain range along the convoluted paths. They fell back into the routine they'd established in the Earth Quarter, so time passed comfortably.

One morning as Marella was sat by herself in the early morning light; she contemplated what might be going on back home. She wondered if her mother had yet forgiven her for going on this quest for the Lords and Ladies, although she still couldn't see how she could have said no, in any case.

Nixie walked to her and rested his head on her bent knees. *"They are all missing you back home and wish you well,"* he said to her.

Marella gently stroked his head and took comfort in his words. "I miss them," she said sadly. "I wish we could have parted under better circumstances."

"That is Riva's lesson to learn. You followed your heart and did as you were asked. It will all come right, you'll see."

Marella and Nixie took the time to enjoy being by themselves and gave each other comfort in their presence.

A hand landed on Marella's shoulder and she looked up to see Daren smiling down at her. She covered his hand with her own, no words spoken. After a moment, Marella could see Lani and Kai join them, along with all four Partners. In silence, they stood together, taking the peace in the moment and reassurance from each other.

Silent moments passed before Daren cleared his throat. "We each have something for you, Marella."

Marella looked at him questioningly. "What's this for?" she asked.

Kai gave a loud burst of laughter whilst Lani giggled. Daren just shook his head in disbelief. "Only you," he said, chuckling.

"What?" asked Marella, looking from one to the other. "What's going on?"

"Marella, if the time is running the same as back home, today is your birthday. It's the Autumnal Equinox."

"Today? It can't be." She looked around in surprise to see the affirmations from the others.

Lani handed her a mug of rooibos tea, the slightly nutty scent filling the air.

"Thank you, Lani. This is delicious" said Marella, sipping the hot brew appreciatively.

"Happy Birthday, Marella, this is from Shaw and I."

Lani handed her a small package wrapped in blue paper. Marella put her drink down by her side and opened the packet. Inside there was a small, diaphanous silver bag with loose leaves inside. Marella looked at the bag, before raising it to her nose and sniffing.

"Lavender and lemon balm?" she exclaimed to Lani's amusement.

"Yes it is. A little bird told us it was your favourite" she smiled.

"A little bird... or a little otter?" asked Marella, cocking an eyebrow in Nixie's direction.

"Does it matter?" said Lani. "There's not much, but we thought you might like it as we travel."

"Thank you so much," said Marella, holding the bag tightly. "It's wonderful."

Daren handed her a small parcel then, wrapped in the same blue paper. Marella smiled at him as she opened it. Inside was an oval, smooth, polished aquamarine stone, rounded on one side and with a thumb-sized indentation on the other. The pale blue stone sparkled with sea-green highlights, reminding Marella of the ocean.

She gasped as she looked upon the worry stone. "Oh Daren, it's gorgeous," she said, as she held her present up to admire it.

"I've carried it with me since we left Charon in the summer. I knew there would be a distinct possibility that we wouldn't be anywhere with people when it was your birthday. I hope you like it. It's hardwearing and it hasn't even received a scratch so it should withstand our travelling."

"It's beautiful, thank you. I can't believe you've carried it all this way," she laughed.

"My turn," said Kai, giving her a large parcel. Marella unwrapped the same blue paper, and opened up a rich, chocolate-brown leather-bound book.

"Oh Kai," she breathed. "This is gorgeous. Did you...?"

Kai nodded to her unspoken question. "Yes, I made it for you. It has one hundred sheets in there, so it should last you a while."

Marella turned the book in her hands as she looked at the hand-stitched crisscross binding and the leather strap that held it closed.

Marella stood up and embraced each of them in turn. "Thank you so much for my gifts. They are all wonderful. I can't believe you remembered and I forgot," she laughed.

"I can believe it," said Daren to the others. "She's never really been bothered about her birthday. It's just been another day for her, which is why I've always tried to get her to celebrate it. I'm thankful every day that the sister of my heart was born."

Tears came to Marella's eyes at Daren's words and she hugged him tightly. "Thank you," she whispered.

Daren squeezed her back. "You're more than welcome," he said.

* * *

They walked for the rest of the day in high spirits, teasing and laughter filling the air. The wind was brisk but sunshine led the way. The cool air made the walking easier, so Marella was truly grateful for it.

When they had set up camp later that evening, Marella was talking and laughing with the others as she enjoyed a cup of her lavender and lemon balm tea, the fresh smell permeating their campsite. Suddenly she stopped laughing and her eyes lost their focus.

Nixie ran to her and put his paws on her crossed legs. After a moment, he relaxed and looked back to the group who were watching him anxiously.

"It's okay, it is Torlan, her father's Partner," he explained for those who didn't remember.

"I wondered if anyone would try to contact her, being as she can hear all Partners," said Daren, a faint bitter tone in his voice.

Daren noticed that Kai was looking at him. He shrugged his shoulders as though to relieve tension.

"It just grates on me, that's all. Marella is doing what she was Chosen for, from birth she was Chosen for this, maybe even before. Maybe that's why she only has one Element – not to make her weaker, but to make her stronger. She can speak and hear all Partners and has never abused that privilege. And yet she has never had encouragement from the Elder of her Element; her own mother. And today, when it's the first birthday she's had away from home, has anyone contacted her? No, not until now."

Daren snapped out his words, showing without raising his voice just how upset and angry he was on Marella's behalf.

Lani reached over and laid her hand on top of his clenched fists. "She's very lucky to have a friend like you, who believes in her so much."

Daren whipped his head around to look at her. "And what about you? Aren't you her friend too? Don't you believe in her?"

Lani stiffened her spine and removed her hand. "Don't you take that tone with me, Daren. Of course I believe in her, and I am her friend. I only meant that you have been friends for so long, it must be a comfort to her."

"Calm down, you two," said Kai, trying to diffuse the tense situation. "Should we really be talking about Marella this way? She is sat right there, and she's crying, just in case you two were too busy sniping at each other to realise."

Daren looked at Marella who did indeed have tears rolling down her face, dripping onto Nixie who was curled up in her lap. Nixie looked back at Daren steadily.

"Is she alright?" Daren whispered to Nixie, receiving a nod from him in answer.

"I'm sorry, Lani. I didn't mean to snap at you." Daren apologised to her.

"It's okay," Lani said, her easy humour restored. "Whatever could be the matter with Marella?"

"Think about it," said Kai to them both. "She's on this challenge without the approval of her Elder, who is also her mother, like Daren said. It's her birthday and we know how much she takes notice of that, because she had forgotten. We've walked all day and now someone contacts her. That is enough to make me cry, without even knowing what is being said."

"Nixie, can you hear? Is she okay?" asked Lani.

Nixie raised his head and looked at them. *"She is okay but feeling emotional. It is her father who has contacted her with birthday greetings from the whole family. She is now hearing about how the wedding preparations for Jorja and Derwen are coming along. She'll be back soon."* With that, Nixie snuggled back into Marella, so that she would know he was with her.

After a moment, Marella sniffed and the others watched as awareness flooded her face. She wiped self-consciously at her wet face and gave a tremulous smile to them.

"I'm okay," she reassured them. "Really, I am. I just wasn't expecting Torlan to contact me."

"And why not? It is your birthday after all," said Daren, trying to smile.

"I know, you all reminded me. I just wasn't expecting it, that's all." Marella looked at Daren curiously. "Have you been getting angry again? We've been through this how many times, Daren? There is nothing you can do or say to change things. This is just a waste of your energy. Use your emotions wisely; don't throw life into feelings that should remain dead."

Daren looked at her, his smile natural now. "Alright, oh wise one. I'll listen… for now. You know it makes me upset on your behalf though so don't ask me to change. It's only because I love you."

"I know you do and I appreciate you and everything you've done for me more than you will ever know." Marella sighed, her smile slipping slightly. "It's just… I know what it's like, Daren. She won't change. Things won't change. I've tried, you know I've tried, but it's just never good enough. There are some lessons you just have to learn and move onwards from. This is one of those for me."

Marella looked at the small group of friends and Partners that had become so dear to her. "Family isn't always about blood. We've shown that through the years, Daren. Now my family had changed again, some are leaving through their own choice, and new members have been found. I will always love my Mama and I will be there for her; but I can no longer live for her. I have to live for me."

Lani went over to where Marella was sitting and wrapped her in a hug. "Stop it," she said. "You're making me cry now." Marella pulled back to see there were indeed tears on Lani's face. Marella gently wiped Lani's face and returned to the embrace.

"It's true, Lani. I have more family now than when I started this challenge and I am thankful every day. I have made my choice, and Riva has made hers. I stand with you and the Chosen every step of the way."

Daren and Kai looked at each other before moving to Lani and Marella and turning it into a group hug. "We most certainly are in this together," said Kai.

After a moment, they all started to laugh and separated. Nixie was wriggling around and trying to escape the huddle he found himself in the middle of. He crawled out as they let go of each other and ran over to where Ula and Kenna were lying, watching their humans.

Lani was still weeping whilst Marella seemed stronger. She smiled at them, delighted beyond all recognition that these personalities had come into her life.

"Come now, let's finish our drinks and head to bed," Marella said, rubbing Lani's arm. "We're nearly at the mountain range. It won't be long now."

In agreement, they moved to sit around the fire and finished their drinks, chatting inconsequentially, and watching sparks from the fire light up the dark sky.

~ 38 ~

"*She handled that well,*" said Ula to Nixie on the general path between Partners.

"*She did indeed. She's getting stronger, less reliant on Riva's approval. It's about time; however, she is taking the strength the others offer her. I am pleased with her.*"

"*She may be taking strength, but she is giving it too. Marella is not selfish, just misguided at times,*" said Ula, her eyes twinkling in the darkness.

"*Aren't they all?*" laughed Kenna. "*They are all doing well though; I'm pleased we are here together too. Marella certainly has a way with words at times.*"

"*She loves Lani, but doesn't treat her like a child. She has my respect for that. Too many treat her that way because of her blonde hair and big blue eyes. They don't see the intelligence that lies behind them.*" Shaw joined in the conversation from the tree where he was roosting nearby.

"*Yes, they are all coming along nicely,*" said Nixie, love and approval threading through his mental voice.

"*And now we move onwards. It will be another week before we find Hynafol at the earliest,*" said Ula.

"*Another harder week,*" said Kenna, wrapping herself up into a bundle. "*Marella is right, by tomorrow we'll reach the ranges, then the weather will change and walking will get harder.*"

"*Bring it on,*" said Shaw, fluffing up his breast feathers.

A variety of grunts and snorts greeted his comment, the Partners all agreeing with him. They watched as their humans sorted themselves out and doused the fire for the night before retiring to their tents.

"*Goodnight, Marella. Sleep well little one,*" thought Nixie to her. "*The morning will be here soon enough, then we walk.*" He felt the love and reassurance from his beloved Marella and snuggled up between Kenna and Ula for the night.

~ 39 ~

The Partners had been right in their thinking. They did reach the mountain range the following day and the weather did get harder as soon as they started to climb. The chill snap in the air of autumn disappeared. Soon snow swirled around them, winter coming early to the mountains, making visibility increasingly difficult as they trudged on.

For over a week, they continued steadily through the mountain ranges, trying to keep on a straight path that would lead them to the Mynydd o Sibrydion. Everything was harder for them, from finding food, to making up a campsite for the night. Shaw even had difficulty flying at times and had taken to sitting on Lani's backpack, trying to keep his seat as the weather engulfed them.

Early one afternoon, Lani stopped her walking, her breaths panting white plumes in front of her. One by one, the others stopped next to her, and looked around to see why they had stopped.

Lani raised her trembling hand and pointed in front of them. "Look, I think that's the Mynydd of Sibrydion - two larger mountains, one smaller one in the middle. It has to be."

The others looked over, peering through the whirls of snow.

"You know, I think you're right," said Kai, excitement in his voice. "We've done it, we're nearly there."

"I don't know about 'we've done it', more like we're getting nearer to the place where we might do it," laughed Daren.

Kai just shrugged his shoulders, "You know what I mean," he said, grinning.

"Come on, let's keep moving. I'm getting colder the longer we stand still," said Marella, practically.

Everyone agreed so they set off once more, their steps lighter now that they could see their destination.

* * *

The wind was bitterly cold and sliced through their clothes like a million tiny knives. Their legs ached from the cold; any body part exposed to the elements felt like it was burning. They were halfway up the middle mountain, and the weather was taking its toll on all of them. They had started to huddle together in one tent at night, preferring to be cramped and sleep sitting up, than lose precious body heat.

They had walked for another week after spotting the Mountain of Whispers, the weather turning worse the higher they climbed. By now it was the last week of Medi, although it could have been mid-Ionawr by the snow that stormed outside their tent.

"I'm sorry," Kai repeated, "I don't know why my talent isn't working properly. I'm allied with Air, it should work here."

They were clustered together in their tent, trying to find respite from the elements, and eating a cold, half-frozen meal to keep their strength up. Everyone was disheartened as they felt no closer to find Hynafol than when they started.

"Try not to get down," said Lani as she tried to sound reassuring whilst her teeth chattered together. "We will find Hynafol and we'll all be toasty warm, I'm sure of it. Kai, please remember that when we were in the Earth Quarter, none of our talents worked. Marella wasn't able to Weave, you couldn't start a Fire and I couldn't move the Air. I'm sure it's the same here."

Daren gave her a smile that showed he appreciated her efforts. He shook out the last sunflower seed and placed it on his tongue, savouring the flavour.

Out of the Partners, it was Ula who seemed to be the most adapted to the weather. With her white shaggy coat and standing tall in the snow drifts, it looked like she belonged in the mountains, whereas Nixie was shivering and struggling. Marella had taken to carrying him, as his short legs made it difficult for him to cross the snow drifts that were in their way.

By the time the first week of Hydref was over, they were in a serious state. Hypothermia was becoming a very real concern and they were all trembling and exhausted. They found it harder and harder to raise their tent each evening and bring it down the following day even though they knew they wouldn't survive without it.

Lani was struggling with, but didn't mention, the voices she heard every evening. They begged and pleaded with her to rest, to not continue on the mountain, that finding Hynafol was not important. They cajoled, encouraged, and wheedled, smoothly persuading her to turn back to Awyr, where she would be safe and warm. She remained firm in her resolve to find Hynafol, but as days passed, it became harder to ignore them.

The companions helped each other wherever possible – mentally, emotionally, and physically. Through this hardship none of them were sure they'd survive, they were actually bound more tightly to each other and the very Elements themselves.

~ 40 ~

One morning, as they struggled against the wind to pack away the tent, the air swirled around them in a frenzy. They looked around, trying to figure out where the danger was coming from, but couldn't see anything in the snow surrounding them.

Suddenly, breaking through the weather, came a burst of tawny brown. Drifting slowly down, as though in a summer's day instead of a winter storm, was Hynafol. He landed before them and folded his great wings behind him as he returned the looks of the Chosen.

He put one leg out in front of him and leaned back on the others, bowing in his fashion to Lani. "Greetings, Chosen of Air, and your companions." His deep voice rumbled over them.

Lani pulled her shoulders back and regally accepted his greeting, the appearance ruined by her shaking body. "Greetings, Hynafol. We are pleased to see you," she replied.

"Come with me," he said to them, walking away, leading them into the whiteness.

They followed him, not having the strength to argue or question where they were going. They walked for about an hour before he led them into a cave they didn't see until they were right next to the entrance.

"Go inside and warm yourselves, there is a fire going in the main hall. I will be with you shortly." With that, Hynafol turned around and walked majestically away from them, his tail swishing behind him.

The companions looked at each other before Lani shrugged her shoulders. "We've come this far, we may has well go all in. At least he said there was a fire."

She walked past the others, and entered a large cave that had a fire burning in the centre of the room, casting flickering shadows along the walls. She walked up closely to the fire and held her hands out to it, feeling warmth in her fingers for what felt like the first time in days.

Daren came up behind and lifted her away from the fire, his arms like steel bands around her waist. She struggled, trusting Daren, but not understanding why he was removing her from the warmth.

"You can't get too close, too soon," he admonished whilst holding her hands in his. He led her to a stone and used it as a seat, pushing her gently down until she sat.

"It was warm there," she grumbled, not happy with being moved.

"If you have frostbite on your hands, you'll do more harm than good," he said, turning her hands back and forth as he inspected them for any signs of white or greyish skin or areas of firmness.

"You need to warm these up slowly," he advised. "If you do have frostbite and get too close to the fire, you won't know you're burning because your hands will be numb. Then you'll have frostbitten *and* burnt hands."

Lani sighed as she realised what Daren was saying. "I really want to get warm," she mumbled to him. He gave her hands a gentle squeeze after finding no signs of injury upon them.

"You will do, soon enough. Let it happen gradually though. Here, let me take your cloak."

Daren unwrapped her cloak from around her, taking care of Lani before he saw to himself. From the corner of his eye, he could see Kai was taking care of Marella, who leaned against him, her head resting on his shoulder.

Kai sat down on one of the stones facing the fire and pulled Marella down so she sat between his legs. He wrapped his arms around her and held her, with Kenna leaning against his legs and Nixie in Marella's lap.

For a few moments, peace reigned supreme in the large cave as the Companions gradually warmed up, exhausted from their efforts.

* * *

Hynafol watched them from outside the room, intelligence gleaming in his warm amber eyes. He was impressed with what he had seen so far, they worked well together and had such a strong bond.

"Ena," he breathed, "they are here. Exhausted and frozen, but they are safe now. I will keep them for a few days so they can regain their strength, however their journey back will be easier. I will make it so. Thank you for telling me when they were close."

"*You are welcome, brother. Treat them kindly and give them my greetings,*" came Ena's reply in his mind.

"I certainly will. Take care, little sister. Until next time…" with that, Hynafol broke the connection with Ena and turned his attention to the frozen humans and animals within his cave.

* * *

Marella looked up as Hynafol entered the cave. She looked at the large, fierce looking creature and saw warmth and intelligence in his face. The strong wings that sprouted from his lion's body looked like they'd be able to carry him for long distances with ease. His hawk's head had long ears, sharp eyes that missed nothing, and fearful, cruelly hooked beak.

Hynafol was by far the most dangerous looking creature she had ever seen, but Marella felt not a moment's worry in his presence. There was something about him that told her she could trust him, a reassurance on a deep level within her. Marella had the urge to tell him everything – everything that had happened to her, everything she wanted to happen, her hopes, her fears. She stopped herself and relaxed back into Kai's embrace, his arms tightening around her as he held her.

Hynafol walked slowly towards them so as not to startle them. The cave echoed as he spoke. "I am glad you are here. You will be safe and warm now; I've made some room for you so that you may sleep here until it is time for you to return. For now, be at ease and rest by the fire. Lunch will be in an hour or so, until then, relax."

He eased his big body down so he lay on one side of the fire, deliberately not blocking the heat or sight of it from any of the companions. He sat there, not speaking, just watching them relax by slow degrees as the warmth permeated their beings.

After a while, Nixie poked his nose out from Marella's lap, his lithe body once again showing his innate strength and flexibility as he thawed out. He jumped off Marella's lap and went over to Hynafol.

Stretching out his front legs as far as he could in front of the gryphon, he lowered his head towards him. As though this was a signal for the other Partners, they joined Nixie and copied his movements as far as they were able. Shaw was unable to do the same so he held his wings out by his side and bobbed his head towards the great being.

Hynafol bowed his head towards the Partners and huffed gently with laughter. The companions eyed each other, wondering what would happen next.

"You have no need to thank me, Partners of the Elements," he said. "It is my honour to help you in any way I can."

"So you say," Marella heard Shaw say, *"but we would not have lasted much longer out there. On behalf of my beloved and myself, I thank you."*

The others grunted in agreement and Marella found herself feeling tearful as Nixie bowed before Hynafol, his body looking tiny before the gryphon.

Hynafol raised his body and shook out his wings before settling back down. He touched his beak to his paws which were crossed in front of him, "Then I am happy to have been of service," he rumbled.

The Partners retreated back to their humans and pushed in, needing the physical contact between them. Hynafol could see the life returning to their tired bodies as they recovered from the constant battering they had taken. He nodded to himself; they would be ready to eat now. Closing his eyes, he sent a mental request through to the kitchen for some warm bread and thick, hot soup.

"I have asked for some food to be brought through for you now. Please don't be alarmed, there is no one here who will harm or betray you."

The Chosen relaxed at Hynafol's words. Upon hearing footsteps behind them in a place they had thought to be empty, they had become tense. Kai and Daren removed their hands from their sword belts.

The meal was carried passed them by a sylph, the rich broth filling the air with aroma. The platter was placed on a table and the sylph left, bowing to Hynafol before returning to the kitchen. The hearty and homely smell immediately got their stomachs rumbling, and Marella looked at Hynafol in embarrassment.

He chuckled at the sounds emanating from the Companions. "Fear not, I would be the same if I had eaten what you have for the past few days. Eat your fill, there is plenty more where that came from."

Without hesitation, the companions went over to the table where the sylph had placed their bowls. On a platter in the middle of the table was some fresh bread, still warm to the touch.

They tucked into the delicious soup, dunking their bread into it and enjoying every mouthful. The Partners also enjoyed some of the soup, although maybe not as much as the humans did. It filled them all with a warmth they thought they had forgotten, and before long, they relaxed completely, replete with food and warmth.

"Come with me and I will show you where you can rest. We will speak more later." Hynafol showed them to smaller caves which were off from the main one. Their backpacks had been placed inside, but all Marella could see was a big fluffy bed that looked so enticing.

She stumbled as she moved towards it, turning before she reached it. "Thank you, Hynafol. I am so pleased you found us."

He smiled at her, looking at the companions. "I am happy I found you too. Rest now, we will talk later when you've had some time to recover." With that, he turned around, his tail flicking behind him, and walked back into the main cave.

~ 41 ~

When Marella awoke sometime later, she was aware of two things. The first thing was she really, *really* needed to find the bathroom and the second, her stomach was rumbling. As she lay there, trying to get herself together before moving, she realised she was actually curled up against someone. *"It must be Daren,"* she thought, smiling. She wriggled a little closer; loathe to move as she was so comfortable, even though she needed to. She felt the arms tighten around her and then breath on her cheek as a voice whispered to her.

"Good morning, Marella. Sleep well?"

Marella stilled, it appeared she had been wrong. She tilted her head backwards so she could look behind her, and saw that it was indeed Kai who was holding her so tenderly. He grinned at her, his deep brown eyes twinkling as they watched her.

Marella smiled at him, blushing. "Good morning, Kai. Yes, thank you, did you?" she replied, also in a whisper.

Kai squeezed his arms gently around her, "I slept like a log, I think we all did."

Marella looked forwards and grasped if she had been more aware when she woke up, she would have realised it wasn't Daren holding her. There, lying next to them, were Lani and Daren, almost mirroring them with their positions.

Marella stifled a giggle as she realised they had all climbed into the same bed. "We must have been exhausted," she whispered to Kai.

"I know we were, but I'm not complaining," he answered. "I kind of like waking up this way."

Marella blushed all the more at his words and said nothing. They lay there for a moment, neither of them moving, just enjoying the peace and being with each other. Then Daren gave a snuffle-snort in his sleep which had them both laughing, trying to keep their giggles inside so as not to wake Lani and Daren.

"I really need the bathroom," said Marella, and gently disengaged herself from Kai.

He moved so she could get out of bed. "I'll go and make us a drink."

Marella nodded in thanks, and moved towards the area Hynafol had said they would need.

Once she had freshened up with some soaproot, and cleaned her teeth with a fresh mint stick, she felt halfway human again. She left the bathroom and followed her nose to the kitchen where Kai had a mug of rooibos tea waiting for her. She grabbed it, inhaling the nutty aroma and smiling. "The bathroom is all yours," she said. "Thank you for the tea."

She sat down at the table in the centre of the room and watched Kai leave. He threw a smile her way before disappearing down the corridor. She wondered how long they had slept for as she felt better than she had expected to. She was lost in her thoughts when a deep voice rumbled through the room.

"Greetings, Marella. I trust you slept well, and now feel rested?"

Marella looked around and saw Hynafol moving towards her, coming in from an entrance opposite the one Kai had taken.

She smiled at him as she answered. "Greetings, Hynafol, I slept wonderfully, thank you. How long was I..." she trailed off, not wanting to appear rude.

"You have slept the day round," Hynafol answered her. "Today is the second day you have been here."

Marella gasped, she hadn't realised they had slept for that long. Without daylight, it was difficult to tell the passing of time.

Hynfol chuffed his laughter, reminding Marella of Nixie. "Do not fear, little one. I wanted you to sleep yourselves out. Fighting the weather the way you did takes more out of you than you realised. By sleeping deeply, you have healed both the exhaustion and the touch of frostbite all of you suffered."

Marella looked down at her hands, remembering they had felt slightly numb. "I just thought I was cold," she said, looking at him.

"You were cold," he laughed, "but if it had gone on for much longer, you would have had frostbite on your fingers and toes, with a high possibility of hypothermia as well."

Marella gulped as she belatedly realised the danger they had all been in.

"You are safe now, Marella, and the way back will be easier, I promise." Hynafol soothed her. He swung his great head around the room and curved his beak into a smile. "The others are waking now, you might want to drink that tea and make a fresh pot. Help yourselves," he said.

Marella gulped back the last of her tea before rinsing her cup out, and set about making a fresh pot for everyone. Hynafol sat down and watched her work.

Kai came back through the doorway and stopped when he saw Hynafol. He smiled at the gryphon, at ease with him. "Good morning, Hynafol, how are you this morning?"

"Good afternoon, Kai. I am very well, thank you. Marella has told me you slept well." Hynafol watched Kai, his eyes twinkling as they saw the way Kai glanced at Marella, before looking back to him.

"Yes, erm, the bed was very comfortable," Kai stumbled over his words. "We were all so tired; I think we just fell in together."

Hynafol laughed and Kai relaxed. "I expected nothing less. You've all been sleeping together anyway; this way was simply more comfortable."

Kai grinned in agreement and then turned as Lani and Daren both walked in, rubbing at their eyes.

"Good morning, sleepyheads," he said to them.

"Urgh, don't speak to me yet," grumbled Daren good-naturedly, as he walked towards the tea pot.

"Sit down, I've made you a drink," said Marella, grinning at them as she pushed Lani towards a seat, before placing two steaming mugs of tea in front of them.

"How come you're up so early?" said Daren, still grumbling as he put the mug to his lips.

"It's not early. According to Hynafol we've slept the day round and it's afternoon."

Daren looked at Marella in amazement before looking to Hynafol to confirm what she said was true.

Hynafol chuffed, his laughter booming around the room as Daren's eyes widened. "No wonder I feel better," he said with laugh.

"No wonder I needed the bathroom," mumbled Lani before flushing furiously when everyone turned to look at her.

Marella patted her hand and laughed, "I was exactly the same, Lani, so don't worry about it."

"I have arranged for some food for you. Do you want to eat here, or go into the dining room?" asked Hynafol.

"If it's okay with everyone else, I'd like to stay here," said Lani. "I've only just sat down and really can't be bothered to move just yet."

With a chorus of laughter, it was agreed they would stay and eat in the kitchen.

"After you have eaten, I think it would be a good idea if we went to the main cave where we can discuss the matters at hand," Hynafol said to them as plates were laid out in front of them. "I will leave you now whilst you eat and will see you shortly."

* * *

The four of them consumed the food placed in front of them and it wasn't long before they felt sated. Lani was sat back in her chair, sipping her drink, and letting the food settle in her stomach as she thought about their journey to Hynafol and what Marella had told her as they ate regarding the frostbite and hypothermia. Of all the things she had thought might happen when she was Chosen, getting frostbite wasn't one of them. She was very grateful that she hadn't listened to the voices in the wind, realising the truth behind Aria's earlier warning.

"Where is Nixie this morning, I mean, this afternoon, Marella?" Lani questioned, realising she hadn't actually seen any of the Partners since she woke up.

Marella laughed, her face full of love as she thought about her Partner. "He's very happy right now," Marella answered. "Hynafol told them where there was a hot spring within the cave network, so they're all there, enjoying the water."

"They slept their fill with us first, Lani," said Kai. "They woke up before us though, and went away so they wouldn't disturb us. Kenna is very happy and says there is even a small hollow that Shaw is using as a bird bath."

"I know he's warm and content," smiled Lani. "I just couldn't get much sense out of him."

"Ula's probably jumping in and splashing everyone, she's good at that," said Daren with a laugh.

"I'm going to ask Hynafol if I can use it before we leave," said Marella. "I could use some water time."

"Wasn't there enough water in that white stuff swirling around you outside?" teased Daren.

"That's not water, that's snow and it's very different, as you well know," replied Marella with a sniff, the effect of which was ruined as she giggled afterwards.

They all grinned at each other, knowing they were once again feeling better if Daren and Marella were teasing each other.

"Come on, let's go. I don't want to keep Hyanfol waiting. We've kept him long enough already," said Lani to the others, scraping her chair as she pushed it backwards so she could stand.

They walked into the main cave area they had seen when they first arrived and once again, a fire was burning in the circular hearth. Kai went over to it and literally ran his hands through the flames. Marella watched in wonder as Kai remained unharmed, not a burn or blister on his hands.

He saw her watching and smiled at her. "What? Fire is my Element, so long as I'm careful, it won't hurt me." He beckoned her closer so she could see.

"It feels good to be within your Element, doesn't it?" murmured Marella fascinated to see Kai's hands within the flames.

"It does. Usually I get enough fire just by being near the hearth or cooking fire, but we haven't had much of those recently, and I'm feeling the need to be close."

"I know that one," she said. "It is how I feel whenever I'm away from water for too long. I need the streams, rivers, lakes. The open water is best because of the sheer strength; however the lake near my home is so soothing for me. I spend hours there."

Kai nodded, understanding what she meant. "It's like that for me at home," he said. "We always have a fire going, even at the height of summer. None of us like the feel of our home without it."

Marella smiled in complete understanding of what it is like for someone to be so in tune with their Element.

"I think I have it the easiest of all of you," said Lani, joining in with their conversation. "After all, I am surrounded by my Element most of the time."

"Which do you prefer, Lani, a cool, gentle breeze or a gale strength wind?" asked Marella curiously.

"Both – I can't choose," said Lani with a smile. "There is beauty and strength in our Elements in all forms. There's no way I could choose just one, the same as you couldn't choose between a stream or the sea."

"Wise words from one so young," came Hynafol's deep voice. "What you say is true, Chosen of Air."

They turned around to see Hynafol resting comfortably towards the back of the cave, where the shadows were the deepest.

"Come," he rumbled, "please take a seat and make yourselves comfortable. There are things we need to discuss." He waited until they were all sat down before he started to speak again. "You are here for the *Plu y Gryphon* and I just want to say it is yours. Have no worries on that account. You will have your Essence of Air without any doubt."

He stopped for a moment as a sigh of relief went through the Chosen. He also saw the Partners come into the room, and sit down in a small group by themselves.

"You know someone is out there, working against you. They were in touch with King Ghobe and they have been here to see Queen Paralda. King Ghobe was taken in by his greed and Queen Paralda, whilst not agreeing with them, is causing as much damage by her inattentiveness. This is not a battle that will be won by sitting on the sidelines."

Marella looked at him expectantly, listening to everything he said as well as taking note of how he said it.

"We don't yet know who it is, although we all have our suspicions. Know that you have the Scions of the Elements on your side, and we will help you in any way we can."

"I'm sorry for interrupting, Hynafol, but who are the Scions? We've never heard of them," questioned Lani.

Hynfol smiled and readjusted his haunches to get comfortable. "I am not surprised by this; we have faded from history faster than I thought we would."

He cleared his throat before continuing, "The Scions of the Elements have been here since the beginning. We are of the same ancestry as the Lords and Ladies, although we take different shapes. You must be aware though; the Lords and Ladies take the shape of what is known to you, so as not to alarm you. They can appear as different shapes to any."

The others looked at each other; that thought had not occurred to any of them.

Hynafol chuckled at the looks on their faces. "Yes, it's true. They take a human shape so as not to scare you with an unknown. Anyway, as I was saying, we Scions have been here since the beginning. We were all brothers and sisters many moons ago, but things changed and it was decided one would be chosen for each Element. I was chosen for Air. Sound familiar?" he asked.

Marella giggled, "Yes, just a bit. It's like our Choosing."

Hynafol agreed with her. "Indeed. If something works, then why change it?" he said to Marella's delight.

"You didn't meet the Scion of Earth, because you had help from King Carrick and High Priestess Alana. Trust me though, if things had gone wrong with that rogue Elemental, you would have seen Cian. You can't actually miss him, he's a giant, you see." Hynafol laughed at his own joke as the Chosen watched him.

Hynafol stopped laughing as he realised the Chosen were not laughing with him. "Hmm, yes, well, carrying on. Meredith is the Scion of Water and she is a..."

"Dragon," interrupted Marella. "She's a sea dragon."

"Yes, she is," said Hynafol, tilting his head as he looked at her. "How do you know?"

"I've been dreaming of her all my life," said Marella simply.

"Of course you have," said Hynafol. "I don't know why I thought anything else. Yes, Meredith is a sea dragon. She can walk on land, fly in the air, but she is at home in the water. The only thing she can't do is tolerate Fire."

"Which leads me to her, you have already met the Scion of Fire, it is Ena," he finished, looking at Kai.

"Of course," Kai breathed. "Born of flame, releases to ash before being born again, the cycle continues."

"You've got it, Chosen of Fire, exactly right," Hynafol said with a smile. "So there you have it, the four Scions of the Elements, all working to help you where we can."

"And we are grateful for your help," said Lani, politely.

"But how does that help you now?" Hynafol asked, reading the looks on their faces. "Well, it means wherever you go, whether it is in the Elemental realm or your own, you only need to call us and we will help in any way we can. The world is supposed to be in balance, no Element stronger than the other. It is why you have opposites as well as those you are compatible with. Earth and Water work well together, as do Fire and Air. Fire and Water are natural opposites, as are Earth and Air. And yet, here you are, four Chosen – one of each Element and you are not only working well together, you are stronger than you would be individually. For your own failings and shortcomings, you have your strengths and successes. This is how it should be; however, someone out there doesn't want that."

He lifted one of his shoulders in a half shrug and continued, "I love being the Scion of Air, but that doesn't mean I don't like living in the Earth, playing in Water, or enjoying the life-giving heat of Fire. No one Element should be above the rest.

The quest you are on is to return balance to the Elements. You are doing this in an obvious way by retrieving the old Essence or finding new ones. However, you are also doing this in the time you've been given. You are working through the seasons, through everything the Elements can throw at you, by going into the Elemental Quarters and facing the unknown. The timing of a year and a day is not coincidental. Can any of you tell me what else has the same timing?"

Hynafol looked at them all. There was some shuffling and clearing of throats before Kai said hesitantly, "It is the same time as the traditional handfasting."

Hynafol beamed at him. "Exactly, Kai, exactly. It is the same time as the traditional handfasting and that, in effect, is what you are doing to help restore the balance. You, you eight magnificent Chosen, are in effect handfasting with the Elements as you traverse your journey. It is one thing to simply say something and another thing entirely to actually live it. You are living it; you are following your thoughts and words with actions. This is what will help to balance the Elements, not just the Essences."

As the Chosen thought about what they had just been told, the Partners moved a little closer. At the movement, Marella glanced around and saw Nixie with the others. "Did you know this, lovely?" she asked him aloud.

"It's not something we knew," he replied, *"but it is something we thought might be true. A year and a day is such a precise time."*

Marella gave a little snort and told the others what Nixie had just said, much to their amusement.

"Well, he's right," grinned Kai, looking around to see where Kenna was.

"Indeed," agreed Daren, leaning back.

"So what do we do now?" asked Lani, looking around the room. "You say we can have the *Plu y Gryphon*, we are marrying the Elements, and someone out there wants to stop us. So what do we do?"

"What you do now is spend the next couple of days relaxing, and recouping your strength. It took a lot out of you, getting here, if you rush back out before you're ready, your body will collapse. You are here and you are safe," said Hynafol.

"Yes, we are you say, but what about our homes and families back on

Wraidd Elfennol?" questioned Lani, not prepared to let it go. "Whilst we were in the Earth Quarter, there was an earthquake that affected a village not far from me. It destroyed Shaw's birth-tree. What will happen whilst we are here? If the balance is broken like you say, then something must be happening."

Hynafol sighed and looked down towards his paws which were crossed in front of him. "Lani, nothing is going to happen for a while because it already has," he confessed.

The tension within their group was immediate. "What do you mean, it already has? What's happened? Are our families safe?" The questions came from all directions and Hynfol raised a paw so he could speak.

"Your families are safe, others weren't so lucky, but no one has been mortally injured. There was a tornado that ripped through Bridd, causing quite a bit of structural damage, just like at Cwmwl."

At Hynafol's explanation, Daren sat up straighter and looked concerned. "How much damage? Is everyone okay?" he asked.

"The damage was extensive, it was a powerful tornado. It wasn't very wide but the winds were fast. Luckily, it didn't last long before it dissipated, but still, damage was caused and injuries did happen."

"Earthquake at Cwmwl, tornado at Bridd," murmured Lani. "That's not a coincidence either, is it?" she asked, looking Hynafol straight in the eyes.

He graced her with a gentle smile, "No, indeed, Lani, a coincidence it is not. You saw quicker than I expected you too."

The others looked between Lani and Hynafol, waiting patiently for the explanation they knew they would get.

"The opposite Element has been the cause of damage to your villages. Earth and Air are opposites, remember. It is not surprising Earth damaged an Air village, and Air damaged an Earth village. As astounding it seems, it's not as unanticipated as you might think. It's quite predictable really, if you think about it."

Lani nodded in agreement with Hynafol's explanation. "Whoever it is trying to stop us from regaining the balance, is using the Elements to attack our world, our homes. I don't know how they are able to do this, but it's an explanation which makes sense. The reason it makes sense is because of what Hynafol has just said. It is our opposing Element that caused the damage. If it were a natural occurrence, would it be that way?"

Enlightenment showed upon their faces as they understood what was being said.

"They had more chance of us believing it to be natural, if they'd used something else," said Kai.

"Exactly, but now we know it is just part of the disruption for our challenge. What can we do about it?" asked Marella.

"You can't do anything except carry on with your quest. My fellow Scions and I will be helping your villages to lessen the damage, or to repair what has been done, although they may not see us. This is our part of the challenge. Perhaps it is once again time for the Scions to be known?" he mused.

"Are the Elders aware of what is going on?" asked Marella, thinking about her mother.

"Yes they are and they are unsure of how to move forward. Do they tell the general population and cause panic, or keep it quiet and hope no one figures it out?"

"Well that's just stupid," replied Marella.

The others looked at her in shock, Daren chuckling to himself. "Come now, Marella. Don't hold back, tell us what you really think," he laughed.

"Well, it is," said Marella indignantly. "By the Waters, our people aren't stupid. They will realise what is going on, then what will happen? Instead of being supported by each other and the Elders, they will become resentful of being kept in the dark. Instead of neighbours helping neighbours, it will become more segregated and mistrustful. I... I... I just can't." With that, Marella threw her hands in the air and stormed out of the room. Nixie looked around at the others before following her.

Kai saw the stunned looks on the faces of the others and smiled to himself. "I'll go after her, make sure she's all right," he said before walking out of the room.

* * *

Daren and Lani looked at each other in silence, neither one sure of what to say following Marella's outburst.

"She may have a point, you know," said Hynafol thoughtfully.

"She usually does," agreed Daren wryly, "you just have to weather the storm with her first."

They sat in companionable silence waiting for Marella, Kai, and Nixie to return. It didn't take long before Nixie came back in, and returned to his place with the Partners. His complete manner of nonchalance was enough to reassure Daren, who looked to see Marella come through the door, holding onto Kai's hand. Daren quirked his eyebrow when he saw this, but didn't say anything.

"I'm sorry," apologised Marella. "I shouldn't have lost my temper."

"No matter," reassured Hynafol. "No harm done."

He waited until both Marella and Kai had returned to their seats before he continued. "I think you may have a point, Marella. If the Elders keep quiet about this and someone figures it out - which they will - then it will work against us, and 'for' whomever it is causing trouble. They seek disruption and distrust. It will be harder for their schemes if everyone is helping each other. I will talk with my brother and sisters, and we will contact the Elders. Don't worry, Marella, it will be okay."

Marella still looked concerned, but she nodded at Hynafol's reassurances, knowing things would now be in the open about what was happening. She couldn't bear the thought of her family not knowing what was going on, especially as they were off to the Fire Quarter next, so whatever would happen, would affect those who lived in Water villages.

"Now," said Hynafol, changing the topic of discussion, "I think it is time for you to relax. You may do as you want – there is the hot springs, I have quite a good library, you may rest if you wish. I even have more than one bed if you would like to spread out." Hynafol's eyes twinkled and everyone laughed as he broke the tension within the room.

"I don't know, I quite like how we slept last night," said Kai, looking at Marella, who blushed as she remembered how comfortable she had been upon waking.

After a few more comments, everyone went their separate ways. Kai and Daren headed to the kitchen area, and Lani followed Hynafol towards his library. Marella and Nixie, with unspoken accord, went down one of the side tunnels towards the hot springs. They stopped briefly in the room where they had slept so Marella could retrieve her swimsuit. Without haste, but not dawdling either, they arrived at the springs.

Marella entered the cavern and looked around. The natural formation of the cave was somehow welcoming, and she could feel herself relaxing, even before reaching the water. She changed out of her clothes and put on her swimsuit. Without further ado, she immersed herself in the water, pleased to find a stone ledge she could sit on. She placed her arms out of the water, leaning back against the stone. She tilted her head back and relaxed, at ease within her Element.

~ 42 ~

When they all met up later, it was obvious everyone felt more relaxed and refreshed than they had been earlier. Lani had spent time in the library whilst Kai and Daren had gone exploring through the tunnels with Kenna and Ula. Marella and Nixie had spent time reaffirming their bond with each other and their Element.

They all sat down to eat a big plateful of noodles and pork, with peppermint tea to aid with digestion afterwards. Once they had eaten their fill, Marella leaned back in her chair and rubbed her stomach contentedly. "Wow, Hynafol, that was delicious, my compliments to your chef."

Hynafol smiled at her from where he rested and bowed his head in acknowledgement, "I'll be sure to pass on your thanks, Marella. To be honest, I think they like having someone else here to cook for."

After they had finished, they followed Hynafol back into the main cavern where the fire was once again burning brightly, casting shadows on the wall.

They sat down, comfortable, warm, and well-fed. "Hynafol," began Lani, "I really appreciate everything you've done for us and have said you will do, but I'm starting to feel like our time here is ending. We need to continue with our challenge. If someone is working against us, which I believe, then we are only halfway through. We still have the Fire and Water Quarters to contend with, plus anything else that is thrown at us. I think we need to get ready to leave. I'm sorry." Lani gnawed on her bottom lip, afraid she would offend Hynafol with her words.

Hynafol huffed gently at her, belaying her fears. "Do not fear, Lani. I have anticipated this. Although you have needed the rest, I didn't think you'd be content to stay here for long. I have packed some fresh provisions for you. Finish out today here and get a good night's sleep. You can set of in the morning and it will be a quicker, and easier, way back. I have spoken with Lord Adaryn and he is going to ensure the winds behave. It will still be cold, but at least you won't have the snows swirling around."

"Thank you, Hynafol," replied Lani, smiling warmly at him.

"There is one other thing you will need though," he reminded them. "The *Plu y Gryphon*."

Lani blushed and gave a startled laugh. "I can't believe I forgot about that," she said.

"Don't worry, I did too," said Marella, giggling.

Daren and Kai just looked at each other before laughing as they realised they too had forgotten. While the group had a moment of madness, the four Partners and Hynafol all shared a look, like parents of wayward children.

Once the companions had calmed down, Hynafol spoke once more. "Lani, please come here."

Lani rose and walked without hesitation to where Hynafol was lying down. He stretched out one large, golden wing before her. "Take what you need, it's okay."

Lani looked back at the others who had calmed down due to the solemnity of the situation.

"Won't I hurt you?" she asked timidly.

Hynafol chuffed at her. "Lani, you know better than that. Your Partner is a hawk, you know he moults and loses his feathers. It doesn't hurt him and this won't hurt me. Go on, get your feather."

Lani reached towards one of the flight feathers that ran along the outside edge of his wing. She knew from being with Shaw she could take one of these, and it would grow back without too much disruption to his flying.

There was a large feather on the top of Hynafol's wing that gleamed in the flickering light of the cave. Lani was drawn to it but, just before she touched it, she stopped. She waited and took a deep breath. *'Lord Adaryn, help me, let me be true,'* she thought.

Lani looked at Hynafol and saw him watching her; respect and admiration shining in his eyes. She took another deep breath and reached forward once more. This time, instead of going for the large, bright feather on the top, she reached towards the underside of his wing. Hynafol raised it slightly to help once he saw where she was headed.

With a swift movement, Lani had plucked a feather from his wing and held it. She looked at it and then up to Hynafol. "Thank you, Hynafol."

Hynafol shook down his feathers and folded his wing against his back. "Good choice, Chosen of Air. You have selected wisely."

Marella, Kai, and Daren came over to where Lani stood clutching the feather and looked at it.

Marella tilted her head. The feather had a strange light about it, as though it didn't quite match the rest of Hynafol's feathers somehow. "Why is it a wise option, Hynafol? And why does it glimmer so?"

Hynafol beamed down at the four of them. "It is a wise choice because it is the right *Plu y Gryphon*, only a true Initiate of Air, chosen by and given Lord Adaryn's blessing, would have picked that one instead of the other."

"You were testing me?" asked Lani, feeling a little hurt.

"No, child, not testing you. The other feather would have worked, it is still a gryphon's feather after all, but the one you have chosen has a stronger connection to Air. That is the original *Plu y Gryphon*, the one chosen by Lord Adaryn himself."

Hynafol bent his head towards Lani and buffed his head against her cheek like Shaw did. The only difference was Hynafol's head was much larger than Lani's so it didn't have quite the same effect. Lani reached up with both arms, still holding the feather, and hugged him instead.

After a moment, they pulled apart and Lani's eyes were suspiciously bright. Trying to give her a moment to compose herself, Marella once again spoke to Hynafol.

"So what is the glimmer then, Hynafol?" she asked.

"Ever the curious one, aren't you Marella," laughed Hynafol. "The reason the feather glimmers is because of it being the true *Plu y Gryphon*. What you see as a glimmer is actually the Essence of Air held within it, and all its correspondences."

"All of them?" questioned Kai.

"Yes, Kai, all them. This feather, the same as the shield Daren retrieved, holds all the correspondences of the Element. So trees, flowers, metals, stones, there is something of everything here. That is what makes the Essence so powerful."

Kai nodded his understanding whilst the others carried on looking at the feather Lani held onto.

Hynafol tilted his head. "Ah, it appears we have another visitor." He smiled at a spot in the cavern that looked empty, "Welcome to my home, Lord Adaryn. Please make yourself comfortable."

Lani gasped and took a step towards the empty space before stopping. She watched as lights started to flicker in and out, and a body started to appear. She bent down on one knee and bowed her head, holding the feather out towards where Lord Adaryn was standing.

"My Lord," she said, "the *Plu y Gryphon*."

Lord Adaryn walked slowly towards them, his long silver hair tied back in a leather thong. His clothing was loose and flowing, changing from silver to shades of blue, yellow, green, and even pink. Marella was fascinated with the changing colours and couldn't stop staring at them. Daren gave her a small nudge and she blinked furiously.

Lord Adaryn stopped in front of Lani and gently placed his hand upon her head. "Rise now, child of mine."

Lani stood up, but still didn't look at him. He placed his fingertips under her chin and tipped up her face until she was looking him in the eyes. "Well done, Lani. You and Shaw have done as I have asked of you and more. I couldn't have Chosen anyone better. You have made me proud."

Tears flowed down Lani's cheeks; however, she made no move to wipe them away. Tenderly, Lord Adaryn blotted them with a linen cloth he pulled from a pocket. "You really should have more confidence in yourself, Lani, but you are still young. I guess confidence will be something you grow into."

Hynafol chuffed from where he sat, catching Lord Adaryn's attention.

"Is there anything you wish to say, Scion?" he asked, arching an eyebrow, his eyes twinkling, as he moved to stand in front of him.

"Not really, oh great Lord of Air yourself, the mighty Lord Adaryn," said Hynafol teasingly.

Lord Adaryn snorted at Hynofol's words, much to the amusement of the companions.

"And since when have you thought of me as such?" questioned Adaryn, laughter plain upon his face.

"Well, I don't, obviously," replied Hynafol. "But your young lady there does. I have seen her heart and she follows you true. She will be your staunchest defender."

Adaryn glanced back affectionately at Lani, "I know, Hynafol, I know. It's one of the reasons I Chose her. Not just for the potential I could see, but also for her faith and belief in me. It is a decision I have not yet regretted, and I don't think I ever will."

"Excuse me," interrupted Lani, her hands on her hips, "but I am still here you know. I'm standing right here and you're both being rather rude, talking about me as though I'm not."

Lani stopped and placed a trembling hand upon her lips, "Oh no, what have I said?" she whispered. Daren walked up behind her and placed his arms around her. Lani leaned into his embrace, resting her head in his shoulder.

Adaryn and Hynafol laughed, and Adaryn walked back to where a trembling Lani stood. "Oh Lani, you were quite right to scold us. We had no better manners than any youngling. Don't worry, child, you haven't offended us."

Lani looked up at him, searching his eyes for the truth. What she saw there made her relax and she smiled.

"Let's get this Essence sent off, shall we?" Lord Adaryn said to her and she nodded enthusiastically.

Raising her hands, she held the feather in front of her heart. With a flash of light, it disappeared, as the scent of lavender filled the air.

"And so the Essence of Air is now held in a monolith in the town square at Alaw, awaiting your return to Charon. Well done, my Chosen, well done indeed." Lord Adaryn smiled, his body language showing how pleased he was with the situation.

"Lord Adaryn, may I ask a question?"

Lord Adaryn turned to Lani and gestured, his arms outspread. "Of course you may, ask me anything."

"Do you know yet who it is working against us? Do you have any idea of what they have planned next?"

The smile slowly dropped from Lord Adaryn's face and he rolled his shoulders. "No, Lani, I'm afraid we don't yet know who it is, although we each have our suspicions. Whoever it is, is good at hiding their tracks and using smoke screens. We fill find out though, and they will be dealt with accordingly, I assure you."

Straightening his shirt and fiddling with the cuff as he spoke, he continued "We don't really know much of anything, however much it pains me to admit it. We're supposed to know everything!" he exclaimed. "What we can surmise, is the Water villages will be hit next as Fire is the next Quarter you must go to, and it has been the opposite of each Element which has been attacked. Oh, pardon me," he scoffed, "I mean natural disaster."

Marella came to stand beside Lani, "Can anything be done to limit the damage, sir?" she asked.

Adaryn looked at her and smiled, "No, Chosen of Water, because we simply have no idea of where or when. Every Water village has been put on high alert; there are already rumblings of factions fighting against each other."

Marella shot a sharp glance at Hynafol, who intercepted it with a wry grin. "Okay, okay, I concede the point," he rumbled good-naturedly. "We have already talked about this, Adaryn, and Marella is convinced the only way to stop this is to be honest with everyone – from the Elders down to the children. Give them as much information as is age appropriate, and let everyone know the consequences. It affects everyone and will stop the rumblings. Marella has argued her case vehemently, and I agree with her."

Adaryn tapped his chin with his forefinger. "I think you may be right. I will speak to the others about this, and we will deal with it straight away. I don't want this to continue. We need to be working together, not pulling apart."

"Anyway, I must go. I will inform Erion and Taren you have been successful; although I'm sure they will know by the monolith. Congratulations again, Chosen."

He held his arm out and with a screech, Shaw came swooping down and landed on his forearm. "Did you think I could ever forget about you, my hawk?" he said, rubbing Shaw's head. "Thank you for everything you have done. I have a small reward for you. I had a small, broken branch from your birth tree. I have spoken with Lady Daire and she has managed to grow it again. It is now in a safe place and is surrounded by the three other Elements, as befits a Chosen. I hope this helps mend the sadness in your heart."

Shaw flapped his wings, causing flurries of air to ripple through the chamber. "*I don't know how to thank you. I never expected this.*"

"I know you didn't and that is one of the reasons I have done it. I think your birth tree still has a role to play, whether now or in the future, I'm not sure. Just think of the fun you and Lani will have as you try to find it." Adaryn grinned mischievously and stroked his finger down the front of Shaw's chest.

Adaryn lifted his arm and Shaw took wing, flying over to Lani's shoulder, where he gripped into the leather pad sewn into her shirt.

"I must go now; there are still lots of things for me to attend to. Good luck, Chosen. You're halfway there and you have done so well. We are very proud of you." With those words, Adaryn faded from sight, the last thing Marella could see were his eyes, still appearing to twinkle as they disappeared.

* * *

Once he was gone, Lani turned to the others and heaved a sigh, a beaming smile breaking across her face. "That's it, we've done it. My part is done."

They all laughed at the relief in Lani's voice although Hynafol shook his head. "Your part isn't done yet; you still have two more Quarters to visit and Essences to retrieve."

"I know, Hynafol," quipped Lani cheekily, "I just meant my time as Leader is done, and that is the part I feel relief over." She looked at the others and her face grew serious. "I just want to thank you for all the support you've given me. You have helped me and my confidence has grown. However, not everyone is meant to be a leader. I'm one of them. I am more than happy to be here with you, however, I am so relieved the burden of leadership is about to be passed on. For me, it wasn't just a challenge, something to attack; it was a weight playing on me. I hope you understand."

Daren, being the closest one to her, pulled her into a hug, his arms reassuring her. "Lani, you have done a brilliant job, but if this isn't what you want, no one here will force you. You are still the Chosen of Air; if that's enough for you, it's enough for me."

Lani closed her eyes at Daren's words, taking comfort from him. When she opened her eyes, Kai and Marella were standing closer to her, smiling.

"We love you, Lani, and only want you to be happy. If you don't want to be leader anymore, then don't worry about it. We'll go straight from here to the Portal, we don't have to stop and see Queen Paralda," said Marella.

Lani stiffened in Daren's embrace and pulled free. She threw back her shoulders and tipped up her chin. Marella cheered inwardly at seeing this reaction but said nothing, waiting for Lani to speak.

"I started this part as Leader and I'll finish it the same. We will go and see Queen Paralda before leaving; it is the polite thing to do. I'll not have her thinking we've snubbed her. Instead of her sitting on the fence, that might be the thing which tips her over and not in a good way." Lani turned so she could see Kai, Marella, and Daren and raised her eyebrow in question. "Does anyone have a problem with that?"

"No, Lani,", "Not at all," "Whatever you think is best," came the replies from the three of them.

"Right, well then, I suggest we rest up as much as we can today for tomorrow we leave." With that, Lani spun on her heel and left the cavern, leaving the others in her wake.

They looked at each other and smiled. "Lani will be fine," reassured Marella.

"Nicely done, Marella," complimented Hynafol. "All Lani wanted to do was leave and go straight back to Wraidd Elfennol, but by your manipulations, she will now meet Queen Paralda and play diplomat before you leave the Air Quarter."

Marella spluttered, "My manipu… Hynafol, I never manipulated Lani," she said indignantly.

"My dear, that's exactly what you did. You played her into doing what you knew was right. That's some power you have. Just make sure you only use it for the good of a situation and not for personal reasons."

Hynafol's words stung Marella and she crossed her arms in defence. "I'm going to the hot springs," she said in a quiet voice and left the cavern, her head down.

"Hynafol, you could have worded that differently," chided Kai as he looked after Marella.

"No, I worded it precisely right." Hynafol sighed, "Marella is very strong in her Element, and as such, she needs to be aware of it. Manipulating Lani is exactly what she did, although she won't call it that. She has to recognise when she is doing this to people, otherwise she will do it all the time. Water is compassionate, loving, flowing; but the negative aspects include being overly-sensitive, insecure and manipulative. If she is aware of them, she can act to change them."

Kai tilted his head as he looked at Hynafol, considering his explanation. "I think you're right. Marella didn't do it maliciously though, you know that, right?"

Hynafol agreed, "Oh yes, I know. I've seen a few people through my time with only a single Element. However, Marella is the most adjusted out of them all. She just needs someone to point out what she's doing at times, instead of coddling her."

Kai laughed. "Oh Hynafol, if only you knew. Marella is as far from being coddled as she can get. Her home life is loving on one side and neglected on the other. She certainly has not been coddled, as you call it."

"Be that as it may, she has, by her best friend if no one else."

At that, Daren started and looked up in surprise to Hynafol. His thoughts had wandered off so he hadn't really been paying attention.

"What? What have I done?" He looked from Kai to Hynafol in search of answers.

"We were talking about Marella being coddled, and unaware she can manipulate people into doing what she wants," answered Kai.

"Well, she's always been able to do so," said Daren in surprise, "I didn't realise it was an issue. It's not something she's ever done for no reason."

"It's not an issue, Daren, just something Marella needs to think about, be aware of. Playing with the emotions of people is not something that should ever be done lightly, and the ends do not justify the means if you are using it without thought." Hynafol stopped; his face serious. He looked at Daren and Kai, knowing his words needed to be heard, not ignored.

"If Marella can think about this, acknowledge what she is doing, then we can all rest assured she will only use it if need be and in dire circumstances. If she is not checked and called on it, she will grow to use it more and more. Do you want her using it on you? Because she will, at some point, if she is not made to realise what she is doing."

There was silence as Daren and Kai pondered Hynafol's warning. Neither of them could imagine Marella doing such a thing, but they both realised they would be stupid if they didn't take his words seriously.

Finally, Daren nodded in agreement. "Okay, Hynafol, so what do we do? Point out what she's doing whenever she does it? How do we handle this?"

"You don't have to point it out as in mention it aloud every time she does. Just be aware of it and if you think it is getting too be too much, tell her. This is something she is doing subconsciously, so will probably deny any involvement. The more she is aware of it, the more control she will have."

Kai let out a deep breath, unhappy with this turn of events. "Okay, I don't like it, but I understand the necessity."

"I wouldn't worry too much, Kai. Marella is now aware and the first thing she has done is to spend time with her Element. Erwyna will speak with her, give her the reassurance she needs right now. You just need to be there to continue it; especially when there is no large body of water around she can immerse herself in."

"Alright, I can do that," said Kai.

Daren smiled up at the gryphon, "How did you get to be so wise?" he asked.

Hynafol chuckled, "When you're as old as I am, you know a few things," he explained.

"Right you two, off you go. There are preparations I need to make for your departure. Go and spend some time doing whatever you wish to do.

You will leave in the morning." With that, Hynafol carefully turned his large body around and left down one of the side corridors.

Daren and Kai looked at each other and grinned. "Back to the kitchen?" Daren said.

"Lead the way, Chosen of Earth, lead the way," answered Kai.

Daren snorted at Kai, leading the way to kitchen, in search of more delights.

The rest of the day passed swiftly, the companions spending time both together and apart as they prepared to leave. Marella seemed a bit quiet and withdrawn, so the others gave her the space she needed and time with Nixie.

They ate a good meal in the evening and called it an early night. None of them were looking forward to the walk back to Awyr to meet with Queen Paralda, although they all knew it needed to be done.

~ 43 ~

The following morning started early as the Chosen and their Partners prepared to leave Hynafol. They had a good breakfast with a hot drink to warm them up on the inside before leaving the caverns and entering the cold, snowy world once more.

"I've made arrangements for you to get you to Awyr today, I hope you don't mind," said Hynafol as they stood near the exit.

"Today?" exclaimed Lani, "We'll never make it today. Have you forgotten how long it took us to reach you?"

"No, Lani, I haven't forgotten, however, I am aware of the passing of time. You need to leave the Air Quarter, as time is not waiting for you. It is already more than halfway through Hydref in your world, there is only one week to go before Samhain."

Lani gasped, "I didn't realise so much time would have passed. We've only been with you for a couple of days. And we still have to see Queen Paralda and make it back to the Portal. By the Air, how are we going to do this?" she panicked.

"Gently, Lani, calm down. This is why I've arranged transport for you. It will also show Queen Paralda you have my support, as well as my feather. Come outside with me and greet your mounts."

Hynafol led them outside where the cold took their breath away. Or maybe it was the sight of four huge eagles, each one with a leather saddle upon its back. "These are Rocs and they have kindly agreed to return you to Awyr."

"What about our Partners?" asked Lani.

"There is room for them too, not even Shaw can keep up with a Roc."

They looked at each other, then at Hynafol. "Thank you for helping us, Hynafol. I'm going to miss you," said Lani, wiping at her eyes.

"It's been my pleasure, Lani. I'm sure we'll meet again at some point. And if we don't, you always know how to visit me," he laughed.

They said their goodbyes and the companions scrambled onto the Rocs, and gingerly sat in the saddles. Their Partners, undaunted by the prospect of a huge flying bird, simply climbed up the front leg Hynafol raised to help them, before making themselves comfortable in front of their companions.

"Honestly, this Roc is so huge, I could lie sideways and I don't think I'd fall off," said Marella as she peered over the side.

"That may be true, but I wouldn't recommend it," said Hynafol, watching her.

"Don't worry, I won't," she reassured him. She held onto the straps and made sure Nixie was safe in front of her. Marella looked around to see if the others were ready. Whilst she wasn't paying attention, the Roc leapt into the air. Her neck snapped back and the breath left her lungs in a whoosh. "NIXIE," she screamed, clinging on to the straps.

"I'm safe, Marella, I'm here. Hold on tight, we're moving at quite a speed."

Marella gulped and held on to the leather as strongly as she could. She moved her head to the sides and saw Lani laughing and whooping as they sped back towards Awyr.

"It's a good job the sky is clear today, I wouldn't fancy doing this in a snowstorm," she thought to Nixie, speech being impossible at the speed they were going.

"I don't think we would have been able to fly through a storm, even with how strong these Rocs are," came Nixie's reply. *"Don't worry; we'll be there before too long."*

For the rest of the short flight, Marella held onto the leather straps in front of her and tried not to move. The previous thoughts of lying down on the back of the Roc had completely disappeared. The end of the flight couldn't come quick enough for her, so it was with great relief when she finally saw the village of Awyr. "Thank goodness," she breathed.

"They are going to land in a field just outside of Awyr, and we will walk the rest of the way," Nixie told her.

"I'll need to get my legs back first," she answered, *"They feel incredibly wobbly right now."*

Marella could feel Nixie's amusement through their bond, and knew this would be something he would remember and tease her about, in the years to come.

After they landed, Marella threw her leg over the Roc's back and slithered down the ground. She hoped she looked a little bit graceful but was sure she looked like she had dropped to the ground like a stone as her legs refused to hold her up.

In front of her, a hand was held out for her to take and she grasped it. It was only once she had been pulled up she realised it was Kai.

"Did you enjoy the flight, Marella?" he asked courteously.

"Not really, no," she grumbled, trying to straighten her clothing.

Kai gave a small laugh and hugged her, pulling back before she fully realised what he had done. "I think the only one who completely enjoyed it was Lani," he said. "She was laughing pretty much the whole way."

Marella shook her head. "She can keep her flying," she said wryly, "I'll stick with water."

"Come on," he said, loping an arm around her shoulders, "let's get this show on the road and get to Wraidd Elfennol."

With Nixie and Kenna running in front of them, Kai and Marella joined Lani and Daren and they headed towards their meeting with Queen Paralda.

* * *

Aria was waiting for them, not far from where she had said goodbye a few days previously, a warm smile greeting them. "It is so good to see you again; I was worried when we heard there was a storm in the mountains. I hope you were okay."

"We were. Hynafol found us before any lasting damage was caused," replied Lani, once again taking the lead.

Aria looked concerned at Lani's explanation. "Lasting damage?" she questioned.

"Yes, we all had a touch of frostbite, but nothing too serious."

Marella wondered why Lani was being almost blasé about their time in the mountains. She felt refreshed after their time with Hynafol, but the horror of that penetrating cold, the numbness of her mind, the loss of control over her limbs, still gave her cause to shiver if she thought about it.

Kai and Daren were walking on either side of Marella as they followed Lani. Kai leaned down and spoke to Marella as they continued to walk. "Lani doesn't want to give too much information away to Aria."

From the other side, Daren whispered "Shaw hasn't said whether or not we can trust her."

Marella looked at them both, her head moving from one side to the other. "I thought all Partners could see into the hearts of those we spoke with."

"They can," replied Kai, "however, it only works if they are true, one way or the other."

"For the Lords and Ladies, or against them. If Queen Paralda is as ambivalent as Hynafol suggested, then Shaw may not know or be able to tell. He has looked into Aria's soul but can't be sure, which is why Lani is being so careful with her words. If they start working against us, Lani doesn't want them to know how close we came to succumbing."

"How do you two know this and I don't?" Marella laughed at them.

Kai shrugged his shoulders. "I don't know; you were there when we discussed it. It was as we were climbing up the mountain to reach Hynafol. Lani asked Shaw if she could trust them."

Marella shook her head. "I feel like I missed out on a whole conversation. Oh well, I'll follow Lani's lead, you know that."

Daren gave her a gentle nudge as they walked along so Marella turned and gave him a small smile.

Marella reached out on a private link to her beloved Life Partner. "*I'll be glad to get back to Wraidd Elfennol, Nixie. I feel out of my depth here. I hope the other Quarters are a bit easier. There's so much double-speak and political manoeuvrings we have to think of here.*"

Marella heard a quiet snort in her mind before Nixie's words flowed through their bond. *"You're doing fine; I'd be surprised if you didn't feel a tad uncomfortable. Kai may be your traditional opposite, but Air is conflicting for you as well. Think about it, Water is emotions and instincts, Air is logic and planning. Communication and miscommunication are also in the realm of Air. Carry on doing as you're doing, follow Lani and look to Kai and Daren if you feel unsure. We'll be home soon."*

"I certainly hope so, then I just have the Fire Quarter to contend with," Marella gave an audible snort and started to giggle, earning her looks from both men at her side.

"Nixie," she said in explanation.

Marella looked around her as she realised they were coming to a stop. She saw they had reached the grotto whilst she had been in conversation with Nixie and Queen Paralda could be seen on the opposite side, sat in her chair with her skirts spread out, just like before. They walked until they were in front of her before coming to a halt. Lani stood with Shaw on her shoulder, three steps in front of them.

"Welcome back, Chosen of Air. I am pleased to see that you have made it unscathed."

"Thank you for your greetings, Queen Paralda. Yes, we are well, and the *Plu y Gryphon* has been retrieved. We thank you for your assistance in this matter."

Marella gave another internal snort at Lani's words. She felt a jab in her ribs and looked to see Daren watching her, his eyes twinkling with his own amusement. Marella gave him a small wink before returning her attention to Lani.

"I am pleased to hear it, may I see it?" asked Queen Paralda, her face showing little warmth.

"I'm afraid not, you see, Lord Adaryn was there, and he has sent it off for safekeeping. We still have other places to go, and it makes more sense than for us to be carrying it around where it could get lost or damaged," explained Lani.

The expression froze on Queen Paralda's face as she listened to Lani's explanation. "I see," she said. "Well then, there's no need for you to tarry here, is there? I'm sure you'll be happy to be on your way. Good day."

With that, she stood up and walked away, her skirts swishing behind her. Aria gave the companions an apologetic glance. "Safe journey, Chosen. It's been a pleasure to meet you, and I wish you well for the next half of your quest."

Lani graciously acknowledged Aria's words. "It has been a pleasure to meet you too, Aria. If ever you need us, please let us know. We will make our way to the Portal now. Thank you for everything."

Aria bowed her head towards them before scurrying after Queen Paralda.

Lani turned to the others as a broad, relieved smile crossed her face. "Let's go," she said happily and led them from the grotto.

"How are we supposed to get back on the ground, Lani? We travelled with Aria to get here," questioned Marella.

Lani just grinned and carried on walking. The others looked at each other, before shrugging their shoulders and following her. She led them the way they had come and when they were back in the field, she reached into her pocket and pulled out a thin tin whistle. She held it triumphantly, a smile lighting up her whole face.

"This is how we're getting to the Portal," she said. She lifted it to her lips and blew, the smooth, soft sound filling the air.

"When did you get that?" asked Daren as the sounds faded away.

"Hynafol gave it to me just before we left. He was concerned we might have difficulty in reaching the Portal." Lani scoffed as she repeated his words, her eyes laughing. "He knew exactly what would happen, and made sure we wouldn't be stranded. This is what he meant about me knowing how to visit him."

The others laughed at Hynafol's wisdom and thoughtfulness, sending their mental thanks through the air to him, hoping he would hear them.

* * *

Within moments, the Rocs returned and they were clambering aboard. Shaw sat with Lani but decided he would fly the last part of this journey, once they were close enough for him to know where the Portal was.

Marella looked down from her saddle as Kai lifted Nixie to her, her face filled with trepidation. Kai gave her leg a squeeze, the warmth from his hand giving her comfort.

"Don't worry, Marella. I'm with you and so is Nixie. It's not a long flight. I'll stay with you."

"Thanks Kai," whispered Marella, her stomach in knots at the thought of flying again. She held onto the leather straps so tightly her knuckles turned white. With Nixie's body pressed against hers, she took a deep breath and waited.

With a massive jerk of his body, the Roc took flight, leaving Marella's stomach on the ground, or so it felt. She swallowed frantically, trying to control herself, squeezing her eyes shut. She could feel Nixie rubbing his head against her chest, but fear held her tight in its grasp.

"Marella, don't worry. I told you I'd be here, and so I am. Open your eyes, Marella, look at me."

Marella frowned in confusion, her eyes still closed. *"Nixie? What's changed? It doesn't sound like you."*

"It's not Nixie. Open your eyes."

Marella peeled her eyelids open and saw Kai was flying as close to her side as the two Rocs would allow.

"Kai?" she gasped aloud, the wind whipping her words away.

"I won't hear you if you speak out loud, it's too windy. Talk through the bond paths." Kai's words were clear in her mind, just like the Partners' were when she spoke to them.

"But how...? I don't understand. I've never heard someone else before, just the Partners? How are you doing this? How did you know?"

Kai gave her a grin as she looked at him, her curiosity winning out over the fear of flying. He could see her body relaxing, as her mind started to ask questions.

"It was written in Hynafol's library. I found a book about the history of Wraidd Elfennol and there was a section in there about how we can speak to each other, as well as our Partners. For some reason, no one knows now we can do this. I thought I'd wait until you needed distracting before I tried it to see if I could do it."

Marella laughed as she heard his explanation. Kai knew how scared she was and instead of telling her to stop it or to pull herself together, he had given her a gift instead. She smiled over at him, thankful for a friend like Kai.

"This is amazing!" she thought back to him, her tone filled with enthusiasm. *"Do the others know yet? Have you spoken to them? What do they think? This is brilliant."*

She could see Kai laughing at her thoughts, but couldn't take offence. She was so excited about the prospect they could all speak together. This made things so much easier.

"I haven't tried it with Daren or Lani yet, so I don't know."

"You spoke with me first?" she questioned.

"You needed the distraction more than they did. They're fine with flying, look at them. Even Ula is hanging over the side of the Roc, trying to see below. You were the one who was scared."

Marella tried to take exception to his words, as she hated to think of herself as the weak link. However, because she could hear and feel the truth in his words, she knew he wasn't trying to be horrible. She could feel the concern in his thoughts, his care for her. Instead of feeling angry, she felt reassured.

Nixie wriggled in her lap and looked up at her, the connection breaking between Kai and Marella as she looked down at him. *"This is a good thing, Marella. I'm glad you and Kai have found the connection. Not everyone can do this, you know. It takes a lot of trust to allow another person into your mind. Well done, Chosen, well done."* With that, Nixie snuggled back down again, tucked away from the chill of the fast flying wind.

Marella gave him a quick squeeze as she contemplated his words. *'A lot of trust, eh. Well, I do trust Kai. I wonder what else is going to change."*

Her stomach flipped as the Roc started to fly lower to the ground. Once again, she squeezed her eyes shut as the sight of the ground rushing towards them was too much. Immediately, she felt warmth reaching out to her. Mentally, she grabbed hold of that warmth and clung to it. She could feel it wrapping around her body so that she felt like she was being hugged. Relaxing into the comfort she felt, she barely noticed when the Roc landed. It was Nixie squirming around, and a whispered *"We're here, Marella,"* that made her open her eyes.

They had indeed landed, right next to the Portal. It had taken them over a day to reach Awyr but just over an hour to return to the crossing. She slid off her Roc and stroked his neck in thanks. His golden eye blinked at her before she moved away so he could take off again.

With a gust of wind caused by the back draft from their wings, the four Rocs took off, headed back towards the Mynydd o Sibrydion and Hynafol.

Daren and Lani were adjusting their backpacks, laughing at each other. Kai came and stood close to Marella, watching them too. "You don't mind, do you Marella?" he asked her, an uncertain note in his voice. "I know it's a private thing that was between you and Nixie."

Marella laughed as she turned to face him, placing her arms around his waist and squeezing tightly. "A private thing?" she laughed. "Only between Nixie and I… and every other Partner out there. I am honoured you tested it with me and your timing was perfect. Thank you."

Kai relaxed at her reassurance and returned the embrace, his arms holding her tightly. "You know, you don't have to worry. According to the books, I won't be able to see or hear everything you think. Your thoughts and feelings are still private. It's only if you consciously speak on the bond path that I will hear you."

"Well that's good to know," she giggled. "I can't have you knowing everything about me."

"I want to know everything though," said Kai in response, his arms tightening around her.

Marella cocked her head, giving him a quizzical look. She pursed her lips and nodded, coming to a decision. "You only have to ask," she said before laying her head against his chest.

Kai tipped his cheek so it rested on the top of her head, a sense of peace flowing through them as they shared a private moment.

All too soon they both broke apart, knowing this wasn't the time or the place. They had a Portal to cross and another Quarter to find. It was, however, with a feeling of contentment they rejoined Daren, Lani, and the Partners before crossing back through the Portal into Wraidd Elfennol.

~ 44 ~

The first thing they noticed, once they crossed over, was how cold the weather had become. They shared a glance before hurrying down the side of the rocks, being careful of the shale and shakeholes. They went as quickly as they could, the cold air seeping through their clothes, although the activity kept them warm.

When they reached the bottom, Kai and Daren went to find the cave where their equipment was stored, Marella and Lani scrambling behind. With Daren's help, they removed the foliage from the front of the cave and retrieved the items from within.

Marella shivered as she sorted through her things, laying her staff across the top of her trundle truck so she could pull with both hands. "We need to get back to a village, find out how much time has passed," she said, her voice shaking as her teeth chattered together.

Daren laughed at her. "Or we could just ask one of the Partners," he reminded her.

Colour suffused Marella's face as she remembered they knew the correct time flow, even when they were in the Quarters.

Kenna gave a small yip, dancing around her paws, her coat a splash of bright colour in the cold, grey light of day.

Marella giggled at her antics and lowered herself down to the ground, crouching on her toes. "Kenna, dearest, is there something you wish to say?"

Kenna stopped her prancing and held herself still. She cocked her head as she sent her thoughts to Marella on the broad path so that everyone could hear her. *"It is the second week of Tachwedd, and there will be snow before the week is out."*

Silence followed her announcement.

"The second week of Tachwedd, already," breathed Daren, shaking his head in disbelief. He finished sorting out his things and prepared to leave as the others did the same.

"This time difference throws me every time," complained Lani.

"We're doing well though, if you think about it," said Marella, shifting her grip on the handles of her truck.

They carried on with their conversation as they set off walking, Partners running or flying around them.

"Doing well?" questioned Lani. "What do you mean?"

"Well, we were given a year and a day from the Summer Solstice to complete this quest and we've done two Quarters before Yule. We're ahead of schedule, if you look at it that way," Marella explained with a smile.

"Let's just hope we don't get behind schedule in the next two," laughed Daren.

"So, are we heading to Hufel, Kai?" shouted Daren as Kai led the way.

Kai nodded his head and turned it slightly so his words could be heard behind him. "I think we need to do the same in Hufel, as we did in Alaw. Speak with Kegan and see if he has any idea on where the Portal for Fire might be. We can rest for the night before continuing. It won't be a long stay though, just a quick stop, re-stock our supplies, and we'll be off."

The others agreed with him and continued on their walk towards Hufel.

* * *

It took them a week of travelling before they arrived, cold and wet in a rainstorm that had besieged them for the past two days. With relief, Kai led them to the Fire Lodge, just off to one side of the town square in Hufel. Kai knocked on the door as they all shivered in the doorway, rain dripping down their travel cloaks.

Adara, Second of Fire, opened the door, and gasped when she saw who it was. She ushered them in, calling for towels to be brought. They stepped through the doorway, but didn't go any further, not wanting to drip all over the floor.

Adara pulled Kai into a warm hug, heedlessly ignoring how wet he was. "Adara, stop," he exclaimed. "I'm soaked through, you'll make yourself ill."

"No worse than you," she snorted at him. "At least I haven't been out in this."

Lani laughed at her words which changed into a sneeze. "Oh, I'm sorry," she apologised, rubbing at her nose.

"Not to worry, my dear, not to worry. Let me take your travel cloaks. We will hang them up to dry for you. Come on, come on, pass them here." Adara spoke brusquely, but warmly, and the companions gladly handed over their sodden items.

The Partners slunk in through the open door having shaken themselves outside to dry off as much as possible. "Oh, now would you look at the state you're in," she said to them. "Áedán, move over, let your guests dry themselves at your fire."

The Partners moved over to the fire where Marella could see a salamander warming himself. He made room and soon the Partners were ensconced in front of its warmth and going to sleep.

"Any more?" Adara questioned before closing the front door to keep out the weather.

Kai laughed and shook his head, "No, no more, Adara. This is it, just us."

Once they had been divested of their cloaks and boots, they followed Adara through to the main sitting room. She bustled around, building up a fire and calling through for someone to make a hot drink for them.

"Adara, is there any chance you could show us where we can sleep tonight," Kai asked wearily. "We're all soaked through, and would like to change clothes before we sit down."

"Of course, why, it's right upstairs. Choose any rooms you want, there's no one else here right now."

Kai led them up the stairs and they all chose a room, not really bothered about their surroundings.

Marella looked around her room as she delved into her backpack for a change of clothing, and saw a door off to one side. She opened it and gasped in delight. There stood a deep, claw foot bath, just waiting for her to fill it. A slow smile crossed her face as she knew what she would be doing before bed tonight.

She changed into a dry pair of trousers and a clean shirt before putting on a soft pair of leather house shoes. She brushed and braided her hair as well as she could, fighting the frizz the dampness had put into it.

When she felt presentable, she went back downstairs to rejoin the others. Kai was sat in front of the fire, holding a hot mug of something in his hands. Marella could see the steam wisping over the top. She sniffed the air and could smell the scents of cinnamon and ginger, along with something else she couldn't place.

Kai looked up at her approach and smiled. She sat down in the chair next to him and sighed as the warmth reached her.

"Here, have a mug of this," said Kai, reaching over and taking a mug from a tray that was at the side of his chair. "It's our Winter Tea, a blend of ginger, cloves, elderberries, cinnamon, lemon balm, black peppercorns, and oregano. It will warm you up in no time."

Marella took the mug from him and wrapped her fingers around it, letting the warmth seep into her hands. She sniffed it appreciatively before taking a small sip and letting the flavours wash over her tongue. Once she'd had a drink and savoured the fusion of flavours, she leaned back in her chair. "I thought you'd all be down here before me. I found a bath."

"I'm surprised you're not already in it," Kai laughed. "I've heard nothing but longing from you and Lani for the past few days, so I thought once you saw the bath, that would be it for the night."

Marella laughed with him, acknowledging the truth in his words. "If we weren't here for the reason we're here, I'd be in there now," she admitted. "I didn't know if Adara would still be around though and wanting to speak with us, which is why I came down as quickly as I could."

"Adara has gone off to rustle up some food for us," he said fondly. "She'll be back soon."

"Where's Kegan tonight?"

"There's a meeting of some description at Bridd, probably to do with the tornado that hit them. All the Elders are there." Kai looked at Marella, questions in his eyes.

Marella lowered her lids before raising her eyes to his and looking at him. "I'm fine with that, Kai, honestly. I have my life now and I know what I need to do. Riva has her own life and will lead it the way she thinks is right."

"Truer words were never spoken," came Adara's voice from the doorway. Marella looked around in surprise and saw that Daren and Lani were also just entering the room.

"I may be out of place saying this, Marella, but Riva is proud of you. I don't agree with how she shows it, but she is. Genna has been in contact with Áedán for the past week, ever since we felt you return to Wraidd Elfennol, wanting to know if you'd arrived here yet."

Daren and Lani sat themselves down near the fire and Kai handed them a drink, which they both took gratefully.

Marella smiled at Adara's words. "Thank you, Adara. That's good to hear."

Adara smiled back at Marella and bustled into the room. "Now, let's get you fed shall we? And then you can retire for the night if you wish. I'm sure you'd like to relax this evening." She raised a hand to halt Kai's protest. "Kai, I know we need to talk, and talk we shall, but not tonight. Not when you're tired, hungry, and probably longing for a bath." She shot a glance at Marella and Lani and laughed at the looks on their faces.

"Come on, come through to the dining area and eat. We shall talk in the morning." With that, she led them to a table where they sat down. Within moments, big bowls of thick, hot meat stew were placed in front of them, along with a plate of warm, just-out-of-the-oven, bread. They dug in and before long the only sounds were of their spoons scraping the bowls.

Once they had eaten their fill, Marella leaned back in her chair and groaned. "I think you may have to roll me up the stairs, I've eaten that much," she said.

Lani laughed at her, "I know what you mean, the stew was so tasty. Thank you Adara."

Adara smiled at them, "I'm just glad you've all enjoyed it. Now, I'm making a pot of valerian tea for each of you, which will be left outside your doors in about five minutes. Go and rest, we will speak in the morning." With that, her portly body disappeared into the kitchen area and they could soon hear the sound of water running.

Kai stood up, turned around, and rested his hands on the back of his chair. "You may as well do as she says," he said. "She won't rest until we do as we're told."

271

"You know her well then, Kai?" asked Lani as they made their way to the stairs.

"She's like my grandmother; I used to call her 'nain' when I was little. She's the one who used to bail me out of trouble before my parents found out." Kai laughed at his memories.

By this time, they were at the top of the stairs, and Kai stopped in front of the room he had claimed for the night. "I'm off for a soak and then I'm going to bed. I don't know about the rest of you, but I feel beat."

After saying their goodnights, the four split off into their own rooms. Marella busied herself with running a bath and soon steam was filling the small bathroom. She opened the little window that was in there to help vent the room, and put some lavender oil under the running water. Soon the scent of the flower filled the air and Marella looked forward to sliding into the water.

Before she undressed, she went and checked by the bedroom door and there, as promised was a tray with a pot of tea and some lavender shortbread. She picked up the tray and carried it into her room, placing it on the table near to her bed.

"Nixie, are you okay downstairs? I'm about to get into a hot bath, so I won't be able to open the door for you." Marella sent her thoughts to Nixie. All she received in return was a feeling of being content and quite unable to move. She smiled and sent her love to him.

She walked into the bathroom and undressed. She carefully lowered herself into the deep tub and relaxed, a sigh of pleasure leaving her as she sunk beneath the silky water. She rested her head against the back of the bath, and let the tranquillity of the lavender oil enter her mind.

Marella stayed in the bath until the water was cool. She let the water out and stood up, grabbed a thick, fluffy towel from the chair and wrapped herself up in it. She snuggled into it as she walked through to the bedroom. She dried herself off before she changed into her nightclothes and climbed into bed. She pulled her book out of the backpack, poured herself a cup of tea and grabbed a biscuit, before sinking underneath the quilt, all warm and toasty.

~ 45 ~

When Marella awoke the next morning, her book was on the floor and her tea was still sat by her bed, only now it was cold. She laughed to herself as she realised she had fallen asleep. The bedside lamp was no longer lit, although Marella couldn't remember dousing the flame. She went into the bathroom and sorted herself out, feeling more rested than she had done for a while. She sorted out her few possessions so that she was ready to go, then opened the door to go downstairs.

The moment her bedroom door was open, the delicious smell of cooked bacon assailed her nose. Sniffing appreciatively, she went down the stairs, trying to be quiet in case anyone was still asleep. She entered the kitchen area and saw Kai leaning against the counter, talking to Adara. He smiled at her when he saw her and beckoned her to come over.

"Good morning Kai, Adara," Marella greeted them.

"Good morning Marella, did you sleep well, dear?" asked Adara.

"I did, thank you. I had a delicious soak in the bath before I crashed out in bed. I can't even remember dousing the light, but it was out when I awoke this morning."

"That was me, I'm sorry. Áedán said everyone was asleep so I made sure no one had any flames lit."

Marella looked at Adara in wonder. "I didn't know anyone could do that," she said.

Adara chuckled as she handed Marella a mug of peppermint tea and a plate with a freshly made bacon sandwich on it. "It's something I do without even thinking about it. It was a handy trick when I had younglings running about. Kai's ability to start fires might actually come in handier when you're on the trail though." Adara shot Kai a glance before looking at Marella. "It's about time that gift of his came in handy, instead of causing me trouble like he did as a child.

Kai flushed as he looked at Marella. "That was a long time ago," he muttered. "And it hasn't been much good up until now. I was unable to start a fire whilst in the Air Quarter."

"That has nothing to do with you; and everything to do with where you were and what you were facing," Adara chided.

Marella chuckled, but said nothing as she enjoyed her sandwich. Just as she finished, Daren and Lani both entered the room. "Good morning folks," called Daren cheerily.

"Morning Daren," smiled Marella. "I take it you slept well."

"Like a baby," he said. "I can't even remember dousing my light, but it was out this morning, so I must have done."

Marella laughed aloud at this before explaining it was Adara's gift which had done that.

"That's pretty nifty," he said as he grabbed a sandwich.

"Good morning, Chosen," came a deep voice from the doorway. As one they turned to see who it was.

"Good morning Kegan, when did you get back?" asked Adara from the kitchen.

"I've just walked in and followed my nose to the smell of bacon," he said. "Is there one for me?" he asked mock-pitifully.

Adara walked out of the kitchen with a plate of bacon sandwiches in one hand, and a cup of ginger tea in the other, both of which she handed over to Kegan. "Come, sit down, and eat properly. You'll all get heartburn, eating standing up. Come on, sit I say."

Without saying a word, but with smiles aplenty, the Chosen and Kegan sat down at the nearest table and finished their breakfast without a word.

As she waited for the others to finish, Marella sent out a tendril of thought towards Nixie, unsurprised to find out he was in the local lake and enjoying himself.

"I've not managed to convince Ula or Kenna to join me yet, but they will, I'm sure of it."

Marella laughed at the image of poor Ula and Kenna sitting shivering at the side of the lake whilst Nixie gambolled like a pup in the water. She explained what she was laughing at when she noticed the quizzical looks coming from the others. "Apparently Shaw is safe because he's in a tree, but Nixie keeps making waves, trying to splash Ula and Kenna, much to their disgust."

Kai laughed with her. "He'll have more chance of getting Kenna into the water if it was warmer. She's a Fire fox, she doesn't like being wet AND cold."

Kegan chuckled at them, his laughter deep and husky. "If everyone has finished, would you please follow me?" He led them back to the main sitting room they had sat in yesterday. "I understand from Kenna you won't be staying long."

"That's right," said Kai. "We need to restock and be on our way. This whole business of time-jumping is making us very unsure. We need to know we have time to finish this challenge."

Kegan nodded as Kai spoke. "Very wise, young Kai. If you get ahead of yourself, then you have time for anything unexpected that might arise."

"That's the idea," said Kai with a grin. "We already know things don't tend to go according to plan, so we're trying to think around that."

"Well, I will make sure you are restocked with fresh food, thick blankets, and the like by lunchtime, although you are welcome to stay another night and start off fresh in the morning."

"Thank you, Elder Kegan," replied Kai, using Kegan's title in a gesture of respect. "I was actually hoping you could 'restock' our information too. Do you have any idea where the Fire Portal might be?"

"'Restock our information', very good," Kegan chuckled. "As a matter of fact, I can help you there."

"Anything would be helpful, just to narrow it down. We have no idea where we should even start."

"The lines I've always been taught are this, 'Seek the King within his circle of fire, your refuge in the forest.' And that's all I have, unfortunately. You could try asking Aine whilst you're here."

"Aine is our Trainer," explained Kai. "I haven't seen Mhia around today, or heard her for that matter," he said to Kegan.

"Mhia is up to mischief somewhere, no doubt," rumbled Kegan. "Don't you worry about her, I'll ask Edana to talk with her."

"Edana is Kegan's Partner, a Collared Lizard. Mhia is a Magpie, and when she was a fledgling, she would often bring Aine 'presents' she had found. Then Aine would have to find out who the original owner of her present was and return it. Poor Mhia didn't understand at first, luckily everyone else did," Kai explained.

Marella giggled at the thought of a magpie, "I can understand the mischievousness," she said. "After all, an otter is hardly serious."

"I'll have you know I can be totally serious," she heard muttered in her mind.

"So you've been listening in, have you? Are you coming back soon?"

"We're on our way back now, and Mhia is coming with us. She has spoken to Aine, who is heading to the Lodge as we speak."

Marella returned her attention to the others and found Kai watching her. "Is Nixie okay?" he asked.

Marella smiled at him, "He's fine and they're on their way back with Mhia. Aine is on her way here now."

"Hello Aine, go on through and join the others, I'll bring you a drink," they heard Adara call out.

They waited for Aine to join them before continuing with their conversation. She walked in and smiled at them. "Hello Chosen, I'm pleased to meet you. I am Aine, Partner of Mhia, and Trainer at Hufel."

The others smiled their greetings and Kai introduced them by name, foregoing the traditional statement of their Partners and jobs. Aine nodded in acknowledgement of them as she took a spare chair and relaxed into it.

"I've just been telling Kai here about the Fire Portal, and the only knowledge we have of where to find it," explained Kegan, bringing Aine up-to-date with what was going on.

"Oh yes, the King of the Forest, does it make sense to you, Kai?" she asked.

"Not really, but then I've not had time to think on it either. I've only just heard of it."

Aine was interrupted as she tried to speak by the unmistakable chatter of a magpie, and Mhia flew through the open window to land on Aine's shoulder.

"She's a beauty," breathed Marella in admiration.

"Don't tell her that, her ego will inflate," laughed Aine, stroking a finger down Mhia's breast feathers.

The others laughed softly so as not to scare Mhia as she bobbed up and down on Aine's shoulder, almost in agreement with Marella.

"Anyway, back to business," said Kegan. "King of the Forest."

"Yes, legend has it the oak tree is the King of the Forest, so if I were you, I'd start my search by looking for a grove of Oak trees. They seem to get hit by lightning a lot, which bursts the sap and the stem apart, leaving the trunk of the oak all gnarled and withered. This isn't enough to kill an oak though and he will continue to grow and thrive even after a hit," explained Aine.

"And where are the oak trees? Which direction should we start heading to?" asked Kai, making a steeple with his fingers, his elbows resting on his knees.

"Why, south of course," laughed Aine. "Surely you've learnt that by now?"

Kai laugh self-deprecatingly, "I guess so."

"So," said Kegan, "when do you want to leave?"

Kai looked at the others, wondering what was best. *"Another night here won't hurt and might do everyone a world of good,"* came Kenna's suggestion.

"I think you might be right, as usual," he replied to her.

"I think we'll stay here again tonight, so long as that's okay with you, Kegan? We'll leave first thing in the morning and head south. Marella, I think it might be time for you to start Weaving once more." As the agreement was reached, Kai chuckled to himself at the look of delight on Lani and Marella's faces. *'It must be the thought of those baths,'* he thought to himself.

***

For the rest of the day, the four Partners were not seen by their humans very much. They all disappeared again after the meeting was over and did not return until after the evening meal had finished.

"Where have you been?" asked Marella curiously to Nixie.

"Just about, here and there," he answered. When he saw that answer wasn't enough for Marella and she would keep on pushing, he added, *"We've been trying to get around and speak to all the Partners. We need to find out who is working against us. So we've been asking for help. It won't hurt us and could help everyone if more eyes and ears are looking."*

"I never even thought of that," she murmured, stroking Nixie's coat. "Can all Partners see into a person's soul, or is it just the four of you?"

"We think it might just be the four of us. No one else we have spoken to has mentioned anything like it. So we've asked them to keep a lookout. Of course, no one is happy at the thought of their human working against the Lords and Ladies but still, they will help and also help spread the word through the villages. By the time we've finished in the Fire Quarter, the whole of Wraidd Elfennol will be looking out for us as well."

"You're a clever pud," she said appreciatively, "don't ever let anyone tell you otherwise."

He pushed at her hand with his head and huffed a breath of air over her hands. *"The only one cheeky enough to do that is you,"* he said with great affection.

The pattern for the evening followed the same as the previous one. They all ate together, then retired early to their rooms. This time, Marella was able to read for a while before falling asleep, and even managed to douse her own lamp.

~ 46 ~

Nixie woke her the following morning by pushing his cold, wet nose against her face until she stirred. She threw an arm over her head as she rolled onto her back, but Nixie just climbed on top of her and carried on.

"All right, okay, yeesh, I'm awake," she sputtered, laughing. "Now get off me, you great oaf."

"Is that anyway to speak to your beloved?" Nixie asked, although Marella could hear the laughter in his voice. *"I must remember to warn Kai about this."*

"Nixie!" exclaimed Marella. "You'll do no such thing. Why would you say that? Honestly, I mean, Kai and I…"

"Are getting along famously and I, for one, hope to see things progressing. Kenna feels the same way too," Nixie told her.

Marella lifted her hands and covered her burning cheeks. "I can't believe you and Kenna have sat around and discussed this like a pair of old women. Honestly, Nixie, Kai and I are capable of deciding for ourselves."

"I know that and so does Kenna," replied Nixie, *"but a little bit of help never goes amiss."*

"You stop this right now, you hear me? Nixie, I mean it. If anything is to happen between Kai and me, then it will be because we've moved it forward, not you two."

"Okay, if you insist. I'll talk to Kenna and tell her we have to behave."

Marella could hardly keep from laughing as her beloved Life Partner put on a show of being dejected and downhearted.

"Go on, off with you. Go and see if the others are ready yet. I'll be down shortly," she said to him, trying to keep the tremor of laughter from her voice. She held the door open and Nixie slipped through and made his way downstairs.

Once she had closed the door, Marella let loose with the laughter that had built up inside. The melodious peal of her giggles floated through the room as she packed her few belongings back into her backpack, before lifting it by the handle to carry it downstairs.

She opened the door and found Lani standing there, smiling. "Good morning, Lani. How are you today?" she asked.

"Good morning, Marella. I'm very well, thank you. I slept like a log again, so I'm feeling ready to hit the road. What had you giggling so early this morning? I could hear you through the walls."

"Is that all you could hear?" asked Marella, a faint flush staining her cheeks.

"Yes, that's all." Lani looked at her questioningly.

"Just something Nixie was telling me. I've had to tell him to keep out of it," explained Marella, trying not to be too descriptive.

"Is this about you and Kai?" asked Lani shrewdly.

Marella gasped. "How did you know? Oh no," she groaned, putting her face in her hands. "They really are like old women. Do all the Partners know?"

Lani put an arm around Marella's shoulders as they walked down the stairs. "I would imagine so," she said cheerfully, "they do like their gossip."

Marella groaned again. "Don't worry, Marella. Daren and I have seen this develop between the two of you. If nothing else, you will have a strong friendship. And if it turns into something else, so be it. At least no one can say you've rushed into it."

Marella gave a weak laugh at Lani's words. "I can't believe we've been the centre of all the discussion between the Partners though. Seriously, isn't this quest enough to stop them gossiping?"

"They take their fun when they can, you know that," reminded Lani. "Don't take it to heart."

"Easy for you to say," mumbled Marella, much to the delight of Lani, who admitted to herself she would love to see something happen between Kai and Marella.

"Come on, let's get some breakfast before we head out to meet the King of the Forest," said Lani, good-naturedly pulling Marella towards the kitchen.

* * *

When they entered, Kai and Daren were leaning against the work top on one side of the room. Marella and Lani walked to the other side, picking up a mug of tea, and went to join them.

"So we just head south and look for a grove of oaks then, yeah?" They heard Daren say as they approached.

Kai shrugged his shoulders. "I think so, we don't have anything else to go on with for now. Not unless Marella has seen something…" He looked at her and she took a moment to have a sip of her drink before answering.

"I haven't seen anything yet, but that is probably because I haven't Woven whilst we've been here. Once we're on the road, I'll start doing it every night again, to see if I can help." She wrapped her fingers around the mug as though to draw the heat right in.

"I think we should get some breakfast and get started then," said Kai. They all bustled about the kitchen, sorting themselves out in companionable silence, preparing and eating their breakfast.

Once they had finished and tidied their things away, Kai looked at them. He cocked his eyebrow in question and said "We ready then?"

Once agreement had been given, he turned on his heel and led them from the kitchen to the front door. Waiting for them was Kegan and Adara.

"Your trundle trucks are ready to go," said Adara, "I've put in as much as I could without loading you down."

"Thank you, Adara," said Kai, wrapping her in a hug.

"You take care now, you hear me?" said Kegan. "You look after each other. You're doing so well. I'll let everyone know about the Scions and that you've been here and gone."

"Thanks Kegan, we appreciate it," said Kai. He put on his cloak, making sure it was securely fastened before looking at the others who had been doing the same, "Let's go."

They said their goodbyes to Kegan and Adara before leaving the Fire Lodge. They walked to their trucks and picked them up, hoisting them until the weight was once more comfortable in their grip.

As one, they started walking together, Kai taking the lead. As they walked, their Partners arrived and either walked or flew next to their human.

"They make a fine sight," said Adara with a sigh.

"They certainly do, I am so proud of them all. They are handling this a lot better than I thought they would."

Kegan raised his hand to them in farewell as they looked back. "Farewell, Chosen. May your journey be blessed."

~ 47 ~

They travelled for just over three weeks, heading south and on the lookout for a grove of oak trees. Marella started to Weave every night, searching for something of use, Kai often sitting with her until she came back around.

The weather turned colder as they entered the month of Rhagfyr and it became a necessity to have a fire that lasted through the night. Marella and Lani decided it would make more sense for them to share a tent for warmth, with Kai and Daren following suit. The temperature continued to drop, the ground became harder, and still the grove was nowhere in sight.

"I can't believe the island is this big," said Lani one evening as she tried to warm up. "I feel like we've been walking forever, and we're still not near the sea. I thought we would have reached the south shores by now."

"It certainly feels bigger than I was led to believe," agreed Daren. "I always assumed it was a small island and you could walk around it in a few days."

"It's been more than a few days," laughed Kai.

"We won't find anything until the time is right, I thought you would have realised that by now," said Marella, walking over to join in the conversation. She sat next to Daren and he put his arm around her shoulders to give her a hug and also to help warm her up.

"So are we walking in circles then?" he asked.

"Not at all, but this island is magical, so things are not always as they seem. We're born with the Elements inside us; we get Partnered with animals, and can hear them; we've walked through Portals to take us somewhere different, where even time is altered. Do you think that is 'normal'?" Marella laughed at Daren and pushed against his side, leaning into him. "You're thinking with your Earth head," she said. "Everything solid, with no surprises. This whole... thing... is not solid though and there are surprises. We just have to go with it until it settles down."

"Go with the flow, you mean, like water?" asked Lani.

"Exactly," said Marella, clicking her fingers. "Don't you see? This whole journey is part of the challenge, not just the going through the Portals and what happens thereafter. I've been thinking on something Hynafol said to us, 'the timing is not inconsequential'. It is the same as the traditional hand-fasting. We need to put our trust and faith in the Lords and Ladies of our Elements, the same as we put our trust in our *Chosen* one. We have been *Chosen*, everyone calls us 'the Chosen', and so we need to act like it."

Marella took a breath and looked at them in turn, "We will find the Fire Portal when the timing is right, and not before. We will deal with whatever is there, when the timing is right. I'm telling you now, based on nothing more than my instincts, we will finish the challenge by the Summer Solstice and not before. It won't be Imbolc, or Beltane, or even the Spring Equinox, but the Summer Solstice."

Daren sighed and his arm tightened around Marella. "I was hoping we'd get this finished before then," he said, a hint of wistfulness in his voice.

"We may do, I may be wrong, but somehow I just can't see it," replied Marella, putting her head on his shoulder.

"I think you're right, Marella," agreed Lani, thoughtfully. "The only thing concerning me is that the time flow will work against us at some point and we will be late. If this is a hand-fasting, then I don't want to be on the receiving end of the Elements, if they think that we've broken our pledge."

"And that is where the trust and faith comes into play again," said Kai, looking at Marella. "Am I right?"

Marella nodded, "We can plan, we can act, we can prepare, but we also have to relax into this. I trust Lady Erwyna. She hasn't ever done or said anything to make me doubt her, even though I didn't believe her in the beginning. She was still truthful with me; it just took me a while to understand that."

"Okay," said Daren, heaving a sigh. "So what do we do now? Carry on walking? Plan for something? Go with the flow? What?"

"That's Kai's call," said Marella with a smile. "We're under his leadership now."

Kai smiled at the group and gave a small chuckle. "Under my leadership?" he questioned. "I think you're doing rather well without me."

Kai looked at them, the smile dropping from his face as became serious. "Actually, I agree with Marella. This is something that has crossed my mind over the past couple of days. I have walked from Hufel to the south shores before, and it's only ever taken three to four days, and that's with a slow walking pace. So yes, I think magic is involved. And no, I don't think we'll get where we need to go before we're supposed to."

He glanced around at their surroundings, his eyes falling on their Partners, and he gave a smile. "What do we do? Why, we carry on as we were before. It's worked with the two previous Quarters. Trust and faith? What better way to show it than to lay ourselves in the hands of our Lords and Ladies."

Kenna stood up from where she had been resting and sat by Kai's legs. He stopped talking for a moment as he rested his hand upon her head. Everyone else remained silent as Kai gathered his thoughts. When he looked up, there was determination spread across his face.

"This does not mean we become lackadaisical though. We have plans and preparations to make. You can have faith the water will boil, but you have to put the water in the pot, and the fire underneath the pot, to make it happen. This is what we need to do." He looked around at the small group of humans and Partners that had come to mean so much to him. "Any questions?" he asked.

"Certainly not from me," said Marella with a broad smile.

"Nor me," said Lani, grinning from ear to ear.

"Nope," said Daren, popping the 'p' and laughing.

"That's sorted then," laughed Kai. "We carry on as we are, planning and preparing where possible. Marella, please keep on Weaving every evening." He looked around at them whilst he huddled into his cloak. "As for now, I propose we eat something hot, and bed down for the night, it's getting cold."

The others agreed with him and made short work of getting something to eat and drink. They were all wrapped up as much as possible and were grateful for the blankets Kegan had given them.

* * *

The following evening, when they had stopped for the night, Marella retrieved her chalice and prepared to Weave. "I'll be with you soon," Kai told her as she prepared to move to the river's edge, near where they had set up camp.

"I'm all right you know, Kai. You don't have to come with me every night," Marella told him.

"I know, but I want to. It makes me feel better," Kai smiled.

"It's all about you," joked Marella, winking at him.

"You got it," he laughed. "I just want to help get some firewood. There's a storm brewing, I can feel it. You start and when you come back, I'll be there."

Marella nodded to him as she made her way over the hard, frozen ground towards the river. She didn't want to twist her ankle at this stage, and in the rough grass, it would be all too easy to do. She set herself up, placing a blanket on the ground to sit on, and getting some fresh water from the river. She sat cross-legged on the blanket with the chalice on the ground in front of her and relaxed into her trance, the sounds of the river helping her.

Marella saw different images flowing through the water, they were going so fast. She tried to slow them down so she could make sense of what she was seeing, using techniques taught to her during her training. She could feel her heart pounding and her breath coming in pants, as she tried to relax and not fight against what she could see.

Suddenly, she felt Nixie there, his strength a cooling balm to her senses. With his help, she was able to slow down the images so she could see. With a cry, she threw herself out of the trance and looked around, her body shaking with the after-effects of what she had seen.

Kai was there and wrapped her into his arms. "Marella, calm down, easy, it's me. What's the matter?"

Marella held onto his arms and burrowed her head into his chest, sobs wracking through her as she clutched onto Kai. He held her whilst looking at Nixie. *"Nixie, what happened? I've never seen her this way before."*

"It was a bad set of visions, affecting those she loves. There is nothing she can do as it has already happened. She feels so helpless right now. Just hold her, she will speak soon."

Kai tightened his arms around Marella and gently crooned to her, until he could feel her sobs easing. He stroked her head and encouraged her to speak with him.

She raised her head and looked at him, her bottom lip still trembling and eyes luminous with tears. "We need to get the others; I need to tell all of you about this."

Kai helped her to her feet and gathered the blanket and chalice, before putting his arm around Marella and leading her back to the campsite. Laughter echoed in their ears as they entered through a gap in the tents as Daren and Lani joked around with each other.

Lani looked over as Kai and Marella came back, a gasp escaping her lips as she saw Marella. She ran over to them and put her arms around Marella. "What happened? Is she okay?"

Kai nodded curtly and looked at Daren. "Nixie says it was a bad set of visions, and Marella said she needed to speak with all of us before explaining."

Daren made a cup of chamomile and gently placed it in Marella's hands after she had sat down near the fire. Marella leaned into Kai as he sat behind her before she started speaking, her voice soft and hesitant.

"By the end of the second week of Rhagfyr, we will find the Fire Portal." Marella stopped and gulped. Kai rubbed his hands up and down her arms, trying to show her his support.

"There has been a firestorm in Ilyn. Quite a few people have been injured, including Bradan, but they are all being helped as we speak. Some people are missing and are being looked for." Marella's voice broke on the last sentence and she took in a shuddering breath.

Daren's eyes narrowed as he looked at her. "Who is missing, Marella?"

Marella looked at him, tears beginning to make silent tracks down her cheeks. "Jorja, together with Salali."

There was silence from the others as the words sunk in.

"I understand that we're on this quest, but why didn't anyone contact us? They know you can hear. Their reasons for this just aren't good enough. Jorja is family and we deserve to know." Daren's voice was shaking with anger and worry. He thought of Jorja as his sister because of how close they all were.

"I don't know, I don't know why I found out through the Weaving, but I did." Marella's voice whispered through the campsite as the sun cast its dying rays through the woods.

Marella sat upright and looked at Daren and Lani. "I'm going to the tent, I'm sorry. I just don't feel like eating today." With that she stood up and looked down at Kai. "Thank you, Kai, for everything."

She squeezed his shoulder as she walked passed and went into their tent, Nixie on her heels. The others looked at each other, not really knowing what to say. Kai busied himself by getting a drink whilst Lani held onto Daren's hands and tried to comfort him.

"It will be all right, Daren. Jorja will be found, you'll see," she said as she rubbed his hands with hers.

Daren gave a sigh and looked at her. "I know she will be found. I can't bear to think otherwise. It is just getting to me how Marella had to find out through a Weave. Even her father hasn't contacted her."

Lani nodded in understanding, "I can see how that must be hard. I'm sure there must be a reason for it though. They know you are both close to Jorja."

Kai came back and sat with them, running trembling hands through his hair. "I've never seen her like this before. The emotions were tearing through her. I can't believe she wasn't told either."

Kai finished his drink and threw the dregs onto the ground. "I'm going to turn in too. I'll see you in the morning."

Without another word Kai disappeared into the tent, leaving Kenna with Daren and Lani. They sipped on their drinks, processing what had happened.

"On a positive note, we will find the Portal soon," mumbled Daren.

Lani cracked half a smile in response. "Yeah, that's good. We're not going to be aimlessly wandering around much longer."

Daren grunted as he prodded the fire and they sat in silence, watching the flames.

~ 48 ~

The following morning, Daren awoke feeling stiff. He realised he had fallen asleep by the fire and had spent the night without the shelter of the tents. He circled his shoulders trying to remove the stiffness from them. He tried to move his legs only to find them weighted down. Ula lay on one side of him, pressed against his legs. He looked down and saw Lani was lying with her head on his thighs. He ran his hands gently over her golden hair before he noticed a blanket was draped over both he and Lani.

A movement by the fire caught his attention and he looked over to see Marella sat by the fire, drinking from a mug and wrapped in a blanket. She smiled as she caught his eyes, the sadness still prevalent upon her face.

"Are you all right?" he whispered to her, not wanting to disturb Lani.

Marella shrugged her shoulders. "I'm as well as you are," she said.

Daren grinned at her before it faded off his face. "What did you see? Did you see it happen or the after-effects?"

"Both," said Marella, gripping her mug tighter. "I saw the storm as it was happening and then once it had passed over. It was horrible, Daren. The heat, the chaos, I could feel the flames licking my face. I've never had Weaves of such intensity. And then to see Bradan injured. A burning support fell on him as he tried to escape from the Water Lodge. His leg is burnt, but I don't think it's broken."

She took a sip of her drink and pulled the blanket tighter around her shoulders. "I need to look for Jorja and Salali. I know I can find them." She looked at Daren and he could see the determination on her face.

"Whatever you need to do, you know I'm here for you."

Marella smiled at him and finished her drink. "I'm glad you said that because I might need your help."

Daren questioned her without words.

Marella stood up from her seat and passed Daren a mug of tea, which he gratefully took from her. She sat down a bit closer to him and continued, speaking softly so as not to disturb anyone.

"I'm going to try something I haven't done before. I'm going to Weave and call for Salali through the Partner bond. I've spoken with Nixie about this and he thinks it might work, but he isn't sure if I'll be strong enough. Will you sit with me whist I try?"

Daren nodded, "Of course I will, you didn't have to ask."

"I'll help too," came Lani's sleep-roughened voice as she raised herself from Daren's leg, groaning as she did so.

"I'm sorry, Lani. I didn't mean to wake you," apologised Marella.

Lani grinned at her. "You didn't disturb me; the rock hard ground with no sleeping mat disturbed me."

Marella returned her grin, "Your head seemed to be okay though."

Lani blushed before she looked at Daren. "Thank you for that, Daren. I'm sure your leg must be dead by now."

Daren laughed as he cocked his knee and rubbed his leg to return some feeling to it. "It's fine, I'm glad I could help."

Kai's head popped through a gap in his tent. "What have I missed?" he asked, as the others laughed at the sight of his disembodied head. He pulled himself out of the tent and shivered in the morning light.

"Marella is going to seek out Salali and she might need our help," explained Lani.

"Anything," replied Kai. "When are we going to do this?"

"We have a week before we find the Portal, so I'm going to try every morning. That's when Jorja has always been more awake. She was always getting up early when she lived at home, so I can't see it being much different now," said Marella.

"You're not doing it before you've eaten, Marella," said Kai, sternly.

She looked at him in surprise, "I beg your pardon?" she said.

"Forgiven," quipped Kai before grinning at her. "Seriously, Marella. You've just said you might need help with this so it's going to take some work. You can't work on an empty stomach. You need to have a good breakfast before you attempt anything like that."

Daren laughed out loud at Marella's face before she too started to laugh. Lani shook her head, smiling at them all and went to the fire to start making a pot of porridge.

Before too long, the oats were bubbling away, Lani overseeing with the occasional stir. Daren and Kai went for a small walk just to collect more firewood that would last them until they left the campsite. Marella went back to the river to collect some water for the Weaving.

After building the fire back up and putting some water on to boil, Daren and Kai put one of the blankets down on the ground. Marella and Nixie sat in the middle and the others sat around them, with the Partners joining them.

She placed the chalice in front of her and looked around in trepidation. "I'm going to go into a Weave first and try to find Jorja. If I can, I'll follow her for as long as possible. When she disappears from the Weave is when I'll try to call Salali through the bond. Understand?"

The others all nodded their heads in acceptance, although Marella could see they didn't fully understand what she had said. She gave an internal sigh; it was difficult to explain how Weaving worked.

With the ease of long practice, Marella sank into her Weaving trance. She controlled the visions that came, seeking the ones she wanted of Jorja and Salali. Her eyes flickered beneath her eyelids as she searched each picture in her mind until she found what she was looking for. There, in the corner of her mind's eye, she saw Jorja, scooping up Salali in her arms and running.

Marella tried to follow, to get closer. She had been trained on how to do this, so why couldn't she? With frustration mounting, Marella continued trying to fight her way to Jorja, the heat from the flames searing her face even as she knew they were no longer real.

It became hotter and harder to reach Jorja until; finally, Marella opened her eyes, gasping for breath. She saw the worried faces of the other three and felt the concern coming from Nixie through their bond.

"I can't get close to her. I've found her, I just can't get close," she said unhappily.

"We'll try again tomorrow, don't worry. We need to leave here soon," said Kai to her.

"I know, I know. I just wanted to…," Marella stopped herself before looking at Daren. "I'm sorry, Daren. I thought I could do it straight away."

"Marella, you will do this. You have our support, but you need to keep your strength up. We'll stop for today and carry on trying to find the Portal or at least the south shore. We'll set up tonight and you can speak someone back home to see if they have any idea on where she was seen last. Then you can try again in the morning."

"Time is passing swiftly, Daren. We need to find her and the longer it goes on the more Jorja will need us."

"I agree with you, you know that. Jorja is like my sister too. However, we can't just put everything into finding her. If we fail in this quest, then it won't matter anyway, it will just be a matter of time before lots more people die due the imbalance of the Elements. We need to keep moving."

Kai and Lani stayed silent as Marella chewed on Daren's words. They could see she was not happy about the prospect of leaving her sister, but she could also see the sense in what he had said.

Her shoulders slumped as she took in a deep breath. "You are right, I know. Come on then, let's try and find the south shore. I'll try again tomorrow."

She stood up from the blanket and gathered her things, putting them away into her trundle truck. She grabbed a water skin and went to the river to fill it up before they left. By the time she had returned, everyone was ready for another day's walking.

* * *

The day passed as they once again tried to find the south shore. They spent time discussing why Marella couldn't get any closer to Jorja in her vision, something she was not used to.

"I just don't understand it," said Marella, a bit out of breath as they traversed the countryside. "Usually, once I'm within a Weave, I can control what I see, and from what angle. I don't understand why I can't get closer to her."

"Perhaps it's *because* it's your sister," said Lani. "Perhaps you are too close to her and that's why your Weaves won't work the same. You don't have the clarity of emotional distance with Jorja."

"You might have something there," said Daren. "Marella, when you've woven in the past, have you ever had Weaves that involve anyone you know, closely I mean."

Marella thought about it before shaking her head. "I don't think so, no. I mean, I've seen people I'm acquainted with - to say good morning to or something like that, but not someone that I'm close to."

"You definitely might be onto something then, Lani," said Daren with a smile.

"But how do we get past that? How do I get closer to Jorja in my Weave, when the Weave is resisting because she's my sister? I need to find her," said Marella, a hint of desperation in her voice.

Kai had been quiet whilst they discussed things, although there was a thoughtful look on his face.

"What troubles you, fy cariad?" asked Kenna.

"Just thinking," he thought back. *"Why hasn't anyone in her family told her about Jorja? It would be understandable that no one contacted her, if they were not used to her ability to speak to any Partner. Her family though, they've known since Marella was thirteen, of her ability. Surely, given the circumstances, you would have thought someone would have contacted her. I honestly don't get it, Kenna. This is their daughter, her sister, family."*

Kenna rubbed herself along Kai's legs as she felt the upset he was feeling through their bond. *"Oh, Kai, I wish there was something I could say to help you understand, but the simple truth is, you've never experienced anything like that before. Marella's family is full of love, but they show it in different ways. Perhaps they think they're doing the right thing and not distracting her during this time. Perhaps they've just been overwhelmed by everything and it hasn't occurred to them. Perhaps... I don't know. I don't have the answers. All you can do is support Marella in this. I'm going to speak with the others, see if we can come up with something to help."*

"Thank you, Kenna. You know I love you," thought Kai, sending love to her.

"I know you do, and I love you too. We will do this, have faith." With that, Kenna scampered off, her tail held high as she caught up with Nixie and Ula, Shaw scouting the skies above them.

"Come on, you three, less talking more walking. We can make a stop for the night soon, but we need to find some water," Kai called back to them, laughing to himself at the looks on their faces at his words.

They stopped shortly after, once Shaw spotted a lake and clearing nearby. They set up camp, each job now easy due to familiarity.

Kai started a campfire using some of the sticks and moss that lay nearby. Daren and Ula went hunting for food. Marella and Lani refilled the water skins, and soon had a pot of water boiling for a hot drink. The time passed swiftly and they were soon sat down, eating a spit-roasted hare with greens, and drinking peppermint tea.

"We're getting low on fresh greens," said Lani to no one in particular. "We'll need to find something else."

"Hopefully we'll be in the Fire Quarter before too long and we'll find them there. I can't see it being as cold there as it is here," laughed Daren.

Lani smiled, "Let's hope so."

"What do you think will be the challenge for this Quarter?" asked Kai, looking around. "We've had a rogue Elemental, the weather working against us, what will it be for Fire?"

"Are you worried, Kai?" asked Lani, gently.

Kai shook his head, "No, Lani, I'm not worried." He coughed as he realised how strong his reaction had been. "Okay, so I might be a tad... concerned, more than I thought."

Lani gave him a kind smile and carried on eating.

"We don't know what we will face, Kai," reassured Daren, "but we're here with you and whatever it is, we'll face it together."

Kai smiled at Daren, feeling thankful for the friends that he had.

Marella stood up and went to her trundle truck, collecting her items for Weaving. She looked over her shoulder at the others, "I'm going to Weave now, I'll be back soon."

"Hang on, Marella, I'm coming with you," called Kai as he tried to stand up, almost tripping over his own legs in the meantime.

"There's really no need," Marella began.

"I know, but I want to be there, I've already been through this with you," replied Kai, cutting off her words.

Daren barked out a laugh, sounding uncannily like Ula in that moment. Marella looked at him and quirked her eyebrows in question.

"It's nice to see someone taking as much notice of you as I do," Daren explained, throwing her a wink. "Doesn't matter what you say, Kai's going to be with you, and Lani and I will be waiting for your return. Fancy mugwort for after?" He grinned at her, knowing she wouldn't be too impressed with him.

Marella just huffed at him and stalked off, giving him a good view of her back.

Kai looked at Daren, "Thanks for that, now she's going to be grumpy at you, and taking it out on me."

Daren laughed again. "No she won't, she may be grumpy, but she's also fair. She won't take it out on you unless it's you she's mad at."

"Stop it, Daren. You're really not helping," said Lani, as she gave Daren a quick punch on his shoulder. "Go on, Kai. Go and make sure she's okay."

* * *

Kai laughed as he made his way towards Marella, leaving Daren and Lani bickering in the clearing. When he made it to the lake side, he could see Marella had already laid the blanket and retrieved some water for the Weave. She was sitting cross-legged and making minor adjustments when her eyes turned to his.

"You're crazy, you know that?" she laughed at him.

Kai spread his hands in front of him, "What have I done now?" he said.

"You do insist on coming with me when, really, there's no need. Nixie is always with me."

"Well, perhaps I feel more comfortable knowing I'm here, instead of just your Life Partner. I'm not trying to take over from Nixie, just help if need be."

"Like I said, crazy." Marella shook her head, still laughing at him before placing her hands on either side of her silver chalice and swishing the water around carefully.

Kai watched her, loving the process of seeing her Weave. It wasn't something he had ever thought of before meeting Marella, but he loved watching her now. There was something so peaceful, so calming, watching her watch the water.

"Are you sure it's the process of Weaving you love watching, Kai?" he heard from Nixie.

Kai grinned at Nixie, who was sat on the other side of the chalice, looking at Marella.

"Well, Marella may have something to do with it too. After hearing about how you and Kenna have been gossiping like old ladies, I can't really deny it, can I?"

Nixie gave a small snort and flashed Kai a look, before returning his attention to Marella. *"She's worried about you, you know. She's not just trying to find the Portal; she's trying to see what your challenge will be."*

"She is?" Kai was surprised. *"I haven't said anything though."*

"I know you haven't. You affect her; she doesn't quite understand it, or rather won't admit to it, but she worries for you. She is doing everything she can to make this Fire Quarter easy on you. Plus she's worrying just how much use she will be once we cross over."

Kai rubbed his chin, *"I must admit I'm worried about that too. I know she won't be able to Weave, and that's okay. Marella usually gives us enough to go on, we shouldn't need it once we cross. I just don't want my Element to hurt her."*

"It won't be easy on her; she doesn't have a secondary Element to help her adjust. You won't find it easy in the Water Quarter either, but at least you have Earth as your secondary. Earth works in conjunction with Water, so that should ease you."

"This isn't about me, Nixie. I want; no, I need, Marella to be safe in the Fire Quarter. Is there anything I can do to help her?"

"I don't know, Kai. I just don't know. The only piece of advice I can give you is just be there for her."

"Thank you Nixie, for everything."

Kai watched Marella's eyelids flicker momentarily before she opened them. She looked around, seeming off-balance before she grounded herself. She looked over to where Kai sat and smiled at him. "Did you see anything?" he asked.

"Not really, although we are going in the right direction. I feel we will be on the south shore in a couple of days. It's a feeling of *rightness* I get when I follow the Weave in the direction we're going."

"That's good enough for me," he said, helping to pack her things away. Putting his arm around her shoulders, he led her back to the clearing, delighted when she looped her arm around his waist. He pulled her to him, and they walked in sync back to the others.

~ 49 ~

The following morning, they had a hot breakfast before Marella spread her blanket on the ground to once again try to find her sister. As she went to get some fresh water for the chalice, Nixie walked alongside her. He said nothing as she filled the chalice and carefully carried it back. Marella placed the chalice in the centre of the blanket and went to sit down.

"Hold on a moment, Marella," said Nixie to her. *"There's something we want to try."*

Marella looked startled and glanced at the others. They too were looking at Nixie, questioning.

"We've been talking, although Weaving is your domain, we think you need the strength of the combined Elements to get to Jorja. Just follow our instructions, please."

Marella looked at Nixie and saw nothing but love and the determination to help her in his eyes. She nodded her agreement and saw the others relax.

"First, Daren – please take your seat in the North," Nixie instructed.

Daren obediently moved to the North sector of the blanket and sat down, making himself comfortable. Ula waited until he was still and then sat next to him.

"Lani, your turn. Please sit in the East."

With a reassuring smile to Marella, Lani moved until she was sat in the East on the blanket. Once she was cross-legged, she motioned for Shaw to join her, leaning back so as to avoid his wings as he landed.

"Kai, you know where you must sit."

Kai first walked to Marella and grasped both of her hands. "You can do this, Marella. You know you can." He squeezed her hands and then went to the South position on the blanket. He sat down so Kenna could join him without delay.

"Now it's our turn, are you ready?" asked Nixie to Marella.

Marella didn't speak, nodding her consent instead, moving gracefully to her position in the West before sitting in her usual Weaving position.

"Now, Marella, you will need to start Weaving as normal but don't touch the chalice with your hands to start the movement. Concentrate with your mind. Once you've entered the Weave, call in the others. Traditionally, you would call in Daren first, however, because you are the last in the circle and first in the Weave, work backwards. Call in Kai, then Lani and finally Daren. Once you are all together, concentrate on Jorja. Do you understand?"

Marella nodded once again, taking a deep breath to steady her nerves. She looked at the others, taking strength from the confidence she saw on their faces. With a second deep breath, she concentrated on the water sat in the middle of the blanket. With her mind's eye, she saw the water swirling deosil, taking her to where she wanted to be. Smoothly, she was there in her Weave. She looked around and saw this was prior to when she had first seen Jorja. She had time to bring in the others before Jorja appeared.

She thought of Kai and his Element – the desire and passion of Fire. She thought of Kai himself and pictured him in her mind. The special look he had when he spoke to her, the feeling of warmth she felt whenever he was near, the twinkle in his eyes when he teased someone. Pouring all she had into it, she concentrated on bringing Kai into the Weave.

She felt his presence, but when she looked next to her, she couldn't see Kai. What she saw was a small, intense flame that quivered and danced next to her. She smiled as she realised it would be the representation of each of them she would see, not they themselves.

Now that Kai was here, she concentrated on bringing in Air – the intellect and wisdom that were such an integral part of Lani. She could hear Lani's laughter filling the air around her, feeling Lani's compassion as they struggled with a problem. With a sound that made her ears pop, Lani was there.

Marella looked to see what shape Lani was and without surprise, saw a silvery-grey feather floating next to the Kai flame. With a bob of her head to the feather, Marella concentrated on bringing in Daren.

She thought of Daren's integral strength, and the protection he had always shown her from such a young age. She felt the stability of his love, and knew that was one thing that would always be constant in her life, no matter what other changes might occur. With a rumble over her senses, Daren appeared in the shape of a sword, shining a lush green, beside Kai and Lani.

Feeling that this might be the moment, Marella took a step forward into the Weave, taking them with her. She walked forward, amazed at the ease with which she walked after how hard it had been previously.

No one else seemed to notice her or her companions as she walked amongst the chaos that reigned supreme. The heat was searing and the noise was deafening. Marella carefully picked her way through the crowd of frightened people, not looking too closely at who she was passing.

Off to her right, she saw Jorja, ducking down as a piece of timber flew through the air, blazing madly. Marella hurried, trying to get closer to her sister. She saw Salali leaping from one of the nearby branches onto Jorja's shoulder. This was more than she had seen last time and it heartened Marella.

Marella walked closer and closer until she could feel her body straining as she tried to follow Jorja, the Weave still not allowing her to follow too closely behind. Without any warning, the air thinned before her and she almost fell. She had been pushing against something that was no longer there, and she could move forward with ease. She gave thanks and scurried after Jorja, who was now running full pelt away from Marella.

'*I know where she's going,*" thought Marella with relief, and swiftly made her own way towards the lake. Marella arrived there, panting and hot, just in time to see her sister immerse herself in the water. Jorja ducked down and put her head beneath the water, coming up and easing her way to the side of the lake, before making her way around the edge towards the opposite side, away from the fire.

Marella ran towards her sister, knowing something else had to have happened. If Jorja had made it to the opposite side without issue, then she would not have disappeared. Out of nowhere came a burning log, tossing and turning through the wind that had whipped through the firestorm; turning it from dangerous to deadly. Marella heard Salali squeak in fear before Jorja held onto him, and pulled him below the surface of the water with her.

With a huge splash, the log belly flopped into the water and fizzled out. Marella stood on the bank, her hand over her rapidly beating heart and waited for her sister and Salali to resurface. She waited and the seconds turned into minutes, and still Jorja hadn't reappeared.

Marella turned to the companions who had kept pace with her throughout. "Something's happened. She should have resurfaced by now. This is why no one can find her." Marella chewed on her lip as she paced back and forth, trying to think of something that she could do. Instinctively, she knew her time within the Weave was running out and she needed to act.

She gasped as a thought occurred to her. This was the lake where she had always come. Indeed, this was the lake where both Nixie and herself were dragged through the spiral under the waters, to meet with Lady Erwyna the very first time.

Marella steadied her erratic breathing and centred herself. She explained to the others what her thoughts were, and what she was going to do. Before her time ran out, she sent a plea to Lady Erwyna.

"Lady of the Waters, please hear me now. My sister is within your embrace, more than that I cannot say. If possible, please return her to us. She is needed here on Wraidd Elfennol." Marella stood for a moment, her head bowed, resisting the pull that would make her leave the Weave and return to her body near the south shore.

She raised her eyes and gazed upon the lake in front of her, desperately hoping to see a sign before she had to go. In the middle of the lake, the waters started to churn, sending spray into the air. Marella held her breath and looked at her companions.

Out of the centre of the agitated waves, the Lady Erwyna gracefully rose and came towards Marella. Her long, black hair whipped around her as she walked across the top of the waves, holding her hands out in greeting.

"Marella, my Chosen, I'm so glad you are here. You have learnt how to make your Weaves even stronger by using the combined powers of the Chosen. Well done." Erwyna clasped both of Marella's hand and gave her a gracious smile.

"I have heard your plea and I have taken Jorja and Salali into my safekeeping. When I saw the danger they were in, and what would happen if I didn't, it was an easy decision to make. It isn't their time to journey on; there are still plenty of things for them to accomplish before then."

Marella hoped against hope that it meant her sister would be okay. She didn't dare ask though as she was afraid it would sound selfish. After all, how many people had the opportunity to talk to Erwyna, Lady of the Waters?

Erwyna gazed into Marella's eyes, searching deep into her soul. She squeezed Marella's hands and smiled at her. Marella's cares and worries didn't seem so pertinent anymore, and she smiled back, a weight lifting from her shoulders she hadn't even been aware of.

"Before I return your sister, I give you a warning. Once you have passed through the Fire Quarter, do not go to Ilyn. You must go from Fire straight to Water. I know this will be hard, especially now as Jorja has been found, or will be very soon. This is imperative though, I wouldn't say it if it wasn't." Erwyna again squeezed Marella's hands, as though she was trying to convince Marella of the importance of what she said.

Marella looked upon Erwyna's face and wondered about this turn of events. However, she remembered Erwyna had already mentioned something similar to her when she had told Marella she wouldn't see her mother again until it was all over. So it was with a clear conscience and a firm decision, she gave her agreement to Erwyna and promised to travel straight to the Water Portal.

Erwyna smiled at Marella, relief showing on her face. "It is time for you to go now; you've spent long enough in this Weave. I will return Jorja to the right time in Ilyn. Three days have passed now and your father is frantic."

"Before I go, and I know I must, please can I ask you why my father never contacted me?" Marella asked.

A gentle smile crossed Erwyna's face. "Marella, he would have contacted you, but he was injured himself, only mildly, but once he was on his feet again, he was constant in his help towards others. He has been searching for Jorja every day. He has also been trying to help get Ilyn back on its feet. He hasn't contacted you because he couldn't bear the thought of explaining to you what had happened to Jorja. He wants to think you as 'separate' from what he was going through. It might not be right, but it wasn't because he doesn't care about you."

Marella thought on Erwyna's words before she nodded her head. "I can see him being like that," she said. "Is he okay now? He wasn't injured much?"

"He's absolutely fine," insisted Erwyna. "He received a bump on the head which temporarily knocked him out. He was never in danger from the firestorm itself."

Marella relaxed as she heard Erwyna's assurances. She could feel the pull of her world calling her more than ever. She looked at Erwyna, "It's time for us to go. I can feel the Weave fraying now."

Erwyna laughed melodiously. "Marella, my dear, the others have already gone. They don't have your strength of Water, and once I came, they left. I'm sure they will have a mild headache, but nothing worse than that. Return to them now. I will return Jorja and Salali to Ilyn and you can carry on to the Fire Quarter."

Erwyna wrapped her arms around Marella and embraced her. "You are doing so well, my Chosen. I'm so very proud of you." Erwyna took a step back from Marella and, as Marella watched, she faded from sight.

*　*　*

Marella sighed, a feeling of satisfaction suffusing her body. They had found Jorja and Salali, and she had also spoken with Lady Erwyna. She felt a tug on her conscious and knew it was time to return. With just a single thought, she felt her soul return to her body. She blinked a couple of times before opening her eyes to see three sets of eyes peering worriedly in her direction. A beaming smile crossed her face. "We did it," she announced.

A chorus of happy shouts met her ears and everyone was laughing and smiling. Marella still sat cross-legged and she knew from experience, it was best to let the feelings return to her legs before moving. She leaned forward, over her legs, and embraced Nixie, hugging him to her. *"We did it, Nixie; Jorja and Salali are going to be okay. They're going home."*

Nixie bumped her head with his and whuffled his whiskers against her cheek. *"I'm so very pleased, little one. It was certainly an interesting experience."*

Marella tilted her head as she looked at him. *"You were there, weren't you? It wasn't just us, it was you as well."*

Nixie nodded to her and she squeezed him tighter, laughing as he wriggled to get free.

"We were linked to you and could feel your struggle to get closer to Jorja. It was Shaw's idea that we add our strength to yours and see if it worked." Nixie gave a sort of shrug with his shoulders. *"It did."*

Marella looked at him, wide-eyed. *"So that's when it went pop – when you were helping me, when you joined in."*

"I would guess so," admitted Nixie, *"but none of us know for sure."*

"I know we wouldn't have done it without you. Chosen indeed, every one of us." Marella smiled until she thought her cheeks would crack. Today would be a

good day, she could feel it.

~ 50 ~

Today was not a good day at all, thought Marella. The day dragged; and she wished she could keep the feeling of happiness from the morning. Instead, a feeling of almost unbearable sadness swept over the group as a whole. Conversation stopped, even between the Partners. Instead, they walked, eyes on the ground in front of them, pulling their trundle trucks behind them. When they stopped for something to eat, they ate in silence. Once they had finished, they walked.

Marella tried to break herself out of the despondency that seemed to drag at them. *"Nixie, speak to me. Help me pull myself out of this funk. It's driving me crazy."*

For a moment, there was silence from Nixie although Marella knew he had heard her. Then she heard a sigh, *"I'll try, Marella. This is hard though. We're never going to reach the Fire Portal. Even if we do, what does it matter? Think of all Wraidd Elfennol has suffered already. Perhaps it would be better if we just let it happen. Stop fighting and it will be easier."*

Marella gasped in shock at Nixie's words. She had never expected to hear anything like that from him. She looked around and saw the body language of her friends as they trudged along. Even Shaw no longer flew, but was nestled in Lani's truck, his head tucked beneath his wing.

The shock of hearing how Nixie felt stayed with her and actually made her feel more aware. Marella fought hard to keep the alertness, struggling against the mind fog that seemed to drift over her.

Kai called them to stop long before he normally would. Apathy was still the main feeling amongst them as they set up camp and prepared food and drink. Marella took charge of the dessert and drinks, hoping against hope that what she had planned would help.

They ate their stew in silence; the only sounds echoing around the campsite were the sounds of their spoons hitting the bowls. The more Marella thought about how they were acting, the angrier she became. She nurtured that feeling of anger, feeding it, until it glowed inside her like an ember.

Once she had finished her stew, she moved to her trundle truck and took out four big oranges. She passed one to each of them. They all pierced the skin and the fresh, citrusy smell suffused the clearing. Marella watched carefully and could see a faint spark return to their eyes. She went and made a peppermint tea for them, handing it around whilst it was still hot, the scent of the mint mingling with the citrus smell of the orange.

Marella waited until they had eaten their oranges and were drinking their tea. "ENOUGH!" she shouted with her mind, using what she hoped was the band that included the humans as well as the Partners. She knew she had succeeded when seven pairs of eyes focussed on her. "You need to snap out of this. This isn't natural, don't you see?" she pleaded with them.

Lani cast her eyes downwards, refusing to look at Marella. "I don't know how you can say that, Marella. Think of everything we've been through. It's a wonder we've survived this long. You can't say it's because of how strong or clever we are. It's been luck, nothing more. I should have stayed at home."

"Don't you dare," hissed Marella. "Don't you dare give in. Who was the one who dealt with Queen Paralda, who spoke with Lord Adaryn?"

Lani nodded her head, despondently. "Yes, I know, it was me. It hasn't helped though, has it? Earthquakes, tornadoes, firestorms – they're still happening. Perhaps we should take a hint and leave it be. It might be better that way."

Marella smiled at Lani's words, causing Kai to look at her curiously. Marella leaned forward and held onto Lani's hands. "You don't really feel that way, Lani."

Lani nodded emphatically. "Yes, I do, I do mean it."

"No, you don't. I don't believe you."

Marella watched as Lani's face started to show her anger. "I do mean it, Marella. Stop telling me what I do or don't feel. You're not my mother. Leave me alone."

"If you're going to continue acting like a child, then I will treat you as one. By the Waters, Lani, listen to yourself. You stood toe to toe with Queen Paralda, and refused to back down, even when she called you out on it. Stop wallowing like a baby who's had a toy taken away."

Lani jumped to her feet, Daren not far behind her. "How dare you speak to me that way?" shouted Lani.

"Honestly, Marella. I'm shocked at you. Why would you speak to Lani that way, it's not on," said Daren, his voice harsh with disapproval.

Marella stood and faced both of them. "You feel that? Do you feel the anger pulsing through your veins at me right now? Keep it, hold it, do what you need to keep feeling."

Kai stood up and stood next to Marella. "Are you sure this is wise, goading them this way?" he asked her, fighting the effects of the malaise himself.

"If it's the only way to make them feel, then yes. This apathy will not win," she declared, looking at Lani and Daren severely. Lani looked at her curiously and Daren stopped mid-rant to look at her.

In a softer voice, Marella continued "I don't know what's going on, but it's affecting all of us. Look to your Partners, see how they are feeling. You care about them, so show it. You've ignored each other, and everyone else, all day. I think this is an attack, the same as you fighting the rogue, Daren. This is insidious, you can't see it, but it doesn't mean it's not there.

Just like the Elements we fought against in the Air Quarter, Lani."

Marella took a deep breath and continued speaking with her mind, 'pathing the feelings through their bond. *"When Nixie said it was better to give in, it shocked me enough to 'wake up', or at least, that's how it felt to me. When you said nearly the same thing, Lani, it confirmed my feelings. We have to fight this."*

She looked at Kai, her eyes pleading, *"Please, Kai, talk to them, please,"* she begged.

Kai stepped closer and embraced her. Standing behind her, with his arms around her waist, Kai spoke to Daren and Lani through the bond too. *"Fire is passion, desire, action. These you all know. Do you know the opposite effects though? Those of jealousy, boredom, and apathy? I think that we are fighting the negative effects of Fire right now. We already know someone is working against us; they've tried in every Quarter so far. What better way to strike than to get us to give in before we've even finished?"*

Marella leaned back against Kai, drawing his strength into her, and watched Daren and Lani. Daren shook his head roughly, as though to physically shake himself free. Lani looked very confused, her body tense and shaking. *"Look to your Partners, love them,"* she whispered across the bond.

Lani turned and saw Shaw lying on the top of her trundle truck. With a cry, she raced over to him and picked him up, nestling him in her arms. He lifted his head up, his intelligent eyes dulled. Lani lifted her arms until Shaw was nearly the same height as her face and lay her face down near to his. When he slowly rubbed his face against her cheek, tears started to flow down her cheeks.

Ula started barking, her sharp cries echoing through the clearing. Nixie unrolled himself and stood to attention, his body stiff. His cries added a synchronicity to Ula's, but then he stopped and looked at Kenna. Walking as though she had been asleep for years, Kenna stopped when she was by Ula and Nixie. With a deep inhale, her yips soon echoed amongst the trees. Shaw lifted his head away from Lani and shook out his feathers. He launched himself away from Lani, swirling in a circle above their heads, before coming back down to earth. He landed on the floor in the middle of the other Partners, held his wings out and gave a screech that sent other birds fleeing into the air, away from the aerial predator they could hear but not see.

Daren and Lani looked at their Partners, blinking as though they had just woken from a sleep, a fugue clearing from their minds.

"By the Earth, what was that?" asked Daren, his body shaking in reaction.

"That was our Partners defying the negative aspects of Fire," said Marella, smiling at the Partners who were now nuzzling against each other. "By doing so, they have given us all the strength to do the same. Once again, we owe them."

Kai squeezed her waist before letting her go and walking over to Kenna. He dropped to his knees and Kenna ran over and jumped, her two front paws placed on his shoulders. They touched noses before Kai dropped his head forward and rested it on Kenna.

Daren had already done the same and Shaw was back in Lani's arms. Marella dropped to the ground and sat cross-legged. Nixie walked over and clambered into her lap. Feeling the physical closeness to their Partners was something they all appeared to need.

* * *

"Well done, Chosen, you are indeed who you say you are."

The words, spoken from behind them, startled them, including the Partners. They looked around to see who it was. Standing a small distance from them was a tall, muscular man. He had long auburn hair that hung loose around his shoulders and his skin was golden in colour. It was his eyes which made Marella gasp though as they were a rich, ruby red and burned with an inner flame. His face was set and had a faint, haughty look to it which set Marella's nerves on edge.

"Who are you?" asked Kai, rising to his feet. Kenna stood to attention by his side, her fur bristling.

"I am Etain, Consort to Queen Djinn. I am here to escort you safely through the Portal." He looked at Kenna and his face softened. "Fear not, little sister, I am not here to harm."

Daren, Lani, and Marella all stood side by side, just to the left of Kai. Their Partners moved so they were stood in front them.

"Was it you?" asked Kai, not elaborating any further.

"Yes, it was," answered Etain. "If you weren't able to recognise the effects of negative Fire, and be able to negate them, what is the point of you coming into the Quarter? As it is, you had to rely on Water to see it for what it was." A sneer crossed his face as he said 'Water' and Marella felt her spine stiffen at the implied insult.

"No one Element is better than the others, Etain. I'm sure you are aware of that. It is something Lord Ethon has mentioned himself, on many an occasion." Kai calmly answered, keeping his attention fixed on Etain, knowing Marella had Daren and Lani with her.

Etain cocked his head in acknowledgement, the sneer still distorting his face. "That may be the common held view, Chosen of Fire, but it isn't necessarily the one everyone adheres to."

"Very true," said Kai. "However, it is a view that I believe in, otherwise I wouldn't be on this quest. We each have a part to play and our strengths and weaknesses are balanced out."

Etain laughed, a harsh sound that set everyone's teeth on edge. "Well, you carry on believing that, Chosen. I'm sure you'll become enlightened one day." With that, turned on his heel and strode across the clearing, ignoring the others. Kai turned around to look at them, quirking an eyebrow.

Daren snorted his amusement quietly, whilst Lani shook her head in amazement and smiled. Marella didn't smile as she didn't find Etain's attitude funny. She found it to be quite disturbing and didn't like the undertones of what he had said. Kai smiled at her and sent warmth through their bond, which reassured Marella somewhat.

"That reminds me," said Daren, slinging his arms across both Marella and Lani. "There's the small matter of you and Kai being able to speak directly to Lani and I. What's going on with that?"

"We'll explain later," said Kai, walking over to them, "for now, I think we need to follow Etain. Come on." He picked up the handles of his trundle truck and started out of the clearing, after Etain who could still be seen striding through the woods. With a glance at each other, they followed after Kai.

~ 51 ~

The Partners glanced at each other. *"This is going to be awkward,"* said Kenna apologetically.

"It seems that way," replied Ula in her calm manner.

"Oh but think of the sparks that will fly," laughed Nixie.

"You laugh now, Nixie, it will be up to you to deal with Marella. It's not going to be easy," Ula reminded him.

Nixie sobered up at the thought. *"I know; I'm concerned for when we cross over. Etain doesn't seem very sympathetic towards other Elements, and Marella doesn't have anything else to help her adjust. I think it's going to hit her hard."*

"We will be there for both you and her," reminded Kenna.

"We'll remind the others too, just in case they've forgotten," said Shaw, flapping his wings to make sure all his feathers were in the right place before he launched himself into the air to follow after Lani.

"We can't do any more than what we have, Nixie. Let's get going and finish this part of the quest," said Ula.

"Lead us onwards, Kenna," said Nixie, bowing his head to her.

She grinned a foxy smile at him, and trotted off jauntily in front of them, her tail held high. *"Show off,"* she heard Ula say, the warmth of their friendship suffusing her small body.

~ 52 ~

The companions followed Etain at a swift pace, but not rushing to catch him up either. Kai led the way, with the others single file after him. It didn't take too long before they came upon a grove of oak trees. The trees were a mixture of young ones with older ones mixed in. Marella could distinguish the younger trees, because they were holding onto their dead, brown leaves whilst the older ones had dropped their leaves around the base of their trunks, where they slowly decayed.

Marella looked around, recognising the grove. She nodded to Kai, telling him this was the place for the Portal.

"Ah, yes, Chosen of Water," Etain smirked. "I wondered if you would recognise this place."

Marella straightened her shoulders and replied to him with dignity. "I do indeed recognise this place, Consort. It is the area I was shown in my Weaves, where we would find the Portal to cross to the Fire Quarter."

Etain looked at her scornfully. "I wouldn't rely on your visions too much, Chosen. They won't work where you're going."

Kai moved to break the look Etain was sending to Marella. Once he had Etain's attention, Kai gave him a tight and controlled smile. "Thank you for escorting us to the Portal, Etain. May I ask, are you going to take us through or do we need to pass through by ourselves?"

Etain smirked at him, before returning his attention to Marella. She stood there, chin tilted and refusing to back down. With a sniff of disdain, Etain turned so that his back was facing Marella, ignoring Lani's gasp of shock.

He clapped his hands together once and the Portal gleamed in front of them. The oak trees, which once stood so strong and proud, slowly warped and twisted, until they formed the curve of the Portal. The creaking and groaning of their branches filling the air, complete with loud cracks as the branches themselves were complaining of their use.

Within the circle created by the branches, the companions could see what appeared to be a swirling ball of fire. They looked at each other in trepidation before Etain saw them and commented. "Oh please, don't tell me the brave and courageous Chosen are scared of a Portal?" He laughed harshly.

Kai straightened his shoulders and, holding his head high, took a step towards the Portal. "After you, Etain," he said, with a sweeping hand gesture.

Etain looked at them and shook his head disdainfully. "Such a ragged crew, not what Queen Djinn was expecting at all. Still, you'll have to do, I suppose. Follow me." With a sweep of his hair, Etain turned around and walked through the Portal with no hesitation.

Kai looked back at the others before grimacing. "Come on, let's get this done with." Pulling along his trundle truck, he walked through the Portal, right through the centre of the burning flames.

Daren, Lani, and Marella all looked at each other. Daren shrugged his shoulders. "You know we have to do this so we might as well get it over with. Come on," he encouraged.

Just then Etain's head reappeared through the Portal. "What's taking you so long? Or is it you are too scared to cross? Perhaps I should close the Portal now and save any indecision."

The moment Marella heard his words, her spine stiffened, and she picked up her trundle truck without a further word. She stalked towards the Portal, defying Etain's smirk as he watched them. Lani and Daren were right behind her, Etain's words having annoyed them as well.

Soon it was only the Partners left in Wraidd Elfennol. *"Come on, you three. We need to be over there to keep them out of trouble. Etain is doing his best to upset them all,"* said Kenna, leading them to the Portal.

"He really is an ass," stated Nixie without preamble.

Ula gave a small bark of agreement with Nixie and they could all feel Shaw's amusement through their shared bond. Together, with Shaw hitching a ride on Ula's back, the four of them crossed the Portal into the Fire Quarter.

* * *

When they reached the other side, the Partners returned to the sides of their humans. The atmosphere was tense between Etain and the companions and Nixie watched Marella carefully, not knowing when the wave would hit her.

"Now that we're all on the right side of the Portal, if you would follow me, Queen Djinn has arranged somewhere for you to relax and sleep for the rest of today. She will speak with you first thing in the morning. I would take your rest whilst you can, if I were you." Etain finished speaking and just looked at them.

"Thank you for your kind hospitality, please send our regards to Queen Djinn," replied Kai courteously, just wanting to get them somewhere they could be alone before the wave hit Marella.

Etain sneered at them once more before walking away, not looking to see if they were following him or not.

"That sneer of his will choke him one day," muttered Lani. "Or I will, I've not quite decided yet."

Daren and Marella chuckled at this, taking care not to laugh too loud lest they draw Etain's attention. Kai threw them a wink and a smile over his shoulder as he walked behind Etain.

He led them to a small dwelling simple in design, a round stone building with a low, overhanging slate roof. There was one door that they could see plus a couple of windows dotted around the building. As far as they could tell, it was only one level.

Etain gestured towards the door. "You may rest here for today. There are refreshments inside. I wouldn't recommend you go wandering about though. This is the Fire Quarter and we wouldn't want you getting burnt now, would we?"

"Thank you," said Kai quietly as he motioned for the others to precede him into the house, leaving their trundle trucks outside for now.

Without another word, Etain turned on his heel and left as quickly as he could, leaving Kai staring after him. With a shrug of his shoulders, he turned around and entered the doorway, just in time to see Marella's legs give out beneath her as she crumpled to the ground.

Kai rushed over to Marella's side, as Daren and Lani caught her before her head hit the ground. She was mumbling under her breath and her arms thrashed about.

"Let's lie her down over there," suggested Daren, jerking his head towards a couch he could see.

Kai and Daren lifted her whilst Lani went to check on Nixie. They put her down on the couch and looked at each other.

"I guess the wave has hit then," said Kai, looking down at her with concern etched on his face.

"Yes, it started a few moments ago but Marella was determined Etain wouldn't see it happen. She's so bloody stubborn. She was swaying on her feet as she fought the effects, whilst you were speaking to him," said Daren, gently smoothing her hair from her face.

"Nixie is okay but he's lying down too. Ula, Kenna and Shaw are with him," said Lani as she returned into the small house.

"Has this affected Nixie as well then?" questioned Kai. "Were Shaw and Ula affected when you were?"

"Shaw wasn't but then I'm not a single Element. I think it's all to do with Marella only having Water. She has such a strong connection to it, and her bond with Nixie is deep. I guess it makes sense that if it affects her, it affects him."

Daren shook his head, "Ula wasn't affected either. I agree with Lani, I think it's because of who Marella is and how deep their bond goes that Nixie is affected. I'm glad the others are with him."

Kai looked down at Marella and a smile tugged at his lips. "I think we should stay with her until she wakes up," he said. "Or at least take it in shifts. What do you say?"

"I agree with you. I know I felt rough when the wave hit me but at least I stayed conscious! You two sort yourselves out, get a drink for us all. I'll take the first bit with Marella," said Daren, sitting himself down on a nearby chair.

"You know, the house isn't that big," smiled Lani. "I'm sure we'd know if Marella needed us, even if we weren't sat here."

Kai and Daren looked at each ruefully, "She's right, you know," laughed Kai.

"I was just getting comfy, too," said Daren, winking at Lani who flushed, Kai noticed with interest.

"I'm going to make us a drink and get some water for Nixie and then I'll be back," said Lani before walking away to the kitchen area.

Whilst Lani was making a drink, Kai had a quick look around the house. It was small but it had everything they needed. There was the main living area which you walked straight into, with the kitchen off the left. To the right there were two bedrooms with twin beds and nothing much else.

Taking a walk outside, he noticed there was an outhouse discreetly placed at the back of the property. As he walked past their trundle trucks, he picked up a few items and brought them inside where they could keep them close. He placed the backpacks inside the two bedrooms.

He walked back to the main area and saw Daren and Lani were sat down on some stools they had found. Lani was near to Marella's head and had laid a damp cloth onto her forehead.

"Is she okay?" asked Kai, concerned.

"She's fine, there's no change really. I just thought this might help," replied Lani.

"So, Chosen of Fire, are you going to explain how you and Marella were able to speak directly to Lani and I?" asked Daren with mock-seriousness.

"Whilst we spent time with Hynafol, I looked through his library, remember?" Kai asked Daren.

"I do, yes. I stayed for a bit but became bored. I take it you found something interesting?"

"Definitely, it was an old book that described how certain people, not all, could speak mind-to-mind directly with each other, without having to go through their Partners all the time." Kai smiled at the look of shock Daren and Lani wore.

"But how... when... I mean," stuttered Lani.

"On the flight back to Awyr, Marella was terrified. It appears flying isn't her thing. I thought about it and decided to give it a go. After all, we've all been Chosen, we keep being told that we're stronger together so I figured if we didn't have a deep enough bond, I didn't know who would."

"So you spoke to her whilst flying then?" asked Daren, glancing at Marella as she lay so still.

"I did, yes. She was very confused to start with and thought it was Nixie. Her curiosity won out over her fear, and it kept her occupied until we landed."

Daren laughed, "That's clever," he said with admiration. "Using her own curiosity against her."

"Yes, well, I wasn't really doing it for that, but it does work. Once you know the paths to use, you can speak to all of us or singularly. And the Partners can hear too if you want them to, or it can be completely private. There are possibilities in this."

"I wonder why we don't know about it anymore," mused Lani. "I mean, we seem to have so much knowledge about some things, and then nothing about others."

"I don't know," said Kai, "It's strange. Who decides what knowledge is kept and taught and which is forgotten?"

"It's probably just down to what is used and when," said Daren, practically. "We were taught things in my training I'm sure I'll never need to use. So when it gets to a point, say, that I'm teaching others, am I going to teach them something I've never used, or will I teach them something I use a lot?"

"I guess that's it," said Lani. "Still, it would be amazing to find out what other 'tricks' we've forgotten about."

"And you thought libraries were boring," smiled Kai. "They're full of fascinating information if you just spend some time in them."

"Okay, okay, point proven," laughed Daren, shaking his head at Kai.

As the three of them sat together, Marella started to twitch. She mumbled under her breath and her head moved from side to side. Lani stood up and went over to her, smoothing her hair and trying to reassure her. Daren and Kai looked at each other worriedly before Daren checked in with Ula to see if Nixie was okay.

"Ula, how is Nixie right now? Marella's started to twitch and shake."

"Nixie too, I was just going to ask you to come here when you spoke to me. I don't like this, Daren. I don't like this at all."

"Ula is worried about Nixie and has asked me to go to them. She's not happy with this situation. Will you watch Marella for me?" he asked Kai and Lani, not really waiting for their assurances before he left to find Ula and Nixie.

It didn't take long before he returned, carrying Nixie in his arms. Marella was twitching and her mumbling was getting louder, although Daren still couldn't make out what she was saying. He put Nixie down on the couch next to Marella, hoping they would both take some comfort from the physical closeness of each other.

He took a step back, placing his hands on his hips as he watched them. Nixie soon moved around and snuggled up to Marella who, in turn, rested her hand on his back. This did seem to soothe both of them; however, it didn't last for long. Marella resumed her twitching and by now, some of her words were audible to the others.

"No, no, no," she moaned, as her head frantically moved from side to side. "You can't do this. It's not right."

They all looked at each other, whatever it was she was seeing didn't sound like it was good. Ula and Shaw came into the room, with Kenna trotting along behind them. They came and sat down near to the couch and watched Nixie and Marella.

"Kenna, I know you can speak with Nixie. Are you able to see what he is seeing?" asked Kai.

"I can't," said Kenna, regretfully. *"I can only share what Nixie lets me and right now, his mind is on lockdown. Whatever it is he's seeing with Marella, he doesn't want anyone else to know about."*

Kai looked helplessly at the others whilst Marella twisted and turned; her movements frenzied. Her moans became louder until she was shouting, her body stiff, and her movements jerky. Suddenly, she bolted upright, her eyes tightly closed. She grasped Nixie's scruff and pulled him to her, holding him tightly. Nixie was making his own sounds of distress and his body was taut with tension. Marella crumpled back, lying down with Nixie still being held closely to her body.

"I don't know what to do," said Lani, tearfully. "This is horrible."

"Kai, try speaking to her through the bond," said Daren. "You're the one who was able to speak with her before. I haven't yet and neither has Lani. Besides, I think you have extra oomph in your bond with Marella. Go on, please," he urged.

Kai nodded and moved closer to Marella. He reached forward to touch her hand, but as his fingertips brushed her skin, she screamed at the top of her lungs, startling Kai so much he fell backwards, landing on Daren.

"KAI! Fire is cleansing, yes, but you can't cleanse him, you'll kill him. Kai, oh no," Marella sobbed, the sound ripping through the others as they froze with shock at her words.

Kai went white as he heard Marella, but he crawled forward on his hands and knees to be by her side, as he covered her hand with his and held on firmly. *"Marella, Chosen of Water, come back to us,"* he commanded through their bond. *"Marella, come on, we need you. I need you. Come back."* His tone changed from commanding to pleading as he pushed his feelings of love, friendship, warmth, and hope to her.

"Keep going, Kai, she's calming down," said Lani to him.

"Marella, if you don't come back to me, I'm going to make your life a living hell," he threatened, desperate to try anything to bring her back. *"I'm going to take you flying on a Roc every day until you come back. You don't want me to do that, do you? So come on back and tell me so."*

He took a deep breath and looked at Daren who urged him on encouragingly.

"Marella, I know we haven't seen eye to eye. You're over-sensitive at times, and I've put my foot in it on more than one occasion, but I'm going to tell you something now. I can't get you out of my mind. Even before I could speak to you like this, I couldn't get you out. I think about you constantly. I've told Kenna that this isn't the right time to be thinking the sort of thoughts I've had - and am having - about you. We're on a quest; we need to work together, nothing else.

And yet… and yet, I find myself longing to be with you, to make you smile, to hear you laugh. I want to be the one who brings you tea after you've woven. I want to see you swim in your lake. Marella, I want us to be together. I don't know where this is going, and I know we need to balance the Elements before we can do anything, but I'm telling you now. I need you. I want you in my life. I want to take a chance with you, and discover where this is going together. I can't do that if you don't come back to me. Please, Marella, please."

Kai felt the burn in his throat, as his words drifted through their connection towards her still form. Tears filled his eyes and he inched closer to pull her hand to his chest. As he reached out with his other hand to caress her cheek, Daren squeezed his shoulder.

"You certainly know how to make a speech."

* * *

Kai froze as he heard Marella whisper through their connection. His eyes darted to their joined hands as he felt a flicker of movement, and his voice echoed in the silence, "Marella?"

Daren took a step closer and peered down at her. Lani, with a small smile, moved so she was back near Marella's head and stroked her hair. Marella's eyelids flickered before she opened them. Her attention moved from her friends, to Nixie who was still lying close to her side, tucked in between her arm and her shoulder.

She ran her hand lovingly down his body, "Nixie, my love. You can come back now, it's safe, I promise." She crooned to him, pushing every ounce of her love for him through their bond as she spoke out loud. Slowly, she could feel the tension leave his body as it relaxed against her, although his eyes were still shut.

"Marella, you can't tell Kai what you saw, it wouldn't be right. This has to play out naturally and it won't if he has foreknowledge," Nixie urgently whispered in her mind.

"How can I not tell him? Nixie, you know what I saw. You were with me too. How can I keep it a secret?"

"You have to, Marella. Say you can't remember, that should give you some time. You know as well as I do that Weave is going to come true and soon. You can't tell

him."

"Okay, Nixie, I won't. I don't like it though." Feeling the truth in Nixie's words, Marella agreed.

Once she knew Nixie was okay and they had agreed on a way forward, Marella returned her attention to the three surrounding her. She tipped her head back and smiled at Lani.

Nixie wriggled and jumped off Marella, making his way over to Ula, Kenna, and Shaw where they spent time rubbing against each other to reassure themselves Nixie was well.

Daren watched them before winking at Marella. "Do I need to do that with you?" he laughed.

Marella snorted, "You can but try." She pushed herself up onto her elbows and carefully swung her legs down to the floor, before sitting upright.

"Are you okay, Marella?" asked Lani, her quiet voice filled with concern.

"I'm fine," insisted Marella, shaking her head to clear it. "How long was I out for?"

"Just an hour or so," said Kai. "Can you remember any of what you saw; it sounded like you were Weaving."

"I can't remember anything, are you sure I was Weaving?" asked Marella, a hint of a blush on her cheekbones.

"It certainly sounded that way," said Daren, watching her with interest.

"You called out for Kai," said Lani.

"Really?" said Marella, the blush high on her cheeks now. "I'm sorry, I can't remember anything."

Daren wondered at the truth of her statement as he watched her squirm with discomfort. When she raised pleading eyes to his, he decided he would help her, although he also had every intention of finding out just what the problem was as soon as he could.

"Come on, Marella. Let's get you up and moving. Carefully now, lean on me until you get the feeling back." Daren helped Marella to her feet, holding her as she wobbled upon standing. He led her out of the room, "We'll just go for a small walk outside to let you get some fresh air."

His voice wafted back to Kai and Lani as they watched them go. Lani looked at Kai, a quizzical look upon her face. "What do you think is going on there?" she asked him.

"I'm not sure, but I get the feeling Marella remembers more than she's saying."

"Then why won't she say?"

"I don't know. I'm hoping she has a good reason. I guess we just need to trust her."

Kai and Lani proceeded to put the small house to rights as they waited for Daren and Marella to return, ensuring everything was where it needed to be and was within easy reach should they need it quickly.

* * *

"So what's going on?" asked Daren once they were out of the hearing of the others, as he led Marella outside. Marella's body gave a slight shudder at Daren's question, betraying the fact she could remember more than what she had told them.

She took a deep breath before turning so she could look Daren in the eyes. "I can't tell you, Daren. Not yet. Nixie and I both agree the Weave will happen soon, but this is something we can't prepare for. Nixie thinks if we say, we will change the outcome and not in a good way. To be honest, I'm not entirely sure what I saw."

Daren was silent as he thought about it. "You've never led me wrong, Marella, not in all the time we've been together, so I have to trust you in this. I don't like it though. I don't like the idea you're keeping secrets from the rest of us."

Marella's eyes shone as the tears threatened to spill. "I know, Daren," she cried. "I don't like it anymore than you do, but answer me this. What would you do if Ula told you not to tell anyone something? Would you listen to your Life Partner or would you go ahead and tell?"

Daren shook his head ruefully, "You know as well as I do I'd follow Ula, so long as she explained why."

"Exactly," Marella sniffled, wiping her nose with a tissue from her pocket. "Nixie is positive we can't say anything, when all I want to do is blurt it out. I'm not sure what I saw, but what I do remember was horrible. I actually hope the Weave plays out soon, because the sooner I can forget about it, the better."

Daren gave her a quick squeeze as they stood together, looking over the small amount of the Fire Quarter they could see. A moment of peace stretched out between them as they relaxed into each other's company. "Did you think it would be like this?" asked Daren quietly.

"The challenge?" asked Marella. Seeing Daren's nod, she tried to put her feelings into words. "Not really, no. There's a lot more walking and waiting involved than I thought," she laughed. "I don't really know what I expected. I'm glad we were both Chosen though, really glad. I don't know if I would have wanted to do it on my own. I admire Kai and Lani for that. They didn't know anyone and yet they've still come." Marella gazed into the distance without seeing, "What about you?"

Daren gave a short bark of laughter, sounding a lot like Ula. "I agree with the waiting and walking, but I think you still would have come, even without me. I think you were born to do this, Marella. Why else would you only have Water?"

"Because I'm a freak," she laughed bitterly. "Come on, Daren, did you never listen to the villagers when they thought I couldn't hear? It's not normal for only one Element," she said, distorting her voice so it was high-pitched and shrill.

Daren bumped her shoulder, "No, I never listen to them because I know you," he reassured her. "You only give them more power to hurt you, if you take their words to heart."

"It's hard not to," admitted Marella, "When you constantly hear something, it will take a stronger person than I am, not to start believing what you hear."

"I understand that, but listen to me, not them. You're not a freak. You're a warm, caring, strong, pain in the ass I am lucky enough to call friend, even though you mean so much more."

Marella smiled at Daren, her love for him shining upon her face. She put her arms around his waist and squeezed as tightly as she could. "I love you," she told him, leaning her head on his shoulder.

"I love you too," he replied, returning her embrace. They stood there for a moment, just taking a moment to enjoy the solitude of being together in peaceful harmony.

* * *

A cough broke the silence and Daren turned his head to see Kai standing in the doorway of the house, a scowl marring his face. Daren grinned and shook his head at Kai. He gave Marella one last squeeze before he let her go. "Someone else needs you more than I do right now," he whispered. "Good luck, be as honest as you can be."

Daren strode back towards the house, clapping Kai on the shoulder as they passed. Kai slowly walked over to where Marella waited for him, his hands thrust inside his trouser pockets.

"You know, I'm sure your Mama would hate to see you walking like that," Marella tried to lighten the tension that had appeared with Kai.

"Do you remember anything, Marella?" he asked her, looking straight in her eyes. "I need to know. You were calling my name and crying out 'no'. Am I going to do something bad? Please, if you do remember anything, please tell me," he begged.

Marella put her own arms around her waist, hugging herself as she tried to find the right words for Kai. She nibbled on her lip as she contemplated what to say.

Kai groaned as he watched her, "Marella, you're killing me here. Either just tell me or don't, but don't just leave me hanging like this."

"I don't want to lie to you, Kai, but I have to be very careful with what

I say. Nixie has warned me against telling you anything as he says it will happen soon and he doesn't want me to influence your decision in any way."

"Well now I know I have a decision to make, so you may as well tell me the rest of what you saw."

Marella stamped her foot to the ground. "Stop pushing me, Kai. This isn't easy. I'm used to sharing what I see, and the fact it involves you, doesn't make it any easier," she said agitatedly.

Kai threw his hands up in the air in disgust. "Stop pushing you? How? How am I supposed to do that, Marella? Answer me that. We're in the Fire Quarter. I'm supposed to be leading our little band, and yet my Weaver has a vision that seems quite important, but she won't tell me what it was about. So you tell me why I'm supposed to stop pushing you?"

"Your Weaver? *Your* Weaver? So that's what I am to you. All that talk before about what you wanted, all rubbish. Well thanks for that, you brought me up from under the wave. Well done you, give yourself a pat on the back," sarcasm dripped from her voice, as she frantically paced backwards and forwards, throwing her hands into the air.

"I spoke from the heart," Kai said harshly, his throat constricting with anger. "Everything I said, I meant. I just didn't realise that within minutes, you'd be taking your Partner's side over mine."

"Do you have any idea how ridiculous you sound right now?" Marella said indignantly. "Of course I'm going to take Nixie's side over yours. Not that this even has sides, but if it did, then I still would. Why? Because Nixie has been my Life Partner for over seven years and he's never led me wrong yet. I trust him with my life. And you, what about you? You come on this quest, spitting sparks at us all, you make me like you and hope for something more. You *tell* me that there's something more, and then you act like this!"

Marella copied Kai as she threw her hands up into the air. "I give up, I'm going back inside. If you decide to start acting as the leader of our group, starting by acting your age, then come back and talk to me. Until then, I'm done."

* * *

Marella stalked back to the house, dirt kicking up at her heels as she pounded away, her chest heaving with emotion. She walked into the house and the door slammed behind her. Lani jumped at the noise. Daren took one look at her and quickly went out the door before Marella could say anything.

"Dare I ask what the matter is?" said Lani wryly, "or shall I just say 'Kai' and leave it at that?"

"Argh," cried Marella. "He's just so… so…, he infuriates me so much. How dare he ask me to choose between him and Nixie, like he ever would with Kenna, not that I would ever suggest such a thing. Just who does he think he is? Arrogant, egotistical, bull-headed, oh so superior… bloody Chosen of Fire," she spat.

"What has he done now?" Lani calmly asked.

"He was pushing me to tell him what I saw within my Weave, starts telling me it's my job to do so being as I'm *his* Weaver whilst we're in the Fire Quarter and then says I'm taking Nixie's side over his! Gah!"

Marella stomped around the room a bit more, her movements agitated and jerky. Lani smiled a small smile to herself whilst she made Marella a cup of chamomile tea in the hope it would help her to calm down.

"You know, Marella, you only ever react this much to Kai. If Daren had said the same thing whilst we were in the Earth Quarter, you'd have come back with some quip or another. You wouldn't have taken it to heart so much."

"What are you saying?" Marella said harshly. "That I'm overreacting because it's Kai?"

"No," soothed Lani, "I'm just saying where Kai is concerned; your emotions are on high alert." Lani gave Marella's shoulder a squeeze as she passed her drink over. "What has you so wound up about this? You knew Kai would be the leader here, the same as you will be the leader in the Water Quarter. Is it the Weave? Talk to me, Marella."

Marella dropped into one of the chairs, her shoulders drooping. She put her drink on the floor by her chair and covered her face with her hands, groaning. Peering through her fingers, she looked at Lani who was waiting patiently.

"Nixie has cautioned me against saying anything to Kai. This Weave I saw is imminent, and if I tell Kai anything about it, it could change the outcome and not in a good way," she explained, worry crossing her features.

"You realise he's already heard some of it though, right?" questioned Lani. At Marella's confused look, she explained "He was sat right by you when you started to talk. He already knows it concerns him as you called his name, more than once."

Lani continued, "I don't want to know what the Weave was about, but I can tell you now, Marella, it didn't sound good. You were talking about Kai, and cleansing, and fire. It was then that Kai tried - successfully I might add - to bring you back. Now I have no idea what he said, as it was said on a private path between the two of you, but whatever it was, it worked. You came back. There is a connection between you and Kai that is visible to the world, should they have the eyes to see it."

Marella blushed at Lani's words, but continued listening, her eyes intent on Lani. "Do you want to hear my thoughts on why you're so upset right now?" At Marella's nod, Lani sank into the chair opposite Marella and leaned forward so she could clasp Marella's hands within her own.

"I think you can remember all of what you saw within the Weave. It's something that is scaring you, and in typical Marella fashion, you're pushing away the one you should be holding tight. Don't you see, Marella? By arguing with Kai and pushing him away, you might actually be affecting his judgement already for this decision he has to make."

A look of shock spread across Marella's face as she considered the implications of Lani's words. "You need to clear the air with Kai, sooner rather than later. We are in the Fire Quarter, leading up to goodness knows what, with a Weave that by right's we shouldn't have as you're not supposed to be able to Weave at all whilst in the Quarters, and now you two are arguing. You need to sort it out."

With that, Lani stood up and brushed down her trousers. "I'll leave you to think about it, but I wouldn't take too long." Lani moved away, going in the direction of the bedroom and closing the door behind her.

* * *

Marella picked her drink up from the floor and sipped it as she thought on Lani's advice. Finishing her drink, she went through the kitchen, rinsed out her cup and placed it upside down on the draining board. Gathering her courage, she headed towards the door, intent on finding Kai and apologising.

Just as she reached for the door handle, the door opened forcefully, making her take a step back to avoid being hit by it. Kai strode through, coming to a stop when he saw Marella.

"Kai, I'm sorry," began Marella.

"Marella, please forgive me," Kai said at the same time.

They both stopped and looked at each other. "Fancy going for a walk with me?" asked Kai, gesturing outside.

"I'd love to," murmured Marella as she walked passed him and through the doorway.

Kai joined her and Marella let him lead her on a small walk around their house, taking care not to trespass too far, as per Etain's instructions.

"I'm sorry you thought I was pushing you or making you choose sides, Marella. That wasn't my intention. I'm just worried," began Kai, catching her hand and linking their fingers together as they walked.

"I'm sorry too," said Marella, not looking at him. "I didn't mean to make it more difficult for you."

They walked together in companionable silence for a short while. Swinging her around so she faced him, Kai placed both hands on her face, holding her tenderly.

"Marella, I meant every word I said when I brought you back. You drive me insane, you make me so angry, I can't form the words I'm thinking, but I still don't want to be without you. I want us to move forward with whatever this is, but what do you want? You never actually said. Am I the only one who feels this way? If I am, tell me now and I'll back off. We'll go back to being just friends, and I won't hassle you about this ever again."

Marella reached up and placed her hands on his arms, gazing deeply into his chocolate brown eyes. She gave a soft sigh and closed her eyes briefly. As she stroked his arms, she looked in his eyes and gave a small smile.

"You're not the only one, Kai. I'm confused about what I feel, and you drive me insane. The timing sucks, you know? The thought of not having you with me, though, that's something I don't want to think about. So, please, I'm asking you now, don't back off."

Kai pulled her close, her body trapped against his and he rested his chin atop her head. Marella pulled her arms tight around his waist before relaxing them, taking ease in holding him and being held.

Standing still, with her head on his chest, listening to the steady thump of his heart, Marella relaxed for the first time since entering the Fire Quarter. Marella tilted her head back to look at him as she felt him move his chin. Kai was watching her, a strange look of longing on his face. "Are you okay?" Marella asked.

Kai just nodded as he lifted a hand and gently trailed his fingers across her cheek and jaw line. He moved his hand around to cup the back of her head, before he hesitantly lowered his face to hers, giving Marella plenty of time to back away if she wanted to. Instead, Marella raised herself onto tiptoes and met his lips with her own. She brushed against his mouth, delighting in the firmness of his full lips, as her heart started to pound.

Kai nibbled tenderly on her lips, before lightly touching them with his tongue, asking permission to take it further. With a sigh, she opened her mouth and they kissed more deeply, their breaths becoming ragged and harsh, as they explored each other's mouths.

Marella's body was pulled tight to Kai as he smoothed one hand up and down her back, whilst he still caressed her head and brushed his fingers through her hair. Marella held onto him tightly, exploring his lean and muscular back with her fingertips.

Slowly, almost regretfully, Kai eased back but kept Marella within his grasp. Breathing heavily, she once again leant her head upon his chest, feeling a sense of joy suffuse her being.

"I know the timing is all wrong, but if you want me to apologise for that, you will be disappointed," said Kai, his voice still husky with desire.

Marella grinned up at him, "Definitely no apology necessary," she said hoarsely, breathing in deeply of his natural scent of pinecones and smoke. "You know, you smell really good. I've never noticed before but you smell of smoke."

Kai chuckled, the sound rumbling through his chest. "Thank you... I think," he said, smiling at her and kissing the top of her head.

After a moment of just enjoying the closeness, Marella pulled away. "I guess we'd better go back in, the others will be worried."

Letting Marella go when he'd just got her, wasn't on Kai's list of things to do so instead of freeing her, he moved to the side and put his arm around her shoulders, immensely pleased when she tucked her arm about his waist. In step with each other, they returned to the house, unaware of Etain's presence a short distance away as he watched them with burning eyes.

* * *

When they walked back into the house, there was a moment's silence as Daren and Lani stopped their conversation and took in the sight of Kai and Marella together. "I take it you two have sorted it out then," said Daren with a twinkle in his eyes as he laughed at the two of them, moving out of the way as Lani tried to elbow his ribs.

"Something like that," said Kai in a satisfied tone.

"Not sure how long the peace will last for though," smiled Marella. "No promises."

Lani giggled at Marella, the sound filling the air as they all laughed together.

"Come and sit down, whilst you two have been smooching, we've been getting some food sorted," said Daren, waving his hands towards the kitchen.

"We?" questioned Lani with a quirk of her eyebrow.

"Alright, well, you did the food, but I did the drinks," Daren defended himself, much to Marella's delight.

"It's nothing fancy," said Lani, "but it should help to fill us up."

They walked over to the table, Lani and Daren dishing up the food and setting the plates down on the table before sitting down themselves. Marella took a breath in of the steam that wafted over her plate. "Mmm, Lani, it smells delicious." Her stomach made a loud, rumbling sound.

"I think your stomach agrees," laughed Daren.

"Oh, shut it you," she said.

"Now, now, children; wait until after we've eaten if you don't mind," Lani said primly.

Kai laughed aloud as he watched Daren and Marella settle down.

Spooning some of the rosemary covered potatoes in his mouth, he found out it was indeed fresh from the oven as it scalded the roof of his mouth. Grabbing a glass of water, he quickly drank it down to soothe the burning sensation. Eyes watering, he looked at Lani and gave a pained smile. "It's really good, Lani, honest."

Everyone followed Kai's example and dug into the potatoes, steak and salad. The silence was only broken by the sounds of appreciation made by them all. It didn't take them long to finish as, one by one, they sat back in their chairs, replete.

Daren rose from his chair and went to the worktop and collected a pot of tea and four cups. He poured the tea and handed them around. Once everyone had one, he looked at Kai. "So what's the plan now then?"

Kai grinned, "Well, Marella and I still have things we need to sort out –,"

"I didn't mean about you two, you numpty! I meant what do we do now we're in the Fire Quarter." Daren laughed long and loud, as a blush spread across Kai's face. Marella groaned before giggling, meeting his glance with a smile.

"All right, all right, settle down," laughed Kai. "It's a simple mistake to make. Right then, as far as being here goes, we're firmly on the 'graces' of Etain and Queen Djinn. We need to wait for them to see us before we can go any further. We're not prisoners here, but we're certainly not welcome. I say we stay prepared for anything, including a quick exit if need be."

Kai shot an apologetic glance at Marella who squirmed uncomfortably, "There is something that is going to happen, but for whatever reason, Marella isn't allowed to say. This means we're in the dark and so we have to go with our own instincts and reasoning."

"I don't know why but I don't think we're going to kept waiting too long. I think Etain wants us out. I have no idea about Queen Djinn yet."

"Etain does indeed want us out and you are right to be wary of him," said Kenna on a broad path so everyone could hear her.

Kai looked at her quizzically, "What do you mean, Kenna? Have you been told something we haven't?"

"It's only what the rest of us have been talking about. Nixie hasn't told us anymore than Marella has told you. However, we do feel like we're not wanted here so our suggestion is to get the Flame and get out."

Lani gave a small giggle at Kenna. "Good idea Kenna, however we can't go any quicker than Queen Djinn will let us."

"I don't think they'll keep us waiting long," said Marella thoughtfully. She looked around and saw everyone watching her. "I know Nixie and I can't say anything, so don't worry. I just feel things will move quickly here. Maybe it's because I'm Water, but it's almost a physical buzz against my skin, urging me to go."

"I know what you mean and it's not just Water that's being affected, it's Air too," said Lani, rubbing her arms. "For now, I think the best thing we can do is actually follow Etain's advice." Lani stopped and grinned at the gasps that accompanied her words.

"Yes, I know, never thought I'd say that!" she laughed. "However, I think we should rest now, it's not long until it will be getting dark anyway. Well, at least, if it follows the same sort of thing as back home. If Queen Djinn does call for us in the morning and things move quickly, we're going to need to be rested and one hundred percent aware."

The others nodded in agreement as they stood up to clear the table. Kai and Daren washed up their dirty plates before putting them to drain. Marella made everyone a drink of valerian tea to take to bed, before both she and Lani disappeared into their bedroom after saying good night to Kai and Daren.

Kai and Daren stayed up for a short while longer, sitting in the chairs near the fireplace where a small hearth fire crackled and popped. "So you and Marella sorted it out then, yeah?" asked Daren, staring into his mug.

"I think so, for now at least. We both want to see where this takes us, but we're also aware the timing sucks." Kai laughed mockingly.

Daren held his mug up in a toast. "To you and Marella, may the sparks burn high."

Kai returned the toast, "And the waters run deep."

They grinned at each other before relaxing back into their chairs, letting the silence surround and enfold them. Ula and Kenna joined them and the four of them spent some quality peace time together before they moved off to bed.

~ 53 ~

The following morning dawned bright and clear. Marella could hear birdsong as she lay in her bed, wondering what today would bring.

"There's no point worrying about it; what will be, will be," said Nixie, shuffling closer to her side and resting his head on her chest.

"I know, Nixie, but I just can't help it. After yesterday, both with the Weave and with what happened between Kai and myself, I fear for what today will bring."

"You don't need to fear about you and Kai, you fit together, both Kenna and I agree and couldn't be happier with how things have moved along. As for the Weave, you know as well as I do, perspective is what counts. What may look like one thing, could be something completely different from a different view. Kai is the one that has to do this. All you can do is support him."

"I don't like it," Marella grumbled, hugging Nixie to her, a slight smile on her face as he wriggled to get free, tickling her cheek with his whiskers.

"You don't have to like it; you just have to do it. Now come on, it's time to rise and shine. Put on your glad rags and don't let Etain get you down."

With Nixie's laughing tone in her mind, Marella dragged herself out of bed and threw a robe about her shoulders. She ducked out of the room and made her way to the outhouse. Once finished there, she went back inside and grabbed a jug of water from the kitchen before returning to the room she and Lani shared.

She quietly opened the door and eased back inside. She glanced over at Lani who had just sat up in bed and was rubbing her eyes. "Good morning, Lani. Did you sleep well?" asked Marella politely.

Lani gave her a sharp look before nodding. "Yes I did, thank you. Why are you being so courteous this morning?"

Marella laughed. "I'm always courteous," she complained.

Lani grinned at her and shifted so that her knees came up and she could put her arms around them. "Well, yes you are, but not normally this early in the morning."

"I've had my orders from Nixie. I need to 'shine' with my glad rags on and not let Etain get on my nerves. I thought I'd practice with you." Marella winked.

Lani giggled at Marella. "Is that what he said? I can just picture him saying that."

"That's exactly what he said, so who am I to disobey?"

"I'll have to let Kai in on that secret then," said Lani, laughing even louder at the furious blush covering Marella's cheeks.

"Phew, it's a bit hot in here," said Marella, waving her hands in front of her face.

Lani chuckled as she bounced out of bed. "Do you know if the outhouse is free?" she asked, changing the subject, much to Marella's delight.

"It was when I left it," replied Marella, shaking out her dress from where it had been rolled up in the trundle truck.

"I'm off then, I hope it still is. See you shortly." With a jaunty wave, Lani skipped out of the room, closing the door behind her.

"Are you sure I need to put this on?" Marella asked Nixie. *"I'm much more comfortable in my trousers and shirt."*

"I know you are, but whilst we are here, you need to be in your official capacity. Keep your staff close by. I'm hearing things about Etain and Queen Djinn that are concerning, although none of my business, to be fair. I want this part done with so we can carry on."

Marella wondered at the tense notes in Nixie's voice. When she looked at him, his body seemed stiff, not as fluid as it usually was. Whatever it was he had heard was of major concern to him.

She dressed, not wanting to waste any more time. She smoothed down her dress and made sure her girdle was hung in the right place. She slipped her feet into her ballet pumps and wriggled her toes. She picked up her staff from where she had placed it under the bed, and looked at herself in the small mirror. "That will have to do," she murmured, before tidying the bed up and opening a window to let the fresh morning breeze sweep away the night's funk.

The door opened and Lani came in, shivering slightly. "Oh, it's brisk outside," she said, grabbing her clothes and changing.

Marella laughed at her. "Lani, you do realise it's Rhagfyr, right? It will be Yule celebrations soon."

"And don't forget Kai's birthday," reminded Lani slyly. "Have you got him anything?"

"When is it his birthday?" said Marella, a hint of panic in her voice. "I don't know."

"His birthday is the thirtieth day of Rhagfyr so you should still have some time." Lani laughed to herself as she adjusted her girdle. She picked up her crossbow and slid it onto her shoulder, patting the quiver of bolts that hung at her waist.

They had both done their hair similarly, loose at the back but kept off their faces by a plait either side, tied together at the back.

Lani double checked herself and looked at Marella. "Shall we go?"

Marella nodded firmly, "Let's get this over with," she said and together they walked out to the kitchen area.

* * *

Marella bustled around the kitchen, putting some water on to boil so she could make a hot drink whilst Lani found some bacon in the cold store.

She was heating the griddle pan and placing strips of the salty meat onto it when Kai and Daren walked in. As Marella and Lani, they were dressed in their formal best. The Chosen of the Elements were ready.

Much to Marella's surprise, Kai walked over and gave her a kiss on the cheek. "Good morning, Marella," he said, his deep voice rumbling over her.

She blushed before turning around and giving him a mug of peppermint tea. "Good morning, Kai," she replied.

She gave a drink to Lani and thrust one in Daren's hands, warning him with a look as he was about to say something. His shoulders quivered with restrained laughter as he tried to behave himself.

Daren cleared his face and tried to act seriously, "So, what's the plan for today, Kai?" he asked.

Kai grinned at him and leaned back against the kitchen worktop. "Well, today we wait for the pleasure of meeting Queen Djinn. Etain said it would be this morning. Once we meet her, I'll wing it." He snorted at Marella and Lani's expressions, "Like you had any more of an idea when you met Queen Paralda, Lani. You can't plan everything, sometimes you just have to see where it takes you."

"Fair point," conceded Daren, raising his mug in acknowledgement.

They ate their breakfast without delay and tidied up the house. Marella double-checked she had everything she needed either in her backpack or in the trundle truck. Rummaging through her backpack, she ran her fingers slowly across the cloth-wrapped silver chalice, feeling the contours beneath her fingertips.

"That won't do you any good right now, Marella. You won't get anything," said Nixie.

"I know," she sighed, *"I just miss it. It's like…"* she bit her lip as she tried to think of an explanation. *"It's like, now that I know I can't use it, I really feel the need to. Does that make sense?"*

"Of course it makes sense, the minute you are denied anything, it's human nature to want it more. We'll be gone soon and then you've have your Weaves back." Nixie reassured her as he went about his business with the other Partners which seemed to involve being under their feet or curling up on top of the trundle trucks.

By the time the sun had crested over the trees, the house was tidy, everything was where it should be, and the Chosen and Partners were sat waiting impatiently. Marella stood up to pace the floor. As she walked from one side of the room to the other, almost like a caged animal, Kai watched her. Daren, catching Kai's eye, smiled and tried to calm her down.

"Marella, rest yourself. You won't do yourself any good fretting like this," he said.

"I know," Marella retorted. "I just think it's rude, that's all. They tell us to be ready, which we are, and then they keep us waiting."

"It's all a tactical game, mind control, pettiness," soothed Lani. "The more upset you are, the more likely you are to give something away."

"I don't have anything to give away," snapped Marella, before turning to Lani with her hands spread in apology. "Oh Lani, I'm so sorry. I didn't mean to snap at you."

Lani shrugged it off with ease, "Don't worry about it, just try to relax. Channel your Element and go with the flow."

"When we finish here, Marella, the first big body of water we come to, you can dive in and spend the whole day there if you wish. That will readjust you to your Element after all this fire." Kai winked at her and she returned his.

"Look what I've found," said Daren triumphantly, "a chess board and pieces." He grinned, "Who wants a game?"

"I will, I'm not very good though," said Lani, getting up and moving over to the table and chairs by the fire.

Daren set up the board, Lani was white and he was black. Lani moved the first pawn and the game began.

* * *

Kai watched them for a while before he became bored. Both Daren and Lani were staring intently at the board and he could see they were both planning moves three or four times ahead of where they currently were. He moved over to the couch where Marella was sat, looking out of the window. He sat next to her and bumped her shoulder with his. "Are you okay?" he asked.

She turned her head and smiled, "I'm fine, honestly. I just feel on edge and want to get this over with. I'm sorry Kai, I know this is your Element, but it puts my teeth on edge. I kept being warned it would hit, but didn't think it would be like this."

"You're handling it fine, don't worry. Marella, I don't like being in the Fire Quarter either, it's not just you. There is something off about being here. Where do the Partners keep disappearing to? Why can't we leave the house or surrounding areas? And what's with Etain's bigoted attitude towards other Elements? I just want to get this done. I'm hoping Ena will turn up," said Kai, his voice lowered so as not to disturb Daren and Lani.

Kai put his arm around Marella's shoulders and pulled her to him. She relaxed into him, her head upon his shoulder. They sat there in perfect harmony, enjoying the moment of peace between them. Kai ran his fingers through Marella's hair and caressed the side of her face and neck. She quivered when he ran a finger across the top of her shoulders, and up her neck towards her ear.

She moved her head as she laughed gently, "Stop that, I don't think this is the right time or place, do you?" she asked, as she tilted her head so that she could look at him, her eyes sparkling.

"No, it's not," agreed Kai, bending his head so that he could rub noses with her. "It doesn't mean I don't want to though."

Marella gave a contented sigh and snuggled back against Kai's firm body, only to jerk upright when a loud knocking came on their door. They all jumped to attention, Marella and Lani making quick adjustments to the fall of their dresses as Kai made his way to the door. After looking around to make sure they were all ready, Kai opened the door to the smirking face of Etain.

"If you're ready, I'll take you to meet Queen Djinn now," he said, his tone implying he'd been kept waiting.

"Yes, we're ready," answered Kai politely and gestured for the others to precede him.

The Partners reappeared and walked to their respective places at the sides of the Chosen. None of them appeared happy and Marella trailed her fingertips down by her sides so Nixie could reach them if he wanted to.

As they walked along behind Etain and Kai, Nixie bumped her hand with his head. *"Marella, be careful. We've just found out Etain is working against us. We're still not sure about Queen Djinn. This goes further than any of us thought, I can't explain it all now, but please be careful. Do not rise to any jibes or provocation. I can tell you now, something will be aimed at you because Etain seems to despise Water above all else, and you are pure Water. Be careful, my Chosen, do not let anything happen to you."*

Marella trembled at Nixie's words. It was one thing to think someone didn't like you, but something else when you found out it was true. She stiffened her spine and tilted her chin.

"We are the Chosen of the Lady Erwyna – called to represent Water and our emotions, giving us the ability to be moved by feelings," she said to Nixie, repeating the vow they had made by the bonfire on the Summer Solstice. With those words, she felt stronger and more confident and her steps gained in strength as she walked towards the unknown.

~ 54 ~

Etain led them to a large, horseshoe shaped open-air arena with lots of stone benches, where Queen Djinn sat on a raised dais directly opposite the entry, looking down at them. Raising her arm, she played with a piece of her fire-tipped auburn hair.

The four Chosen stood in front of her, side by side. As one, they bowed their heads to her for a moment before looking up at her. Marella gripped tightly to her staff and noticed for the first time Kai and Daren were carrying their swords.

Queen Djinn raised herself so that she was standing, the folds of her bronze-coloured leather skirts dropping into place as she did so. The corset of her dress was the same shade of bronze and had a diagonal criss-cross pattern going from her waist up to the top of the bodice. She was dressed for a reaction, and a flicker of annoyance crossed her face when Kai refused to look anywhere apart from her eyes.

"So, you're the Chosen of the Elements, I see." She placed a long fingernail against her thin lips, pulled back in a tight smile. "I presume you want something from me."

Staying in line, Kai raised his voice to be heard. "Yes, my lady. We seek the *Fflam Eiriasedd*, the Flame of Incandescence. We have been sent by Lord Ethon himself to retrieve it, by your permission, of course."

"Of course," she sneered, looking over them. A calculated look settled on her face as she made a show of considering what Kai had said.

A movement caught Marella's eye and she discreetly turned her head so she could see all the seats were being filled by the other Fire elementals. *"Kai,"* she whispered through their bond. *"Prepare yourself; I think we're the main attraction."*

"I know, little one, I've seen. You just look after yourself, you hear me?" he spoke back, showing his concern for her through their bond.

"There is a way for you to get the *Fflam Eiriasedd*, however, it won't be easy. I'm not actually sure if you're up to it," Queen Djinn said with mock concern. "What do you think, my lord Etain?"

Etain stepped forward so he was between his Queen and the Chosen. In a voice loud enough for everyone in the arena to hear, he said, "I have already given you my thoughts, my Queen. I do not think the Chosen of Fire is strong enough to retrieve the *Fflam*. He is reliant on the other three Chosen with him, and seems to have an especially *close* attachment to the Chosen of Water."

"Hmm, this may be a problem then," said Queen Djinn, drawing out the game. "For the *Fflam* can only be retrieved by a Fire Elemental. I wonder if being Chosen will be enough?"

"My Lady, I came here to retrieve the flame and that is what I shall do. Tell me what I need to do and I will do it," Kai said firmly.

"Such confidence," she scoffed. "Okay, if you are so insistent, when would you like to try?"

"Now is as good a time as any," said Kai, much to the surprise of Queen Djinn and the surrounding Salamanders, as a murmur went through the arena.

Marella turned her head sharply to look at Kai, before seeing Etain watching her with a look of expectation on his face. She kept her mouth shut and her face stoic, and was rewarded by a look of disappointment falling across his face.

"You may rest over there for five minutes whilst I arrange things," said Queen Djinn dismissively, gesturing over to a table. She walked off the dais, calling Etain to her as she did.

* * *

The four Chosen and their Partners walked confidently to the table where they saw a jug of water and four mugs. Under the table were four bowls of water for the Partners. Everyone had a drink without speaking.

"You be careful out there, okay Kai?" said Daren. "I don't know what her game is, but she's playing one. How did they know about you and Marella?"

"I don't know, yet I presume we've been watched from the moment we arrived. I will play along though; this is something I need to do. We can't not get the *Fflam*, Wraidd Elfennol needs it. Look after Marella for me, and don't let her do anything stupid." Kai winked at Marella as he spoke so she wouldn't take offence at his words.

Marella smiled tremulously, fear ravaging her body. "Kai, I'm so scared right now," she admitted. Lani reached for her hand and held it tightly, knowing Kai could do nothing with an arena full of people watching them.

Kai grinned as though she had just said something funny, and they could hear the murmurs pick up again around them. "I know you're scared, but you need to stay strong. You know I will do this, you've seen it."

"But I didn't see the outcome," she cried quietly, "I don't know how it ends."

"Then have faith in me," Kai said to her, looking into her deep blue eyes. "I will be doing everything I can to come back to you. We have a date at your Lake, remember? Trust me, Marella." Using their bond, he pushed a wave of love to her, filling it with the emotions he felt for Marella.

She gasped and swayed backwards on her feet as she felt it, colour returning to her cheeks. She took a moment, whilst Daren and Lani remained silent. She looked at Kai, hoping he would see how much he meant to her, and said, "If you don't come back to me, I will haunt you and make your afterlife a living hell, do you hear me? Don't think dying will allow you to escape from me, because it won't. You get the *Fflam*, wipe the sneers of the faces of Etain and Queen Djinn, and come back to me."

Daren, Kai and Lani burst into muffled laughter at her words and Kai nodded. "I'll come back to you, Marella. I promise, from my heart to yours."

"Only you, Marella, could tell someone how much you love them, using threats like that," Daren laughed. "Kai, do your thing. You know we have you insomuch as we can."

* * *

"If I may have your attention please," came the sound of Etain's voice booming through the arena. "The man you see before you is a Chosen of Fire, Lord Ethon's representative. He needs the *Fflam Eiriasedd*, but to do this, he will need to triumph over fire itself."

A loud wave of noise started all around the arena as everyone started to talk at once. Etain waved his hands until silence reigned once more.

"Queen Djinn has decided it would be fairest to all if the trial took place here, so then no one can be accused of 'foul play'." He threw a glance over towards Daren, Lani, and Marella to see what effect those words would have. Instead of outwardly showing a reaction, Marella tilted her chin up and stared him down.

Daren, staring straight ahead at Etain, spoke out the corner of his mouth. "Take it easy, Marella, he's egging you on."

"I know, I know. By the Waters, I want to get out of here." Marella moved her feet to relieve some of the tension flowing through her body, adjusting her grip on her staff to make sure she had it securely.

Having no reaction to draw attention to, Etain carried on. "Kai, Chosen of Fire, will be cleansed. If he survives, he will be given the *Fflam*. If he doesn't, well, he can't have it, now can he?" Etain gave a sharp, mocking bark of a laugh and hesitantly, the crowd joined in.

"He has them well and truly whipped, doesn't he?" said Lani, keeping her voice low.

"If it wasn't clear before that he was working against us, I'd say it's clear now," said Daren, his voice thick with disgust. "Marella, are you okay? You've gone very pale. Marella?"

Marella looked up to Daren and Lani, who shuddered at the look of anguish on Marella's face. "I know what this trial is. This is what I saw."

Daren's sharp intake of breath was the only indication he had heard as he kept his eyes trained on Etain, who was now directing people around as they made ready a square made of logs with Kai stood in the middle.

Lani held Marella's hand tightly. "There is nothing we can do, Marella. Have faith in Kai and Lord Ethon. He wouldn't have sent him here as a sacrifice."

Shaw landed on Lani's shoulder at this point and rubbed his head against her cheek. *This is a travesty, Etain shouldn't be allowed to do this, but Queen Djinn won't stop him. She's just as bad. Kai can do this, although he shouldn't have to.*

Nixie rubbed against Marella's legs. *He will be okay, Marella. Use your love for him and guide him back.*

Marella trembled with anticipation and foreboding, as the logs were piled waist high around Kai, before the men walked away. Etain watched with glee at the discomfort on their faces.

Stand steady, Chosen. I will get the Fflam *and return to you. Do not give them any opportunity to take this away from us.* Kai spoke through the bond on a broad path, so that they could all hear him.

Marella took a deep breath, letting it out slowly, as she braced herself for what she knew would come. Daren and Lani exchanged glances before turning to face Kai. *He's not doing this without me,* Kenna said fiercely before jumping over the wooden barricade to be beside Kai.

They could all see Kai arguing with her, trying to convince her to leave, when Etain stepped up to him. Ignoring Kai completely, Etain spoke only to Kenna. "Little sister, you do not have to be cleansed. You are the purest of fire. This is for him alone."

Kai stopped arguing, and listened to Kenna, as she answered Etain on a broad path so that all the Chosen could hear.

I am he and he is me. If I am pure, then so is he. If he must be cleansed, then so must I. He is my Life Partner, and that means I am with him through life and all that it entails - the good, the bad, the loves, and the loss. Perhaps one day you'll find a Life Partner of your own, Etain, Consort of the Salamanders. I will stand by my Partner as you conduct this travesty against the very fabric of Fire itself. I am sure Lord Ethon is now aware of what you are trying to do against his Chosen. Be very careful, Consort, as fire can burn.

Marella couldn't contain the small smile that blossomed over her face at Kenna's words. *Well done, Kenna,* she sent to her, and felt the warmth of acknowledgment rush back.

Etain had stiffened with shock as he listened to Kenna, and now his face was rigid with fury. He obviously didn't appreciate being spoken to in that manner, and the fact others had heard, just made it harder for him to bear. With a furious look directed at the three Chosen, Etain waved his hands in the air to once again take control of the crowd.

"Light the fire and let the Cleansing begin," he shouted, and a procession of four torch-bearers entered the arena. Marella's body was taut with tension as she recognised the scene unfolding before her eyes. She knew the fires would be lit with Kai inside, and just couldn't see how he would survive it.

Kai turned around so he was watching them. Only the tip of Kenna's tail was visible where it was pointed into the air, coming to just below Kai's waist.

Marella's breathing increased as the torch-bearers approached Kai. A cold sweat broke out over her body as she watched Etain rub his hands together in apparent glee.

Just as Marella was about to hyperventilate, a calmness descended over her. Strength flooded her body, and peace settled in her veins. She looked at Daren and Lani. Daren winked at her and Lani smiled, a profound sense of joy on their faces. She turned back towards Kai and saw him smiling.

Daren took a step forwards and raised his voice to be heard as he said "By the Earth that is Her body." He stood there, watching Etain and Queen Djinn.

Lani took a step to stand by Daren. With her hair glinting in the torchlight, she said with a voice powerful beyond recognition, "By the Air that is Her breath."

Kai couldn't stand with them but he joined in, in a voice strong and true, "By the Fire that is Her bright spirit."

Marella took her step to stand on the other side of Daren. With her voice proud and full of love, she finished her part of the blessing, "By the living Waters of Her womb."

By now the torch-bearers were next to Kai, waiting for the signal from Etain or Queen Djinn to light the flames. Etain's whole body was now rigid with rage, and he gave them leave to lower the torches.

As the flames caught hold and the wood snapped and crackled in the morning light, the four of them said the blessing in unison. "The circle is open yet unbroken; Merry meet, and merry part, and merry meet again."

The silence was as thick as syrup by the time they had finished. Marella stood bravely watching the flames get closer to Kai, reflecting their light in his eyes. Just as it seemed he was about to be consumed by fire, something caught Marella's eye. Turning her head, she saw Ena heading for Kai, shooting out of the sky like an arrow.

When it looked like she was about to land on Kai's head, she spread her legs slightly and landed on his shoulders instead, one foot either side. A shocked sound echoed through the arena which became louder as people realised that something unexpected was happening.

Marella watched the flames grow closer and higher to Kai. Just as they were about to cover him, Ena's wings seemed to grow, being fed by the fire, instead of consumed by it. She wrapped them around Kai and Kenna, completely covering their bodies with hers.

"Look at Etain and Queen Djinn," breathed Lani, a note of

satisfaction running through her voice.

Marella turned her attention to them and saw with pleasure they both looked very worried at what had just happened. Queen Djinn was speaking rapidly to Etain whilst his posture was defensive.

"Good," said Marella, "They deserve to be worried."

"Is this what you saw then, Marella? In your Weave?" asked Daren, still watching the flames burn through the logs.

"It was, but it is different now." Marella tried to explain without anyone else hearing them, so she switched to their mental path instead. *"I saw Kai in the square and the fires being lit, but I never saw us give the blessing or Ena arrive. I don't know what happened to change it, but I'm glad it did."*

"I don't understand though, why couldn't you tell Kai about this? Surely it would have helped him?" thought Lani.

"Would it help you, Lani? If Marella had told him what she saw, he would think that he would burn to death. She's just said she didn't see Ena arrive and it's only Ena who is keeping them both safe right now," said Daren.

"Oh yes, I forgot about that," said Lani, an apology threading through her thoughts.

"Don't worry about it," reassured Marella. *"I'm just glad it happened this way. The alternative doesn't bear thinking about."*

"When will this be over, do you think?" asked Lani out loud.

"At the rate those logs are burning, another half an hour will see them turn to ash. I can't imagine the intensity of the heat in the middle of that square right now," said Daren.

They waited patiently for the flames to die down and release Kai and Kenna. The more peaceful they became, by contrast the angrier Etain and Queen Djinn appeared to be.

Marella could hear some of the shouts coming from the crowd now, and it appeared Kai had a few fans out there.

"Give the *Fflam Eiriasedd* to the Chosen, he surely deserves it," she heard one man shout.

"The Phoenix is here. Give the *Fflam* to the Phoenix or the Chosen," shouted another.

Marella looked around as the shouts grew in intensity and volume and felt a surge of satisfaction run through her. Etain and Queen Djinn may be working against them, but it seemed they had some friends within the Salamanders.

The flames surrounding Ena slowly started to die down and more of her body became visible through them.

"Won't be long now," said Daren, his hand clenching in anticipation.

With a loud snap echoing throughout the arena, the last of the logs split in half and the flames fizzled out. The embers glowed, but Ena was now clearly seen, her wings covering Kai and Kenna. With a loud screech of defiance, she slowly opened her wings which shrank back to their normal size as she did so. Kai stood there, with Kenna by his side, looking like he'd just spent the time having coffee and cake. He looked unruffled, but relieved to see them again.

He carefully picked his way through the embers, lifting Kenna over ones that still burned, until he could make his way back to the others. Upon reaching them, Daren reached forward and grasped his forearm in a warrior's greeting.

"By the Earth, but it's good to see you again," he said with broad smile.

"You can't get rid of me that easily," joked Kai, holding firmly onto Daren's arm.

Lani stepped to Kai and raised herself onto her tiptoes to kiss his cheek. "Welcome back, Chosen of Fire," she said, a hint of a smile touching the corners of her mouth.

Kai leaned down and returned her kiss. "Thank you, Chosen of Air; it's good to be back."

Kai turned as Marella came to his other side. She copied Lani and kissed his cheek. "You just wait until we leave the Fire Quarter," she said, sotto voice. "I think I might have to make you pay for putting me through that."

Kai laughed with her, seeing the playfulness and relief in her eyes. "Once we finish this quest, you can make me pay any time you want," he promised her, seeing her face light up with pleasure.

* * *

Kai stepped back and took his place in the line-up of the Chosen, their Partners by their sides after having their own reunion with Kenna. Kai raised his hands to calm the crowd and it became silent as they waited to hear what he would say. "Queen Djinn, ruler of the Salamanders, and Etain, Consort to the Queen; I have completed your trial."

"With help," spluttered Etain, no longer looking in control.

"Be that as it may," agreed Kai, "but complete it I did. I did not request Ena to come to my aid, although I will be eternally grateful she did. You agreed that if I was 'cleansed' I would be allowed to take the *Fflam Eiriasedd*. It is what your people are calling for. Are you going to go back on your words, on your honour, and deny me that?"

"Well, by rights, it was that you needed to be cleansed. I don't feel you have, just because a phoenix wrapped its wings around you," said Etain, much to the disgust of the crowd, who began jeering at him.

"We stood in the middle of your trial by fire, for the duration of the burning, and have walked out with nary a singe. And for your information, the phoenix is called Ena. Although I didn't think I would have to introduce you being as she is a Scion of the Elements."

The jeering from the crowd became louder once they heard Kai introduce Ena. She had been sat off to one side, ignoring the proceedings as she rearranged her fiery plumage. She flapped her wings a couple of times, drawing attention to herself as sparks flew from them.

She launched herself up into the air, in the middle of Kai and Etain. She hovered, defying gravity with the slowness of her flight, yet staying aloft effortlessly. "Queen Djinn of the Salamanders, you appear to have made a grave mistake. The trial by fire was not within your rights to insist upon for someone who is not from the Fire Quarter. Lord Ethon is unhappy with this turn of events and will be here soon. Do you have anything you wish to say?" Ena's words filled the arena with ease.

Queen Djinn stood up and took a moment to rearrange her leather skirts. She was looking pale now, her face tight with anxiety. "I did but follow the advice of my Consort, Etain, although it appears it was the wrong thing to do." Her voice rang out like a bell, clear and full of sincerity, although Marella had her doubts as to the truth of it.

Gasps of shock filled the arena from those sat there, but no one looked more shocked than Etain, whose step faltered at her words. The colour drained from his face as Etain faced the phoenix and raised his voice to the sky. "I thought that if someone was claiming the *Fflam Eiriasedd*, even if they said it was with Lord Ethon's approval, it would be better to make sure they were pure, rather than just give it to anyone."

"And do you still think that was your right?" Ena asked him clearly.

Etain looked around, wildly glancing for support from his Queen, but she looked at Ena, refusing to glance his way. His whole body stiffened as he realised he was being made the scapegoat. With as much dignity as he could muster, he looked back to Ena.

"Yes, I still think was right. To be Fire is to be pure. Only the purest should be able to claim the *Fflam Eiriasedd*. It has been in our safekeeping for eons. Why should I give it to the first person who comes along and tries to claim it in Lord Ethon's name without checking first?"

"There are other ways to check the authenticity of someone's claim, Consort. You seem to have become misguided through these eons you speak of. I'm sure Lord Ethon will want to speak with you about your views on the world," Ena told him. Etain's head drooped as he realised he wasn't going to get out of this without serious consequences.

"Queen Djinn, I do not find you blameless in this affair either, and will be telling Lord Ethon why. Perhaps, if you are only able to follow the advice of your Consort without putting thought into your own actions, you are no longer fit to rule the Salamanders? We shall see."

By now, Marella was working hard to contain her mirth at seeing

Queen Djinn and Etain dealt with like naughty younglings. She struggled even more when she saw Ena cast a glance her way, and felt amusement come through the Partner bond.

The crowd was as silent as a tomb, waiting to see what would happen next. Tension built as Ena continued her slow flapping without speaking any further. The confidence had drained out of Etain and Queen Djinn was nervously plucking at her clothes as she waited.

The embers from the square which had nearly gone out, started to glow. Brighter and brighter they became, until all four sides of the square lit up like a bonfire at night. Just as quickly they died down and went out completely. In the middle of the square stood a tall man, muscular and broad of shoulder. His long, red hair was wild, although he had tried to tame it by tying it back with a leather thong. He was dressed similarly to Kai, except his red leather surcoat had flames embroidered in gold all over it.

He stepped forward, out of the fire square, and looked up to Ena who was hovering above him. "My thanks, little sister; I can take it from here."

Ena bowed her head to him and then to Kai before flying off, upwards towards the sun.

After watching Ena leave, he strode forward, his black leather boots kicking up puffs of dust with every step. Marella breathed a sigh of relief that Lord Ethon had joined them at last as she immediately felt safer.

"Fear not, Chosen of Water, nothing will happen to you. Erwyna would never forgive me," Lord Ethon sent to her, along with a wink Marella was convinced no one else saw.

"Queen Djinn, I believe you have something for my Chosen. I am relieving you of the burden of responsibility of the *Fflam Eiriasedd* as it is too much for you to control. I am sure you will be happy to pass it on to my Chosen instead." His voice filled the arena, smooth, low, and full of power.

Queen Djinn looked like she might protest, but after a moment's hesitation, bobbed her head at Lord Ethon. She walked off the dais and stepped onto the arena floor, trying to control her features in some semblance of normality, even pleasure.

Once she was in front of Kai, but not too close, she stopped. Looking at Lord Ethon once, who nodded in her direction, she cupped her hands together in front of her, closed her eyes and concentrated. Slowly, a spark appeared within her hands. She blew upon it to encourage it to grow. As Marella watched, the spark grew into a flame which flickered and danced within the palms of her cupped hands.

A defiant look flashed over face, so quickly Marella thought she had imagined it. She held her hands out to Kai. "Here you are, Chosen of Fire, the *Fflam Eiriasedd*. The responsibility for this is now yours."

Without any hesitation, Kai stepped forward and held his hands out to accept the flame. Marella watched as the flame jumped from the hands of Queen Djinn, into Kai's. He turned around and presented his hands to Lord Ethon, who stood with a proud smile on his face.

"I think you know by now what you must do, Chosen of mine, so whenever you're ready." Lord Ethon took a step back so he stood with the other Chosen, as Kai slowly, reverently, held his hands up to his chest and waited.

With a flare of light, the flame disappeared and Kai let out a sigh of relief. He bowed his head to Lord Ethon, "It is done, my Lord."

"It is indeed, well done." Lord Ethon then raised his voice so it could be heard by everyone. "The *Fflam Eiriasedd* is now in the protection of the Lords and Ladies. A monolith showing the flame will rise in Hufel, in honour of the task undertaken, and successfully completed, by my Chosen."

A round of applause echoed around the arena, along with some cheers and cries for the Chosen.

"I have one thing to say before the Chosen and I depart from Danau. No one Element is bigger, stronger, braver, or better. We stand firm in our belief, Lord Adaryn and I, together with Ladies Daire and Erwyna. The Elements should always be in balance. We work better together, compensating for each others' weaknesses, providing strength and support. One Element by itself might succeed for a while, only to consume itself and be extinguished for good.

You, my Salamanders, are my Elemental representatives. You are of Fire and I am so very proud of you. Do not, I beg of you, allow the misrepresentation of yourselves. Do not allow someone else to make decisions for you that you don't agree with. Fire is passion, fire is strength. Use these qualities to help Wraidd Elfennol as a whole and the Fire Quarter will prosper. Use these to segregate the Fire Quarter and you will become weak."

Lord Ethon turned as he surveyed the whole arena. "I stand before you in the presence of eight of the finest examples of Elemental behaviour than I could ever have hoped for. Only two of these are claimed for Fire. Does this mean the others are lacking in some way?" he asked.

A resounding 'no' echoed back from those sat in the stands. Lord Ethon smiled in satisfaction. "That's right, my friends, no, it does not. I am proud of you, proud to have you represent Fire. Do not make me regret it." His voice was chiding, like that of a parent talking to a child.

Marella wondered at the ease with which he controlled the crowd. *"The practice of eons, little one,"* she heard and she choked back a laugh.

"We must take our leave from you now, Salamanders of Danau. Time has played a cruel game upon my Chosen, and so it is with haste I must take them with me, and deliver them through the Portal."

The Chosen looked at each in bewilderment. Just how much time had they lost? This was the first time any of the Lords and Ladies had directly involved themselves.

Lord Ethon waved to the crowd for a few seconds more, encouraging the Chosen to do the same. Their Partners made a quick display of interwoven bodies, high jumps and spectacular aerial displays, much to the delight of the crowd.

"Queen Djinn, I look forward to speaking with you some more about this, very soon," said Lord Ethon, his words ringing with a clear warning. "Etain, you can come with me now."

Etain walked over to join the Chosen, standing in between Lord Ethon and Kai. The others were directed into a circular shape and instructed to either hold hands or have bodily contact with each other before Lord Ethon could start.

Lord Ethon stamped his foot to the ground, puffing up a small dust cloud. From his stomp appeared a glow, which began moving around them, moving faster until it looked like they were enclosed within a wall of orange-hued light.

"Farewell, Danau, I will return to you shortly," Ethon shouted, and then they were gone. The light slowly stopped spinning and the wall dissipated. Lord Ethon, Etain, and the Chosen were gone.

* * *

To the Chosen, there was no sense of movement. They were just inside the wall of light, waiting for something to happen. Before long, the light faded and Kai's eyes widened with surprise. They were back at the Fire Portal, their trundle trucks ready and waiting for them.

Ethon smiled but it quickly faded. "I'm afraid your luck with the time paradox has run out whilst you've been in the Fire Quarter." He looked at them sadly.

"Just how much time have we lost, Lord Ethon?" asked Marella, wondering if it was already too late.

"It was Rhagfyr when you entered the Fire Portal, correct?" he asked. Seeing their nods of affirmation, he told them sorrowfully, "Yule, Imbolc and the Spring Equinox have all passed. The months have changed from Rhagfyr through to Mawrth. We are coming to the start of Ebrill."

"Ebrill?" asked Kai, a note of disbelief in his voice. "It can't be. We spent the shortest amount of time in the Fire Quarter. We were only there for one day."

Marella had paled with Ethon's words and was leaning on her staff for support. Lani was stunned whilst Daren swayed on his feet.

"It is true, Chosen. We are in the last day of Mawrth. Once you go back through the Portal you will see the change in the seasons for yourself. Everywhere is in bud and bloom again. You will see. That is one of the reasons why I have transported you here, to get you back to Wraidd Elfennol as quickly as possible. You still have time; you still have until Solstice at Mehefin."

Kai shook his head as the words sunk in. He straightened his spine and gave a quick but respectful bow to Lord Ethon. "Then by your leave, we need to go. The sooner we are through the Portal, the quicker we can be on our way to the Water Quarter."

Lord Ethon nodded, "By all means, be on your way. We will meet again soon. Well done, Kai. Well done indeed."

With a simple nod at Lord Ethon, Kai looked at the others. "Are you ready to go?"

"Definitely," said Marella with more than a hint of relief in her voice, making Kai smile.

"Ready or not, we need to go," said Daren, straightening his shoulders in anticipation.

Lani just nodded her acquiescence as she readjusted the straps on her backpack.

Kai returned his gaze to Lord Ethon. "Thank you, for everything you did back there."

Lord Ethon looked fondly at Kai. "I didn't really do much; Ena is the one who protected you. I did not believe anything like that would have happened. I wouldn't have sent you in without prior warning if I'd have known, trust me."

He shot a sharp look at Etain, who was now looking different from the haughty, over-confident man who had greeted them. He hung his head in shame at Ethon's words, but kept his silence.

Lord Ethon jerked his head towards the Portal which glimmered a few steps away from them. "Go on, get going. Have fun in the Water." He grinned at Kai, who smiled back.

Turning around, he hitched his shoulders and started walking towards the Portal, Kenna by his side.

"Go with my blessing, Chosen of Fire," Ethon blew a kiss in the direction of Kai and a flicker of red and gold shot through the air, splitting into two and landed on the back of Kai and Kenna's heads.

Not noticing anything, Kai directed Daren through the Portal first, followed by Lani. He motioned to Marella to go next but she turned around and ran back to Ethon. She threw her arms around him and gave him a quick squeeze before reaching up to kiss him on his cheek. Marella quickly made her way back to the Portal and crossed through without any hesitation.

Kai cast a glance over his shoulder just as he prepared to cross, and saw a smile beaming across Lord Ethon's face. He raised a hand to his Lord of Fire and walked through the Portal with Kenna by his side.

Lord Ethon waited until they were gone and safely through the other side before he turned his attention to Etain. "You are coming with me," he said, "and we're going to have a little talk about your attitude."

With a blink of an eye, they were gone, and the Portal was silent once more. A black mist rose from one of the trees, swirling with agitation before dissipating into nothing.

~ 55 ~

Once through the Portal, Marella moved out of the way and looked around her, her eyes showing her surprise and disbelief at what she saw before her. The oak trees that had stood proud with their winter coat, now stood in all their Spring finery. Marella saw the new leaves on the branches and acorns growing.

She sniffed the air and relished the smell of petrichor in the air - the earth, growth, dampness, and life-giving rain. She sank to the ground and pushed her hands into the wetness beneath her, crumbling the earth in her hands.

Daren chuckled at her as he pulled her to her feet. "Come on you," he said. "We have to get a move on. I can't believe it's Ebrill tomorrow. We need to get to Ilyn."

"We're not going to Ilyn, remember. We're not allowed." A shadow crossed Marella's face as she reminded Daren they needed to make their way directly to the Water Quarter.

"How are we going to find it?" wondered Lani as she readjusted her grip on the trundle truck.

"That's a good question," said Daren. "We've always been given a hint from the Elders to help us find it."

Kai made his way to them and ran his hand down Marella's back to let her know he was there. "I don't think that finding the Water Portal is going to be difficult," he smiled at them. "Not when we have the Chosen of Water with us. I'm more than sure Marella can Weave to find the location unless, of course, Nixie is already aware of it?" He grinned slyly at Nixie and felt a wave of annoyance come from him.

Marella looked at him, confused. "What do you mean about Nixie?" she asked.

"Nothing, Marella, I just assumed that being as you were so strong in Water, and Nixie was Chosen for you, he might have an inkling of where we needed to go, that's all."

Marella's face cleared as Kai's words made sense to her. She smiled at the others, feeling at ease with herself and the others now that they were out of the Fire Quarter. "Come on, let's go. We still have daylight left, so we may as well be walking. The closer we get to it, the easier my Weaves will be." With a spring in her step, she picked up the handles of her truck and set off, not noticing the amused looks on the faces of the others.

"Nixie, when are you going to tell her?" Kai asked as they walked along.

"I'm not, not unless I have to. That's something I want to keep separate. How did you find out?"

"It's something Ena told me about whilst the cleansing took place. She seemed to

think it might be relevant."

Nixie gave a snort, causing Marella to swing her head around to check on him. *"Interfering, meddling Scions,"* Nixie grumbled to Kai. *"I'm hoping it won't come up, but if it does, I'll be the one to tell her, not you. Understand?"*

"I understand, Nixie, don't you worry. I just thought it might be better if you told her before we get to Teimladau, rather than after."

"I'll think about it," said Nixie before breaking the connection and running forward to be with Marella.

"Crazy otter," laughed Kai to himself as he pulled his trundle truck behind him, following his companions and friends on the last leg of their journey.

* * *

They set off to find the Water Portal by heading to the Western most point of the island. For three weeks they travelled, and were besieged by the storms of Gwanwyn.

As they set up camp for the night, another storm blew up around them. Daren and Kai pegged down the tents and tried to form a wind break with their trundle trucks. The campfire which Kai had only just lit, sputtered out beneath the onslaught of the wind and rain.

The four Partners huddled up inside a tent, the only one to venture out was Nixie and that was only so he could nudge Marella to get her inside too.

All eight of them huddled together in the tent as the wind whipped around outside, billowing the sides of the tent in and out. Marella sat close to Kai with his arm wrapped around her. They had taken the time to talk during their walks, and now Marella felt she knew almost as much about Kai as she did Daren. The silence was heavy inside the tent, with only the rustle of clothing or a murmur from a Partner.

"I never thought I'd say it, but I've had enough of the rain," grinned Marella, trying to lighten the atmosphere.

Daren looked at her before a small smile tugged at his lips. "I thought you loved the rain, sweet?"

"I do, I love being outside in it and I love watching it from the inside of home. I've just had enough of three weeks of this and I'm no closer with my Weaving. This Spring is a rough one, it's all cold rainstorms and howling winds. Where is the gentle sunshine that helps with the growth? Everything is just going to get covered in moss and mildew at this rate."

Lani chuckled at Marella's exaggeration. "So now we've left the Fire Quarter, you decide you want some sun and heat in your life? Typical," she laughed.

"Yeah, looks that way, doesn't it?" Marella snuggled a bit more into

Kai, his arm drawing her even closer as she did so.

"Well, it looks like you have your own furnace to keep you warm now, Marella," said Daren, nodding his head to the two of them.

Marella's smile widened as she tilted her head back to look at Kai. He smiled at her and dropped a quick kiss onto the tip of her nose, before she looked back at Daren. "I'm one lucky lady," she said.

"Oh please," said Lani in mock disgust. "Let me out of this tent, I can't cope with it anymore. I think I preferred it when they were snapping and snarling at each other."

Everyone laughed and the tension that had been weighing them down felt lightened. Marella pushed herself up, and tried to move which was difficult given the size of the tent.

"What are you doing?" asked Kai.

"Where are you off to?" asked Daren at the same time.

"I still need to Weave, we're nearing the end of Ebrill now, it's only another week until Mai and we still haven't found the Portal," replied Marella, struggling to move within the confines of the tent and the people and animals within.

"Wait until after the storm has finished," suggested Lani. "We can't go anywhere, anyway. It's seems pointless you getting wet to retrieve your chalice when we can't move."

"No, I need to do it now, I know I do."

"Let her go," said Kai to the others, "You know she won't settle until she has."

Marella flashed him a grateful look as he manoeuvred so she could exit the tent. Marella crawled out of the tent flap, ensuring it was shut after her so the others didn't get wet. As she stood, the wind pulled at her hair, making it fly around her head in a halo of wet tendrils.

She moved to the centre of the campsite, to where the fire had been set up. Acting on instinct alone, she threw her head back to the sky and lifted her arms out to the side of her body. The elements attacked her exposed areas, and stuck her trousers and shirt to her skin, lowering her body temperature immediately.

"Marella, what are you doing? Get back in here before you catch your death." She vaguely heard Daren shouting at her, but it seemed like it was from so far away, she paid no attention to it.

"*Marella, little one, what are you doing?*" she heard Nixie ask, just moments before she felt his body entwine about her legs. Marella didn't answer; knowing he would feel it soon enough.

"*Ahhh, I see,*" sighed Nixie, relishing in the power of the storm.

As she stood with her arms outstretched and the rain coated her face and body, a series of Weaves made themselves known to her. Her body stiffened as each image was sent into her mind and Nixie's.

Marella relaxed, allowing each image into her consciousness, feeling at ease with what she saw and where she must go. Slowly, she lowered her arms to her sides and bent her head forward, her hair covering her face like a drape. "Thank you, Lady Erwyna," she whispered.

The wind and rain abated as Marella stood there in silence, enjoying a momentary meditation with the elements of the storm. The Air changed from bitter and cold, to warm and playful; the Water changed from pounding to trickling, whilst the Earth stayed constant and strong. A ray of sunshine broke through the clouds as they started to disperse, and filled the grove with warmth and light. Marella knew herself to be blessed by the Elements.

With peace in her heart, she turned around to go back to the tent. Facing her, were Daren, Kai, and Lani, all looking at her in awe.

"What?" she asked, "what's the matter?"

Kai came over and embraced her. "Do you have any idea what you looked like then?" he asked, running his hands over her hair and caressing her face. Mutely, she shook her head. "You looked like a Goddess of the Wilds. So strong, so powerful, and yet, in balance with the Elements surrounding you. By the Flames, Marella, you continue to amaze me every day."

"Move you big oaf," Marella heard and peered around Kai to see Lani swatting at him with her hands. "I want to give her a cuddle too. Shift!"

Marella chuckled as Lani manhandled Kai out of the way. Lani took Marella's hands in her own and peered closely into her eyes. "Are you okay?" she asked.

Marella nodded, "I'm fine, I promise. I know where we need to go now, at least."

Daren came up behind both of them and crushed them both in his arms. "One of these days, you'll listen to me when I tell you to stay out of the weird and freaky weather," he grumbled, a smile breaking across his face.

"Me? Listen to you? I doubt that somehow," said Marella as she laughed, lightly jabbing her elbow into his stomach.

Laughing together, they broke apart and saw that Kai had lit the fire and water was now bubbling away. He had pulled out a waterproof blanket and put it down on the ground so they had somewhere dry to sit.

They all sat down and Marella gratefully received the mug of skullcap he had prepared for her.

"So, what's the plan?" asked Daren as he took his mug from Kai.

"We're nearly there," she said bluntly.

Excited exclamations bubbled all around her as she took a sip from her drink.

"We are looking for a medium sized lake that has lily pads growing on it. The Portal itself is in the middle of the lake, which can be accessed by some large, boulder type stepping stones. There are bulrushes by the water's edge, and alder and willow trees surround the banks."

"That's great," smiled Lani. "How far away do you think we are?"

"Only a couple of days, if that. In the Weave, the moon was full and she's gibbous now. So unless we have to wait a month before we find it, which wouldn't surprise me right now, I think we're close."

"Are we asking the Partners to scout again, like we did with the Earth Portal?" asked Daren.

"So long as you, and your Partners, don't mind. I think out of us all, Shaw is most likely to see it from afar."

Lani nodded, "I'm sure he won't mind, but I'll ask him." Lani concentrated for a moment, her eyes glazing as she spoke with Shaw.

A smile lit her face as she said excitedly, "Shaw thinks he has already seen it. He was flying earlier today, and went further afield than normal and he says he saw the sunlight glinting off some water. He's going to have a look first thing in the morning. If it is, then we can head off as soon as he returns."

Everyone smiled at the news Lani shared. "This is wonderful," said Daren. "I hope we can be there before too long."

"I hope it won't be too hard on you, once we cross over," Marella said to Kai.

He just grinned back at her, "Don't you worry about that. I have Earth in me too which will help. Let's just get to the Portal found first and then we can worry about the other things."

The rest of the evening passed by pleasantly and it wasn't long before they were off to bed.

~ 56 ~

Marella was putting on some water to boil when she heard Shaw screech in the stillness of early morning. She gazed upwards to see him flying into land, just as Lani came out of the tent.

"You're up early again, Marella," she greeted her with a smile.

"I know, I'm not sleeping too well at the moment. There'll be plenty of time to catch up when this is all done, I hope," she said.

Daren poked his head out through the tent flap. "Did I just hear Shaw?" he asked.

Lani held up her arm and Shaw alighted there, flapping his wings to help him get his balance.

"That's a yes then," laughed Daren. He crawled out of the tent with Kai at his heels.

"Good morning," Kai said to them all, a smile crossing his face when he saw Marella. She smiled back at him before turning to Lani.

"What does Shaw think, Lani?" Marella asked.

Lani stroked down his breast feathers, appreciating Marella had asked her, even though she would hear him anyway if Shaw wanted her to.

"Shaw thinks we need to head off in a north-westerly direction and we should be there by lunchtime."

The companions grinned at each other, excited by the prospect of finding the final Portal. They prepared a quick breakfast before starting off in the direction given by Shaw. As they walked along an easy trail, with bluebells growing either side of the path, Marella thought about who it could be that was working against them. They hadn't really discussed it or even thought about it much.

"Have you thought any on who is against us?" she suddenly asked Lani, who was the closest one to her.

"I've not really. I don't like the idea of anyone working against us. It seems so improbable. If the balance between the Elements is upset, the whole island suffers, like we've already seen. The idea someone might be doing it deliberately just beggars belief." Lani shuddered as she walked, imagining a world without balance.

"We've just seen a prime example of it though," pressed Marella. "Look how Etain was. He wanted to burn Kai to make sure he was 'cleansed'. It that's not out of balance, I don't know what is. Someone must be encouraging it."

"Or more than just some 'one'," said Lani, thoughtfully. "We've been beaten to every Quarter so far. I can't see how Water will be any different. Can it be just one person... or a group of people?"

"That's even worse," exclaimed Marella. "Thinking one person was behind this was bad enough, but to think now it could be more…"

"I know," agreed Lani. "We will figure this out, Marella. The Lords and Ladies are with us. Whoever it is can't stay hidden forever."

"Look," shouted Daren, pointing to the opposite side of a meadow. "Marella, is this the right place? Have we found the lake?"

With a nod to Lani, Marella pulled her trundle truck a bit quicker until she caught up with Daren. She looked over to where he was pointing, glancing around the surrounding area to match it up with the Weave. After a moment, she grinned at Daren.

"It certainly looks that way, come on, let's get closer." They walked through a meadow of spring flowers as they approached the water. The border of trees gave way to luxuriant growth of grasses and other plants. The meadow gave way to the water, with bull-rushes easing the transition from earth to water.

"Where are the boulders though?" wondered Daren.

"I don't know, I saw them before even though they're not here now. This is the right place though, I'm sure of it," replied Marella, looking out into the water.

"Well, Shaw was right. We are here by lunchtime, and I, for one, suggest we get something to eat before we search for the Portal. Who knows what time it will be when we cross or how many days we will lose? I need food in my stomach if I'm going to deal with all of that," said Kai with a smile, starting to set up the campfire.

After a quick but hearty meat stew, followed by a peppermint tea, Marella and Kai walked deosil around the lake whilst Daren and Lani walked widdershins, searching for any sign of the boulders. They returned to the campsite at the same time.

"I couldn't see any boulders," said Lani softly, with Daren nodding in agreement.

"No, we couldn't either," said Marella, looking around. "I know this is the right place, I know it."

"*Of course the boulders aren't there,*" said Nixie sleepily from where he was curled up near the fire.

Marella glanced at the others before crossing over to him and crouching down next to him. "What do you mean, Nixie? Why aren't the boulders there?"

"*Is the Portal there, little one? Use your noggin! Do you think the Water Quarter wants anyone just walking through at any time? What time of day is the time associated with Water?*"

Marella gasped as she realised what Nixie meant. "Of course," she exclaimed. "The Portal will appear at dusk." She cast a reproachful look at Nixie. "You could have told us that before," she said.

"*Why bother? You were having too much fun and besides, no one asked me.*"

With that, Nixie stood up and stretched, before running to the lake and smoothly entering the water, disappearing beneath the surface.

Blushing at his reprimand, Marella faced the others and told them what he had said. "It's true, too. He's Chosen just as much as I am, and yet, once again, I never thought to ask him if he knew anything."

"Don't worry, Marella. I'm sure if it was something important he would have told you anyway," said Kai, gazing over at the water where Nixie was last seen.

"Come on, we can grab a quick snack, and talk about what we're going to do next." Lani put her arm around Marella and together they walked over the trucks and the campfire.

Daren watched Kai, a questioning look upon his face. "What's with Nixie?"

Kai startled, "How would I know?" he asked Daren.

"I don't know, but I get the feeling something is going on, and you know more about whatever it is than even Marella does. In fact, I think Marella is in the dark more than normal. Don't you dare hurt her, Kai, not after everything, not now. You hear me?" With that, Daren stalked off to the campfire and the girls, changing his mood to smiles and laughter when they looked at him.

"Nixie, you need to sort your head out," Kai thought to him. *"I know you can hear me. You knew before we even arrived here that the boulders wouldn't rise until the evening. Don't make Marella feel any more guilty than she already does, especially over something that has nothing to do with her. Tell her or don't, I don't really care right now. But don't you dare try to lay your guilty conscience upon her, and make out it is her lack or failing. You know better than that."*

After watching the water and getting no response except silence through their bond, Kai spun on his heel and made his way to the campfire as well.

From the water, an otter's head broke through the surface and looked over to the companions. He saw Ula, Kenna, and Shaw watching and waiting for him. *"I'm sorry,"* he thought to no one in particular, taking care not use the paths to Kai and Marella.

He dove back beneath the water, seeking the oblivion of play, before he had to go back out and resume his responsibilities. Responsibilities that were about to become harder. He just hoped Marella understood.

~ 57 ~

Later that afternoon, no one commented as Nixie slunk back into camp. He made his way over to the other Partners and sat by them. He looked as dejected as it was possible for an otter to look.

"You need to tell Marella, Nixie. She's going to find out anyway," Kenna said to him, rubbing his coat gently with her nose.

"I thought you might know, Kai can't keep anything to himself," said Nixie grumpily.

Kenna gave him a small nip on his flank. *"Stop feeling so sorry for yourself, and stop taking it out on Kai. He has kept your secret; he hasn't even mentioned it to me."*

"Then how do you know?" asked Nixie, his curiosity getting the better of him.

"I was with him, numbskull," exclaimed Kenna. *"I was with him, protected by Ena, as we went through Fire's Cleansing. Ena spoke to us both."*

Shaw and Ula politely stayed out of the conversation. Nixie's eyes flickered to them and back to Kenna. *"Does everyone know?"* he asked.

"If, by everyone you mean the Partners, then no. I haven't told them, but I think you should. I think you should tell everyone. I'll be honest with you, Nixie. I have absolutely no idea why you're keeping this a secret. It just doesn't make sense to me."

"It wouldn't do, not unless you knew everything, which you don't," said Nixie, acerbically.

"Yeesh, Nixie, dial it down, will you? I'm trying to help you here." Kenna turned around and walked away from Nixie, her tail showing her displeasure with him.

"We don't know what's going on, Nixie, but whatever it is, you can talk to us, you know," said Ula before walking off to check on Kenna.

Shaw said nothing, watching him with his amber eyes glowing with intelligence. Nixie had an uncomfortable feeling he already knew.

"After all we've been through, from the day we were Partnered to now, it is this stupid secret that has me so fearful," thought Nixie to himself and he hunkered down into a ball of unhappiness, misery soaking through his every bone.

During the afternoon, everyone sorted through the things they would need through the Portal, including their formal wear. Daren and Kai stowed away their trundle trucks, camouflaging them with branches and leaves that Daren twined together to disguise their presence. That evening, just as the light began to change, the waters of the lake started to churn and bubble. The companions stood on the bank of the lake, watching the boulders appear from beneath the surface.

Marella grinned at the others, "They surely weren't there when I went swimming this afternoon," she said.

Kai and Lani both laughed whilst Daren just shook his head at her, a grin breaking across his face. Slightly to one side, the Partners stood together, watching both the companions and the waters of the lake.

"You still haven't told her then?" questioned Kenna, her attention forward.

"You know I haven't, it just never seemed the right time. It's too late now, I guess. I'll just have to deal with it if it comes up."

"When it comes up, Nixie, not if." Kenna gave a small yip and Kai shot a glance over to her. He smiled at her and she felt his constant love through their bond. Kenna watched as the Portal shimmered into sight, appearing like it had always been there, even though Kenna knew it had not. She watched the excitement on Marella's face as she turned to squeeze Kai's arm at the appearance of the Portal.

"Right then, Chosen. This is the last Portal we need to go through," she said to them, smiling broadly. We need to get the *Dagrau y Crochan* from King Nixsa, return home, and it's all done. Let's go."

Laughter filled the air at her simplistic explanation which made the grin on Marella's face stretch even further.

"Come on then, Chosen of Water," said Daren, once again shaking his head at her as laughter filled his tone. "Lead on, oh watery one."

With her head held high, Marella called Nixie to her. *"Come on, Nixie my love, let's go and meet King Nixsa."*

Nixie felt his insides squirm as he ran forwards to be by her side as they crossed. He cast one look over his shoulder at Kenna before both he and Marella went through the Portal.

***

Once everyone was on the other side of the Portal, a surprise waited for them - that consisted of a crowd of people. Marella looked around in surprise as Kai stepped to her side.

She looked at him, "Are you okay?" she asked.

"I'm fine," he grinned. "It won't hit me this soon, you know that."

Marella returned her attention to the group of people in front of her and wondered what she should do.

A regal-looking lady stepped forward and the crowd parted for her. She was wearing a deep-blue silk dress that rippled when she walked, like waves upon the ocean. Her most striking feature was her long, snow-white hair. From where Marella stood, she could see that even tied back in a plait; it still fell to her hips.

She nodded her head to Marella and the rest of the Chosen. "Greetings, Chosen of the Elements. My name is Aneira, and on behalf of King Nixsa, I would like to welcome you to Teimladau." Her voice was deep and fluid, melodious in tone and Marella found herself taking an instant liking to her.

"Thank you, Aneira. I am Marella, Partnered by Nixie. These are my friends, Daren and Ula, Chosen of Earth; Lani and Shaw, Chosen of Air, and Kai and Kenna, Chosen of Fire." Marella pointed out the pairs as she introduced them. "I have to admit to being slightly surprised to see you all here," she said as she looked at them. "We only made it to the lake this morning."

Aneira gave a little chuckle, "We knew when you had arrived, Marella. The swans saw you and told us, so unlike you; we have had time to prepare for your arrival."

Aneira then introduced some of the people who were with her until the names were awhirl in Marella's head. Aneira stopped and laughed at herself. "My apologies, Marella. I'm running away with myself here. You'll never remember all the names. Come, let me take you to Teimladau centre where you can refresh yourselves in the home we've prepared. We are having a feast tonight in the square which we hope you will join us for."

A bit bemused, Marella and the rest followed Aneira to the main square in Teimladau. Everywhere Marella looked; she could see water features or hear the sound of water tinkling over stones. She felt a deep sense of relaxation come over her and smiled at the others, watching Kai for any sign of him being affected by the wave.

Aneira led them down some smaller, quieter streets to a simple stone building with a thatched room, backed by a courtyard with its own fountain. She showed them inside which had a large living area with open kitchen and wooden, circular stairs that went up to the first floor.

"There are two bedrooms with two single beds in each, and a bathroom up there," she explained whilst Marella looked around the living room. "I'll leave you to refresh yourselves. Please feel free to join us whenever you're ready. Just follow the flags, you'll find us easy enough." With that, Aneira left them to it.

"Well, this is different," said Daren wryly. "I think, no I know, this is the first time we've actually been met and welcomed."

"It does make a nice change, doesn't it," said Lani as she shook out her dress.

Kai said nothing, but went into the kitchen area to pump out some water. He splashed some on his face, the droplets running down and splashing onto his white shirt.

"Are you all right, Kai?" Marella asked, gently running her hand across his back as she joined him.

Kai reached around and pulled her to him, bending his head and taking a deep breath in. "You always smell so good, like a fresh ocean breeze. I love it," he said.

Marella laughed as she leaned back to look at him. "Are you okay?" she repeated, determined he wasn't going to wriggle out of answering her.

"I'm fine, stop fussing," he said a bit harshly before he ran his hand across his face. "Okay, so maybe fine is a bit much, but I will be. I'm not as bad as you were, anyway," he winked.

"That may be true, but you're forgetting two things," she smiled at him.

"And what's that?" he asked, distracted as he ran his fingertips over her cheek towards her hair.

"That just may be what brought us together, for one," she said. "And for two, you don't have to suffer in silence, you big lug. We've all been through it now, you're the last one. Okay, so I was a bit out of it when it hit me, but I'm sure Daren and Lani understand how you feel. Don't fake it, love, talk to us."

Kai's fingers stilled within her hair. "What did you just call me?" he asked.

"I called you a big lug," Marella laughed.

"No, the other part."

"Oh, that part. I called you 'love'. I also told you to talk to us, but I'm guessing you didn't catch that part."

"So is it just a name for me, or something else?" Kai asked as he gazed into her deep blue eyes.

"What do you think?" responded Marella as she leaned up on her tiptoes to give him a quick brush against his lips. She stepped back before he could take it any further and Kai groaned.

"I think that I have fallen absolutely, completely, and forever, in love with you, Marella, Chosen of Water. I think we need to have a talk about our future when this is over, as I know for sure I need you in it." Kai placed his hands on her face and gently placed kisses all over her face and neck, much to Marella's delight.

"Then talk we shall," she said, "But first, let's finish what we set out to do." Giving him a squeeze, she stepped back and picked up a jug from the side and pumped some crystal clear water into it. Searching around brought some glasses to her attention so she grabbed them in one hand, the jug in the other, and made her way back to the living area, looking over her shoulder and sending Kai a wink as she did so.

* * *

"Is he okay?" asked Daren, reaching for the glasses and setting them down on the oak table in the middle of the room.

"He's okay, the wave is hitting him, but he seems to think he can handle it," replied Marella, casting another look into the kitchen where she could see him splashing water on his face again.

"Do you want me to talk to him?" Daren asked as he filled up the glasses with the water.

"No, I think he'll be okay," said Marella, reaching for her glass. "You'll be sharing a room, so if he wants to talk, you'll have the opportunity."

Daren nodded as he swallowed back the entire contents of his glass. "By the Earth, but that water tastes good," he said. "Here, Lani; taste this." Daren handed her a glass and watched as she too drank it down.

"Wow, that really is good," sighed Lani blissfully.

Marella watched as Kai walked back into the main room, his colour better than before. He helped himself to a glass and drank deeply.

"So," she said before she became too distracted by the sight of him drinking, "who's going to use the bathroom first? We really shouldn't spend too long getting ready, being as they've been so nice to us."

"I'll go," said Lani. "I won't be long." She placed her glass back down on the table and went up the curved stairs, grabbing her backpack as she did so.

* * *

The others drank some more water as they waited, before Marella went upstairs to sort out her things, ready for when Lani had finished in the bathroom.

When she opened the bedroom door, she found Nixie curled up on the floor. *"What's the matter, Nixie?"* she asked, crouching down and stroking his fur.

"I have something to tell you and I don't think you're going to like it," he answered miserably.

"Well I won't know unless you do tell me so come on, spit it out," she encouraged as she made herself comfortable on the floor.

"This isn't the first time I've been in Teimladau," he said, resting his head upon her knee.

"Okay," said Marella gently running her fingers across his head. *"Surely there's more to it than that. That wouldn't upset me."*

"There is more," he said dejectedly, *"I'm King Nixsa's brother."* He waited for her reaction, his body stiff.

"That's it?" asked Marella, lifting his head up so she could see his eyes. He nodded, unable to speak to her.

"You really are a numpty when you want to be, silly otter," she said, rubbing her cheek against his head. *"Do you think I'm surprised? I thought there might be a connection between you from the moment I heard his name. Nixsa – Nixie, there's not a whole world of difference."*

Nixie's body slowly relaxed as he realised Marella was taking this far better than he had expected.

"Is this what has been upsetting you?" she asked him gently.

"Yes, Kai and Kenna know as Ena told them during the cleansing. Sorry, Marella," said Nixie as Marella shuddered at the memory.

"The others don't?" she asked, seeing him shake his head. *"Do you want me to tell them or will you?"*

"I should do it, he's my brother," Nixie answered, feeling better than he had done for a while.

"So, I have to ask, but how is he your brother when you're an otter and he's… not?" asked Marella.

Nixie gave a small chuff as he laughed. *"Do you remember when Erwyna first called you? You weren't too happy about it, were you?"*

Marella grinned as she remembered what a drama queen she had been. *"It's a good job you stuck by me,"* she said, *"but what does this have to do with you and King Nixsa?"*

"I'm getting to it," Nixie laughed. *"You were right in that I had known about you being special for a long time, before you even took your Test. Erwyna came to us when you were born, Marella."*

Marella gasped as she realised this was indeed something that had been building up over the years. She looked at Nixie and waited for him to continue.

"Erwyna came to us and explained how a girl-child would be born, only of Water. She told us that a Partner needed to be found for her, one who would help and guide her until such time as Erwyna called for her. I volunteered to be that Partner."

"So is that the only reason we're together then?" Marella asked, feeling a twinge of hurt go through her, no matter how she tried to ignore it.

Nixie stood up and rubbed her nose with his, *"No, little one, it's not. Of course, I didn't know you before you took the test, but Nixsa kept an eye on you, he told me how strong your abilities were getting. He also told me I'd have my hands full with you, and he was right. When I volunteered to be your Partner, I lost the ability to transform to an animal from a human form, and back again. For the length of your lifetime, I am only an otter."*

"You are more than 'only' an otter, Nixie," Marella said indignantly. *"What do you mean though, for my lifetime?"*

"I'm an Elemental, from the same line as the Scions. I will live many human lifetimes before it is my time to move on."

Marella thought about this before smiling broadly and throwing her arms about Nixie and squeezing him tight. He wriggled out of her arms and looked at her. *"Just what are you doing?"* he cried.

"Okay, so this may sound a bit crazy, but I'm actually glad you won't die. The part about me dying I'm not so keen on, but at least I know you'll be living again and happy when I do pass."

"Crazy woman," Nixie chuntered to her. *"How can I be happy when you pass? I'm your Life Partner, Marella. It will tear me up inside when you go."*

"You said it yourself, you will live many lifetimes. That gives you the time to grieve for me before time eases the rawness of loss. Nixie, you know as well as I, that the pain of losing someone never fades but the pain changes. It changes into something you get better at dealing with. And so it will be for you." Marella tried to reassure him through their bond at the same time as she explained what she meant.

Nixie remained disgruntled with her for a moment as he tried to understand what she meant. It seeped through their bond that Marella was actually happy with him, not angry as he had feared. He couldn't quite understand why she was happy, but he wasn't about to refute the feeling.

* * *

"Marella, are you okay in there?" There was a loud knocking on the bedroom door which startled both Nixie and Marella. They looked at each other before Marella started to giggle, as she went to open the door. Stood outside the doorway were Kai and Daren, both looking worried. They peered into the bedroom, their eyes darting around the room before falling on Marella.

"You've been gone for a while; I tried to speak with you but couldn't seem to reach you. You scared me," said Kai, all in one breath.

"I'm fine, Nixie's fine, we're both fine," she reassured the pair of them. "We needed to have a talk without everyone else being here. We'll be down soon now. I just need to have a quick wash and get changed."

"Okay," mumbled Daren before going back downstairs, leaving Kai leaning against the doorframe with his arms crossed.

Marella looked at him quizzically. "What's the matter with you?" she said, "I need to get ready, so go on, shoo!" She waved her hands at him as though she was waving on an animal. Kai just grinned at her and stayed where he was.

Marella put her hands on her hips, "What are you grinning for? You look like a prize baboon."

"You know lots of smiling baboons, do you my love?" Kai asked her as he grasped her by her waist and pulled her close.

Marella rested her hands up on his chest and smiled up at him. "The grand total has just gone up by one," she said.

"You're a fool, Marella," he said to her, holding her tightly.

"Aye, a fool for you, more like," she sighed. "Go on, now, I really need to get ready."

Kai gave her a quick kiss that left her breathless. He grinned at her as he turned around. "Don't be too long or I might have to come back to help."

He laughed and ran down the stairs as Marella grabbed a pillow from the bed to threaten him with. Still laughing, she closed the door and finished sorting out the more formal attire of the Chosen, before heading to the bathroom to refresh herself.

It was only a matter of minutes before Marella closed the bedroom door silently behind her and followed Nixie down the stairs. The others were waiting in the living room, all properly dressed and ready to go.

"Before we go, Nixie has something he needs to tell you which is relevant to who we meet tonight," she said, effortlessly drawing their attention.

Nixie made quick work of explaining that King Nixsa was actually his brother. He saw the looks of relief on Kai and Kenna's faces that they didn't have to pretend anymore. He looked at Daren and Ula as he had known them the longest and saw nothing but pleasant surprise as they heard his story.

Lani came over and stroked his back. "Thank you for telling us, Nixie, although I'm not sure it makes much difference. We still need to get the Cauldron, whether he's your brother or not."

Marella laughed and slung her arm around Lani's shoulders, being careful to miss her hair. "That's it, Lani, tell it how it is," she said.

Lani blushed and tilted her head forwards. "It's true though," she mumbled.

"It certainly is," said Daren, "and on that note, perhaps we should go. With one thing and other, we've been here for nearly an hour."

They all left the house and went out into the street where they could already see people milling about. With friendly waves and greetings, the Chosen made their way down a cobbled street, following the flags as directed to the main square of Teimladau.

~ 59 ~

In the centre of the town square stood a tall pine tree with most of the branches cleared away except for a few near the top. Attached to the top were red and white ribbons which fluttered gently in the breeze. As they approached, music started to play and men and women ran forward to catch the ribbons.

As Marella watched, the men caught red ribbons and the women caught the white. They started to dance around the maypole in time to the music, weaving in and out, intertwining the ribbons as they danced.

King Nixsa sat at a long wooden table, watching the dancing. As he caught sight of the Chosen, his cerulean blue eyes lit up with pleasure. He stood up and clapped his hands which stopped the dancing and the music.

King Nixsa was a tall man with long, silvery hair with blue tips. He was of lean build, but there was a strength in him Marella could see. He reminded her of the Willow tree, sinewy and supple which would bend with the wind rather than break. At his side sat Aneira who also stood up and smiled with pleasure at the sight of the Chosen.

As silence fell over the square, King Nixsa announced "Ladies and Gentlemen of Teimladau, please join me in welcoming the Chosen of the Elements. They have finally made their way to us and their timing is perfect as we start our Beltane Festival. Eat, drink, and be merry, for tomorrow we have a Cauldron to find," he joked.

He gestured for the Chosen to join him at his table. He nodded to the musicians and the music started up again, with the dancing quickly following suit. They sat down at the table and the Partners joined them. Nixsa looked at them all in depth, before he nodded his head, appearing satisfied with whatever it was he had found.

Marella made the same introductions as she had done previously to Aneira. Nixsa smiled at them and made them feel very welcome. Before she could thank them, someone had placed platters on the table filled with food to make her mouth water. There were honeycakes and bread, green herbal salads, cheesecakes and an abundance of red fruits, including cherries, strawberries and raspberries. There was mead to drink, as well as a red wine punch.

Marella looked at the display in front of her before she turned questioning eyes to Aneira. "Can it be…?" she started before Aneira nodded her head without Marella having to finish the question.

"Yes Marella, this is all to celebrate Beltane. Today is Beltane Eve which is why Nixsa said your timing was perfect."

Marella took a sharp breath in as she realised time was already slipping away from them. It was only yesterday, by her reckoning, when they had said Beltane was a week away and now here it was, tomorrow. By the silence on either side of her, she knew Daren and Kai had heard too, and by their muttered exclamations, they were none too happy with the time difference.

Lani broke the silence, "King Nixsa, are you aware of the passing of time in Wraidd Elfennol?"

He nodded to her, his eyes gentle with understanding. "Yes Lani, and trust me, although I would be more than happy for you all to remain here, safe and relaxed; I am also aware of the time limit imposed upon you. I shall have you out of here as soon as possible, but only on the understanding you are all welcome to return as and whenever you want."

"So what do I have to do to retrieve the Cauldron, King Nixsa?" Marella asked curiously.

"Now now, my dear, let's not ruin the celebration by talk of business. We're here to enjoy, to relax. Eat your fill, dance with your beloved, the morrow will come soon enough. Besides, it will give me chance to talk with my brother," he said, winking at her.

Marella gave a slight huff as she wanted to know what she had to do, but relaxed as Kai linked their fingers together under the table. Smiling at Nixsa, Marella said "Of course, I'm sure there's plenty of *time*."

Nixsa gave a shout of laughter that had heads turning in their direction. "Aneira, did you hear that? She means to remind me of time even though we've only just spoken of it. She is determined, this one, a one-track mind."

"And you should be glad she is," defended Kai. "Marella has helped all of us to retrieve the Essences and now it is her turn. The safety of our world and yours is dependent upon these; surely you recognise the importance of this?"

With Kai's words, King Nixsa had grown very serious and Marella was afraid he was offended. Instead, a slow smile broke through and Nixsa nodded his head. "Well said, Chosen of Fire, and Fire you have indeed. I do recognise the importance, however one thing I know which you do not. You are safe here and I will not let time slip away. Ask your Partners if I am true, don't ask Nixie because he is biased, but I do not think it is Marella with the doubts."

To Marella's embarrassment, Kai called Kenna over to him. "Kenna, please can you tell me if King Nixsa is true or if he has ulterior motives?" He looked at Nixsa, "I'm asking Kenna as she is your natural opposite."

"If I have anything to hide, Kenna will surely find it," agreed King Nixsa. Aneira sat by his side, nibbling on a piece of Beltane bread, at ease with what was happening around her.

Kenna was silent for a moment as she took the King's measure, but instead of answering Kai, she leapt across the table to the surprise of everyone and licked the king's nose. King Nixsa jerked backwards in surprise, nearly toppling off the bench as he did so. Aneira burst into peals of laughter, soon joined by Marella and Lani.

Daren and Kai looked at each other ruefully, "I guess that means he's okay," said Daren, chuckling.

"I would guess so," agreed Kai before standing up and offering his arm to King Nixsa. "My apologies, your Majesty, however after the Fire Quarter, I needed to make sure."

Nixsa waved the apology away but took Kai's arm in the warrior's greeting, "Don't be silly, Kai, I understand, no need to apologise. I was quite shocked when I heard what Queen Djinn was up to with that crazy Consort of hers. I wonder what Lord Ethon will do with him now?"

"I don't know, but I hope he changes his attitude with whatever it is," Kai said.

"Hmm, yes, that attitude. Well, unfortunately, that attitude seems to be gaining popularity. Not here, you understand," he added to reassure them. "The Sylphs are supposed to be the ones to hear the whispers on the wind," he said, smiling at Lani, "but the rumours going around about how the Elements are not in balance, and this one is better than that one, have even reached beneath the waves to us."

"What can be done though?" asked Marella, a hint of desperation in her voice.

"Not much, I'm afraid," replied Nixsa sadly. "You can only make it plain to your people you do not think that way and why. They will form their own opinions regardless. You just have to hope they will agree with you."

"Don't they realise what will happen if the Elements are out of balance though?" questioned Lani as she delicately ate some berries. "Haven't the recent storms been enough proof for them?"

"You would think so, wouldn't you?" said Aneira as she patted her mouth with a napkin. "Unfortunately although everyone has eyes, not all can see. We can guide or advise but we can't, and we won't, dictate."

There was silence for a short while as they concentrated on eating whilst thinking about what had been said.

"So," said Marella suddenly, "I know I keep going on about this, but what is going to happen tomorrow. King Nixsa, please can you tell me anything?"

"You will be going for a swim, Marella. It's as simple as that. Nixie will be with you, although I somehow doubt if I could prise him away from you anyhow. Aneira, I, and your companions will be watching and waiting for your return. Once you return, you will have the Cauldron. I would like it if you would stay for the final festivities of Beltane, but I do understand if you can't. We will be burning the Bel-fires atop the hill and I know some of us will be jumping the flames. You are welcome to join us if you wish."

He stopped and looked at Aneira. A warning look passed between them, before mischief alighted upon Nixsa's face. Aneira shook her head and sighed. "Of course, the Greenwood Marriages might be more to your liking," he said slyly, laughter threading his voice.

Marella groaned and sank her face into her hands, not daring to look at Kai. Daren's snort could be heard loud and clear, as could the slap on his arm that Lani gave him.

Keeping a straight face and his voice serious, Kai addressed King Nixsa. "Sir, although I would love to participate in the Greenwood Marriage, I somehow think my beloved's father might be a bit peeved."

Daren choked as he imagined Edlin's reaction being described as 'a bit peeved'. He stifled his laughter to hear the rest of Kai's tongue-in-cheek explanation, but instead of continuing with the laughter, Kai turned the conversation to a more serious note.

"Besides," Kai continued, "we do have a quest to finish and, as has already been pointed out to me, 'the timing sucks'. So, finish the quest we shall, and then I will be sorting things out to ensure we have the 'right' time, for us. I have told Marella I want her in my life, that I need her in my life. I don't just mean for the old one lunar month handfasting, or even the longer year and a day one. I need Marella in my life for the rest of my days, and I will do whatever I can to make sure that happens."

Kai clasped Marella's hand and brought it to his lips, giving it a gentle kiss as he looked into her eyes, the rest of the table disappearing until it was just the two of them. "I love you, Marella," he whispered to her, watching as the colour rose in her face.

"I love you too," she whispered back, her heart full of emotion.

"That just serves you right," Marella heard Aneira say to Nixsa, as they came back to their current surroundings.

Nixsa was watching them both, a tender look on his face. "You are constantly surprising me, Kai. I was expecting an answer full of laughter and instead you give me one from the heart." He looked at Marella and nodded approvingly. "Marella, you've caught yourself a fine one here. Although you don't need it, you have my blessing. May the two of you be forever as one."

"Thank you King Nixsa," said Marella before a smile broke through. "He is a good one, although I have no idea how I 'caught' him, as you say. We could barely speak with each other to start with."

"Ah, well, where would we be without a few sparks in our lives, eh?" Nixsa laughed. Looking at Aneira, he said "We've had a few of our own, haven't we, love?"

Aneira laughed, looking at him lovingly. "We certainly have, usually because of your mischievous ways."

"You wouldn't want me any other way," Nixsa stated confidently before glancing at her.

"Really?" joked Aneira. "Are you sure about that? Let me think. Hmm, maybe you're right, although you could tone it down some."

Marella laughed at the interplay between the two as the colour rose in Nixsa's cheeks at Aneira's gentle reprimand. "My apologies, Aneira. When we first met, I didn't realise that you were with King Nixsa," Marella said.

"Not to worry, it's not something I talk about a lot. He has enough to deal with, without me as well." Aneira smiled at the group as Nixsa put his arm about her shoulders and pulled her closer.

"Don't listen to her," he said. "She is with me every step of the way and we discuss most things between ourselves that we deal with. She just lets me be at the forefront so if anything goes wrong; it's me that gets the blame instead of her."

Laughter sounded around the table as Aneira twisted beneath his arm and pinched his ribs. They continued to relax and talk for the rest of the evening, enjoying the companionship and the music before they headed off to their house for the night, promising to return early the next morning.

~ 60 ~

As the sun rose the following the morning, the Chosen were already awake, breakfasted, and waiting for the appointed time for them to return to King Nixsa and Aneira. Marella had put on her bathing costume beneath her gown and was sipping contentedly on a mug of her lavender and lemon balm tea. She watched the others as they moved around the kitchen and living area, reminding her of bees in a hive.

"Why are you all so frantic this morning?" she asked, as she lazily reclined back in her chair with Nixie curled up in her lap.

"Why are you so calm?" retorted Daren as he made his way to the kitchen.

"I'm calm because this is nearly over. I'm calm because all I have to do is go for a swim which I've been doing since before I could walk, as you well know, Daren." Marella looked at him critically. "So I ask you once more, why are you so frantic?"

Daren stopped and the air puffed out of him as he put his hands on his hips and faced her. "We're worried, okay?" he said, grimacing.

"Why?" she asked. "Daren, you had to fight a rogue Elemental, Lani had to contend with the Elements themselves, Kai got Cleansed! By the Waters, Daren, what do you think is going to happen to me when I'm swimming?" Marella's voice rose with each question, Nixie shifting agitatedly on her lap.

"I don't know, all right?" Daren shouted in response, making Marella gaze in shock at him with her mouth open.

Kai poked his head in from the kitchen area, "Is everything okay in here?" he asked, looking from one to the other.

"Yes, Kai, we're fine, everything's okay," said Marella without taking her eyes from Daren.

Kai nodded and added "Lani and I are just going for a short walk to see if anything is happening yet. We'll be back soon." He exchanged glances with Lani and they both left by the back door, mutually agreeing that going by the front door might just be a bad idea.

Once they had gone, Daren sank into a chair with his head in his hands. "Marella, I'm sorry. I just... I don't like it. I don't want you hurt. You've only just found happiness with Kai, and I don't want to see anything jeopardise that."

Marella went over to Daren and crouched in front of him, pulling his hands from his head so she could see into his eyes. She spoke softly, reassuring him with her tone, and by holding onto him.

"Daren, dear heart, this is something I need to do. Just as you needed to fight to get the Shield, I need to swim to get the Cauldron. We knew from the start this would be something we couldn't be involved with for each other, but something we would have to do for ourselves. I had to watch you fight the rogue even though I hated every moment of it. Now it's your turn to watch."

She squeezed his hands and continued, "There is one big difference though, between your fight and mine. In Naear, we only knew Carrick and Alana were to be trusted and everyone else was an unknown. From what we saw and were told last night, by our Partners too, it is the other way around here. We can trust Nixsa, Aneira, and *most* of the Undines. Those we can trust outnumber those we cannot."

She stood up, pulling at his hands until he stood up too, "Nixsa and Aneira will keep you well fed and amused, I'm sure. I will be fine and Nixie will be with me. Trust in me like I trust in you." She wrapped her arms around his waist and squeezed with all her might. Daren returned the embrace and they stood there in silence, just drinking in each other's presence.

Marella heard the back door open and close quietly a few moments before she felt two pairs of arms join in the embrace. She recognised the feel of Kai behind her and could see Lani's blonde hair catching on Daren's shirt. She took a deep breath, feeling a sense of rightness that they were all here. Slowly, they drew apart until they were stood in a circle, holding each other's hands.

Lani smiled at them before dropping the hands she was holding. "It's time to go, Marella. People have started to arrive at the square."

Straightening her shoulders, Marella took a deep breath and smiled at them all. "Let's go then, time's a-wasting."

* * *

The short walk from their house to the square took longer than expected, as it seemed like everyone had come out to watch them. The streets were full of people who cheered as they watched the Chosen walk by in full, formal attire.

Marella led the way with Nixie by her side, holding her staff in her right hand proudly, as she walked, smiling at the crowd and thanking them for their well wishes. In a row behind her, walked Daren, Kai, and Lani, with Ula and Kenna walking beside them, and Shaw swooping through the air, impressing the crowd with his acrobatics.

They arrived in the main square and King Nixsa rose from his seat at the same bench as last night and strode across to meet them. He clasped Marella's hand and smiled down at her. "I hope you slept well last night."

"Yes, thank you, really well. I don't think I'll be going camping again for quite a while after we've finished this quest," she laughed.

"Hmm, yes, I can understand why," Nixsa chuckled. "I like my home comforts too much to go camping, I must admit." He turned to greet the rest of them and bade them join him at the table.

"A little bird told me that lavender and lemon balm was your favourite tea, Marella, so I hope you don't mind, I ordered a pot of it. Here we go," he said as he poured some of the aromatic tea into a cup and passed it to her.

"Thank you King Nixsa, you were told correctly." Marella sniffed appreciatively before taking small sips of burning liquid.

"Right, onto business," Nixsa said abruptly, "I know you won't appreciate any delays so I'll tell you now that Aneira is just sorting out a few things, and then she'll be joining us. Once she is here, we will take a short walk to the lake which is where most of my Undines are already."

He looked around and saw the quick flash of worry pass Daren's face. He smiled at him reassuringly. "Once we get there, I will take your companions with me and we will sit down and await your return. All you need to do is to walk into the lake and follow Nixie, which is what you are used to, from what he tells me."

Confidence shone from Marella and she laughed at Nixsa's words. "I suppose you'll tell me the water is nice and warm too, just like he does, when in fact it is exceedingly cold."

Nixsa chuckled and shook his head at Nixie. "Shall I tell Marella about the time you fell into the lake during the Yule celebrations? You didn't claim it to be warm that time."

Nixie gave a shudder that rippled through his entire body, much to the delight of Marella. She gave a small laugh and nudged him with her leg. "Oh, Nixie, I think I like it here," she giggled. "I'm learning all sorts about you. It's fantastic."

Nixie snorted his disdain and then his gaze focused on something behind Marella's shoulder so she turned to see what he was looking at. Aneira gracefully approached them, a beautiful smile upon her face. "Good morning Chosen," she addressed them and received a chorus of greetings back.

"Shall we go then?" asked Marella, fidgeting in her excitement.

"Slowly, Marella," laughed Aneira. "Finish your drink first, then we'll go."

Marella took a gulp of her drink, blinking furiously as the heat hit her mouth, making her eyes water.

After burning her mouth, Marella finished her drink in a more sedate manner which made Kai laugh to himself. Her knee was jiggling up and down under the table, so he discreetly reached down and placed his hand upon it, stopping the movement. Marella bit her bottom lip as she realised what she was doing and smiled at Kai. He stroked her knee before removing his hand and placing it back on the table.

Nixsa looked around the table and saw everyone had finished so he stood up. "Shall we go to the lake then?" he asked and gestured for Aneira to precede him from the table.

They walked serenely down to the lake, hearing greetings once again. "Everyone seems really friendly here," Marella commented as they approached the water.

"Yes, well, we have our moments. You're lucky that you're here during Beltane, you're a Chosen, *and* you're about to put on a show for them. They're naturally inclined to like you," Nixsa laughed.

"Thanks for that," said Marella, her lips twisting into a smirk. "It makes me feel a whole lot better."

"I thought it might," laughed Nixsa and showed them where they would be sitting whilst they waited for Marella.

As the sun rose higher in the sky, more people turned up and found somewhere to sit around the lake. Marella waited nervously for King Nixsa to tell her when it was time. Nixie stayed by her side, his sides quivering with every breath he took. When it appeared no one else was coming, and the sun reached the zenith, King Nixsa stood up and called for everyone's attention.

"My friends, we are honoured today by Marella, Chosen of Water, who will be retrieving the *Dagrau y Crochan* from our waters and sending it to safety. This is to ensure the balance, not just of the Elements, but of our world itself. Circumstances have been difficult for them, so I am hoping that this will be an easy task for her to finish on."

He surveyed the crowd, looking for pockets of discontent amongst his people and was pleased to see that everyone he could see looked relaxed and happy.

"Marella is going to enter the lake now, and beyond that, I don't know what will happen. It may be over in a matter of moments or it may take longer. Your guess is as good as mine, so I ask you to show patience. Remember, we do not know what will be happening beneath the still waters of our lake."

Nixsa turned and held his hand out to Marella, smiling as she rose with fluid grace. She smiled at her companions, winking cheekily at Kai before slipping off her dress. "Keep my seat warm," she said as she stepped down to the water's edge with Nixie by her side.

* * *

Standing with her toes barely touching the water, Marella waved to the crowd that had gathered. She took a deep breath and walked slowly into the water. Once the water was to her mid-thigh, she gave a small jump and dove forward into the water. She went down just enough to wet herself through and then came up again, her hair streaming down her back.

"Dagnabbit, Nixie, I forgot to put my net on," she grumbled as she started a strong, yet steady, breast-stroke.

"You'll be fine," he reassured. *"The rate you're swimming, your hair will be behind you all the time anyway."* Nixie was rolling and paddling through the water, keeping pace with Marella.

"Do you know what we have to do, Nixie?" Marella asked, using their private path. *"I can't just swim around here all day."*

"You don't have to. Remember your lake? The spiral? Dive below the surface here and you'll see another one, although this one is a bit larger. I've been training you to swim here since we were first Partnered although I never thought it would under these circumstances," Nixie thought to her.

A smile broke across Marella's face and she sent a surge of love to Nixie, thanking him for his help. Her breathing easy and her strokes swift, she quickly made it to the centre of the lake where she trod water momentarily as she looked back to the shore.

She could see Kai and Daren standing there, their hands shielding their eyes from the glare of the sun on the water as they watched her. Lani was a tiny figure in between them but Marella could still see her golden hair blowing in the gentle breeze. She raised her hand in acknowledgement before taking a deep breath and diving beneath the surface to find the spiral.

Her eyes adjusted to the dim light beneath the waves as the muffled sounds of the lake hit her ears. *"Whoever said it was silent under the water had obviously never swum underwater,"* she thought as she dove deeper.

She heard Nixie's laugh in her mind and saw his body undulating up and down as he aerodynamically cut through the water. *"There it is, Marella, do you see it?"* Nixie asked.

She turned her head, feeling her breathing strain slightly as she continued deeper. She could see the glow of the same white stones that lay beneath her lake and felt reassured by the similarity.

"Go on up and control your breathing. Be in command before filling your lungs and coming back down. Swim as quickly as you can when you come back down. You will need all the air you can to swim this spiral."

Marella nodded her understanding and shot upwards like an arrow. She wasn't that far from the surface so it wouldn't place too much of a strain for her to come straight back down. Her head and body broke through the surface of the water and she bobbed up and down for a short while, making sure she didn't move too far from her current position.

She stayed on top of the waves for a minute or so, just long enough to calm her thumping heart and get her breathing back under control. She deliberately didn't look around for the others. She could feel them through their bond, and she knew all the Partners were keeping tabs on her so there was no need. She needed her full concentration on the matter at hand, so simply blocked out anything else.

Feeling ready, she took a deep breath, filling her lungs as much as she could, before diving once again beneath the surface. She quickly dove back down to Nixie, feeling through their bond that he was still in control of his breathing and not in distress.

"I've got about one minute, one and a half, before I need to breathe again, Nixie. I wish I could hold my breath for five minutes like you can. It would make this easier."

Nixie laughed through their bond and reassured her. *"You'll be fine, the spiral is right here. I have a couple of minutes left before I need to surface but I won't leave you down here by yourself. If you don't complete it this go, we'll both go and breathe and try again."*

Marella acknowledged his words through their bond, admitting to herself she didn't want to have to try again. She could do this, and would do this, first time. Finding the leading stone was easy as it glowed in the dim light of the water. The moment she touched it, Marella felt a calmness descend upon her, her worries and anxieties washed away.

Trailing her right hand over the stones, she followed the spiral round into tighter and tighter circles, making sure her fingers kept contact at all times. Right in the centre of the spiral was a large milky-white stone that pulsed with an inner light. *"You need to lay your left hand on the centre stone, whilst keeping your right in contact with the leading stones,"* Nixie instructed.

Marella maneuvered her body so she was facing the correct way to follow Nixie's commands and laid her hand down onto the centre stone. It pulsed out a bright beam of light before everything went black.

"Not again," she thought.

~ 61 ~

Marella opened her eyes and looked around, unsurprised to see she was back in the same place as where she had met Erwyna before. She was lying down on a couch so she pushed herself up and looked around to find Nixie lying in some rushes nearby. As she swung her legs forward and off the couch, Erwyna walked into the room, smiling broadly and reaching out to hug Marella.

"Marella, my dear, it's so good to see you. Let me look at you," Erwyna cried. She gave her a brief hug before taking a step back and looking Marella up and down. "You've lost some weight, Marella," she said with a critical eye.

"That's what happens when you've been camping for nearly a year," Marella said with a slight acerbic twinge to her voice.

"Of course, of course," said Erwyna, hiding a smile.

"My Lady, please don't think I'm being rude, but please don't tell me you're going to give me the Cauldron here? Where you could have done it months ago?"

"No, Marella, not at all," Erwyna couldn't hide her laughter now and the peals rang through the room like bells, waking Nixie who stretched out his body and gave a great, big yawn.

"Hello Erwyna," he greeted her, *"fancy seeing you here."*

"Tsk tsk, Nixie, sarcasm doesn't become you," said Erwyna, laughing once more. "What am I saying? Of course it becomes you. I've never know you to be anything different to me."

Marella cleared her throat, wanting information about the cauldron, not a walk down memory lane. Erwyna returned her attention to Marella and rebuked her with just a look. Marella felt a blush making itself known as her cheeks heated. She lowered her head and looked down to the ground.

"Now, about the cauldron," said Erwyna, continuing as though nothing had happened. "The original *Dagrau y Crochan* has been destroyed by those working against us. They seek the permanent imbalance of the Elements, leading to strife, arrogance, and superiority."

Marella shook her head in dismay. "So what are we to do?" she asked. "Is this it? Is it all over and we've failed?" Marella felt despondency settle upon her as she thought of being the one who didn't get the Essence. A feeling of guilt, of letting the others down, crashed over her and she sank back down onto the couch, a groan escaping from her mouth.

Erwyna sank onto the couch next to Marella, held onto her hands and rubbed them briskly. "All is not lost, Marella. Have a bit of faith," she chided. "We just have to make a new Cauldron, that's all."

"Right," Marella snorted. "A new Cauldron, that's all. I'll just click my fingers."

"Honestly, Marella. I thought we'd moved past this attitude of yours. I really believed you had grown during the time spent away, however, at the first hiccup, it all comes rushing back."

Marella was silent for a moment, resenting the rebuke, before her sense of fair play came back. "I'm sorry, Lady Erwyna," she said, raising her head to look her squarely in the face. "You are correct. I'm jumping ahead again and not listening to what you have to say. My apologies."

Erwyna waved her hand, "Perhaps you have grown after all. The Marella I met here last year would not have apologised, but would have clung to her anger for days."

Marella blushed as she remembered that it was indeed what she had done to Nixie after their last visit.

"Now, if you will let me, Marella, I'm going to slip into your mind and show you what you must do to make a new Cauldron. This must be done now, before your feet touch the Earth again. Only by being immersed in, and surrounded by Water, can this be done."

Marella nodded her consent and sat still as Erwyna leaned forward and placed her fingertips at Marella's temples. She closed her eyes and relaxed, as she felt Erwyna gently place the information she needed in her mind. Erwyna leaned back and removed her fingers. Marella opened her eyes and smiled.

"Here is the vial you will need. Once you have used it, give it to Nixie who will return it to me." Erwyna smiled at Nixie who bobbed his head to her.

"Go now, before the others worry about you too much. You must tell King Nixsa to beware. Currents are moving beneath the surface of his kingdom and he needs to know about them. Tell him to seek out Dylan, Hafgan, and Morwenna who will help him find the truth."

With these words, she kissed Marella's forehead before pulling her to her feet. "Remember, do not touch the Earth or you won't be able to make the Cauldron."

"I understand," said Marella. "Thank you for all you have done and shown me. I will do my best."

"I know you will," smiled Erwyna. "Now if we can just get that attitude sorted, we'll be fine." She winked at Marella to let her know she was teasing. "If you swim straight upwards, you'll find yourself in the middle of the lake again."

"Straight on up?" questioned Marella before her head was tilted upwards by Erwyna to gaze at the ceiling.

There was no ceiling; it was the water of the lake that acted as one. Marella could see the vegetation on the lake bed which appeared like it was some sort of hanging decoration.

"Straight on up," confirmed Erwyna, her eyes twinkling. "We will meet again, Marella, and soon. Until then, know I am very proud of my Chosen and everything you have achieved."

Marella bowed her head and straightened her shoulders as she felt the warmth of Erwyna's blessing flow through her.

"Goodbye, Lady Erwyna, I shall look forward to seeing you soon," Marella smiled and pushed herself upwards as though she was jumping. She didn't fall back to the ground, but continued upwards, poking a hole into the spongy film that enclosing Erwyna's rooms. It sealed itself behind her with nary a drop passing through.

She saw Nixie swimming strongly by her side and felt his happiness through their bond. *"Are you ready to make the Cauldron, Nixie?"* she asked him, clutching the vial in her hand.

"Of course, should be interesting," he replied, his tone light.

* * *

Marella and Nixie crested the surface of the lake at the same time and Marella drew in a deep breath. Even in the middle of the lake they could hear the cheers as the people watching saw them surface. She swam towards the shore, being careful not to drop the vial or loosen the stopper. As she moved closer, Daren, Kai, and Lani came rushing to meet her.

She stopped where she could still tread water, and stayed there, seeing the confusion on their faces.

"The Cauldron has been destroyed," she shouted, her voice carrying beyond the waves.

The people closest to her gasped in horror and Marella could see the news being passed on as those that had heard told those that hadn't. She saw Kai take a step back before he turned on his heel and went to King Nixsa, who hurriedly came to the shore to speak with her.

"Marella, come to shore so that we can talk. Kai tells me the Cauldron has been destroyed. Is this true?" Nixsa sounded horrified and Marella could empathise with how he was feeling.

"It is true, King Nixsa," she said respectfully, "but I'm afraid I can't come to shore yet, as the Lady Erwyna has given me the means to create a new one. I must do it before my feet touch the Earth again."

Nixsa looked intrigued, but nodded his head to Marella and Nixie. "Okay then, Chosen of Water. Do what you must."

Marella turned her body in the water so that she faced Nixie. *"Ready?"* she asked.

"Yes," came his simple reply.

Still treading water, Marella loosened the stopper at the top of the vial.

With steady hands, she took out the dropper from the top of the small bottle and watched as six drops of indigo-blue liquid fell to the surface of the water in front of her.

Instead of dispersing, as ink tended to when dropped in water, Marella watched as the six drops bound themselves together. The waves started to come with a bit more force and Marella had to fight against a current to keep her distance from the shore. The six drops slowly enlarged and the edges turned upwards to the sky. Marella smiled when she saw this and knew they were ready for the next stage.

"Nixie," she called and he swam over to her, being careful not to touch the drops.

When he was within range, he moved so he was looking away from Marella. She reached out and plucked a single hair from the scruff of his neck. Nixie shivered as she did so and dove underwater to realign his fur.

"Silly otter," she thought fondly, *"one hair won't make a difference."*

"Says you," he snorted. *"Your turn now, come on."*

Using her other hand, she reached up pulled a hair from her own head before reaching forward towards the blue splodge that still floated in front of her. As she touched the hairs to the sides of the mass, the waters churned and bubbled. Her legs were now aching from treading water, but she fought to maintain her place.

The blue globule started to change shape and the sides rose up. It curled and bent, becoming larger and more solid as it did so. Both of the hairs were consumed within the mass. The Cauldron was now a deep, pot-bellied vessel with a handle either side, and three legs for it to stand on. She held the vial out for Nixie, who carefully took it in his mouth, before diving down below the waves.

Marella started to wonder just how she was supposed to get this to King Nixsa without her feet touching the Earth. *"I should have thought of that earlier, huh,"* she thought to herself.

Nixie was back with her, watching the Cauldron as it grew to a decent size. Marella draped her arm across his back carefully so as not to disturb his body's movement. Marella felt something beneath her feet and panicked, thinking she had drifted too close to the shore, but Nixie soon calmed her down. *"It's okay, Marella, this is part of it."*

As Marella watched a giant bubble appeared, enclosing herself, Nixie, and the Cauldron. She was now able to stand, as the bubble leisurely ascended into the air and moved towards King Nixsa and her companions, who were watching with open-mouthed astonishment.

When it reached them, Marella held out her hand to the King. "King Nixsa, if you wouldn't mind coming in?" she asked with a twinkle in her eye.

He reached up and grasped her hand, taking a quick breath as she pulled him up and inside the bubble. He looked beneath his feet before he looked at her. "You know, seeing the ground some distance from my feet is making me feel a bit queasy."

Marella grinned at him. "Well let's make this quick then and you can return to the solid Earth."

King Nixsa changed his attitude from joking to being serious. "What you are doing is amazing, Marella. I just wanted you to know. Nixie, I can't believe this is happening to you, brother. I thought you a fool to volunteer as Partner to the Chosen. It appears the joke is on me. Anything you need, you only need say." Nixsa thumped his clenched fist over his heart and bent his head.

Marella wondered what that was about but didn't ask. Instead, she looked at them and said, "Yes, well then, that's excellent and I'm sure Nixie is over the moon. However, to complete the last stage of the Cauldron, I'm afraid I need one of your hairs."

Nixsa looked startled, "One of my hairs?" he asked.

Marella sighed and put her hands on her hips. "I know this may sound like a strange request, but nothing of what we're doing right now is normal," she said, exasperation clear in her voice. "We're floating in a giant bubble with a Cauldron I've just made using drops of goodness knows what, and some hair. So yes please, a hair... from you... and we can finish this."

King Nixsa laughed at her and made a show of reaching up to pluck a single hair from his head. He pulled one long silver strand and passed it to Marella who dropped it into the cauldron. As they watched, the hair was integrated into the blue of the body and became a braid that wrapped itself around the outside of the cauldron.

"Is that it?" Nixsa asked, his voice quiet and filled with wonder.

"No, there is just one more thing," answered Marella, reaching up to pierce the bubble above her head.

Nixsa grabbed her hand before she could break it. "What are you doing? You can't touch the Earth, remember?"

"I know, there's enough time, don't worry," she reassured him, gently disengaging his hand, and reaching up once more. She pinched the top of the bubble between her fingers and gave a sharp tug. A small hole appeared at the top and the bubble started to disintegrate around them. Still holding her fingers pinched together, Marella held them over the cauldron before opening them.

A single drop of crystal clear water dropped into the cauldron, causing it to shine with a dazzling blue light. As Nixsa, Marella, and Nixie shielded their eyes from the glow right in front of them, the light spread out so it encased the whole cauldron.

Just before the bubble disappeared completely, the light faded from the Cauldron and a simple triple spiral now shone from the side of the cauldron. The last of the bubble dissolved, and their feet touched the earth beneath them. Marella breathed a sigh of relief that the timing had worked and sent thanks to Lady Erwyna.

Kai, Daren, and Lani rushed to Marella, giving the gown back to Marella to get dressed in, whilst Ula, Kenna, and Shaw welcomed Nixie back into their fold. Aneira moved more sedately than the others, but with no less purpose. As soon as she was close enough, she stared at Nixsa before running her hand across his cheek. "Nicely done," she said.

"Marella, celebrate later, we still need to send off the Cauldron," Nixie reminded her.

She turned to the others, "I'll be with you in a minute. I need to finish this as Nixie has just reminded me."

Picking up the Cauldron with both hands, she lifted it above her head, hearing cheers from the people surrounding them. Raising it to her chest, she looked at Kai as the Cauldron disappeared in a flash of light.

"The four Essences are now reunited and balance shall once again prevail," King Nixsa said gravely.

"That reminds me, is there somewhere we can talk privately, King Nixsa?" Marella asked him. "As in all of us here, but where ears can't listen in without being noticed?"

Nixsa nodded, "Yes, of course. Come with me and we shall retire to our home." He addressed the crowd and told them the Chosen were now going to have a short rest before rejoining them later. He led them away from the lake, hearing the jubilation behind them fade away the closer they were to his home.

* * *

He opened the door of a standard looking house which blended in with the rest of the surrounding homes. As they walked in, they saw it was the same layout as the house they had stayed in last night but on a larger scale.

"Please take a seat," said Aneira as she moved towards the kitchen. "I'll make us all a drink of chamomile; I think we need it after the excitement of this morning."

They sat down, Kai sitting next to Marella, with Daren and Lani perched on chairs next to them. The Partners had all made their way into the private garden at the back of the house, and Marella could see them through the window, soaking up the sun.

She waited for Aneira to return before she started to speak. "Nixsa, Lady Erwyna told me things are happening here you aren't aware of, but you need to be. She gave me three names and told me to tell you to get these people to help find the cause of the trouble."

Nixsa looked troubled but accepted what she said. "What names were they?" he asked.

"Dylan, Hafgan, and Morwenna," Marella answered.

Aneira nodded her head, "They are solid Undines, Nixsa. They will help. Everyone speaks in front of Morwenna because they forget she is there. She knows a lot more than people give her credit for."

She explained to the Chosen that Morwenna was an older lady who had unfortunately lost her hearing due to an infection. "She sits down by the fountain in the main square most of the time and she's become such a part of the feature people will talk about anything in front of her. She can read the barest movement of lips though and will be able to find out just who is saying what."

Marella nodded at Aneira's wisdom. "It sounds like these are people who can help. We can leave this in your capable hands then," she said. "Regrettably, I get the feeling we shouldn't tarry here any longer. It feels like we've spent the shortest amount of time here but also the longest."

Nixsa nodded his head sadly, "I thought you might say that and I completely understand. It is true, time isn't being kind to you whilst you are in the Quarters. Spend the rest of today here and we will take you back to the Portal for when it reappears this evening," he promised them.

"That sounds good to me," yawned Marella. "I feel so tired all of a sudden. I could do with a nap, I think, or I won't have the energy to walk anywhere when we get back to Wraidd Elfennol." She finished her chamomile tea and returned her mug to the table. "Thank you Aneira for your hospitality."

"You are most welcome, my dear," replied Aneira. "Go and get some rest, you have shadows beneath your eyes."

Aneira showed them out, leaving Nixsa sat with his finger steepled together, deep in thought. "He will be okay," she reassured them. "We'll get this sorted, never you fear."

They made their way back to their house, with Kai holding Marella up for the last part. They stumbled through the door and Kai managed to get her upstairs and on top of the covers before she fell asleep. He smiled down at her as she relaxed, curled up like a youngling. He pulled off her ballet pumps and placed them neatly on the floor by the bed. With a final look at Marella, he gently closed the door and went back downstairs.

"Is Nixie asleep too?" whispered Lani.

"I don't know, he's not here," answered Kai. "I think he's still in Nixsa's garden."

"Yes, they all are," said Daren smiling. "Apparently they've all earnt an afternoon lazing in the sun, so that's what they intend to do according to Ula."

Daren and Lani sat on the couch and Kai took one of the deep-wing chairs for himself. They sat back and enjoyed the tranquillity. Kai started to feel sleepy himself and he could see Lani's eyes were drooping. Daren started to snore from where he was sat, his arms folded across his chest. Kai gave a mental shrug and relaxed, feeling sleep claim him as it had the others.

~ 62 ~

Marella woke up and stretched out her body. She felt so much better than before. She lay still and reached out to Nixie, but he wasn't speaking. She knew he was warm and comfortable so she let him be. She listened for sounds around the house but could hear nothing. Her curiosity rising, she rose out of bed, freshened up in the bathroom and made her way downstairs.

As she stood in the doorway, she smiled at the sight she saw. Daren and Lani were curled up together on the couch and Kai was sat in one of the chairs, his head resting on the top.

She walked past them into the kitchen area where she filled up the kettle from the pump and put it on to boil. She picked up some mugs and the peppermint tea. While she waited for the kettle, she stared out of the kitchen window into the courtyard beyond. Two arms snaked around her waist and pulled her back against a hard body. She nestled into the warmth of Kai and rested her head back against his shoulder.

"Do you feel better now?" he asked quietly so as not to disturb Daren and Lani.

"I do, much better. Do you?" she asked, twisting around in his arms so she could face him.

"Yes, I didn't realise how tired I was," he said, smiling at her.

The water began to boil, so she returned her attention to it, lifting the kettle off the oven top and pouring the hot water into the cups. As soon as the water hit the tea bags, Kai sniffed the air.

"Peppermint?" he asked. At Marella's nod, he eagerly lifted a cup to his mouth and took a sip.

"Be careful, you'll burn yourself," she warned, laughing at him.

"Peppermint is just what I need to wake up," he said, blowing across the top of his mug. "I don't like taking naps during the day, they make me feel groggy. This is what I need to wake myself up. Thanks love."

"Will you carry mine please, whilst I take in Daren and Lani's?" she asked, picking up two mugs from the side. Kai grinned and picked up a second mug, walking through to the living area behind her.

"Wakey wakey, sleep heads," she called, wanting to wake them up but not wanting to scare them.

Daren and Lani both stirred, Lani moving out of Daren's arms when she realised where she was, a blush colouring her cheeks. She reached for the tea without looking at Marella.

"Um, thanks Marella," she mumbled, taking a sip and trying to create some distance between herself and Daren without it being obvious.

"My pleasure," Marella grinned. "Did you sleep well?"

Kai nudged Marella and whispered, "Stop teasing."

"Spoilsport," she whispered back.

"Not at all, tease Daren if you wish, but Lani is a bit more self-conscious about this so be gentle."

Marella looked at Lani and realised Kai was right. It wasn't just shyness written on Lani's face. She was very uncomfortable with being found in Daren's arms. Taking pity on her, she said "Lani, I'm going to make some sandwiches for us all – what would you like?"

Lani placed her cup of the table and jumped to her feet. "I'll help you," she said before scurrying off to the kitchen.

Kai winked at Marella as she walked passed him and returned to the kitchen. He could hear a low murmuring coming from the two of them and hoped Marella would soon put Lani at ease.

Daren still lay on the couch, one arm thrown carelessly over his eyes. "Feeling okay there, Daren?" Kai asked.

"Shut it, you," Daren grumbled before lifting his arm off his face and laughing at Kai.

"Want to talk about it?" Kai laughed.

"Who are you? Marella in disguise? No, I don't want to talk about it!" Daren exclaimed, pushing himself upright and reaching for his tea.

"Don't worry about it," Kai said, "You were both tired and you got comfy whilst asleep. It happens. Nothing else did, because I was here."

"Yeah, some guard dog you were." Daren grunted as he took a sip of the hot drink. "I didn't 'get comfy whilst asleep' as you put it. I pulled Lani to me. She seemed uncomfortable as she sat there so I was trying to help. Now she can't get away from me quick enough."

"Ahh, now I see," said Kai thoughtfully. "I didn't realise you felt that way."

"No one did," Daren still grumbled. "And now you do, and Marella knows, and it will get complicated which is what I didn't want."

"No worries," soothed Kai. "I'll talk to Marella, she'll understand and keep quiet, no teasing. You and Lani can sort it out between you, no interference, I promise."

"Thanks, Kai, I appreciate that." Daren carried on sipping his drink before he changed the subject. "I can't believe we all went to sleep like that. Marella yes, I'm mean; she did the whole freaky floating in a big bubble thing this morning. I don't know why we all dropped off though. I felt fine until we came back here."

"That's true and something I hadn't thought of," Kai rubbed his chin. "I think we should speak with Nixsa about this. Come on, you can come with me, it was your realisation."

* * *

They told Marella and Lani where they were going and left the house. As they walked along, Kai looked around curiously. "What do you see, Daren?" he asked.

Daren looked around and saw nothing out of the ordinary. "Houses, the street, water features, what should I be seeing?"

"What day is it? What happened this morning?" Kai prompted.

"It's Beltane and we know what happened." Daren stopped and looked up and down the street. "It's Beltane which is a major festival. Marella remade the Essence of Water this morning. There should be celebrations going on, people moving about. Where is everyone? What's going on?"

"I don't know, but I don't think it's good," said Kai. "Come on, let's find Nixsa."

With determination in every step, Daren and Kai strode forward to Nixsa's house. When they arrived, it too seemed deserted, just like every other home they looked at. Kai started to bang on the door, shouting for Nixsa to come and open it.

Finally, Nixsa threw open the door and demanded to know what they were doing. "You've just woken up Aneira. Have some consideration, Kai, Daren. What could be so serious?" He spoke abruptly, displeasure oozing from every pore.

"My apologies, your Majesty," said Kai, making it obvious with his use of Nixsa's title they were here officially. "We were just concerned as we have all just woken up from a sleep none of us intended to have. We thought Marella was tired from her work this morning, but we all slept too."

A look of concern spread across Nixsa's face and he looked up and down the street before gesturing for them to enter. They walked inside and Aneira entered the kitchen to make herself a drink of tea to help wake her up. Nixsa waved his hand at them to sit down. "Now, talk to me. Tell me what you're thinking."

"To start with, we didn't think of anything. We just assumed that we were all tired from the past year and that was it. But then Daren made a comment that he didn't know why he went to sleep and it made me think. I've tried to contact Kenna, but all I can get from her is she is comfortable and cosy."

"Kenna is fine," soothed Nixsa, "they're all here in the garden."

"Be that as it may," said Kai, "we should still be able to wake them. On the way here, we passed no one in the streets. There are no celebrations, nothing. Everywhere is as still as the grave. Now you can't tell me that is normal for Beltane, let alone one with a special event like what happened this morning."

"No, that's not normal," Nixsa looked very worried by now. Aneira had walked through during their explanation and rested her hand on his shoulder, a troubled expression upon her face.

"Has Marella or Lani noticed anything?" she asked.

"Not that I know of," replied Kai. "The minute Daren and I thought of it, we came straight here."

"Come on, I think we need to go out," said Nixsa. Aneira nodded her agreement and they quickly put on some shoes and left the home.

"We'll go down to the lake," said Nixsa as he walked along. "If there's a party going on, it will be there, especially after this morning."

They walked until they were back at the lake but instead a party, silence greeted them. Everyone was asleep, some were lucky enough to have a blanket over them but some appeared to have gone to sleep where they fell.

"This is not right," Nixsa said to himself. "So wrong, so wrong."

"We need Marella," said Kai. "I'm going back to get her, you wait here," and off he ran, leaving Daren, Nixsa, and Aneria talking amongst themselves.

* * *

He was only halfway back to the house when he saw Marella and Lani hurrying towards them. "I'm glad you're here," he puffed, getting his breath back. "I think we need the Chosen."

Marella nodded curtly and carried on towards the lake as Lani walked slightly slower with Kai. "This is really strange, Kai. No one is awake," said Lani.

"I know, we'll sort it out," he said, trying to comfort her.

"Why is everyone asleep? Why did we go to sleep? What time is it?" The questions poured forth from Lani, and Kai had no answers to give her. Together they hurried after Marella, who was now speaking animatedly with King Nixsa and Aneira, as Daren ran past them in the direction they had just come from.

Marella turned to them as they approached. "No one is awake yet apart from us. This whole situation is off, everyone's asleep and none of the Partners are answering. We need to contact Erwyna. I don't think a simple Weave will do it, so I'm going to try something I've only read about. It's an old ritual used to call the Lords and Ladies whether they wanted to be called or not. I'm hoping this way we can break through whatever it is keeping everyone asleep."

"That sounds like a good idea," agreed Kai. "Is there anything I can do to help?"

"Not right now," Marella said. "Daren is going to collect my staff and chalice, but more than that, nothing physical. I will need you once I start Weaving though, so if you need a drink or anything, I'd do it now."

Kai grinned at her before walking away to sort out whatever it was. Lani stayed with Marella, nerves stretched with tension.

"I really don't like this, Marella," Lani said. "I can't speak with Shaw, no one is around, it feels surreal. I don't think this is a good thing."

Marella smiled at Lani, "I don't think so either Lani, but now is not the time to be panicking. We need to speak with Erwyna to try and find out what has happened." Marella looked around; trying to find something she could ask Lani to do to distract her from her worries.

"I know," Marella clicked her fingers. "I'm going to be Weaving differently than normal, and once I start, none of you will be able to move. Could you go and get us some water to drink please? I don't know how long I'll be under and you might get thirsty."

Lani agreed and scurried away towards Nixsa so she could ask him where she could get a jug and some cups.

It didn't take long before everyone was back and they cleared a space beneath one of the willow trees. Marella asked Kai to draw a large circle in the dirt. Daren put down a blanket he had also grabbed from the house, and Lani placed a jug of cold water and the cups down to one side.

Marella then explained what she was going to do. "I'm going to do a circle of protection around us, which is why I've said you won't be able to leave the circle before I'm finished. You are the Chosen of the Elements, so I want you to sit in your honorary positions within the circle, as representatives of each Quarter."

She looked at Nixsa and Aneira. "I would like you two to join us, if you don't mind?" she queried.

"What do we need to do," said Aneira without hesitation. "Tell us and we'll do it."

"I don't actually need you to do anything that I know of" Marella said. "It's more for what you represent. As King and Queen of Teimladau, you balance out Water. I am there as the conduit to Erwyna, so your help will be invaluable."

"Right then, is everyone ready? Remember, once I cast the circle, you can't leave until I say so," Marella warned.

"We understand," murmured Daren and the others.

Marella stood in the centre of the blanket with her staff in her hand and a chalice full of lake water by her feet. She took a moment to compose herself before starting the ritual which hadn't been performed in Wraidd Elfennol in over two generations.

"Element of Earth, Guardian of the North, I call upon thee to be present during this ritual. Please join me now." Marella nodded to Daren who joined her on the blanket. He sank down to the ground and made himself comfortable.

"Element of Air, Guardian of the East, I call upon thee to be present during this ritual. Please join me now." Lani walked with poise to the blanket and sat down, showing no sign of the previous nerves.

"Element of Fire, Guardian of the South, I call upon thee to be present during this ritual. Please join me now." Kai joined them, his face solemn and yet proud as he took his place.

"Elements of Water, Guardians of the West, I call upon thee to be present during this ritual. Please join me now." Nixsa and Aneira joined everyone on the blanket and sat down; waiting with anticipation to see what Marella would do next.

Holding her staff out so it was above the heads of those sat down, Marella turned deosil three times, saying "I ask that the God and Goddess bless this circle so we may be free and protected within this space," as she did so.

Everyone watched with amazement as a silver dome rose up from the ground and enclosed above their heads. They could see translucent silver swirls moving before them. Marella muttered "As above, so below," as she stopped turning and held her staff down by her side.

Marella gracefully sat down, laying her staff by her side. She nodded to everyone in the circle. "I'm going to Weave now and I don't know how long I will be. Help yourselves to drinks whilst I'm gone but please, whatever you do, don't leave the circle."

The others watched in silence as she held both hands either side of her silver chalice. The water started to swirl although none had seen her touch it. Without a further word being spoken, Marella's body slumped.

"That's her gone," confirmed Kai who had watched her often enough, he knew even better than Daren did. "Lani, please would you pass around the drinks? I don't really want to move from my position here although Marella only said not to leave the circle."

Lani reached over and grabbed the jug and cups, pouring water into them all and handing them around.

"So now we wait?" asked Nixsa.

"Now we wait," agreed Kai, keeping his eyes on Marella.

Marella sank swiftly below the surface and entered her Weave. Her very soul protested against the death and destruction she saw. Reluctantly, she turned her back on that Weave and closed her eyes. She sent a call out to Erwyna, a plea from Her Chosen.

"Marella, I'm so glad you've made it," she heard Erwyna say, relief prevalent in her voice.

Marella opened her eyes and saw for the third time, she was in Erwyna's rooms. She ran over to her and Erwyna enveloped her in a hug, holding tightly. "What is going on? We all fell asleep and now we can't wake anyone up. There's only the four of us plus Nixsa and Aneira. Even Nixie and the other Partners are sleeping. None of us can rouse them."

Erwyna led her over to the couch Marella was familiar with and sat her down, reaching for a glass of water which she handed to Marella. "Drink this whilst I explain what I know," she said.

Marella obediently took a sip before waiting for Erwyna to start.

"Okay, so I'll start with the obvious," said Erwyna gathering her thoughts. "What you thought was simple tiredness from the swimming and the Cauldron, was in fact, an attack against not just the Chosen, but all of Teimladau and Wraidd Elfennol."

Marella gaped at her, the glass forgotten in her hand. "Drink, Marella, you will need your strength," Erywna encouraged. "So, those who were happy to embrace the change of one Element being more important than the others, were free to go and they left through the Portal the very afternoon you fell asleep. The ones who remain in Teimladau are the ones loyal to King Nixsa and Aneira."

"Hold on, you said 'the very afternoon' – what day is it now? I thought it was the same day?" asked Marella, worried and unsure if she even wanted to hear the reply.

Erwyna closed her eyes briefly before looking at Marella with sadness etched into her face. "Marella, today is the Summer Solstice." She waited for that to sink in, for Marella to understand that over a month had disappeared.

Marella put her glass down and paced around the room, shaking her head. "No, no, no, that can't be right. I just went to sleep this afternoon. We still have to get back to Charon." She stopped and looked at Erwyna, feeling like a small youngling once more. "We brought the Essences back," she cried. "This isn't fair."

Erwyna strode over to her and grabbed her shoulders, giving her a small shake. "No, Marella, it isn't fair. You did get the Essences, you did your part. However, no one ever said that everything is fair. The person behind this is stronger than we ever anticipated and is receiving help from a source we dare not think of yet."

Marella looked bemused at Erwyna who sighed and tried to explain. "Listen to me; you know that we, the Lords and Ladies, are the so-called rulers of the Elements, right?" At Marella's nod, Erwyna continued.

"You also know we celebrate eight festivals throughout the turning of the wheel in honour of the God and Goddess, right?" Marella nodded once more.

"Everything and everyone has balance. We are all made from the God and Goddess, male and female, emotions and intellect, light and dark. It's all about balance. Now we fear that something within the dark is rising, drawing power from the light and tipping the balance in their favour." Erwyna dropped her hands from Marella's shoulders and walked a small distance away, her arms hugging herself around the waist.

"Everyone from every Quarter who is against us, has gathered at the Portal to Teimladau." Erwyna's voice dripped with sorrow. "Everything from rogue Elementals to goblins, sylphs, and salamanders. It was the contingent from the Undines who told them where to go."

Marella gasped as she realised the extent of what Erwyna was telling her. "So it's everyone against us, then?" she asked. "Is no one able to help us?"

"You will have those from Teimladau, the Scions, and us. From the moment I lost contact with you, we have all been trying to re-establish some connection with any of you. We informed Charon of what had befallen you, or what we thought had befallen you, and it was through their responses we found out who it was working against you all this time. Since then, we haven't been able to contact anyone there either."

Marella looked at her, needing and yet dreading the answer she was about to hear. "Who was it, Erwyna? Please tell me now; I'm going to find out very soon anyway."

Erwyna looked at her, judging whether to tell her or not, before she sighed and said "It is Elder Demi who has worked against you from the beginning. She has been sending representatives to each Quarter before you, trying to turn the tide and stop you getting the assistance she thought you might receive."

Marella stood still, her expression blank as she tried to process what she'd been told. "Demi?" she murmured, her tone questioning as she looked at Erwyna for confirmation.

"Demi," said Erwyna firmly.

"By the Waters, how is Daren going to cope with this. She's been almost a member of his family for years." Marella paced once more as she tried to think of how she could break it to Daren without hurting him too much. She stopped abruptly and faced Erwyna. "Is it wrong of me that I'm glad it's not Riva?" she asked.

A small smile graced Erwyna's face. "I wondered if you suspected her, and no, it's not wrong. It's a completely human thing to do. What you need to do next though, is inform Daren straight away. Don't try to keep this from him, or postpone it until a better time, there is no better time.

Speaking of which, it is time for you to go back. Don't worry, as far as the others are concerned, you've only been under for a couple of minutes. It was a good idea to bring Nixsa and Aneira in the circle with you, that really helped me break through."

"What do you want me to do?" Marella asked, feeling out of her depth with the knowledge she now had.

"Tell the others everything, the Portal, Demi, everything. They need to know. Nixsa will know what to do with his Undines. Now that you've broken through, everyone else should start shaking off the influence of sleep and wake up. Arrange for them all to have a drink from the lake before you head to the Portal. We will see you back in Wraidd Elfennol." Erwyna gave Marella a quick squeeze, "Go now," she said, "close your eyes and return to the others."

Casting one last look at her Lady, Marella closed her eyes. Within seconds, she felt herself back with the others. As she opened her eyes, she looked around to see them watching her. Lani had a cup held up to her lips, as though she had just been about to take a drink.

"Marella, did you get through?" asked Kai, his voice low.

Marella rolled her head to the sides, just to give herself a moment before she had to tell them what she knew. "I spoke with Lady Erwyna. I know what's been going on and I know why. Let me break the circle and I'll tell you all everything I know."

Standing up and holding her staff once more, Marella turned three time in a widdershins direction. "As above, so below, the circle is open, yet unbroken. Go with blessings."

Everyone gave a shiver as the energy dispersed, raising the hairs on Kai's arms which he absentmindedly patted down as he watched Marella.

"Shall I go and make a hot drink?" asked Aneira, getting ready to leave her place on the blanket.

"Please don't, not yet," said Marella. She looked around at the group in front of her. "I have news to share that I would prefer only saying once."

Everyone remained seated and waited expectantly for Marella to continue. Taking a deep breath, she filled them in on what she had found out from Erwyna. After she had finished, she remained silent, gauging their reactions.

Daren closed his eyes and dropped his head into his hands. Lani reached over and put a gentle hand upon his back. He groaned at the contact and looked up at the others, his expression full of anguish. "I can't believe Demi is the one behind all of this. How long has she felt this way? And why did no one pick up on it? Not even the other elders? Is Erwyna sure?"

Marella nodded, her heart hurting for him. "Yes, she was sure. I don't know how it was hidden, but it was."

"And everyone who is against us, is knocking on my front door," stated Nixsa grimly.

Marella nodded again. "Yes, that's also true." She looked at them and wondered just how they could turn this around. They would be no good at all in the state they were in. "Everyone who was asleep will now be waking up, if they're not already awake. We need to make sure they all drink from the lake before we head to the Portal. Erwyna was insistent upon that."

Aneira stood up and dusted down her backside. "Well then, let's start. Nothing will happen if we just sit here. There's work to be done. I'll not have a bunch of ingrates telling me how I should behave to other Elements. If it's a fight they want, it's a fight they will have."

She looked at them, her expression fierce and determined. Nixsa raised himself to stand by his Queen and gazed upon her lovingly. "My fiery Water Queen, you know I'll fight by your side."

Nixsa looked at the others. "Let's go back. We've done all we can here for now. We need to get organised with those we still have. We will pass by the lake before we go, never fear."

They gathered up their belongings and trudged back to their houses, feeling the weight of worry upon their shoulders.

* * *

The companions arrived at the house and started to look around. "It's pointless packing anything," said Marella. "Time has run out. I'm sure Nixsa will return any of our belongings afterwards."

No one said anything at the implication they would survive the coming battle.

"What are you going to take with you, Marella?" asked Lani, her voice trembling.

"Just my staff, I don't have any other weapon like you three." She looked down at her worn leather trousers, her shirt that had seen better days, and the thin-soled boots she wore. "This will do, I'm certainly not heading into a battle wearing my formal gown," she said with a grin.

The others looked down at the clothes they wore and grinned. "You may have a point there, Marella," laughed Kai.

The sound of running footsteps halted the conversation. As one, they looked to the front door which they had left ajar. In bounded Ula, nearly knocking Daren over with her enthusiasm, with the other Partners on her heels.

"I'm so sorry, Daren. I didn't mean to fall asleep. It was just so warm and comfortable." Ula's words were very fast and Daren struggled to understand. He wrapped his arms around her and held her until he could feel her rapid heartbeat slowing down. Looking around, he saw the others were also consoling their Partners who all seemed to be carrying a burden of guilt.

"Listen to me, all of you. This wasn't something caused by any failing of you. This is something that was done to everyone. Let me link with you and you will be up-to-date with what has happened." Marella looked around at the Partners, not moving until she had eye contact with all of them.

She closed her eyes and connected with all four of them, showing them her memories of what had occurred. She felt the shock and anger flowing through the bond and knew that the stakes had just been raised. She looked back at the others and smiled. "They're up to speed now."

A soft tapping could be heard from the front door which was still open. Marella turned around and saw Nixsa standing there. "Come on in, Nixsa. You don't have to knock on your own front door."

"This isn't my front door, it's yours." He winked at Marella and said "this house is yours now, a gift from Aneira and I, to you. We hope you'll be able to come back and visit us once this mess is over. Without worrying about falling into a forced sleep, that is."

Marella grinned at him, surprised at his gift, but pleased as well. "I'd be honoured to come back here," she said. "It's wonderful, thank you so much."

"Well, with everything that's going to happen, I would prefer it if you looked forward to something, rather than being all gloom and doom," he said, looking around at them all. "Are your Partners still feeling guilty?"

"I don't think so, not anymore. They know what's happened and what is coming. They're more angry than anything else now," answered Marella.

Nixsa crouched down and faced Nixie. "You come back to me, you hear me? Don't be all bloody heroic and do something stupid." He stood up and looked at them, seeing the surprise on Marella's face. Nixsa shrugged his shoulders. "He's my brother," he said as though that explained everything, which in a strange way, it did.

"I've brought you all a gift as well," Nixsa continued, looking at Daren, Kai, and Lani. "I didn't think you would have come prepared for a fight; so I've had a hunt around and found these, which I think will fit you."

He handed them each a stiff, hardened leather jerkin to try on. Daren and Kai found theirs fit perfectly, whereas Lani and Marella's hung down to their knees. "Oh well, we have extra protection," Marella winked at Kai, liking how he looked in his.

"We're all about ready to go, if you are," said Nixsa. The others sobered up at the thought of the coming battle. Kai and Daren picked up their swords and scabbards, fitting them around their waists. Lani holstered her bow and checked her quiver of bolts.

They looked at each other and then at Nixsa. "Let's go," said Daren.

As the last one out of the door, Marella closed it behind her, her fingers trailing on the wood as she wondered if she would return to it again. Shaking herself to get rid of the maudlin thoughts, she scurried after the others as they walked down the street, holding her staff firmly in her hand.

Nixsa led them back to the lake where Aneira had drafted in some helpers to make sure everyone had a drink of the cool water before they headed to the Portal. The Chosen joined the line behind other Undines, who were similarly attired.

Not a word was spoken as they lifted their cups in unison, raising a silent toast to each other. The Partners joined in too, only drinking from their bowls when the others did.

Suddenly, Lani caught her breath. She looked at the others with excitement on her face. "I'll be right back," she said before dashing back the way they had come.

The others looked at each other before looking at Shaw. He just remained unflappable, perched on Ula's back and waited for Lani to return. Within moments she had returned, clutching a bag in her hand. She stopped, bending over at the waist as she puffed and panted, trying to get her breath back. The others patiently waited for her to recover so she could tell them what she was so excited about.

Once she was recovered enough, she stood up, her eyes shining, and opened the pouch. Without saying a word, she emptied the bag into her hand. Out rolled a small hazelnut and an acorn. With a quick intake of breath, Marella stared at the objects in Lani's hand. Feeling excitement build in herself, she watched as Lani crouched down to the ground and covered the acorn and the hazelnut with earth.

"Alana, Carrick, I call upon you now," she said. "I hope you can hear me, and are able to come to our aid. We will be at the Water Portal if you can." Lani patted down the earth covering the seeds of hope, and stood up, dusting her hands together. "Now we can go," she said firmly.

With one last look at the dark patch of earth that had so recently been turned, the eight Chosen walked away.

Nixsa stood by the Portal, refusing to let anyone through until he knew it was as safe as it could be on the other side. "I'll not let you go through and be slaughtered like cattle," he argued with Daren, who was insisting they be let through.

"They don't know we know they're there," Daren argued. "They're expecting the Chosen, us," he gestured wildly, "to walk through. If we go, we can see what's facing us. Nixie can speak with you, can't he? He is your brother. So then you will know what's happening as well. It's a win-win situation. We can't cower behind the Portal any longer."

Fury filled Nixsa's face. "How dare you call me a coward? It is my Undines that are here to help you!"

Marella stepped between them and placed her hands on them, drawing their attention to her rather than each other.

"Emotions are running high; it's no good taking it out on each other. Nixsa, Daren is right. We do have to go through. How you follow is up to you. You can wait for Nixie to give you the lay of the land, or you can come with us. It's your call. They're your Undines, like you say."

Nixsa took a breath, calming himself. "You're right, I apologise Daren. I'm not thinking straight."

Daren shook it off and clapped Nixsa on the back. "So what are you going to do?"

"The sensible thing and let you go through, with only yourselves and your Partners to keep you safe." Nixsa spoke as though he had swallowed something very unpleasant. He disliked the idea, but couldn't think of anything better that would protect the majority.

Daren smiled grimly and nodded at Nixsa, who looked away. Marella gave his arm a reassuring squeeze. "It's the right thing to do," she said as Daren walked back to the others. "You're their King, you need to put them first."

"I know, it doesn't mean I have to like it though," said Nixsa, before he dragged her into a hug.

With the Undines milling behind them, the Chosen were anxious to get through the Portal. Even now, knowing they had failed in their quest, they still couldn't bear the thought of just running and hiding. They looked at Nixsa, Aneira, and the Undines and saw strength and courage reflected back at them. With a look at each other, the eight Chosen stepped through the Portal together to meet a battle they had never wanted.

~ 64 ~

They crossed through the Portal and returned to the land of Wraidd Elfennol. They could feel the warmth of Mehefin on their faces as they traversed the boulder stepping stones.

Looking around, they couldn't see any sign of the army that was supposedly waiting for them and looked at each other in surprise. Daren held out his hand for Lani to take as she made the last jump onto solid ground. The Partners all leapt after them and shook themselves down.

The meadow looked very different to when they had passed through on their way to the Portal. The spring flowers had made way to those of the summer, including St. John's Wort making a proud display of its vivid yellow petals and green, oblong leaves.

A moment of uncertainty prevailed as they didn't know what to do. Things were very different from what they had expected. As they stood there, wondering what to do, a voice called out to them from the cover of the trees.

"You thought you were oh so clever, didn't you, *Chosen*," spat a familiar voice. "Ooh, look at me, I'm going on a quest because I'm so wonderful," the voice mocked.

Marella saw a look of hurt flash across Daren's face before it hardened with determination. "Why don't you come out from behind the trees, Demi? We know it's you," Daren called, raising his voice.

Marella shared a glance with Nixie and she knew he was passing on what was happening to Nixsa and Aneira.

Demi made her way to where the Chosen could see her. She was surrounded by Gnomes and Salamanders. There were even some Elementals there, similar to the one Daren had already fought. His eyes focused on them for a moment before returning to Demi.

"Why, Demi? I thought you believed in the balance of the Elements. One cannot exist without the other."

"Oh, I'm so sick of hearing that pretentious crap," Demi snarled, her face twisting with rage. "Why should I have to rely upon anything else apart from me? You just get let down by other Elements. The Earth provides food, everyone would starve if it wasn't for the Earth. Why didn't you just let her go?" she asked, pointing to Marella. "This would all be over now, with Earth ruling the Elements, if it wasn't for her."

"What do you mean, Demi?" asked Daren. "You know that isn't true," Daren said, striving to remain calm as more people joined Demi from behind the trees. "Crops cannot grow without water, air and fire. It takes all four to feed people, not just one."

"Rubbish," scoffed Demi. "That's just what you've been told and you blindly believe in it. Well, I'm telling you it's different. I won't let the Elements be balanced again. It's worked just fine for the past year without you, without balance. If you had left her before you reached the Air Portal, none of you would have been hurt." A hint of madness appeared in her voice and Daren felt his heart fill with sadness at the knowledge she was lost to him.

"It was you that attacked Marella! But how, why? You've known her since she was a child. Why would you do that? You call earthquakes and firestorms working just fine?" questioned Daren, his voice incredulous. "People you know were hurt in those storms, don't you care?" he asked, trying one last time to get through to her.

"It's just a shaking down period. It will soon settle, then everything will be fine. People get hurt every day, they'll recover." Her words were a callous as the look on her face.

"I can't let you do this, Demi. I'm so sorry, but this is wrong. This is not how I was raised; it's not what I believe in. I'm sure there are plenty of others who agree with me." Daren pulled his sword out of his scabbard and held it ready in his hand.

Demi laughed, a cold, mocking sound that sent shivers up Marella's spine. This wasn't the same woman she had seen from afar in Bridd. "Am I supposed to be scared now, Chosen of Earth?" Demi mocked. "The four of you against all of us? It will be a slaughter and I'm not talking about us."

"Four of us?" said Daren, "I think you need to recount. There are eight of us here, Demi. Or do you discount the Partners so lightly? Where is Eade? I would have thought he'd be by your side and I don't see a Red Angus bull anywhere."

A flicker crossed Demi's face at the mention of Eade. "Yes, well, it would have been a bit far for him to come so I left him at Bridd, where he'll be safe."

"Safe?" questioned Daren, "But you just said it would be a slaughter for us. Surely Eade would be safe on the winning side?" He tapped his sword against his leg. "Perhaps it's more like Eade doesn't want to be associated with you as he knows you are in the wrong."

"Don't you dare question the loyalty of my Partner," Demi screeched, her control unravelling by the second. She looked sideways at some of the Goblins standing nearby. "I've had enough talking now, Daren. It's been nice knowing you, but you're standing in my way." She dismissively turned her back on Daren, gesturing for the rest of them to move forward and attack the Chosen.

"Leaving so soon, Demi?" Daren shouted as he crouched down into a fighting stance with Ula moving to protect his left hand side. She ignored him as she continued to walk towards the back of the crowd now surging forward towards the Chosen.

Kai gave Marella a quick, hard kiss before he moved away to give himself room to swing his sword without hurting anyone other than who he was fighting with. Kenna moved to his side, giving his hand a quick lick as she did.

Lani removed her bow and calmly started to load it as Shaw took wing and flew high into the sky.

Marella and Nixie shared a loving glance before Marella raised her staff and held it in both hands.

* * *

With a roar, the opposing horde of people attacked the Chosen. Those that were in the front attacked with vigour, striking at Daren and Kai, and soon their swords were covered in blood.

Marella and Lani fought off their attackers back to back. Nixie and Shaw were attacking any that came too close and Shaw's battle screech could be heard over the clearing where they fought.

Within seconds of the fighting starting, Nixie spoke to Marella, *"Keep going, Marella, Nixsa is on his way."*

"Nixsa is almost here," she gasped to Lani as she hit an opponent in the stomach with the end of her staff, before lifting it up with a quick strike under his chin. He dropped to the floor like dead weight and someone else took his place.

The fighting eased momentarily as the sound of arrows flying through the air took everyone by surprise. Suddenly the clearing was filled with the sounds of suffering, as the enemy were pierced by the archers accompanying Nixsa.

A row of twelve archers stood tall and proud, as they fired off arrow after arrow at the enemy in front of them. "Go," said Marella breathlessly. "Go and be with the archers, you'll be safer with them and see the targets easier."

With a quick nod, Lani ran off and took her place at the edge of the line up before the archers rearranged themselves so Lani was in the middle. Marella watched from the corner of her eye to make sure she was as safe as she could be.

Sweat dripped down her face and her ears rang with the deafening cacophony of men shouting, animals screaming, and the striking noise of steel on steel. Marella couldn't distinguish now between friend and foe as all around her seemed to blur into a whirlwind of chaos and colour.

She blindly continued to fight anything that came before her until a hand grasped her wrist, preventing a paralysing blow to the side of the neck of her opponent. Struggling to break free, she focused on who she was fighting, her relief flooding her body as she recognised Carrick.

She threw her arms around him, "You came," she cried. Carrick grunted as he sliced the stomach of a Gnome that had snuck up behind Marella. Setting her back on her feet, he grinned at her.

"I told you we would, now defend yourself, girlie. There's a fight to be won." Carrick stayed by her side, swinging his sword with dexterity, cutting into flesh and bone.

Marella's body ached from the knocks she had taken. Her sense of time was confused as she felt like hours had passed, when they had only been fighting for moments. She had lost track of both Kai and Kenna, and Daren and Ula. Although she could hear vicious growling and snarling coming from somewhere behind her, she dared not look to try and see.

However hard they fought, those opposing them seemed never-ending. Marella couldn't believe that this many were opposed to the idea of balance. Her body moved methodically as she fought to stay alive. The fight was evenly balanced now that the majority of the Gnomes and the Undines were fighting with them. Marella saw Salamanders and Sylphs change sides, and she realised not everyone believed what they had been told.

The air started to spin faster and Marella watched with amazement as a tornado appeared out of nowhere but only seemed to attack the enemy. Using a lull in the fighting to her advantage, she looked around, and smiled broadly as she saw Hynafol controlling the whirlwind from a position high on her right.

Elsewhere, Marella could see bursts of flame and could hear the screams of agony from those burning. A long tendril of water appeared out of the lake and whipped around a dozen or more Salamanders that were getting too close to the archers. With a flick, the Salamanders were thrown into the water, their screams turning to gurgles as their natural opposing element drowned them. Marella squinted until she was sure she could see the shape of a dragon's head and smiled. It must be Meredith, the Scion of Water, making her presence known.

"And how many other water dragons do you know," she heard Nixie say as he ripped and tore into the legs of the soldiers in front of him.

Marella snorted but began fighting again as the lull stopped and a fresh wave of people faced her. She heard Lani scream and from over on her far left, she saw a spot plummet from the sky. Her heart ached for Lani as she realised it was Shaw.

A rumbling noise started, way down deep in the ground, causing everyone to stumble and fall as their balance was affected. Momentarily, it appeared as though the fighting had stopped as everyone looked around, trying to find the cause of the noise.

With a sound like thunder, Cian joined in with the fight, clearing throwing his weight behind the Chosen. He swung his arms left and right, the bodies flying through the air, as he made his way to fight against the rogue Elementals.

Marella spared him a glance as she fought, her arms now felt like lead. He was taller than she had imagined with a thatch of deep brown hair. His skin was the colour of someone who spent a lot of time in the sun which made Marella laugh to herself, feeling the edge of hysteria.

"This needs to end, Marella. Link with the others and take Demi. Give her to us and we can make sure she doesn't cause you any more trouble."

Marella heard the voice of Erwyna and saw what she wanted her to do. "Carrick," she shouted, striving to be heard above the noise, "I need to link with the others, are you okay?"

With a jerk of his head, Carrick acknowledged her and continued to fight, clearing a path so she could run towards Lani. After knocking loose the hands that tried to grab at her as she ran, Marella was able to pull Lani after her as she drew closer to Kai and Daren.

From what she could see, Shaw was the only one injured, and Marella hoped that it wasn't too serious. Stopping near to the water's edge, Marella shouted to Nixsa that she needed Kai and Daren. He fought his way to their sides and helped them dispatch a couple of skilled Sylphs who had nearly succeeding in gutting Daren.

Kai and Daren made their way to Marella and Lani, striking out with their swords as they did so. "You pick your times," Daren huffed at her as he moved closer.

"Not. My. Idea," said Marella as she swung her staff downwards, clobbering a dark-haired Salamander on the head.

* * *

The four Chosen were soon surrounded by their friends who gave them time to act. Marella grabbed hold of Kai and Lani's hands, making sure they were on the correct side. Daren grabbed hold too and Marella swept them all away in a powerful link that surged through them, letting them know what was to be done. The Partners were also linked with them, by bond if not physically, lending their strength, love and loyalty.

The sounds of the battle fell silent as their minds blocked out the noise. Their focus changed from trying to see the battle as a whole, to trying to find a singular source of contention.

"Over there," spoke Daren calmly through their merge. The others looked, seeing Demi shouting orders from the safety of a nearby boulder.

"Lani, stop the fighting please," requested Marella.

Lani nodded and, concentrating, gave a blast of air that sliced through the opposing forces, stopping the fighting instantly.

As the opponents wondered what was happening, Daren began his part of the binding ritual. "We are the Chosen of Lady Daire – called to represent Earth, the senses and our ability to manifest our desires. To be the Earth is to be silent."

Lani said "We are the Chosen of Lord Adaryn – called to represent Air, our thoughts and our ability to have a sense of self. To be Air is to know." Her voice was strong and passed easily through the crowd who watching them, rather than keep trying to fight.

"We are the Chosen of Lord Ethon – called to represent Fire, our passion and ideas, giving us the ability to make decisions. Those that are Fire, have the will." Kai stood proud as he repeated the words he had said so long ago.

Marella completed the binding, feeling a sense of fate holding her tight. "We are the Chosen of the Lady Erwyna – called to represent Water and our emotions, giving us the ability to be moved by feelings. To be Water is to dare."

"We charge Elder Demi, of the Earth village Bridd, to have wilfully tried to sabotage the balance of the Elements, together with a mission given to us by the Lords and Ladies we answer to. She has caused strife and unrest, physical injury and emotional pain. We call upon the Lords and Ladies of Wraidd Elfennol to take Demi into their care, for her to be stripped of all powers and rights as Elder."

Daren took up his turn again. "We have travelled to the Earth, we were silent."

"We have flown through the Air, and we knew," said Lani.

"We were cleansed by Fire; we have the will," replied Kai.

"We were birthed from the Water, and we dare!" finished Marella, throwing emphasis on the last word, a challenge to all opposing the balance of the Elements.

A subsonic boom clapped through the meadow, dropping people to their knees. The Lords and Ladies appeared before Demi who was still clinging to her boulder.

Lady Daire stepped forward and gazed upon Demi with sorrow on her face. "Demi, you have heard the charges against you, what say you?"

Demi clambered to her feet and spat insolently on the floor. "I acknowledge no charges made by those upstarts. They will see the truth one day. They will see that the Elements are not meant to be in balance, but in opposition instead. I will be revered, a ground breaker."

Daire shook her head, "You are so wrong, child of mine. The Elements need the balance to survive. An abundance in any may cause a short term flourish in certain areas, but will wilt and die before too long."

Demi stood there, her shoulders back, defiance in every bone in her body.

"I find her guilty as charged," said Daire, stepping back in line with the others.

"I, too, find her guilty," said Adaryn, shaking his head sadly.

"Guilty," said Ethon, a stern look upon his face.

"I'm afraid I find her guilty as well," said Erwyna.

Daire stepped forward once more, "Demi, as your Lady, whether you still acknowledge me or not, it is my right to take you with me. You will stay with me until such time as I see fit. You will no longer be part of Wraidd Elfennol. You have caused enough damage."

With that, a flash of lightning lit the sky and people turned away, shielding their eyes. When they could see again, they saw the Lords and Ladies had disappeared, along with Demi.

~ 65 ~

The Scions stood by the Chosen as they looked around the once beautiful meadow. The vivid yellow flowers that had once stood so proudly were now soaked in scarlet blood, which dripped from their sagging leaves.

"Go home," said Marella to those left behind, bone weary to the very core of her being. "Go home and think on what you have done, what you have lost. None of us will walk away from today unscathed."

Slowly, people started to back away, slinking into the forest, disappearing from sight.

Kai sank to the ground, groaning as he did so. Kenna limped over to him and curled up in his lap, licking at the blood on her leg.

Nixsa carried Shaw over to Lani who was now able to inspect him for the injury that had caused him to fall from the sky. "It's a broken wing," she said to Marella, her grey-blue eyes full of anguish.

Marella crouched down and stroked Shaw carefully on his breast. "He will heal, Lani. The healers will take care of him, you'll see."

Daren still stood, staring at the boulder on which Demi had stood. Ula walked up beside him, her white fur now tinged with red. He looked down at her, *"Are you okay?"* he asked.

Ula stood next to him, *"Yes, Daren, I am fine. None of this is mine,"* she reassured him.

"So what happens now?" asked Kai, moaning as he moved his injured leg.

"I don't know," admitted Marella. "Did we fail or not? We retrieved the Essences, but we didn't make it back to Charon on time and we definitely won't now."

"I wouldn't concern yourselves any longer," came Ena's voice that they knew so well. "The quest has been completed; although not in the manner we expected. The Elements are once again in balance and will remain so, thanks to your hard work. The place of the Essences will remain secret but the monoliths will remain as a reminder of what should be. Instead of each stone having but one symbol on it, now they will hold all four, carved into the stone for all eternity."

"So what do we do now? Can we go home?" asked Lani.

Hynafol joined them and smiled kindly down at her. "Yes, Lani, you can go home. Your family will be pleased to see you."

"Why weren't any of them here?" asked Daren. "We've been doing this and yet there is no one here that I know from home, or from Ilyn where I've spent just as much time. Where are they?"

"Just as you were thrown out of time in Teimladau, so too have they," said a rough, gravelly voice.

Daren turned around to see Cian easing himself to the floor. Although he was still the size of a house, it made it a bit easier to see his face. "The day after Marella was successful in making the *Dagrau y Crochan* is the last that they can remember. By the time you return home though, they will be aware of exactly what has happened and what you had to do."

Daren bowed his head in acknowledgement, sinking his fingers into Ula's ruff.

"Lani, would you bring Shaw to the water for me, please," said a voice none of the Chosen recognised. Lani looked around but smiled when she saw Meredith's blue head sticking out of the water.

She gently picked him up, suppressing a grimace of her own as he gave a chirp of discomfort.

"Place him into the water," Meredith directed. Lani lowered him gently to water, holding him in her cupped hands as the waves washed over him. The mighty Scion of Water leaned over him and blew upon his feathers, ruffling them in the breeze she caused.

Shaw twitched and then jerked as he tried to stand up. Lani lifted him out of the water and cradled him against her body.

"Lani, it's fixed. My wing, it's healed," Shaw told her with delight. To prove his point, he flapped his wings out, gusting the wind around them before launching himself into the air, flying high and swooping low.

Tears poured down Lani's face as reaction set in. Seeing her beloved Shaw healed and in no pain allowed the emotions to run free that she had suppressed whilst fighting.

Marella hobbled over to her on a body now stiff with aches and pains. She gathered Lani in her arms and the two cried together, allowing their emotions to have free reign for the time being. Daren and Kai joined them, holding the two girls closely.

"Let's help clear away, shall we?" suggested Meredith to the other Scions. "I don't really want to leave all this here."

The other Scions looked around at the devastation that filled the meadow and nodded. With the four of them working in harmony with each other, there was soon a new hill in the middle of the meadow and not a body or speck of blood to be seen.

"Chosen of the Elements, it has been my honour to be with you once more, but I am needed back in Naear," Carrick said gruffly from nearby. "I have left Alana there, holding the fort, but I must return."

Marella broke free from the embrace and went over to him. She knelt before him and embraced him too. "Thank you so much for coming, Carrick. We couldn't have done it without you. I'm sure Alana is doing fine; please pass on our regards when you return."

"Alana is doing very well, but there's a reason I must return, you see." Carrick's weather-beaten face suddenly turned red as he shared his news with them. "She's having our baby any day soon, and I want to be there for her."

Carrick's hands were soon being pumped by both Daren and Kai as they loudly congratulated him and wished Alana well. Lani came over and embraced him once they had finished, turning his face red once more.

"Yes, well," he coughed, "as nice as that may be, it's time to go. You still have some seeds, in case you need me again?" he questioned.

"We do indeed," soothed Marella. "Now go, be off with you. Go and regale Alana with tales of how many you knocked unconscious." She winked at him and he smiled in return.

"It was good to see you all again. Please feel free to visit whenever you can." With that, Carrick turned and called to his contingent of Gnomes that it was time to return home. He led them to the forest's edge and clapped his hands five times. A Portal, similar in appearance to the one the Chosen had used, appeared between the trunks of two Alder trees.

With a last look around at them, followed by a jaunty wave, Carrick watched his Gnomes go through the Portal before stepping through himself.

"It is time for us to go too," said Nixsa as he approached them. "My people will heal better in the waters of home."

Marella looked at him and then down to where Nixie stood by her legs. "You know, people will never believe me when I tell them you're brothers," she laughed.

"Brothers we were and brothers we will always be," confirmed Nixsa, laughing with her. "Remember, that house is yours, so return as and when you can." He clasped Marella in a warm hug before saying his goodbyes to the other Chosen.

He walked slowly back to Aneira and his Undines, most of who now had makeshift, bloody, bandages wrapped around various parts of their bodies. He looked back at Nixie and smiled. "Don't be a stranger anymore, Nixie. We miss you."

Nixie darted passed Marella's legs and climbed up Nixsa's leg before he even had chance to realise it. He held onto Nixie, stroking the fur on his back. Nixie leaned up and, ever so gently, nipped at Nixsa's nose, making Aneira laugh with delight.

Nixsa, Aneira, and the rest of the Undines moved back through the Water Portal, until it shimmered away from sight.

"We must be going too," said Ena. "We still have things we must do to find out how deep this canker is. Our job is not finished, but it has been made a whole lot easier by you. So for that, I thank you." She spread her fiery wings and took flight, flying away.

"We will see you again," said Hynafol, raising himself to his full height and stretching out his wings. "I'm afraid to say that your trundle trucks and supplies didn't survive the battle," he added regretfully.

Cian grumbled and groaned as he pushed himself up, his brown eyes twinkling in the evening light. He lifted up a hand in farewell before walking away. With every step he took, he shrank from sight, much to the amazement of everyone.

"One last thing before I go," said Meredith, "regarding when you were attacked before the Air Portal. You heard Demi confess that she had caused it, but there is another reason for the colours that you saw, Marella. Yellow was because you were attacked in the Air realm, green is because it was instigated by Demi. The red was Etain, he was watching the attack. Indeed, it was that show of strength that convinced him to join Demi in the fight against you. He thought you were too strong together. I hope this helps answer your questions." Meredith blew bubbles in the water before she too departed.

"So that's that then," said Marella, looking around. "Everyone's gone, it's nearly dark, we don't have our tents or food. Great, just great."

"What about that cottage over there?" said Daren with a grin on his face. "Come on," and he led them to a small house that Marella definitely hadn't seen there a moment before, with a welcoming plume of smoke coming from the chimney.

They ate some of the food that was already prepared and steaming hot before collapsing into their beds, their Partners close by and just as exhausted, glad to finally have finished their quest.

~ 66 ~

The following morning, the Chosen and their Partners slept themselves out, restoring some of the energy they had lost. A multitude of groans could be heard as they tried to get up from the cosy beds as the aches and pains from the day before made themselves known.

They pottered about the house for a short while, enjoying a hot breakfast before restoring order and tidying up any of the mess they had made. Marella cast a longing glance behind her as they closed the cottage up and made their way out.

* * *

"It feels funny, walking like this," said Lani as they comfortably walked along.

"What do you mean?" asked Daren, glancing over from where he had been watching Ula.

"Well, we're not in a rush, we're not looking for anything, but most of all, we won't have to pull the trundle trucks. I've got used to having that fixed to my backside."

Everyone laughed as they realised the truth of Lani's words. "You're right," agreed Marella. "It does feel different." She was silent for a moment before asking "So, are we going back to Charon now?"

"We don't have to, we could just go home," said Daren, not looking at anyone. "I mean, the quest is completed, Ena told us that. We could just go home," he repeated, longing clear in his voice.

"Daren, if you want to go home, then do so," Kai said gently. "I'm not though, not yet. I made a promise to complete this quest back at Charon, and that is what I'm going to do. Besides, my family will probably be waiting for me there anyway."

Daren was silent for a moment as he thought about the significance of Kai's words. He shook his head, "No, you're right, Kai. We started this together, we will end this together."

They slowed down as they came to the meadow. Apart from a few trampled flowers, and a new hill, nothing seemed out of place. Lani pointed at something, "Look over there, what's that?"

As they got closer, they could see that it was a plaque in front of the hill. Words had been engraved in it, in both the old and new languages of Wraidd Elfennol.

"Bydded y maeth y ddaear yn eiddo i chi,
Bydded eglurder o olau fod yn eiddo i chi,

Bydded y rhuglder y môr yn eiddo i chi,
Bydded amddiffyn y hynafiaid yn eiddo i chi.

May the nourishment of the earth be yours,
May the clarity of light be yours,
May the fluency of the ocean be yours,
May the protection of the ancestors be yours."

Marella smiled at the words, recognising an ancient blessing given for those who had died. She gazed from the plaque to the hill and her smile faltered. "So many lost," she mourned.

They all shared a moment's silence to remember those from both sides that had lost their lives the day before.

Kai put his arm around Marella's shoulders and pulled her towards him, offering comfort. "Hopefully this won't happen again. Demi is with the Lords and Ladies and I think most of those who followed her were here."

"Do you honestly believe that's it then?" asked Lani as they started to walk away in the direction of Charon. "That's the fight finished?"

"I hope so," said Kai "but somehow I doubt it. I can do my best to help prevent it from happening again though. I don't know how yet, but I'll think of something between now and then."

They walked away from the meadow and the hill, setting a comfortable pace. They walked for most of the day, taking plenty of rest stops as their bodies recovered, before their surroundings became familiar.

"I don't think we're far away from Charon now," said Marella, looking around as they drank some cold water from the nearby stream. "I'm sure this is one of the old roads that we used to use when we came from Ilyn, but then a straighter one was built so everyone uses that instead."

"What do you want to do then?" asked Daren, looking at the others. "We can carry on and make it to Charon tonight or we sleep here and arrive in the morning. It's up to you."

Lani groaned as she stretched her legs out, "I know it's not taken half as long to get back as it did going – and I'm not even going to try to comprehend that little nugget," she added, "but we don't have our tents or anything. I, for one, would love to spend another night in a proper bed. So I vote we push on."

Marella grinned at her, "I'm with you, Lani, completely agree."

"It looks like we're walking then, Daren," said Kai, laughing at the pleased expressions that crossed the faces of both Lani and Marella.

Kenna yipped and jumped into the air, causing laughter to explode out of everyone. "I'd say it's not just us that wants to get back," said Kai, laughing at his Partner.

Daren and Kai pulled the girls up to their feet and they continued towards Charon, their steps quickening the closer they got.

~ 67 ~

Evening was just starting to fall when they arrived, walking through the streets towards the main square and the Lodges. Daren and Kai checked the straps and scabbards to make sure they were properly fitted and dusted down their clothing as much as they were able. Lani readjusted the holster of her bow which had moved as they walked, whilst Marella patted off the dust from her shirt and trousers and held onto her staff proudly.

It wasn't too long before they were spotted and the whispers soon spread like wildfire as people realised the Chosen had returned.

With their heads held proudly, the Chosen and Partners arrived in the main square of Charon just as the torches were about to be lit. Standing side by side, they looked at each other before the Partners moved to stand in front of them. Lani and Marella held hands, with Kai and Daren reaching for them too.

As one, the eight friends moved to the centre of the town square where a huge stone monolith now stood. They moved around the stone until they were stood in their correct elemental positions.

* * *

Daren gazed silently at the symbol of Earth on the northern side of the monolith. He placed his fingers on Ula's head and sent a wave of love to her. *"We did it, Ula. Together, we did it."*

Ula turned her head so her amber eyes gazed upon him. *"We will always be together, Daren. I'm glad we did this, but I am also very glad to be going home."*

Daren laughed at her words, appreciative as his heart now yearned for home too.

* * *

With Shaw on her shoulder, Lani looked at the symbol of Air. She felt she had come off the lightest with her part of the quest, but she recognised it was just a part of the whole. If she had listened to those persuasive voices, or if they had succumbed to frostbite or hypothermia, the quest would have ended there.

Shaw brushed his head against her cheek and fluttered his wings. *"It's all about balance,"* he reminded Lani. *"We couldn't have done one part without the others. None of us could have done this singularly. I am pleased to have been a part of this."*

Lani nodded her understanding and stood silent, but proud, before the sigil of Air.

* * *

"You've changed, Kai," said Kenna as they stood before their side of the monolith. *"You are no longer the 'arrogant jerk' who arrived here with a chip on his shoulder."*

Kai laughed at her words, and thought back to how he had acted when he first met the others. *"I really was. I'm so glad things have worked out the way they have."*

"Yes, now you not only have me, but you have Marella and Nixie too. I'm so very pleased for you. I don't know if I've had time to say that yet." Kenna wriggled her body so it brushed against his legs and she licked the tips of his fingers.

"Thank you, Kenna, that means the world to me," he thought. *"I don't know what will happen, but I'm looking forward to finding out."*

"It will be interesting, that's for sure," agreed Kenna before turning her gaze back to the stone.

* * *

"Did you think when you took the Test all those years ago that this is what would happen?" Nixie asked Marella as she gazed up on the swirls of the Water sigil.

A smile tugged at Marella's lips, *"No, Nixie, I can honestly say I didn't expect this at all. I can't quite believe it's over though. I'm going to miss everyone."*

"Do you believe that this is it? You're going to be seeing them just as often as before but now you'll have your own beds to sleep in. You are the four Chosen, your responsibilities will be different now, you'll see."

"Eight Chosen," reminded Marella firmly, *"none of us could have done this without you, all of you."*

As they had stood there, the crowd had grown around them. As the Chosen gathered their thoughts and moved to stand beside each other, they were greeted by the sight of the Elders facing them.

A pang shot through Daren as he saw Slade standing in for Demi. Lani reached over and gently squeezed his hand, giving him her support. He squeezed back and held on tight to the woman who had quietly stolen his heart.

Riva was stood stiffly in front of Marella, her face blank. Marella drew in a breath and leaned on the bond between herself and Nixie to provide her with the strength to face her mother. And yet, as she stood there, she could feel not just the bond with Nixie, but the one with Kai and Kenna, Daren and Ula, and Lani and Shaw. The bond pulsed and glowed like a golden thread within her being, seven separate strands that wrapped and wove around her own. At that moment, Marella realised due to their friendship and the experiences they had shared, this bond was theirs for life.

Marella was surprised to see a tear trickle from Riva's eyes and make its way down her cheek, before dripping to the ground. Riva's emotions broke through the mask she had tried so hard to maintain.

"I am so sorry, Marella. I should have been there for you when you left, and afterwards. The choice you made was the right one, and I was completely wrong. I wish I could change things but that is impossible. All I can offer you is my apology and my hope for a chance to make things better between us."

Marella listened to her mother's apology, surprised she had received one. It seemed like she wasn't the only one to have changed over the past year. She smiled confidently, no longer the youngling desperate for her mother's approval. She stood with poise and assurance with her peers, her friends, her fellow Chosen.

Riva held her arms open and Marella stepped into them, no longer the Chosen of Water, but simply Riva's daughter. That broke the solemnity of the occasion, and the Elders all embraced and laughed with the Chosen, the crowd smiling and talking as they were welcomed home.

A harmony of barks, yips, screeches and other noises sounded above the general cacophony in the main square as all the Partners gathered made sure their Chosen were welcomed home in style.

Riva took a step back and smiled at Marella. "Look at you, you've changed," she said proudly, before wrapping her in her arms again.

"A lot has changed," agreed Marella.

The long-term rift between Marella and Riva wouldn't be sorted out overnight. They had a lot of work in front of them to make a healthy and happy relationship as mother and daughter, but for now, it was enough for Marella to see the love and pride that Riva had hidden for so long.

"Riva, I think we should bring this to order," said Erion from close by. Riva nodded her agreement and caught the eye of Kegan, who in turn motioned to Slade. Letting go of the Chosen, the four Elders took a step back and the crowd quieted down.

"We would like to officially welcome you home, and congratulate you upon the success of your quest. We offer our apologies for missing the battle you have so recently fought. We understand that you must be tired, but there will be a feast tonight in your honour, if you would like to join us?" said Kegan.

"We still need to eat," Kai answered cheekily, causing a ripple of laughter through the crowd.

Kegan shook his head, laughing at Kai, nearly dislodging Edana who was sat on his shoulder.

"Your families are all here in Charon and you will be able to spend some time with them before we eat," said Erion, grinning as Lani whipped her head around to look for her mother, father, and brother. When she spotted them, she waved with enthusiasm, before returning her attention to the Elders.

"We would like to hear your accounts of what has happened to you over the last year, whenever you feel able to," asked Slade with dignity. "We have heard the reports from the Scions, but I would feel better with a bit more detail."

Daren nodded his head, acknowledging the pain Slade was in. He made a note to speak with him as soon as he could about Demi, and how she had been at the end.

"For now, relax and be welcome. Go and greet your families." Riva turned around so she faced the majority of the crowd and spread her arms. "People of Wraidd Elfennol, I present you with the Chosen of the Elements," she cried and the crowd once again showed their appreciation, the noise deafening.

Marella pushed her way through the crowd that surged forward to stand by her mother's side. "Where is Papa?" she asked excitedly.

"I'm here," she heard before she was swooped into the air. Edlin held onto her tightly, "I'm so very proud of you," he whispered in her ear.

"Put her down, Papa, it's my turn now." Edlin gently lowered Marella to her feet where she was swept into Jorja's warm embrace.

"Thank you for saving me," said Jorja, holding Marella tightly. "I know it was you." Tears poured down their faces as the sisters embraced, other arms soon enclosing them in a family hug.

Marella briefly caught sight of Kai being swept away by the crowd and by his family. He cast a look over his shoulder and winked at her. She smiled back at him, pushing her love through their bond. She felt Daren and Lani reciprocate the feeling and knew that no matter how crazy life might get and how much distance was between them, with their bond they were always together.

The rest of the evening passed in a blur as people came to greet them and everyone tried to catch up on a year's worth of stories. Food and drink were consumed and laughter filled the air. It was the early hours of the morning before everyone went home and the Chosen were led to the Lodges to get some rest.

~ 69 ~

It was early the next morning when Marella awoke and slipped quietly out of the Lodge, making her way to the monolith.

"I thought you'd be here," Marella was greeted by the sound of Lani's voice. She looked around to see Lani sat on a bench to one side of the square, munching on an apple.

Marella walked over and sat down beside her. "I just needed a moment to myself," she admitted.

"It was a bit much, wasn't it?" said Lani, taking small bites out of the fruit. "For so long, it's been the eight of us, interspersed with different people in the Quarters, but even there we had *our* time."

Marella nodded in agreement. "True, last night it felt like everyone wanted a piece of me and all I wanted to be was be back with you."

Lani smiled, "That's exactly how it felt for me too." She was silent for a moment as she finished her apple. "What do you suppose will happen now?" she asked.

"I don't know," pondered Marella. "Will you continue your training to be a Silent Messenger?"

Lani shrugged, "I guess so, it's what I've always wanted. It just seems so...," she paused, unable to put how she felt into words.

Marella gently bumped her shoulder. "I know what you mean, don't worry about trying to explain. I remember the day all this started; I was writing about a Weave that I had seen. I can remember being all excited, because I was going to be shown how to make the ink that the Weavers use. I'd be able to make my own, instead of having to request more from the Lodge here every time I ran out. But now, the idea of going back to getting excited about ink, well...," she trailed off, frowning slightly.

"We'll sort it out, you'll see," reassured Lani, linking arms with Marella. "Where's Nixie, by the way? I thought he'd be with you."

"Oh, he's off in the lake with Torlan," replied Marella. "He told me not to wait up for him last night." Marella snorted as Lani laughed, shaking her head at the playful otter.

"There you are." Daren waved his hand in greeting as he and Kai made their way over to the bench. "I've just been to the Air and Water Lodges, looking for you two."

"We're having a moment," whispered Lani before winking.

Kai and Daren laughed as they plopped down on the grass near the bench. "It was crazy last night, yeah?" said Daren.

"Just a bit," agreed Lani. "Marella and I have just been saying that."

"And wondering where we go from here," added Marella, smiling at Kai.

Kai shifted before darting a glance at Daren and nodding. Marella watched them curiously, whilst Lani grinned next to her.

"Marella, you know how I feel for you. We've had a year of being together, albeit in unusual circumstances. The story of our life is only just beginning and I would like to write our own happy ending. Please would you do me the incredible honour of Weaving your life with mine?"

Marella gasped with delight and threw herself off the bench and into Kai's arms which he wrapped around her and held on tight.

He lowered his head into her neck and kissed it tenderly as he felt her shaking body next to his. "Are you okay?" he whispered.

Marella didn't speak but nodded her head, her hair brushing against his face.

Lani clapped her hands with delight, her eyes overflowing with happy tears. Kai looked at her and smiled. Daren leaned over and clapped him on the back.

"Congratulations you two," he said, approval radiating from him. "You're going to drive each other crazy and I can't think of another couple who deserve it more."

Kai laughed and continued to rub Marella's back. "You say that," Kai said with a wink, "I can think of another couple just as worthy." He directed a pointed look at Lani and watched as her glance darted to Daren as colour rose in her cheeks.

"Marella, love, sit back for a minute. I have a present for you." Kai gently moved her so she was sat next to him before he reached out and handed her a blue, velvet covered, hinged box.

She slowly opened it up, gazing in wonder at the beauty before her. She raised glowing eyes to Kai. "Is this for me?" she whispered as Lani tried to see what it was.

Kai nodded, "It's my wedding gift to you. I hope you like it."

Marella gazed at the twinkly teal blue stones on the antiquated copper necklace. She carefully lifted it out of the box so Lani could see. The necklace was absolutely stunning, with copper hearts, beads and teal stones decorating it. There was a drop at the front where a solitary teal crystal hung from a delicately twisted knot design. The chain was approximately seventeen inches long, so the drop would sit nicely in the neckline of Marella's formal gown.

Marella carefully replaced the necklace before kissing Kai soundly as Daren and Lani laughed. "It's stunning, Kai, I love it. Thank you. How did you get it though?" Marella asked him.

Kai smiled at her, "It was actually a gift to me, for you," he said. At Marella's quizzical look, he explained further. "It is something Aneira gave me whilst we were in Teimladau. She said she would be honoured for you to have it."

Marella trailed her fingers over the necklace once more. "Thank you," she said, her eyes brimming with emotion.

Daren, grinning, stood up. "Come on you crazy kids. We've got Elders to greet, parents to meet," he said, winking at Kai. "Futures to sort out, evil to vanquish, blah-di blah-di blah."

Lani stood up and linked her arm through his as they strode away towards the Lodges. "Evil to vanquish? I thought we did that yesterday?" Their voices faded as they moved further away from Kai and Marella.

Kai sat forward and gently kissed her nose. "We'll sort this out, the future is ours. I just wanted you to know how I felt before the craziness happens again, like last night."

Marella snuggled into Kai, secure in his love. "I don't care about the crazy I deal with during the day, so long as I have you as my own personal crazy to come home to," she laughed.

Kai tickled her, laughing as she squirmed out of his hold before jumping to her feet. She held her hand out to him and, grinning, he took it and let her help him up. Once he was stood up, he kissed her before they sauntered off after Daren and Lani, ready to face the day... together.

~ Epilogue ~

The past six months had gone by in a whirl, thought Kai as he stood with Daren. Jorja and Derwen had married and Jorja had just announced that a baby was on the way.

Slade had taken over officially as the Elder of Earth and, to everyone's surprise, had called AuraLeigh to be his Second. Kai grinned at the memory of Marella's reaction to that snippet of news.

Daren had gone with Lani to help find Shaw's birth tree. After they had returned, he had proposed to Lani at the Samhain festival and they were now planning on a Beltane wedding.

Their lives had all changed since they had been Chosen. None of them returned back to what they had been doing, although they did all return for training. They had become Ambassadors of the Elements, trusted by the Elementals and humans alike, as they worked to clear misunderstandings and imparted knowledge on how the differing Elements supported and worked with each other.

Lani was now a fully qualified Silent Messenger too, which helped with their travels. Marella had at long last learnt the secret of the ink, and now took great pleasure in making her own and trialling different berries and leaves to see what she could come up with.

Daren gave Kai a nudge, bringing him back to the present, as the sound of the harp started to play.

Kai looked up and saw Marella appear in the doorway, looking stunning in a deep blue gown that was fitted in the bodice but flared out softly as it dropped to the ground. Her necklace twinkled in the soft glow of the lights that were hanging from the trees.

Her hair was loose and she wore a copper tiara upon her head, a beautiful design of twists and loops that matched her necklace. She carried a small bouquet of white roses and white amaryllis, the delicate scent drifting towards where Kai waited for her.

Kai's breath caught in his throat as he looked at her. He watched her walk down the path, through the chairs that had been placed outside for the occasion. He held his hand out and as soon as she was close enough, she grasped his fingers. Holding her hand high, he walked the last few steps with her before they stood in front of Erwyna and Ethon.

Ethon waited until everyone was quiet before he started the ceremony that would bind Marella and Kai together for life.

"Marriage is a bond to be entered into only after considerable thought and reflection. As with any aspect of life, it has its cycles, its up and downs, and its trials and triumphs. With full understanding of this, Marella and Kai have come here today to be joined as one in marriage."

Erwyna continued "Please join hands with your betrothed, and listen to that which I am about to say. Above you are the stars, below you are the stones, as time doth pass, remember …

Like a stone should your love be firm, like a star should your love be constant. Let the powers of the mind, and of the intellect, guide you in your marriage. Let the strength of your wills bind you together. Let the power of love and desire make you happy, and the strength of your dedication make you inseparable. Be close but not close. Possess one another yet be understanding. Have patience with one another, for storms will come, but they will pass quickly. Be free in giving affection and warmth."

Together, Ethon and Erwyna concluded the ceremony by saying "May your love so endure that its flame remains a guiding light unto you, and may it be as vast as the ocean. By the power vested in us, we now pronounce you husband and wife."

Cheers erupted from those that had watched as Kai leaned forward to kiss his wife. Smiling, they turned to face their friends and family. Before they could move, Ethon tapped Kai on the shoulder, making him turn back to them.

"One more thing before you go and celebrate," said Ethon with a smile.

"It wouldn't be right for our Chosen to join without receiving our blessings," smiled Erwyna. "Please join hands."

The crowd went silent as they watched the Lord of Fire and the Lady of Water, bless the young couple who stood before them.

Ethon and Erwyna spoke together, "We give you our blessings as your Lord and Lady. It is with honour you have asked and it is with honour that you receive. May you each and together be blessed with health, happiness, harmony and love."

From Erwyna's hand, light blue swirls appeared, surrounding Marella and Kai. From Ethon there came deep red triquetras. Floating towards Marella and Kai, the red and the blue intermingled until they appeared purple to those sat behind.

From within the swirling mass, two spirals and two triquetras made their way towards Marella and Kai. Lifting their joined hands together, Marella and Kai watched as one each of the symbols made their way to their hands. The symbols landed on their hands and shrunk down in size until they were side by side. With a bright flash of light, the sigils permanently etched themselves into the skin of Kai and Marella, one in gold and one in silver.

Marella and Kai gazed in wonder at the backs of their hands, before Marella lifted her eyes to look at Erwyna and Ethon. "Thank you," she said. Kai put his arm around her shoulders. "Yes, thank you," a broad smile across his face.

"Now we've finished with that," said Ethon with a smile to include everyone, "let the feast commence."

With that, Marella and Kai walked back towards the Lodge, getting showered by rice the guests threw at them. Daren and Lani walked along behind them, smiling happily at their friends' contentment.

The wedding feast lasted all day and for most of the evening. Everyone enjoyed themselves and danced until their feet were sore.

Kai and Marella retired for the evening in the Fire Lodge before heading off the next morning to spend some time in their little house in Teimladau. Nixie and Kenna would be sleeping over with Nixsa and Aneira, to give the newlyweds some space.

After they had spent a full moon in Teimladau, they were going to move into their new home that Kai had built, with a little help from Daren and his Chlorokinesis. It was built next to a small lake, midway between Hufel and Ilyn. It was a beautiful cob house with a front door designed by Lani of a gorgeous oak tree in full leaf.

Time faded away from them all as they enjoyed the festivities and what was to come. For a while, everyone enjoyed the harmony that the Chosen had fought for, and won. Relations with the Quarters was tighter than ever, and peace reigned throughout Wraidd Elfennol.

There was one, however, who did not approve of how things had turned out and continued to work against them. As time went by, people grew older and memories grew fainter. A new generation was born, and the old one moved on.

"You may have won the first battle but my memory is long. Enjoy it whilst you can, people of Wraidd Elfennol, for I will be coming again very soon."

An unseasonably chill wind swept over the island, causing those outside to pull their cloaks tighter whilst those inside huddled closer to their fires. In a small Air village far away from Alaw, a tiny girl youngling, thin and scrawny, huddled into the corner of her room as she heard the words on the wind. She put her head into her hands and wept.

Glossary
Characters (in alphabetical order)

NAME	PARTNER	RESIDENCE	ROLE
Adain	Caelia (Falcon)	Awel Ysgafyn	Lane's Father
Adara	Áedán (Salamander)	Charon	Second of Fire
Adaryn			Lord of the Skies
Ail	Eithne (Dormouse)	Bridd	Trainer of Earth
Aine	Mhia (Magpie)	Hufel	Trainer of Fire
Alana		Naear	Priestess of Daire
Aneira		Teimladau	Queen of Undines
Aria		Awyr	Paralda's Sister
Bradan	Orabel (Duck)	Charon	Second of Water
Bram	Unknown	Awel Ysgafyn	Lani's Brother
Branwen	Cari (Crane)	Awel Ysgafyn	Lani's Mother
Carrick		Naear	Guardsman
Cian			Scion of Earth
Cináed	Oriana (Rooster)	Hufel	Kai's Father
Daire			Lady of the Land
Daren	Ula (Wolf)	Bridd	Chosen of Earth
Demi	Eade (Bull)	Bridd	Elder of Earth
Derwen	Blasa (Ram)	Bridd	Jorja's Fiancé
Djinn		Danau	Queen of Salamanders
Edlin	Torlan (Beaver)	Ilyn	Marella's Father
Ena			Scion of Fire
Erion	Aveline (Hummingbird)	Alaw	Elder of Air
Erwyna			Lady of the Waters
Etain		Danau	Consort of Salamanders
Ethon			Lord of the Flames
Ghobe		Naear	King of the Gnomes
Hynafol			Scion of Air
Jorja	Salali (Squirrel)	Bridd	Marella's Sister
Kai	Kenna (Fox)	Hufel	Chosen of Fire
Kegan	Edana (Lizard)	Hufel	Elder of Fire
Lani	Shaw (Hawk)	Awel Ysgafyn	Chosen of Air
Lianna	Fia (Cat)	Hufel	Kai's Mother
Logan		Naear	Gnome Official
Marella	Nixie (Otter)	Ilyn	Chosen of Water
Meredith			Scion of Water

NAME	PARTNER	RESIDENCE	ROLE
Murtagh	Meara (Kingfisher)	Ilyn	Trainer of Water
Naida	Ren (Frog)	Bridd	Daren's Mother
Nixsa		Teimladau	King of Undines
Paralda		Awyr	Queen of Sylphs
Riva	Genna (Marsh Wren)	Ilyn	Elder of Water / Marella's Mother
Siorus	Broc (Badger)	Bridd	Daren's Father
Slade	Awel (Dove)	Bridd	Second of Earth
Taren	Vail (Dog)	Charon	Second of Air

Welsh Translations

ENGLISH	WELSH	SABBATS
January	Ionawr	
February	Chwefror	Imbolc
March	Mawrth	Spring Equinox
April	Ebrill	
May	Mai	Beltane
June	Mehefin	Summer Solstice
July	Gorffennaf	
August	Awst	Lughnasadh
September	Medi	Autumnal Equinox
October	Hydref	Samhain
November	Tachwedd	
December	Rhagfyr	
Spring	Gwanwyn	
Summer	Haf	
Autumn	Hydref	
Winter	Gaeaf	
Mountain of Whispers	Mynydd o Sibrydion	
Shield of Earth	Tarian y Ddaear	
Feather of the Gryphon	Plu y Gryphon	
Flame of Incandescence	Flam Eiriasedd	
Cauldron of Tears	Dagrau y Crochan	

~ ABOUT THE AUTHOR ~

When I first started Water Weaver, I had no idea how much it would take over my life. Luckily, I had the support of friends and family, who were there as sounding boards for me, even though they had no idea what I was talking about.

Writing Marella's story opened up a whole new world for me; and I don't just mean in the novel. Finding out how supportive the Indie Community is as whole – whether that is bloggers, authors or designers – was a blessing to be held closely. I could not have made it this far without the encouragement and advice given to me by too many people to name individually.

I would like to give thanks to some other authors who helped me out when I was feeling lost.

- Beth Barany
- Celeste Prater
- Dahlia Donovan
- Dean Murray
- Deborah Camp
- Echo Shea
- Jamie Summer
- Jen McConnel
- Julie Farrell
- Lynn Stookes
- Lynn Vroman
- Rachael Slate
- Randi Cooley Wilson
- Raven Williams
- Sara Burgess
- Sharon Gibbs
- Shawn McGuire
- Sheila Kell
- T.E. Ridener

These authors cover a wide range of genre, and all come highly recommended by me. I love their stories, as well as their help. If I have left anyone out, my apologies! Trust me, this community is one that welcomes in new authors, and provides friendship every step of the way.

I would also like to thank my Street Team (although I don't like that name) for their friendship and support as I tried to get my name out there. Thank you for taking a chance on a new author!

I would also like to say thank you to Saskia Castro, Sharon Gibbs and Amy Shelton for beta reading Water Weaver, in its roughest format.

I would like to thank Amy Shelton and Debbie Attenborough, for all their advice for the book, but mainly for being there for me – when I've wanted to cry, been frustrated, been loopy – they've put up with me and helped me out.

My final thanks go to you, the reader that has made it this far, that took a chance on a new author and read my book. I know you have invested a few hours of your life in my book. If you enjoyed this book, please take a moment to write a review, even a star rating on Goodreads is helpful; or contact me at m.j.sheppard2014@gmail.com. I'd love to hear from you!

15433165R00247

Printed in Great Britain
by Amazon